1/24

# Pretending

Caroline Williams has worked in various capacities with theatre, books and websites. She currently works with the Irish Theatre Institute, as director of the Irish Playography. She lives in Dublin with her daughter. *Pretending* is her first novel.

# Pretending

CAROLINE WILLIAMS

PENGUIN

IRELAND

PENGUIN IRELAND

Published by the Penguin Group
Penguin Ireland, 25 St Stephen's Green, Dublin 2, Ireland
(a division of Penguin Books Ltd)
Penguin Books Ltd, 80 Strand, London WC2R ORL, England
Penguin Group (USA) Inc., 375 Hudson Street, New York, New York 10014, USA
Penguin Group (Australia), 250 Camberwell Road,
Camberwell, Victoria 3124, Australia (a division of Pearson Australia Group Pty Ltd)
Penguin Group (Canada), 90 Eglinton Avenue East, Suite 700, Toronto, Ontario, Canada M4P 2Y3
(a division of Pearson Penguin Canada Inc.)
Penguin Books India Pvt Ltd, 11 Community Centre,
Panchsheel Park, New Delhi – 110 017, India
Penguin Group (NZ), cnr Airborne and Rosedale Roads, Albany,
Auckland 1310, New Zealand (a division of Pearson New Zealand Ltd)
Penguin Books (South Africa) (Pty) Ltd, 24 Sturdee Avenue,
Rosebank, Johannesburg 2196, South Africa

Penguin Books Ltd, Registered Offices: 80 Strand, London WC2R ORL, England

www.penguin.com

First published 2006
1

Copyright © Caroline Williams, 2006

The moral right of the author has been asserted

Set in 13.5/16pt Monotype Garamond
Typeset by Palimpsest Book Production Limited, Polmont, Stirlingshire
Printed in Great Britain by Clays Ltd, St Ives plc

A CIP catalogue record for this book is available from the British Library

ISBN-13 1-844-88061-4
ISBN-10 1-844-88061-3

For Sorcha

# PROLOGUE
## September 1993

# Hatching

Ciara would make shadowy versions of her toy dinosaurs on the ceiling, until the grey monsters grew so large they scared her. Then she'd pull them away from the light until they grew tiny, and she'd gobble them with her hand. The monsters would tumble to the ground, defeated.

Eleanor switched off the lamp and kissed her twice on the forehead. Her daughter wriggled under the covers to avoid a third kiss. Ciara loved this bed, this room, these shadows – it was what she knew best. They had lived with Eleanor's parents since Ciara was born. It made sense, until Eleanor finished her studies and until she got on her feet. They were moving out in a few weeks, but Eleanor hadn't told Ciara that yet.

'Do you know how old I'll be when I wake up, Ellie . . . ?'

Eleanor smiled.

'How old, honey?'

'Five . . . A whole hand!'

As soon as Eleanor reached the door, Ciara called her back.

'Ellie . . . pretend I've just hatched . . . like a dinosaur. I know I came from your tummy, but pretend – just pretend – you see me cracking open my egg. You see my long neck stretching out . . . Say what you'd say, Ellie, if you saw me for the very first time.'

# I
# January 1996

# Kaleidoscope

When Cuan was four, he said he wanted to be a pilot, but they weren't listening – so he jumped off the top of the stairs with his toy aeroplane and broke his arm. When he was six, he said he wanted to be a girl, but everyone ignored him – so he kept a shoe box in his bedroom of glittery things that he found, mostly hair slides and glassy beads. He put in his mother's old lipsticks because he liked their smell. At night when everyone was asleep, he'd sit in the corner of his bedroom wearing his soft flannel dressing gown and play with his glitter-box. He was an odd child; too sensitive, they said, out of sync. His brother Michael was three years older, and was steady and solid, as if he was made from less permeable material. When Cuan was seven, their dog Bessie was hit by a car. Michael sat and held her, calmly binding the gash on her leg with Cuan's T-shirt. Cuan shivered. Purple blood was leaking all over the cartoon tyrannosaurus. He saw Bessie's eyes go milky distant, and he vomited.

'Get Mum!' Michael shouted, but Cuan ran and hid for five hours.

Cuan's girlfriend Eleanor got pregnant when they were both seventeen and still in school. It seemed impossible to Cuan. They weren't even boyfriend and girlfriend, really. When he was told he said nothing; in fact, he said nothing for several days. Eleanor's family moved to Galway that Easter, within weeks of finding out the news. Her sister Nancy ran into Cuan in Golden Discs in Dun Laoghaire Shopping Centre, two days before they left. She shouted abuse at him until the security guard told them to leave. He had bought some Joni Mitchell for Eleanor, but never got around to giving it to her. He sat his exams that June in a daze. Michael was in his third year at medical school and gave him some drugs to keep him awake, and some to make him sleep.

Eleanor gave birth to Ciara that September and Cuan visited them twice, before her family decided that it would be best for all concerned if he had nothing more to do with Eleanor or her daughter. He's just a kid himself, they said. Cuan walked away, never having held his daughter, and started up another shoebox with 'Ciara' on the lid. He wrote poems and drew pictures for her and put in a small teddy and a toy dinosaur.

His parents sent him to a psychiatrist. She had short blonde hair and a German accent. Cuan spent most of the sessions wondering was she wearing a wig and letting the books on her shelves go slightly out of focus so the spines danced, making a kaleidoscope of army greens around her blonde head. She sent him to a psychologist, a man so dependent on cliché that Cuan ran rings around him. Mr Knowles had a smile that was too full of teeth, and grey eyes that drilled for contact. Cuan hated him. After three sessions the clichés came to an end when Knowles announced he was going on a spiritual journey to India. Cuan smiled for the first time in months.

He got enough points in his Leaving Cert. to do an arts degree. He wandered around the campus for two weeks, and managed not to speak a single word to anyone. The crowds frightened him. He scaled the concrete slants on the side of ugly buildings like a cat. He dropped out and took a job in a second-hand music shop for a couple of years. He lived with his family in Blackrock, but he hardly ever ate or talked with them. Michael won prizes and put them on the mantelpiece. Cuan hung posters of Bob Dylan and John Lennon on his bedroom wall.

At twenty-one he left home. Beforehand he climbed up to the attic and buried the two shoeboxes under a stretch of fibreglass. He took a dinosaur from one and lipstick from the other and put them in his pocket for luck. That night at dinner he told his parents he was going inter-railing around Europe. He showed them the ticket and a red book of train arrivals and departures. They offered him money, but he said he had saved up enough from his job. Three weeks later he sent them a postcard of the Eiffel Tower with a German stamp to say he was fine, happy enough, then he disappeared for about two years.

In September 1993, Michael tracked him down in Berlin, and cajoled him into coming home. He arrived back in Dublin dazed from drugs, his long fair hair blowing in his eyes. As the ferry pulled into Dun Laoghaire, he was unsure of the month and the year. He checked with Michael and discovered that it was the day before Ciara's fifth birthday.

'Time you got your act together,' Michael said.

'It's not an act,' Cuan said.

'Just quit the semantics, Cuan! I'll get you off the drugs, but you have to do the rest.'

While they waited for the DART to Blackrock, Cuan felt another panic attack coming on. Michael had taught him breathing exercises on the ferry, but they simply weren't working. Cuan went around the back of the shelter. Michael watched him from three feet away, through the Perspex. Cuan crouched on his hunkers and started to retch. Michael felt the pain at his throat. A nurse from the nearby hospital stopped to help. She spoke gently to Cuan and began to rummage in her handbag. Michael came quickly to his side.

'It's OK,' he said, 'I'm his brother.'

She glanced at him, and though it looked unlikely she accepted the fact.

'He may need a doctor,' she said.

'I am a doctor,' Michael replied, and she handed him a small packet of tissues and walked away.

They got on the crowded train and sailed past the stop for Blackrock. Michael brought him to his flat in town. Cuan stayed there six months, and did most of what his older brother told him. As the months went by he became more solid, as if he was inhabiting his body again, cell by cell.

He went to the pub occasionally with Michael, and he had the kind of fragile good looks that attracted attention. When women drifted towards them, he became shy and let Michael do the talking. Michael chatted politely to several beautiful women while they gazed upon his silent brother. The more Cuan drummed his fingers on the side of the glass, the more interesting they found him. Sometimes Sinead, Michael's girl-friend, came.

'Make a bloody effort, Cuan,' Michael would grunt.

When Cuan spoke, Sinead looked at him with great concentration, as if she didn't speak a word of the language, but was too polite not to try her best to understand.

Eventually he was ready to move on. He took up computer programming. He had a natural aptitude and there was no shortage of work. He got a well-paid job in a bright open-plan office, where everyone drank at least six coffees a day and talked about computer games incessantly. He moved into a bedsit on Pearse Street, and added four freshly cut keys to his bunch. He liked to feel their weight in his jacket pocket, and the complex music of their rattle.

After a year working with computers, he was still lonely and restless. He had friends in work, but he'd sooner e-mail them three desks away than talk. One grey January evening in 1996, he turned on his television to drown out the sound of the students in the basement. He settled upon an arts programme, in which people were stopped in the street and asked about their favourite books. A woman stood on the Ha'penny Bridge, and the wind made her long brown hair fly towards the camera like an anarchic halo. She described a children's book he'd never heard of, and she told the story so well it made him laugh out loud. The caption read: 'Martina Casey, Setanta Arts Centre.' Cuan bought the book the next day and read it through the night. He loved it, too. He loved it so much that he took a maintenance job at the arts centre where she worked, two weeks later.

# Wishes

When she was small Martina had a secret – she had no wishes. She knew this was strange, that most children had them because she was always being told to blow out birthday candles, close her eyes, or snap a chicken bone. When she tried to make a wish, all she ever saw was a blue darkness. You never have to tell your secret wishes, so she made it through her childhood without anyone knowing. When her friends started to talk about boys a lot, she realized she had no wish for a boyfriend. To placate them, she fixed on Robert Redford as her heart's desire. She gambled that Redford would never come to Dublin to shoot a film, so they'd never know she was lying. She made up dramatic stories about what would happen when they cast eyes on each other for the first time. She could make her friends roll around the floor with laughter or wind them up with innocent erotic suspense. At twelve she learned she had an excellent ability to make people laugh and to pretend to feel things.

Martina grew up strong and independent. She worked in the arts, freelance, taking whatever random work came her way. She was open to things and generous to a fault. She had complicated relationships with difficult men and was nearly thirty before she learned how to let things go. At twenty-nine she ended her third and lengthiest relationship. She had no regrets leaving Richard in that dilapidated farmhouse in Gougane Barra, West Cork. If it had to come down to one petty thing, it was the way he had taken up watercolour painting that winter. He painted for thirteen hours a day, badly, and never left the house. The paint spread over everything they owned – there were daubs of insipid colour on clothes, on mugs, and on books. Martina left on a Friday. The man she had spent the past four years of her life with was destined to be a bachelor; she should never have intervened. She could no longer pretend to love him. She bought an orange Volkswagen Beetle for £300 and drove to Dublin, untaxed and uninsured, with an angry roar.

She was pregnant when she left Richard, but she didn't know that at the time. As soon as she found out she left for London. She rang her friend Karen from Gatwick; Martina knew it was too late for her to come to her, but she needed to tell someone, just in case . . .

'In case of what, Martina?' Karen's voice was full of panic. But Martina didn't know.

The abortion was the loneliest time of her life. When she woke she felt like she'd been kicked between the hips. She asked to see what they took away, but the nurse shook her head and said it was too late. She pictured the thin doctor scraping her womb into the bin, like congealed lasagne leftover from a dinner party, festering and unwanted. She couldn't cry. She rocked with the pain and muttered to her mother to forgive her and to hold her, over and over. Her mother had died four years previously. When Martina tried to see her face all she could see was that blue darkness.

When she came back to Dublin she stayed with Karen for two weeks, until she found a flat and until she felt stronger. Then she moved on to a house-share in Rathmines that had cheery occupants, rising damp and a hallway full of bicycles. There were three ballet dancers in the basement, and for a while she worked as touring manager for their dance company. She travelled the country in her Volkswagen and ended up getting the exhaust fixed, so she could have a conversation without turning off the engine.

*

At thirty-two she was offered a job managing the Setanta Arts Centre. The Setanta had been open two years at this point, and had become a hotbed of emerging artists and experimental theatre. It was housed in an old building on Eden Quay beside O'Connell Bridge – the only bridge in Europe as wide as it was long. The Setanta's artistic policy was equally broad, and Martina's decision to take the job was an easy one. She was wonderful at managing the place, exuberant and creative. She loved the randomness of it – a new theatre show one week, a new exhibition the next. She was over a year there when she first met Cuan. A video installation was opening in an hour. She was blindly busy. She rushed towards him to ask him to mop the floor and he fell over, knocking down a metal bin in the process. She laughed, and he blushed.

'Sorry, but I didn't think you were going to stop,' he said, maintaining his position on the floor.

'I'm Martina,' she said, still laughing as she crouched down to help him pick up the rubbish. 'I run here.'

'I'd say you run just about everywhere,' he said, grinning and shuffling out of her way.

Cuan became her closest friend within hours, and she had no idea how it happened, or that such a magical thing could happen. He was on contract – they had six months to play together. It was a small arts centre; people talked. When she told them there was nothing between her and Cuan, for once she was telling the truth – for the first time she felt so close to someone she could feel no wall, nothing. She could touch him as easily as she'd touch her own face. But it was a secret. She hadn't touched him, not in any sexual way, and she hadn't told him, though she told him almost everything else that mattered to her.

# Tricky Questions

'Ellie, do monsters really exist?'

Ciara was bouncing on the bed, asking a question on every rebound.

'No,' Eleanor replied emphatically, before she realized Ciara's game.

'Then why do we have a word for them? Do traffic lights change even when there are no cars around? Do people still have birthdays after they die? How old were you when your Nana died? When will my Nana die, do you think? Who do you love more: my Nana or me?'

'Shush, Ciara, you'll make my head explode!'

Eleanor wasn't rushing so much this morning. Ciara saw her smiling to herself when she found her red cardigan in the hot-press. Ciara continued to bounce on the bed while Eleanor got dressed, miming her mother's exploding head in the mirror. Usually Ellie would make her stop. Sometimes Ciara could make Ellie give out to her in her head. Right now she'd say things like, *You're much too old to be jumping on beds. You're seven, Ciara. S-e-v-e-n. You should be making your bed, not jumping on mine* . . . blah, blah, blah – except she was in a very good mood today, for some reason.

'What time will you be at Nana's, Ellie?'

'I'm going to be late tonight, honey. I'm going to a film.'

'Ohhh, can I come . . . ?'

'No, I'll pick you up in the morning, OK?'

'Can I have Coco Pops for breakfast?'

'Sure.'

'Can I bring my dinosaur video?'

'OK.'

'Wow, you're in a good mood! Can I sleep over at Sophie's house tomorrow night?'

'Maybe . . . We'll see what her mum says.'

'Cool!'

Eleanor was waiting for Ciara to ask her who she was meeting, but she didn't. She had practised saying the answer as casually as possible, almost throwaway. *Beth. Do you remember Beth from the bookshop?* Ciara had met Beth once, about a month ago. Eleanor had brought her in to buy a Roald Dahl book, and to see how they got along. Ciara was impressed with Beth. She asked her as many tricky questions as she could manage about *The Simpsons*, and Beth got them all right. Beth and Eleanor hadn't asked each other any tricky questions at this point. They were just letting things unfold, to see what might happen.

Eleanor had met Beth first almost six months before. She had gone into Foley's to browse during her lunch hour. It was an excellent bookshop – a worn wooden floor and a selection of books that looked as if they'd been handpicked, rather than ordered from catalogues or pushy book reps. Beth appeared from the storeroom carrying a large cardboard box. Eleanor somehow got in her way, and Beth had to try to manoeuvre around her, without knocking over the book displays. Eleanor apologized, and Beth smiled.

'People think that working in a bookshop is some kind of idle intellectual pursuit, but most of the time it's lugging shit about!'

Beth carried the box up to the till, and began to price the books, pausing to flick through the ones that interested her. For the next fifteen minutes Eleanor glanced at her in the security mirror, as often as she could without drawing attention to the fact – and without appearing like a shoplifter. Beth

16

had curly dark hair and sallow skin. She seemed about thirty, but she could have been any age. She was wearing frayed jeans and a black vest. She sounded Irish, but looked more like a free-spirited backpacker, passing through. She had freckles on her nose. Eleanor, who dealt with a couple of hundred strangers each day, had never noticed anyone so vividly. Usually so measured and deliberate, she did something impulsive. She picked up a lesbian magazine and walked towards the till. From a cursory glimpse at the cover she knew it was a lifestyle magazine that had a feature on women tennis players. She knew nothing about tennis and even less about whatever else might be inside the magazine. She didn't want the magazine; she wanted Beth's attention. And she got it.

'Two eighty . . . please.' Beth smiled at her again, as Eleanor fumbled for the right change.

'God, I handle money all day. You think I'd be better at this!'

Beth looked at the navy bank uniform and shook her head with a bemused grin.

'Well, I'll have to test you so, sometime,' she said.

And for six months that's exactly what Beth did. She took to making lodgements for the bookshop every few days, and queuing at Eleanor's counter. Eleanor went into the bookshop at least twice a week, and she got to know the stock better than half of the staff did. They began lending each other books, their favourite books, to see how close they could get before touching. They had wildly different taste, but that didn't matter – impassioned arguments were exactly what two headstrong people needed to bring them together.

# Bolt

Cuan fixed everything at the Setanta – light bulbs, switches, computers, fax machines. He made things that hadn't worked for years come to life. Everyone took to him, and he seemed to become more and more confident as the months went by. The two teenage girls who worked in the coffee shop on Saturdays would chat to him and giggle. James, the artistic director, flirted with him outrageously. Cuan just grinned and lapped up the attention. Martina teased him – she was never certain how much was deliberate charm on his part and how much was accidental.

When his six-month contract was up, he was offered promotion to production manager. James and Martina had a cagey grown-up meeting and decided that he was the obvious candidate. They both encouraged him to take the job. He did, and for the next few months he and Martina moved even closer. They could spend ten hours working together and go for a pint and let three more hours trip by while they talked. They could talk about everything. They could bicker about anything, especially trivial things. They could agree on important things without even finishing a sentence. They locked other people out unintentionally. Mostly Cuan spoke to Martina as he thought, in wild metaphoric twists and turns. She followed him effortlessly, delightedly. Other people would try to pin him down to reality, scared he'd get them lost, or that he was trying to shake them off. Martina had none of these fears, and nothing he said scared her.

They talked about their families, relationships, friendships.

Initially she presumed he was gay; most people did, and he rarely said anything to contradict that presumption. He told her of some girl he'd been in love with in Berlin, and though they'd never had a physical relationship he reckoned that Jeanette was the one. When they had serious chats, Martina always fixed on her mother, Cuan on Jeanette. After a while Martina gave up the practical advice such as why don't you write, or ask her over. Martina sensed Jeanette was his Robert Redford, but she didn't tell him that. Sometimes she didn't say things because she knew he needed to find his way there by himself. Some days she felt decades older than him.

They had worked together eleven months when the first Christmas came around. The Setanta was madly busy. There were two shows in the theatre – a children's play which ran twice in the afternoon and comedy improv at night. The set for *The Tin Soldier* had to be struck daily, to make way for the comedians. It was all hands on deck. Martina was footing a ladder for Cuan, while he fixed the lighting rig. He was comfortable as a cat fifteen feet up, and quite probably could have managed on his own, but Martina enjoyed this stuff more than filing and phone calls.

'Just don't sue me personally if you fall. I've no assets!'

'No worries. I'll do my Batman trick.'

Cuan lifted the sides of his T-shirt, mocking wings. When Martina looked up at his bare stomach, she felt lightning chase through her blood. It was so sudden and so violent, she thought they'd both been electrocuted. When she realized that they weren't, the only other explanation was clear, and it meant trouble. The lighting gel slipped out of Cuan's fingers and he dived forward to catch it. The ladder shuffled, but Martina's weight kept it upright.

'For fuck's sake, be careful!' she shouted.

He glanced down, oblivious to the danger.

'Relax, I'm fine. Hey, don't look so spooked. I wasn't going to fall.'

He climbed halfway back down the ladder and sprang to his feet.

That evening she rang Karen and told her.

'Jesus, Martina, he's just a kid,' she said, and Martina agreed.

She tried to block it. For the rest of the week she tried to measure a distance between them, a safe distance, but it was impossible. It seemed irreversible – like a trip switch, except the opposite – and, when the voices in her head started to explain it in his language, she knew it was time to bolt. That weekend she wrote a letter to her board of management to say she was going to quit and move to County Clare, citing personal reasons. They urged her to stay, but she was adamant. So she moved to a similar job in Ennis the following month.

Cuan was devastated. They'd planned to teach each other things. Cuan was going to teach Martina more computer stuff. Martina was going to teach Cuan to drive.

'We'll see each other, right?' Cuan asked, twice, because she ignored him the first time. He sat in her office, deflecting her attempts to send him off on various errands. Martina was sifting through her computer files, deleting any personal ones. She shook her head, and kept her eyes on the screen.

'Nope, not for a while. I need a fresh start, I'll be up to my eyes . . .' she said, trotting out every hollow excuse she could muster.

Two nights before Martina left, Cuan was working overnight to paint the theatre floor black for a dance show the following day. Martina stayed and chatted with him until 2 a.m. She told him things she didn't really remember. How her father drowned when she was four, while she was waiting on the shore for him with his towel. She told him about her abortion. He told her about the lipstick and the hair slides. He told her that he had panic attacks when he was in Berlin and spent six weeks in a psychiatric hospital there. They pumped him full of drugs, and he was nine months getting clean of them. He put no one down as his next of kin, but Michael came over and found him. He didn't tell her about Ciara, but he came close.

# Stones

'Ellie, is there such a thing as a princess knight?'

Ciara was shouting from the top of the stairs, waving a makeshift sword.

'Sure, honey, bound to be.'

'Cool!' Ciara shouted, and she went back to fight whatever creature she had made from a dressing gown and several scarves.

Eleanor was downstairs drinking coffee with her mother. She had just got back from work and she was exhausted. She had been on the foreign exchange desk all day and spent most of it bickering with customers over exchange rates and bank commissions – customers who were flying off to interesting places, and should have been better humoured.

'He's back in Dublin,' Anna said. 'Nancy saw him in some arts centre down the quays – looks like he works there.'

They hadn't talked about Cuan for years. Eleanor knew her mother was only saying this because Nancy would. Nancy had already left two 'Call me' messages on her answering machine.

'So ... ?'

'Well, I just thought you should know, that's all. He may try to contact you. Forewarned is forearmed.'

'Oh, for God's sake, he's not some psycho!' Eleanor said, but Anna was on a roll.

'I blame the parents. They always indulged him. They never took a firm hand with him. You had to grow up. He didn't – never will. Brains to burn and they let him go to that comprehensive, and they weren't short of a few bob. He spent half his time drawing pictures and the other half campaigning for animal rights – that's not an education. Probably still walking around with multicoloured jumpers and a Walkman stuck in his ears.'

'You wanted him out of our life – what do you expect from him? He's history. I hope he's happy.' Eleanor sighed – how could they still argue over him, the same argument eight years on? Anna let it go.

Eleanor felt exhausted. Ciara came running downstairs.

'Are we staying for dinner?'

'No, not tonight.'

'Awwwww!' Ciara protested. Eleanor snapped at her, and Anna frowned.


That night Eleanor went to bed at nine-thirty, quietly, so that if Ciara was awake she wouldn't hear her and come and join her. Sometimes on a Friday they went to bed at the same time and read. Tonight she needed some space. She thought about Cuan, and the Christmas they conceived Ciara. They were both virgins. He was terrified at first.

Eleanor was head girl at her school. College guys asked her out, but she had no interest. She had a boyfriend, Paul, when she was fifteen, but he meant nothing to her. She kissed him and let him touch her, but something like a scream followed his hand underneath her skin. Cuan was different. He was like a magical creature. His body was like liquid. They shared books and music. He seemed to have no interest in asking her out and so she fell in love with him a little. They stayed over at a friend's house in November. They watched a video and slept on the floor, surrounded by umpteen others in sleeping bags. In the middle of the night Eleanor moved closer to Cuan, and he leaned closer to her. The sound of the sleeping bags touching crackled like lightning. Eleanor ached for him to touch her, but he didn't.

From that night on, she planned where and when they'd touch. She stayed over at his house at weekends. His parents were too cool or too busy to care. Her mother objected, so she lied and said Louise, her most sensible friend, was staying, too. He lit candles and put on their favourite music. His body smelt of Imperial Leather, the soap his mother always bought. His heart beat impossibly fast. She loved his body so much she wished she could draw him or paint him. At school she'd look at brown things to remind her of his eyes. They had a wonderful two months.

She knew her mother was right. Cuan wasn't remotely practical; how could he be a parent? She was scared. Before she told either of them, she got Michael to confirm the pregnancy test: she couldn't believe that a thin blue stripe on a ridiculous white plastic tube could be wrecking her plans. Michael had access to labs, and facts. He looked grey in the face when he told her the results. He was kind and frank. Eleanor just shook her head.

'Does Cuan know anything?' he asked.

'No, I'll tell him . . . soon.'

'Jesus, Eleanor, you don't have to go through with this . . . I could lend you money if that would help. You could nip off to London . . .'

'Just fuck off, Michael. It's not your problem.' Eleanor cried because she was thwarted, and because it was her problem. She wouldn't let Michael hug her, so he shrugged and leaned over and patted her arm. He smelt of that soap. Eleanor threw up.

Her father got transferred to UCG. Instead of waiting for the next academic year to begin, the whole family moved to Galway straight away. Some afternoons she'd mitch off her new school. The nuns let her come and go as she pleased, given her 'condition'. She'd get the bus out to Salthill and walk on the rocky beach. She'd find stones the colour of

Cuan's eyes and fling them out to sea in the hope that the pain would cease.

That night she dreamt that Cuan cycled past her car and smiled in at Ciara. A fox ran out on the road and the car swerved and she knocked it down. Ciara screamed. She stopped the car and got out and saw Cuan lying still in the ditch, semiconscious. His head was bleeding, and his eyes were Ciara's. She got up at 4 a.m. and wrote him a letter, addressed to the Setanta Arts Centre. She wouldn't post it, not for a week or so at least. He was two weeks younger than her. He'd be twenty-seven next Tuesday. Eleanor felt ancient.

She hadn't talked to Beth about Cuan. When Beth asked who Ciara's father was, she just shrugged and said, 'Oh . . . he's out of the picture.'

# Juxtapositions

Once Martina left, all the colour seemed to go from the Setanta. Cuan felt a pain in his chest for five days. Though he still chatted with everyone, he seemed distracted. He wasn't sleeping and was coming in late. The Setanta held no meaning for him without her – the job had turned mundane overnight.

He thought about going back to IT or travelling. Everything for the past year had been about Martina. Every book he read, every film he saw, every CD he bought – he'd filter for her, for them to share. He'd often go to the same film twice, so she could see it. He made her tapes for the car, tracks so cleverly juxtaposed that maybe only she would understand. He could make her laugh out loud in the middle of traffic by running some Dusty Springfield song into The Smiths. He'd never write out the track listings, so she'd ask him questions, and so he'd know which songs caught her attention. He was giving her clues, signs, maps, but Martina just accepted them as random gifts. When he became earnest about music, sometimes Martina would laugh.

'I don't need to listen to *Blood on the Tracks* to understand you! You weren't even bloody born in 1966!'

''Seventy-five! *Blood on the Tracks* was 1975 – I was five! *Blonde on Blonde* was Sixty-six – you're nearly ten years out!'

'Clearly! Now since you're so clever with dates, when is the get-in for the Mamet play?'

'Friday twelfth,' he said.

'Top of the class ... Let's ring them and make sure they know that our fire door is bust, so they have to bring their stuff through the foyer.'

'Does "Let's ring them" mean me ring them . . . ?'

'Yep. Their production manager's a sweetie – you'll love her.'

'What do you mean?'

'Oh, Cuan, just make the fucking call!'

He learned things from her, from the way she said things and from the way she could unpick people's bad habits. She'd hang up the phone in a temper.

'He's in a fucking meeting – well, why take the call? I bloody hate that – when you ring someone and they do that . . . so I end up whispering and apologizing like I've done something bad.'

He knew that feeling exactly; he just couldn't put it into simple words in the same way she could.

He liked the way she noticed him. He could feel it sometimes like a kind of light. One day she noticed him smelling his armpit – it was just a fraction of a movement – and she rummaged in her bag.

'Do you want to borrow my deodorant? It's not a girlie one . . .' she explained as she threw it over to him.

'It smells like toothpaste,' he said, before he'd taken off the lid.

'Brat!' she said, as she watched him fumble with it. Sometimes she watched him so closely it was like she was filming him. He knew she knew things about him – details that no one else knew, such as the way he opened an envelope, the shape of his hands, or the precise blond of his hair.

Sometimes when she went out for a message, she'd borrow his leather jacket. She often forgot her coat when she drove to work. He loved watching her put it on, then pull her long hair from behind the collar and shake it down her back. She'd grin at him and put her phone in one pocket and her wallet into another and say, 'What treats will I bring back – a KitKat or a Danish?'

When she looked at him it was like no one else. There was no exasperation, no disapproval, no pity in her eyes. Mostly she looked at him as if he was a magical child. He had no idea how he could live without her.

Showing her stuff on the computer was the best. They both looked forward to huddling up together in the little office. It was like being in a tent. Cuan got a chance to be older, more competent and patient. Martina got to be a little vulnerable, and less bossy. Though she picked it all up quite quickly, sometimes she'd forget a step and be cross. She'd bump her head against his shoulder and say, 'Nope, start again!'

She'd rest her forehead on him for ten or maybe fifteen seconds while he got it back to the start. He wanted time to rewind to one of those moments. He wanted to feel the weight of her head, her hair brushing against his arm and maybe, somehow, hold her there.

# Lines

Martina was bored in Ennis. She felt half dead. Her new colleagues were fine, but they were like cardboard to her. There were relentless, turgid meetings that seemed entirely unnecessary, and she found it almost impossible to concentrate during them. After two weeks she discovered that Gerry Doyle, the previous manager, had resigned over a misplaced apostrophe. The bi-monthly poster of events at the Ennis Art's Centre was spotted by a member of the board in his local dry cleaners. He led a witch-hunt, and several rows ensued. The fact that this particular member of the board hadn't been to any event in the centre for nine months didn't seem to matter. He ran two businesses locally, so he had clout. Gerry left, and ensured that everyone in the building knew the reason. He met Martina on the street and told her.

'I can't believe you left the Setanta for this kip,' he said.

Martina learned to watch her punctuation, and to watch her back.

The centre was much less busy than the Setanta and it had better resources, so she didn't have to get stuck in like before. She hated sitting at a desk. She wrote five letters to Cuan and posted none.

Eventually he rang her and said,

'So . . . Danish or KitKat?'

She didn't know what to say to him. He said her voice was odd, hollow; she told him she'd a cold.

'Well, that's it decided, then. You have to come back to the city. It's not good for you down there in the country.'

'Ennis is a town, you fool,' she laughed, and relaxed. 'Come visit,' she said, almost without thinking.

He was silent for a moment.

'I can't. I'm working on something,' he said.

'Fine, fuck off and paint the floor so.'

'No, it's not that. It's my own stuff.'

'Well, bring it down. Show me.'

'No, Martina, really I can't.'

'Then don't ring me any more,' she said.

She hung up and broke two of the tapes he had given her, with difficulty. When the plastic refused to crack under her feet, she unravelled them into the bin. All those twisted love songs reduced to a tangle of shiny plastic, like a preposterous wig, When she saw them later, she was embarrassed by her spite and felt about fourteen.

For the first time in over a year she felt distant from Cuan. She was angry with him for being young, for having a family. People who had parents really had no idea what it was like to have nothing, no back-up. He could fuck up all he liked and that house in Blackrock would still be there. He could fall down the stairs at work and break his leg and he'd have somewhere to go, someone to cook for him. He could run up a credit-card bill and they'd bail him out. He could fall off his bike and hit his head and go into a coma and they'd all be waiting by his bed for him to wake up. Maybe she was going crazy.

She went for a pint with Matt O'Rourke that night, just to take her mind off things. Matt was a local – an alcoholic playwright whose third play had opened to bad reviews the week before. He made a pass at her and she told him what an ugly, talentless moron he was, though she knew he was too drunk to comprehend it.

She walked out of the pub and the town seemed claustrophobic. The narrow streets felt dull and overfamiliar, though she'd only been there a couple of months. The country? 'Fuck him,' she muttered, 'he hasn't a fucking clue. There's gridlock outside my door, Cuan, every bloody morning!'

Her flat was above a pharmacy. It'd had the same window display since she moved in – the bottles of moisturizer with faded labels had probably been there for years. She felt like smashing the glass so they'd have to change it. The whole building smelt like a pharmacy. Sometimes her flat reeked of antiseptic and very strong vitamin tablets, or sickly perfume. The shower dripped cold water – as soon as you washed you had to jump out or it spoilt everything.

Next morning she drove to Lahinch and went for a walk on the beach. The tide was out and the light brown sand was furrowed like an angry forehead. At the edge of the water the sand was smooth, apart from where gulls had etched a pattern with their feet. She watched as the light waves made the lines soften, then vanish. She suddenly felt an urge to look in a mirror, to see if age had begun to scrabble into her face. She tried feeling for lines, but her fingers were too numb from the breeze. Her face just felt warm and marshmallow soft. She splashed it with the icy sea water.

She visited the aquarium, but left after ten minutes because Cuan wasn't there. She wished he was beside her, his face pressed up against the glass tanks, watching the grace of the stingrays, the comedy of the octopus, the tragedy of the lobster.

# Fingertips

Cuan had spent four days being shadowed by Don, the trainee production manager. Don had a plodding, literal approach to all the tasks, and Cuan just gabbled explanations and did jobs too quickly. Don made Cuan nervous. He stood too close to him and tried to follow him up ladders.

Cuan was taking a break from the Setanta. He had no idea what he was going to do, but he knew he needed to get out. The day he was due to leave, he picked up a letter. He presumed it was from a theatre company to say thanks, or an invitation to a show. He carried it around in his pocket for an hour before he opened it.

His hands shook as he held the photo of a beautiful eight-year-old between his fingertips, slightly crushed from his pocket. She had brown eyes and two plaits with different-coloured hair bobbins. He walked out of work at 11 a.m. and got on the train. He rang Martina from the station at Ennis. She picked him up ten minutes later. He was still shaking. She brought him to her flat and made him tea. He handed her the photograph. This time she was shocked. It seemed impossible to her that this person who looked eighteen could have fathered a child. The photograph made no sense to Martina, as if it were wildly out of focus.

'Do you want me to read the letter?' she asked.

'Yeah, read it out loud, could you? The lines keep jumping around when I try to get through it . . .'

Dear Cuan,
Ciara is now nearly eight and getting to an age where she

may want to find out more about you. I've told her very little and, though she asks questions a lot, she hasn't looked for any details. But if she wants to meet you in the next few years I wouldn't stand in her way. Where are you at? Have you any interest in making contact? I suggest you write rather than phone. Write to her directly if you like – she's a great reader. If I don't hear back from you I won't write again.

I don't blame you for anything, we made the best decisions – Ciara was meant to be. She smiles like you and frowns like my mother. Things were tough in the beginning, but they're fine now. I'm starting a new relationship. It's summertime in Galway.

Eleanor


'Jesus, what are you going to do? Do your parents know? Have you not heard from her in eight years?'

He just rocked and sipped the tea. When he put down the mug she held him and he sobbed gently. She loved him at that moment, perhaps more than she'd ever loved anybody. He was sad and broken. She kissed his head like a child. For the first time in weeks he was ready to sleep. He slept for hours. She left him to go to a meeting at six. When she got back, he'd fixed her shower.

'You want me to help you write the letter?'

He nodded.

'You want me to drive you back to Dublin at the weekend?'

He shrugged his shoulders.

'You want to stay here until then?'

He nodded again.

'For fuck's sake, Cuan! You can talk most people under the table. Say something!'

'Did you bring back any chocolate?'

\*

33

Over the next few days Cuan told Martina almost everything about Eleanor. How Jeanette was real, but most of the time the feelings were about Ellie. How he hadn't slept with anyone since. How he climbed off a moving train in Paris because some Frenchwoman wanted him to have sex with her. Martina laughed.

'It's OK to laugh at that part, right?'

Cuan smiled, like the girl in the photo.

He bought a sleeping bag and slept on the couch. He wrote a letter to Ciara two days later. He put Martina's address on the envelope, and gave it to her to post.

She didn't drive him back that weekend. Instead they went to Doolin and watched a dolphin for two hours. Cuan wanted to go swimming with it, but Martina freaked, and persuaded him to go to the pub instead.

There was a session on. A local fiddler and one from Donegal were trying to match rhythms and find common tunes for which they had different names. An earnest young American was playing acoustic guitar, gently and with reverence. A man who looked at least eighty was playing bodhrán with a steady beat, oblivious to the cultural negotiations. Martina and Cuan sat squashed together and whispered over their pints of Guinness.

They shared a bag of pistachio nuts from Cuan's pocket. After a while Martina found it intolerable being so close to him. He was jigging his knee against hers in time to the bodhrán. She asked him straight out:

'So, why don't you want to have sex?'

'Martina, I can't . . .' he said, and he looked down at his glass and swirled the dregs of his pint around and around.

It was a careful question, despite being blunt. He could have interpreted it numerous ways. Any answer, no matter how vague, would have given her some clue, but he chose not to. She went to the toilet, not wanting to be pressed against him any longer. She was angry with him for playing his game again – flirting, then turning into a kid and denying it, making himself taboo. She was angry with herself for wanting him, and for not managing to ignore it, and she scuffed her knuckles against the pebbledash wall to feel anything other than that dull, familiar ache. When she came back she sat opposite him, and tried to focus on the music. He'd drawn two faces on the pistachio shells and pressed them into his index fingers – they were dancing and playing.

'Let's go back,' one said.

'If you promise not to jump out of my car while it's moving,' Martina replied.

They went to bed that night and said no more about it.

At 3 a.m. she got up and made some tea, quietly. She watched him sleeping on the couch, his bare shoulders and arms, his hands, his long fingers. Why did she want to touch him? She had had three serious relationships, where the sex was just background music. She had had umpteen one-night-stands, before and during her time with Richard, but none since. They meant nothing. She didn't regret any of them, apart from Frank the conceptual artist, who seemed to turn up in every pub or pizza restaurant when she was least able to deal with him.

Cuan stirred in his sleep, and turned so his bare back was facing her. She sat on her hands, and traced the contours of his back slowly with her eyes. He was so thin. Even though he was a little taller than her, she must weigh at least a stone heavier. She wanted to touch him just once. She knew he was on his way somewhere else, maybe gay or maybe he just needed some young fragile woman, just out of her teens, that he could love to distraction. Wouldn't that break her heart. She joked about it with him when they worked at the Setanta. If they hadn't seen each other over the weekend she'd quip, 'Where did you go? Did destiny show up?' Sometimes he'd

35

joke back, but other times he'd get annoyed with her for pushing him. He'd grow sulky and petulant and say:

'Thanks, Mum, but I'm able to do this by myself.'

'Good,' she'd say. 'Well, get on with it!'

But he didn't, or he couldn't. He flirted with her relentlessly, but she knew he was just playing. It didn't mean she had the right to touch him. He played with everyone. He was undecided, and it tantalized her, and perhaps that was all there was to it. She convinced herself that if he started seeing someone, male or female, she could let him go. She got up and went back to bed, shaking the pins and needles out of her hands. She fell asleep before the blood found its way back to her fingertips.

# Baggage

'Toothbrush?'

'Yep!'

'Nightie?'

'Yep!'

'Archie?'

'Yep, and Bluey and Shelly!'

'Ahhh, Ciara, you don't need three cuddlies!'

'I do!'

'OK. Just don't leave any of them behind –'

'I won't!'

'Don't expect Nana to remember to pack them up tomorrow . . .'

Eleanor glanced at Ciara in the rear-view mirror and Ciara winked, as if she knew. Eleanor had planned this carefully. Beth shared a flat with friends from work. If things were to happen, it had to be in Eleanor's house and Ciara had to be elsewhere, ideally Eleanor's parents' house. So while Ciara was tucked up in Eleanor's old bed, reading her battered copy of *Black Beauty*, Eleanor set about seducing Beth.

Though Beth was older and more experienced, she was letting Eleanor do all the work – she was being careful. They went for a meal, then a walk by the river, and she waited for Eleanor to kiss her first. Eleanor hadn't said she was lesbian, and Beth had decided quite some time ago that she wasn't messing about with straight women, even ones as beautiful as Eleanor.

Eleanor never got around to saying it. They were squabbling about the film they had seen the previous week – they

37

disagreed on just about everything. They even argued about who should walk by the edge. Beth was insistent that she should, but Eleanor had walked that stretch so often with Ciara, she wasn't happy until she was the one on the outside.

'And what makes you less likely to fall in?' Beth asked, letting Eleanor get her way.

'Everything!' Eleanor said, then she asked Beth back to her house. Beth said yes, and forgot about all that had been said or not said.

When they made love for the first time that night, there was an urgency and a certainty to it, and nothing to argue over. If Beth had any more questions, she knew not to ask them directly, just to let Eleanor answer by the way she touched her, or the way she held her fingers when she came.

The next morning Eleanor snapped her eyes open at seven, as if it were a school morning. Beth was still sleeping, but stretched towards her, a sleepy arm as confident as Ciara's that it would reach her. Suddenly Eleanor felt scared by the intensity of the night before, and all that it implied.

'Let's not rush things, Beth . . .'

Beth woke smiling. This was the first time she'd seen Eleanor unsure, but this was the kind of uncertainty she could deal with.

'You've read the propaganda so?'

Eleanor shook her head and looked puzzled.

'Oh, come on, everyone has – what does a lesbian bring on a second date?'

Eleanor shook her head again.

'Her suitcases. Don't worry, I'm not that sort of dyke. Anyhow, I've been burned before by bisexuals.'

Eleanor got defensive.

'What do you mean? Why do you say I'm bisexual?'

'Oh, El, take it easy! You've a kid – you must be into men, or used to be anyhow.'

'I was seventeen, for fuck's sake!' Eleanor started to get dressed.

'You're so competitive! You want to be the best lesbian now. Well, take a break, you're not! You've the whole coming out thing ahead of you. Last night was great. The next time might be great, but have you thought the whole thing through? What about Ciara's questions or the other mummies at the school not letting their kids back to play . . . ?'

'Christ, this isn't Holy Catholic Ireland of the fifties, Beth. Ciara goes to a multi-denominational primary school, for God's sake! Her teachers wear Birkenstocks and tie-dye dungarees – male and female. I'm the one that's out of place with my prim bank uniform . . .'

Eleanor sat down on the bed; she'd put her work blouse on by accident. Beth was still naked, and not running off anywhere.

'OK,' Beth sighed, 'let's just shut up and have breakfast or more sex before your mother gets here . . . Aha! See, that last bit made this anxious look flash across your face!'

'If I thought my mother approved, I'd send you packing now,' she said.

Beth kissed her, and took off the blouse. She undid Eleanor's bra with one hand and practised dexterity – Eleanor felt herself falling off the edge and she didn't care.

# Separating

The new production manager at the Setanta fell off a ladder and broke his leg in three places. James rang Martina to see if she had a contact number for Cuan, or any other delicious guy in his mid twenties who wore Levi's and tight T-shirts and could do a half-decent job.

'I'm seeing Mr Right later. What can you offer him?'

'The sun, the moon and my arse,' James laughed.

Actually, Marina was looking at a sleeping Cuan while she spoke, but decided she wouldn't say that to James. He probably wouldn't understand the game they were playing – he might tease her for seducing Cuan, or he might tease her for not doing so. She chatted with him for about twenty minutes, catching up on the Setanta gossip, hearing wild tales about his social life. She and James had a close friendship, a friendship often fuelled by bitter laughter at life's disappointments. He had been upset when she decided to leave her job so suddenly, but he never tried to stop her and he never asked her why. She wondered had he guessed.

'So, can I have the cute boy back, please, if you're quite finished with him?' he asked before he hung up.

Cuan woke to the sound of her laughter.

'You want three weeks'§ work back at the old place? James has two dance shows and the Gay Pride photography exhibition to deal with and he broke the production manager.'

'Yeah, why not,' Cuan said. 'I'm sure you could do with your life back, right?'

This is my life, she thought, this is the bit that feels real – but she said nothing. She went into the kitchen to cook them breakfast. Cuan took a shower. Martina could hear the water splashing on his body, and pictured the thousands of drops of water dancing on and off his pale skin. When he fixed the shower Cuan discovered that the water pressure was so bad in her flat that, if you ran a tap in the kitchen, it stopped the flow in the bathroom. Martina stood at the sink and ran the hot tap. Ten seconds later Cuan shouted as the shower turned stone cold.

They were quieter than usual over breakfast. Cuan wanted Martina to listen to a Pakistani singer he'd just discovered.

'It's devotional music. He's a Qawwali master.'

'It sounds much too lively and rhythmic to be a prayer . . . Is he celibate?'

'Umm . . . He's dead, actually.'

After breakfast Cuan went out to investigate the bus times. Martina had a timetable somewhere, but she didn't try to find it. She wanted him out of her space for half an hour, so she could say goodbye to him properly – not just snap and push him away. He'd slept on her couch for three weeks. Since he arrived she had felt a constant underlying arousal, a buzzing beneath her skin, like an overdose of caffeine or like the noise a light bulb makes before it's about to blow.

She unzipped his sleeping bag and lay under it on the couch. She masturbated and smelt traces of his skin, while the zip's teeth gnawed into her neck. From the time she was fourteen she could masturbate to orgasm in about two and a half minutes, a useful skill, particularly as she had yet to encounter a man who could navigate around her body and bring her with him on the trip.

She wondered if Cuan masturbated much during the three weeks – or if sex had ever entered his head, or irritated his blood. He never talked about sex. He talked about music incessantly, as if it was sex and religion rolled into one. She'd seen music flood him like desire – it made his heart beat faster, his palms sweat and his body tremble. Morrissey's voice or Joni Mitchell's could touch him, engulf him for weeks. How could she compete with that?

She rubbed her fingers around the mouth of the sleeping bag, hoping he'd pick up her scent. She stood up muttering to herself. That's it, he has driven me completely nuts. I'm reduced to some fucking pheromone witchcraft.

She was having a cup of tea quite serenely, when she heard his key in the door.

'The next one's in a hour.'

'Cool. Go pack. I'll drive you to the bus.'

He began to extract her key from his bunch.

'Hold on to it. The landlord doesn't even know it's cut.'

He packed in about two and a half minutes. He had hardly any clothes with him. He'd taken to wearing her denim shirt and a couple of her T-shirts. All he'd brought were a few CDs, and they were still scattered around her machine. They left early so they could stop by the Saturday market and rummage around the book stand. When Martina got back to her flat, she felt utterly drained. She headed towards her bed and spotted his sleeping bag on the couch. She picked up a corner of it and dragged it into her bed.

# Magic

'Ellie, I think I might be magic – a witch,' Ciara said. 'What do you think? Now seriously, what do you think? Have you ever seen me doing anything unusual or magical . . . ?'

Eleanor snapped open her eyes and looked at her watch.

'Ciara, it's six forty-five and it's Saturday!'

'I know!' Ciara said. 'Isn't it great. We're going to Salthill with Beth later, right?'

Eleanor groaned.

'Not if I don't get two more hours' sleep. Go put on a video.'

Ciara pranced downstairs like a cat and pounced on a letter in the hall, which had been lying there for two days unnoticed. She flipped it over with her teeth – and squealed when she saw it was addressed to her.

'Ellie, I got post!'

She ran back up to the bed. Eleanor was wide awake this time.

'Ciara, we have to talk –'

'OK, Mum, but I've to read my letter first.'

She opened it, smiled at the drawing and read:

Dear Ciara,
My name is Cuan and I'm twenty-seven. I'm your father. I have brown eyes like you. I like music and drawing. The cat in the corner looks a little bit like me when I was your age. I'd love to meet you some day whenever you choose. I'd love to write to you and send you more pictures if you'd like that.

Say hi to Eleanor for me.
Love, Cuan


'Ellie, where does he live? Can we visit him?'

'I don't know,' Ellie said, and picked up the envelope. 'Huh, Ennis!' she said, surprised.

'Is Ennis far away, Ellie?'

'About forty miles,' Eleanor said.

'Oh, that's really far,' Ciara said. 'We'd have to take the car.'

Later that day Ciara found a giant lobster claw at the beach. She put it over her fingers and swiped the air around Ellie and Beth.

'Can I keep it for Cuan, Mum? Does he like this kind of thing, too?'

'Whatever you like, honey. I'm sure he does,' Ellie said, too distracted to flinch.

Beth made a low mutter. She didn't like the way Ciara mentioned Cuan every five minutes, as if he was going to be her next best friend.

'Why did he wait so long, El?' she asked, when Ciara was out of earshot.

'Because I told him to,' Eleanor replied.

'Yeah, but something so important – his own daughter! I know you can be fairly intimidating but, Jesus Christ, I wouldn't let you stand between me and something so important.'

'I told him it was for the best. He loved me enough to stay clear.'

'Don't go building her hopes up too much, huh? He might disappear again before you get a chance to meet him.'

Eleanor got cross with Beth for nagging, so Beth stopped and took some photographs. Her photo of a rock fissure in the Burren was selected for an exhibition in Dublin next month. She hadn't got around to telling Eleanor and Ciara, and now it seemed trivial.

Eleanor was preoccupied. She was trying to figure out a way to tell her mother about Cuan's letter, before Ciara did, and she wasn't looking forward to it. She thought about asking Ciara to keep it secret, but decided against it. She'd never asked Ciara to lie, or not to say things – and was anxious that she might have to soon over Beth.

'Mummy, Beth, I found a hermit crab. Look!'

Beth braced herself to see something ugly; she wasn't really the outdoor type.

'Oh, look, it's got caught in that sea anemone. Who do you think will win, Beth? I think the anemone's going to have a nice crunchy snack!'

# Blackouts

Anna dropped the bombshell first. She was sitting at the kitchen table making a list. Eleanor glanced over her shoulder and read: toothbrush, pyjamas, small radio.

'Your father's going into hospital. He's been having blackouts. The doctor said that it might be the beginnings of a stroke.'

'When?' Eleanor asked.

'Four o'clock today. There's no point in delaying things. The ambulance is booked.'

'Where is he now?'

'Out in the garden,' Anna replied, standing up and holding out her list like a map, ready to follow the detailed instructions as if someone else had set them.

Eleanor looked out the kitchen window and saw her father pottering at the far end of the garden. He was examining his blackcurrant bushes, pressing the fruit gently between his fingers, and tasting an occasional one. He upended his wheelbarrow and used it as a perch to reach the bush closest to the back wall. Eleanor shook her head. His wiry body was agile, not frail. Her mother must be fussing unnecessarily.

'I can't think of the blasted name of this shrub, Ellie, can you? It's taking all the sun from my blackcurrants.'

'I'm not Ellie! I'm Ciara, Granddad!' she giggled, opening her mouth to try a berry.

'Oh, of course you are, pet. I'm just a bit dotty today. We planted this just last year and it's a special type of – blast it, I can't think! See if you can find me the plant encyclopaedia on the bookshelves and we'll sort it. Good girl, Ellie.'

Ciara trotted inside, her fist full of smudged fruit for the others to try.

Eleanor came out with the book.

'Here you go, Dad. How are you feeling?'

'Oh, I'm grand. You know your mother, she's just fussing again. You're the only one she can't rattle, Ellie. The rest of us are putty in her hands. Now where did I leave my glasses? Lord, I sound like a doddery old fool these days. I'm sixty-eight, Ellie. Surely that's not old, is it . . . ?'

'Oooh, Granddad! There's an ambulance here for you. Can I come, too?' Ciara shouted, running down the garden towards them. David hugged his granddaughter, and Eleanor sent her inside to watch cartoons.

Eleanor watched as her father, slightly bewildered, climbed into the back of the ambulance. It was silent, but flashing. Maybe it has to flash always, she thought, even when it's not an emergency. He sat on a chair with his coat and fishing hat on, and it looked all wrong. Anna followed with the bag she had carefully packed for husband, and her handbag. She paused to give an instruction to Eleanor about locking up the garden shed, and a strange look crossed her face. Eleanor saw her mother falter for a moment and glance towards the ambulance. Maybe she could do something now to reverse this drama, bring those helpful paramedics in for tea and biscuits. Call a halt to tests, and the waiting around for results. But it was too late. She handed the key to the shed to Eleanor, and climbed aboard. The nice uniformed man ensured the door was secure and the ambulance pulled away quietly.

David had a severe stroke the following morning. The hospital could do nothing, just let it take its course they said. He lost his speech and the power in his right side. They gave him sloppy food and a drink in a beaker. He couldn't work the fork. Eleanor watched a young nurse guide his hand to his mouth, then gently push down his chin to lever his mouth open. Then she explained swallowing, in a dazzlingly cheerful presentation, as if it were some clever new trick he could pick up. When he didn't take to it straight away, the nurse cajoled him to try harder.

Eleanor took a week off work and sat with him in the mornings. When his meal arrived, she fed him from a spoon. He had tears rolling down his face, and Eleanor was terrified that he would choke on the mince and grey mashed potato. They told Anna things might improve. There was a rehabilitation hospital in Dublin that offered speech therapy and physiotherapy. He could transfer there in about three weeks if he continued to recover. They put him on Prozac. When Anna queried this, they said it was standard procedure for geriatric patients.

'Sixty-eight is hardly geriatric,' she said angrily. 'The man hasn't even retired!'

They gave Anna Valium, but she threw them in the bin. After a few days David's motor coordination improved a bit so he could feed himself, just about. But he couldn't crack open a boiled egg. The engineering department in UCG sent flowers and a basket of fruit. Ciara ate all the grapes and hugged her granddad. She told him that when she grew up she was going to study sea creatures and how they made their shells. Would that make her an engineer like him or more like a vet?

# Images

Martina came up for the opening of the exhibition. Her car had broken down, so she got the train. She had a few bits and pieces to do in Dublin, but mostly she wanted to see Cuan. He was back staying at his parents' house and asked would she stay, too.

'Cuan, I'm going to be thirty-five next month – I think that's a bit old to sleep on your floor like a teenager.'

'You can have an entire bedroom. There's loads of space,' he said. 'Come on, you'd get on with them . . . better than I do, anyway.'

She had nowhere else to go. Karen had a new boyfriend and was muttering about getting engaged. James had his busy social life, even if most of it was just talk. She didn't want to get in the way if he did manage to pull some handsome twenty-year-old.

So mom and pop it would have to be, she decided. They lived on Newtownpark Avenue, an ugly compound word and an incongruously simple address. She told Cuan not to meet her at the DART because she wanted to guess the house. She surveyed the detached residences, squinting her eyes so she couldn't read the names, and she guessed right. Hy-Brassil was red-bricked, with variegated ivy, weeping willows and quirky phallic orange flowers.

'Er . . . Sarah and Brian,' Cuan said, their Christian names tripping a little uncomfortably on his tongue, 'this is Martina.'

Sarah was beautiful. She had sharp cheekbones like Cuan, and she had the same light, frenetic movements.

'Coffee? Oh, good, I'll make cappuccinos. Most of my

friends are detoxing at the moment – they frown like I'm offering them double whiskey.'

And Cuan's humour, evidently. Brian had Cuan's brown eyes and Michael's square jaw and confidence. He had his coat on and a neatly packed overnight bag open at his feet. He was a television producer, issue-based documentaries mostly. Cuan had warned her he was always preoccupied by the current project – whether it was the heroin problem in Glasgow, the homeless in Dublin or the racism against refugees in rural Ireland, it would be all that he really wanted to talk about. This time around it was effluent in rivers. Really, there's a limit to how much that can be tossed about, but he did his best.

'You see, the extraordinary thing is that most people like you say, living in the city, aren't aware of the devastation these factories are causing –'

'Martina lives in Ennis, Dad –'

'Oh, yes, yes, that's right – now take the river Fergus, there's an interesting example . . .'

And ten minutes later, he'd left for Sligo to meet some fisheries expert. He kissed Sarah, winked at Martina and tousled Cuan's hair. The house seemed instantly quiet. It was like someone had turned off the bass button on the CD player.

Martina was a little edgy, but they seemed genuinely pleased to have her stay. Cuan looked about seven.

'Here's the hard stuff and a KitKat,' Sarah said, beaming at Martina and unable to mask her utter approval. 'Cuan tells me you like them.'

Martina sat in the living room, drinking excellent coffee, looking at Michael's trophies and eating her third fun-sized KitKat – life was becoming more and more surreal, she thought.

*

They went on the DART to the exhibition that evening. Cuan was wearing a short white T-shirt. When he leaned to open the window on the carriage, his T-shirt rode up and Martina could see the band of his boxer shorts above the top of his jeans.

'Cuan, are you gay?' she asked. The train lurched and Cuan landed back in his seat with an exaggerated bounce.

'Do you think I'm gay?'

'How the fuck would I know? It's your body, your feelings – you should know.'

'Well, I don't,' he said. 'I doubt it – I mean, I'd know by now, right?'

'What about tonight? You know there'll be dozens of handsome gay men prancing about – is that why you dressed like this?'

'Like what? I always wear jeans. Jesus Christ, Martina, I bring you to my parents' house and in five minutes you turn into my dad!'

She felt old – she hated when he turned peevish. The brakes on the DART shrieked. She got off at Landsdowne Road. She left too suddenly for Cuan to follow her, but he probably wouldn't have anyway. He had to fix the lighting rig at the Setanta before the exhibition kicked off. There was a rugby match just over and drunken fools whistled at her. She walked up to Donnybrook, muttering and stamping his name into the pavement as she went.

She went into a café. There was a girl with fair hair at the table next to the window who looked so like Cuan that Martina thought she was hallucinating. The woman with her had curly hair and sallow skin, and looked about five years too old to be Eleanor. I'm cracking up, Martina thought. I've buried both my parents and endured all sorts of awful times, no problem, and some fucked-up boy-child is wrecking my life. She left the coffee shop and went into the pub next door.

She ordered a Ballygowan and a basket of chips. Both tasted stale and disgusting. I'll go back and tell him, she thought, face it. Tell him I want no further contact with him.

# Aperture

The girl at the table next to the window was making a tiny hole with her hands and holding it close to her eye.

'Apterture ...'

'Aperture,' Beth corrected, patiently. 'That's for the amount of light. Here, you can see it on the camera if you tilt it in the light.'

Ciara's eyes opened wide.

'Cool! Oh, here's Ellie. Can I take a picture?'

Eleanor walked into the coffee shop, looking exhausted.

'Sorry, guys, I had to talk with the doctors,' she said. Beth reached for her hand, but Eleanor pulled away.

'Have you still got time to get to your exhibition?'

'Just about,' Beth said. 'You guys coming?'

'No. Someone here has got to get to bed early for a change.'

'Awwwww ...' Ciara protested, and looked for an ally in Beth – but Beth knew better than to intervene.

'We can go tomorrow, Ciara,' Eleanor said. 'It's running for three weeks.'

'How's your dad?' Beth asked.

'Improving. Talking a bit – frustrated when the right word won't come. Mum looks shattered, though. I hope she'll take a few days off and go to stay with Nancy.'

Eleanor's mother was changing – almost as much as her father had in the past few weeks. She was ten years younger than her husband, and for the past few years she had argued incessantly with them all. Now she had a focus for her energy and, however awful it was for her to see the man that she loved so vulnerable, she knew what to do. But Eleanor didn't.

'How are you?' Beth asked. When she saw Eleanor glance sideways at Ciara she realized that, whatever answer came, it would be a censored one.

'Fine. You should go, right?'

'Yeah, I suppose,' Beth said. 'My five minutes of fame.'

'See you back at the guesthouse . . .' Eleanor said.

'Yeah, don't finish Harry Potter without me!'

As they were going out the door Ciara asked, 'Can I send the photo to Cuan if it comes out? It's my first proper black-and-white photo. Do you think he likes photography, Ellie?'

'Yep, sure does,' she said, sounding a little exasperated.

When they got back to the guesthouse Eleanor sent Ciara up to bed and she watched the nine o'clock news. After the first item her attention wandered, and by the time the weather came on she realized she'd learned nothing. Anna watched the news religiously; she knew about every flood or famine, and the minutiae of every political scandal. Eleanor insisted that Ciara shouldn't be subjected to the six o'clock news on a daily basis. She remembered as a child knowing way too much about the bad things in the world. Anna felt it was important to keep up with things. Eleanor knew that skimming the surface of murders and explosions meant nothing. She went upstairs to check on Ciara. They were all sharing a room, primarily because it was much cheaper. There was a double bed and a single. Ciara had crawled into the double and fallen asleep diagonally across it.

Her father was recovering, but very, very slowly. She could understand his speech, like she could understand Ciara at two – even when the sounds made no sense to others. This hospital was better, specialist and more respectful. When he was in the general hospital Eleanor had watched two nurses make his bed, chatting about boyfriends above his head as if he didn't exist. He had looked from one to another, utterly bewildered. When she visited him, there was just a fraction

of a delay before he recognized her. It was almost imper-
ceptible, like the delay on a long-distance phone line. When
Eleanor saw his face flood with recognition and relief, she
felt utterly loved by him.

In these past few weeks she had talked more to him than
she'd ever talked. She told him about Beth, twice. The third
time he asked her, 'Who's Beth?'

She just shook her head.

'A friend, Daddy. Just a friend.'

# Abstract

Martina got to the exhibition at about ten-thirty. It was just finishing up. James had left ten minutes before with a handsome bleached blond on his arm. Cuan smiled when he saw her.

'I kept you some wine,' he said. 'It's good stuff. The French Embassy donated it . . . the new ambassador's a dyke, apparently.'

'What made you think I'd show up?'

'Ah, I knew those hulking rugby types would bore you after a while.'

Martina ignored the glass of wine he held out, and took the bottle from the counter, swigging from the top as she went upstairs to the gallery. Cuan pulled the metal shutters down, locked up the main door, and followed her.

'Martina, come and look at this photograph. It's from the Burren. It's taken so close up it looks abstract.'

He traced the rock fissure slowly with his fingertips. Martina kept her distance.

'It looks like a vagina from where I'm standing,' she said. He smiled and made the glass steam up under his touch.

He took off his T-shirt and wiped the glass clean. He was beautiful and clearly flirting with her. But she was tired, too tired to play.

'OK, Cuan, we need to talk –'

'Hold on, I've two guys waiting for blow jobs in the toilets.'

'Shut up!' she said, and turned to walk away.

'Will we go for a pizza?' he asked, putting back on his T-shirt, and hiding under it as he spoke.

'What about getting back to your parents' house?'

'I have a key, Martina. I'm not really seven.'

Yes, you are, she thought – you're seven, or seventeen, or twenty-seven whenever you fucking want to be – but I'm too tired to walk away tonight. He pretended to get his head stuck in the sleeve of his T-shirt, and yelped towards her like a puppy.

'OK! OK!' She sighed, adjusting it for him. 'Let's go to South Street.'

'Cool,' he said, pushing his head out with a loud pop.

They turned off the lights on the drag queens, biker girls and abstracts like Beth's rock fissure.

Martina spotted Frank in the corner of South Street Pizzeria. He was holding his wine glass with both hands and had put some candle wax inside. He was explaining to a blonde in her twenties about his first 'work'. He had posted glass phials with various substances – all treatments for depression – to himself over a period of nine months. The only one that survived intact was the herbal remedy St John's wort . . . She looked bored. Cuan said she looked Swedish and that she probably hadn't a clue what the word 'depression' meant.

Cuan found it odd.

'You slept with him . . . Why on earth would you want to have sex with someone who looks so bitter and twisted?'

'Because, Cuan, that's what grown-ups do! It was fine – we enjoyed it.'

He winced.

'What is it with you?' Martina said. 'You're like a nine-year-old when they first hear about sex . . . Ugghhh, I'll never ever want to do that.'

'Fuck off, Martina, stop being so mean.' He went to the toilet, huffily. He brought her back a story about some drunken man in a cubicle, crying because his best friend was marrying his sister next week. They split the bill and realized they'd no money left for a taxi.

'Jesus Christ, I'm thirty-five in two weeks' time,' Martina said. 'If I was a proper older woman I could afford a nice hotel room.'

'If you were a proper older woman you wouldn't be wearing my jacket,' he said.

On their way out the door Martina spotted Frank, now chatting to the waitress – the blonde had obviously been bored to death. He had his finger stuck in the glass stem vase and was wriggling it about earnestly.

'Probably his second exhibition,' Martina said. 'He made a giant Perspex penis and wrote to fifty male celebrities, inviting them to have their photo taken naked inside it, to deconstruct the gender thing. They all refused, so Frank appeared himself in a dress made from the refusal letters.'

Cuan shrugged.

'Seems like you found a lot of time to talk as well as fuck that night.'

She kicked him like a brother.


The night was clear and warm. They walked the five miles out of town. They'd gone past the point of being tired and were giddy and energetic. They went by the coast, stopping at Sandymount to look at the moon. The tide was out, so they walked the rest of the way back by the beach. Cuan asked her to carry his rucksack for a moment. She put it on her back, muttering about the weight of it and why on earth he needed to carry so much crap around with him.

He flipped over and walked on his hands, very steadily.

'Martina, I have to tell you something . . .'

'That you were a circus performer in a past life?'

'Nope, something else . . .'

'Oh, no, no, Cuan, not another secret!'

'No, not exactly. I saw you on television reviewing that book —'

'Jesus, did they re-run that thing. That was years ago.'

'No, I saw you before I met you —'

'Oh, aren't you cute to remember! Was I very good?'

'Oh, forget it.'

'No, tell me.'

'I saw you and liked you . . . first.'

'No way! I picked you out first. I loved you from the moment you fell at my feet.'

Martina was too distracted by his antics to make sense of what Cuan was telling her. They'd have time to talk in the morning, she thought. They got back to Blackrock at four.

They sneaked up the stairs quietly, so as not to wake Sarah. As they parted on the landing Martina glanced into Cuan's bedroom. She suspected it was exactly the same since he was a teenager. There was a neat pile of clothes on a chair just inside his door.

'Jesus Christ! Did your mother leave those out for you?' she asked.

'Actually, I iron my own clothes,' he said, and she wasn't certain whether to believe him.

'Really?' She looked in his eyes, to see if he still wanted to play, but he glanced away.

'Really! Goodnight!'

She had a fitful sleep in Michael's room — surrounded by posters of lymph nodes and musculature.

# Intact

Martina woke at eight. She lay in bed because she couldn't face making polite conversation with Sarah. She knew Cuan wouldn't wake for hours. Unless he had to work he could lie in like a teenager. Martina gazed around the room. She couldn't make sense of it. Although Cuan would obviously come and go a bit, Michael was thirty. He'd recently bought a house with his girlfriend. He would probably never sleep in this room again. So why was it so intact? Why not convert it into a guest bedroom or an office? Was it nostalgia? She wondered if Sarah or Brian meandered in and out of these rooms when the house was empty, to sit on the beds, or smell the faint musky boy smell that lingers about and think, This is our family; these are our sons.

The only possible change to the room was a shelving unit that was filled with video copies of Brian's documentaries. She remembered Cuan claiming to have seen only one or two. There must be close to fifty. Brian had narrated most of them. Martina browsed through the topics, and reckoned she should watch a few of them at some point – there were lots of political and social issues she should brush up on. Though she wasn't certain how much of that sonorous authoritarian voice she could take. Cuan had often made scathing remarks to her about his father's politics – the stripped-pine, DART-line socialist as he termed him – but then, Cuan had probably never voted in his life.

The phone rang at nine. Sarah answered it and called Cuan. Martina came out and listened on the landing when she heard his tone. James had been knifed on O'Connell Street at

1 a.m. He was out of intensive care, and stable. His wallet was intact so it looked like random violence. Sarah lent Martina her car and they went straight to St Vincent's hospital to visit him, as he'd requested.

James was groggy and pale, with a drip in each arm. Cuan was shocked and said very little. Martina was full of questions, but she didn't want to press James too hard.

'I'm OK,' he said. 'I don't remember it. Actually, it's all a bit of a blur.'

He showed them the wound. Martina felt a flash of pain when she saw the five black stitches across his soft tanned stomach. Cuan looked away. James rustled in his bag and handed a set of keys to Cuan.

'I know you're due a day off, but I want you to open the gallery today. The local comprehensive has group-booked the summer project gang to the exhibition. Media studies. I suggested it and when they realized it was the Pride exhibition all hell broke loose. The Parents' Association battled against the board of management. But they came around, eventually. It's a big step. Out of sixty 12- to 14-year-olds, maybe one or two fewer will top themselves if they realize there's a world out there for them.'

'Sure. I can open the gallery in twenty minutes,' Cuan said. 'I was planning to go in anyhow . . . and, um . . . I have keys.'

'I know you've keys – he didn't whack me on the head! These are keys to my house. I want you to go get a pile of worksheets – they've all the numbers of the various organizations on them. Just hand them out. That way they don't have to question if they are allowed to take one or not.'

'No problem,' he said.

'Well, it is – my house is miles out of your way – but it's important.'

'We've Sarah's car,' Martina said, 'but you'll have to give me directions. I always get lost once I cross the Liffey.'

'It's OK,' Cuan said, 'I know exactly where it is.'

'Excellent,' James said, and he mustered a joke about the handsome Indian doctor who passed by. Cuan and Martina hugged him gingerly and left.

# Coming out

James pretended he was straight until he was twenty-five. That was about ten years of pretending. He suspected as a child he might be gay, but he wasn't certain until the age of fifteen, when he fell headlong in love with the captain of the hockey team. They were on the junior team together. The attraction was so intense, James found it almost impossible to concentrate during training, and matches were a disaster. He didn't make it onto the senior team, but he became their most loyal supporter, and that was even better. Being able to watch Mark in action, cheer from the sidelines, and all those congratulatory hugs or commiserating claps on the back; the feeling of his thick cotton shirt, wet with sweat. He got to touch Mark once a fortnight, and he savoured those brief moments of contact. Sometimes he might not catch him at the end of a match and would pop into the showers, as casually as possible, to shout 'Well done' over the steam and hiss of the water. He'd try to catch a glimpse of a different part of him each time – one week his upper thighs, another his stomach with its curly hair around the belly button. He didn't dare look at his crotch – silly, perhaps, as Mark would have hardly noticed a quick glimpse. Mark was besottedly in love with a young woman called Hazel and entirely blind to James's feelings. Probably for the best, James often thought in retrospect, as he would never have had the privileged access to him if Mark had known the truth.

James left London and moved to Dublin in the early 1980s, shortly after he came out. He worked with independent theatre companies, production-managing and directing.

Within six months of being in Dublin, he knew hundreds of people in the arts community and the gay community. He was out every night. He pre-empted an alcohol problem, joined AA and made dozens more friends. When the Setanta opened in 1992, he was an obvious choice to direct it. He was universally welcomed, and in turn he welcomed many so-called marginal interests groups to consider it their space.

When Martina joined the crew a year later they became a great team. She was full of energy for projects – a little untidy and administration bored her to death, but she was an excellent catalyst for getting work off the ground. For knowing what work was important. She could interview artists who were looking for exhibition space or theatre space, and have a sixth sense for which to back, which to reject. Unlike him, she was never dazzled by the flashy, articulate ones with the well-typed proposals. They shared an office. Everyone else at the centre called them Ma and Da.

She had been away for a couple of days when Cuan applied for the job two years previously. James remembered interviewing the shy twenty-five-year-old who looked eighteen, Walkman earphones dangling out of his pocket like a wayward spider. He'd push one bit back in and another would dangle out. Well, at least he's into music James thought. That's a start. Bashful and handsome, probably gay, James wondered had he seen him picking up the paper. The Setanta was one of the main places where people picked up the gay community newspaper, with its listings and personal ads. Sometimes on a Saturday when the coffee shop was open 200 or so would be picked up. Occasionally people too scared to bring one away would sit having a coffee, reading, looking up every so often at the people picking from the pile. Sometimes you could almost see relief on their faces – imagine, all those other people are gay.

'So, why do you want to fix things around here, Cuan?'

64

James browsed his CV. With his IT background, Cuan was way overqualified to paint the floor and wire up microphones. How many system analysts does it take to change a light bulb?

'I just want a change,' he said.

'Mmm, but you may not find this work very stimulating. Why is the IT world not doing it for you?'

'Computers get boring after a while. Everyone I know works with computers. They get a bit boring, too.'

He was cute, undoubtedly a bit fucked up, but not a drug casualty as far as James could tell. He needed the job for some reason, so James hired him.

Martina took him under her wing straight away and he blossomed. James knew what was going on between them. He could see it a mile off. He'd been there himself many times with women — that intimacy can be so seductive and confusing. Martina was observant and tough, but utterly blind when she wanted to be. He was forty-two, a father figure of sorts — even so, anything he said to her would fall on deaf ears, so he said nothing.

He knew Martina had no family, and he told her it felt the same for him. She got angry with him and said, no matter how prejudiced his mother and brother were, they existed. At any time he could try to build a bridge — London was an hour away. She hadn't that option, particularly as she didn't go in for that voodoo seance shite. He argued it out, talked of his friends being his family now.

'Well, I hope you don't regret it,' she said. 'When my mother died we left a lot of stuff unresolved, and that's the hardest thing — I'd tell her stuff now that would allow us to under-stand each other a bit better, but I can't.'

As he lay in St Vincent's Hospital, with a drip in each arm, he knew that she was right. What if things had gone slightly differently last night and he'd bled to death on the street. When he hit the ground with a searing pain in his stomach, he thought he was dying and a colourful funeral flashed in front of him, which they wouldn't have attended. They would never have known how he died and, even if they had, they would have thought such a death was a by-product of his 'lifestyle', as they would term it. They would never have known that he lived a happy, fulfilling life – that he loved and was loved. They needed to know these things. His mother was seventy-five; his brother forty-four. Time they grew up a bit.

A nurse came in, looking a little flushed.

'I'll cope without the bed pan for a little longer I think,' he said.

'No,' she smiled, 'you have a visitor.'

Last night's date, a bleached blond Greek god, appeared from behind the curtain with a bunch of tulips.

# The First Time

The teenagers arrived on time, and they made an extraordinary amount of noise in the high-roofed gallery. The boys were jostling and jeering each other; the girls were giggling and making smart remarks about the boys.

'Christ, they shouldn't be allowed have sex for at least a decade!' Martina said.

'They're probably grand in twos,' Cuan said. 'It's a group thing.'

They handed out the worksheets, which were stuffed into bags or pockets by most, discarded by some, made into three paper planes and one balled missile – all in all, a reasonably successful circulation.

The teenagers dispersed an hour later. When the crowd thinned Martina saw a familiar-looking girl with blonde hair staring at the rock fissure . . .

'It's great, Beth,' she said. 'Like a perfect cave!'

Martina looked to Cuan, who was watching this confident child also, and trembling. Eleanor spotted him straight away, as she'd expected.

Ciara was looking at the photos of couples on Harley-Davidsons, oblivious to the drama. Eleanor walked up to Cuan.

'You ready?' she asked. He nodded.

'Is she?' he asked.

'I think so . . .' Eleanor called Ciara and she skipped over.

'Ciara, this is Cuan. He works here.'

'My Cuan?' she asked, a little startled.

'Yes, your Cuan,' Eleanor replied.

She got a bit shy and said, 'But . . . but . . . I thought you lived in Ennis.'

'I live here mostly,' he said. 'In Blackrock.'

'Oh. Is there one?'

'One what?'

'A black rock?' she enquired.

Martina smiled in recognition. Cuan often played word games with her, especially when it was easier to twist syntax than attend to the meaning.

'Well, no, not exactly, but it's by the sea.'

'Oh, like Salt Hill?'

'Yeah,' he said, understanding her now, 'and Grey Stones.'

'I like the sea. I've got a lobster claw for you at home in a box, but Ellie made me put it in the garden 'cos it smelt like rotting fish.'

'I've some things in a box for you, too,' he said.

'Oh, in Blackrock. Can we go there?'

'Maybe soon, if your mum doesn't mind.'

'I've to go and visit my Granddad, but maybe sometime after that . . .' she said, and Ellie nodded.

She cocked her head exactly like Cuan and grinned.

'That's some coincidence . . . don't you think? All those place names, and they're all by the sea.'

And she took Ellie's hand and Beth's, and they left.

Martina and Cuan locked up the gallery at five and drove back to Blackrock. They were too tired to talk. Cuan was almost catatonic, but Martina couldn't let it go.

'What do Sarah and Brian know?'

'I'm fucked tired, Martina. Can we leave it for now?'

'Just tell me that, Cuan, and I'll leave it.' Martina was crunching the gears in the unfamiliar hatchback. Cuan was wincing at the noise and staring out at the sea.

'Nothing. They know nothing.'

'How could they know nothing – you were in school?'

'They weren't involved. They'd never met her parents and they thought we'd just broken up. They liked Eleanor, she was so . . . capable. For a few months they pushed me to contact her or try to find out what had gone on, then they just stopped. Sent me to a shrink.'

'I suppose you said fuck-all to him as well!'

They got to the house and Cuan took to his room, playing music a little too loud like a grumpy adolescent. Martina and Sarah watched television together for an hour. They had coffee and ate more KitKats with that slightly relieved way parents have when the kids have gone to bed. Martina got up before Cuan the next day and headed back to Ennis. She had breakfast with Sarah at about eight.

'No, don't wake him,' she said, realizing when she said it how ridiculous it sounded, for a twenty-seven-year-old to be nudged awake by his mother. 'I'll phone him later.'

In fact, she didn't speak to him for four months.

# Refuge

When she got back to Ennis, Martina didn't go to work for two days. She rang in sick. It was a half-truth – her stomach was churning and she had a rotten period. She pieced together the preceding few days and realized that Cuan must have known he was going to meet Ciara, maybe for quite a while. How could he not have told her that he was going to meet her? Their friendship was a sham.

She was furious with Cuan. He just seemed to lead a charmed life, where everything had a fairy-tale ending. All the women rallied around and made things perfect . . . even Ciara. She greeted him so open-heartedly and with such interest, like he'd just come into her classroom, a boy from another country who should be welcomed. Why did no one ever blame Cuan for not doing things, or not saying things? How could he not have told Sarah and Brian? Even when he did, Martina knew they'd accept it. They'd invite Ciara and Eleanor for Sunday lunch, play happy families and love him all the more because of it.

She picked up the phone to ring Sarah, to thank her for having her stay, but it was cut off. That bloody job isn't paying me enough, she thought. She hated Ennis Arts Centre – the atmosphere was so different from the Setanta. The theatre shows were tame and predictable. Nobody had any interest in commissioning new work. The women's poetry circle was the worst – all well-heeled Fine Gael supporters who liked 'nice' women poets who'd never write about bodily fluids or charming male ones who'd drink like fish but be full of flattery.

Martina changed jobs fairly shortly after that. She began working on arts projects in a women's refuge, just outside Limerick. She did jewellery-making and pottery with the women, and drama and art with the children – and she loved it. When they were turning pots the women would often share their stories, sometimes telling particular instances of abuse for the first time. She'd look up and see three or four women with tears rolling down their faces, into the clay. She never cried, but she didn't feel like an impostor there.

She rented a small, grim house in the sprawling suburbs just outside Limerick. She managed to get a six-month lease, which suited her better than a yearly one – a year seemed much too long a stretch of time to commit herself to. The house was cheaper than many of the apartments she had looked at, mostly because the owners wanted someone in quickly. The house belonged to an elderly woman – she had been living there up to quite recently, until her daughter decided that she wasn't coping. The estate agent who was so forthcoming with this information shook her head with unconvincing empathy.

'They're only charging rent to cover the cost of the nursing home,' she said. 'It's a nice place. They even let her bring her dog.'

Martina looked at the twenty-year-old in the crisp red suit – nope, not a flicker of sarcasm.

'Gosh, that was nice of them,' she said, and the estate agent beamed with delight.

She took the house, and hoped it didn't make her complicit in the incarceration. There was an unhappy feel to the place and Martina didn't know how to make it better, or if it was just lingering guilt. Most of the furniture and almost all of the personal paraphernalia had been removed, but the crockery was clearly that of an elderly lady. Martina couldn't bear to use the thirty-year-old willow-patterned plates – they were too full of history. She went to the pound shop and bought bright yellow ceramic plates and bowls, and she took down all the net curtains. That was as far as she would go towards personalizing the place – it was not her home and never would be. She signed up for a few night classes to get out in the evenings – French conversation and one entitled 'Your Rights as an Irish Citizen'. She abandoned the latter after a three-hour discussion on proportional representation – the mathematical end.

She started dating an academic who was recently divorced, and brushing up his French. Though he looked ten years older than Cuan's father, he was in fact forty-eight. Seamus McMahon. God, he even sounds like an old man – that was Cuan's voice in her head, still there but fading. He had two teenage boys he hardly ever saw, and had had a vasectomy when he was thirty-five. He was a sweet man, impractical and romantic. He loved her cooking. Martina cooked grown-up food at his apartment – pasta with blue cheese and wild mushrooms, exotic vegetables, crisp salads. They drank good wines. She realized she'd hardly ever cooked in Dublin – she lived on frozen pizzas or beans and chips in Bewleys.

The first time she stayed over, Seamus popped out and bought croissants for breakfast. He made tea by heating up last night's brew in the microwave. She could never love him, but he loved her. He was a thoughtful, gentle lover, which was what she wanted. He'll do fine, she thought, once I teach him how to make a decent cup of tea.

# Fissure

'Play Barbies, Beth!'

It was 7.45 and Eleanor was having a shower. Beth was waking up on the sofa, evicted from Eleanor's bed about three hours earlier, before Ciara came bouncing in. Beth grudgingly played along with this celibacy charade, but after several months of broken sleep she was unconvinced by Eleanor's reasoning, or promises that things would change. Beth didn't have to be at work until eleven, even a quarter past eleven was fine as long as she turned up with a bag of muffins for the tea break. She'd crawl back into the double bed when the house was empty. It would be still warm and scented by sex, unless Ellie had stripped the sheets in a fit of efficiency. Ciara climbed on the sofa and emptied out about a half a dozen dolls and lots of pink accessories.

'OK, you be Kelly.' She handed Beth a doll with cropped hair. Beth stretched out a sleepy arm.

'I cut her hair so she'd look more like Mummy . . . I even named her like her . . . Kelly/Ellie, see? I'll be Ken – he's her boyfriend and they're going to a party.'

Beth looked at his plastic smile. He was naked, but his crotch had some moulded Y-fronts. Does anyone make male dolls anatomically correct, she wondered. Kelly had a pink flowery crotch, perpetual knickers. God, it was very early in the morning.

'OK, I'll get dressed and call for you. Kelly, are you listening? Keep your eyes open! Only you'll tell me to go away, 'cos you don't really like Ken as a boyfriend. You're waiting for Action Man to come along.'

Eleanor came in, cross.

'Ciara, I told you to get dressed – you know you're not allowed play in the mornings!'

Ciara scampered.

Eleanor scowled at the toys strewn on the sofa.

'God, she hasn't played with that stuff for over a year. Nancy gave her a Barbie every Christmas and birthday for about three years. She said I'll thank her one day – that Ciara would have nothing to kick against if I brought her up wearing gender-neutral clothes and buying her carpentry sets.'

Beth was still just waking up.

'Come away with me next weekend, El. My brother's rented a boat on the Shannon. His girlfriend's Spanish. They're good fun.'

'Is he the computer programmer?'

Beth laughed.

'No, that's Peter – he's strictly the clubbing type. He wouldn't be caught dead doing anything wholesome. I must ring him. We haven't talked since Christmas. No, John. He's a teacher in Kilkenny, remember? He's great. You guys would get along.'

It always amazed Eleanor how casual the whole sibling thing was for Beth. She had two brothers and two sisters, no rows. They'd often let months skid by without talking to each other. Then they'd hook up like long-lost friends – no guilt trips.

'What about Ciara?'

'Well ...' Beth took a deep breath. 'I thought just us. A lot of the fun is berthing the boat and going for pints ... it wouldn't really be good for Ciara.'

'I dunno, Beth. Mum is going up to Dublin next weekend, to visit Dad, and Nancy's looking to buy a house in Greystones.'

'Christ, how old is she? Twenty-four? Why on earth is she buying a house?'

Eleanor frowned. Beth knew the signal: don't criticize my perfect family.

'Well, Ciara could go with her maybe . . . ?'

'Yeah, but there's the whole Cuan thing. Ciara might have questions, and Mum won't give her the right answers –'

'What "right answers", Eleanor. There are no right answers! You have to let go a little. You'll suffocate her with all that stuff. Lighten up a bit. It's just one weekend.'

Eleanor got angry.

'Easy for you to say – you haven't a clue about responsibility –'

'Ellieeeee! I can't find any socks,' Ciara called from downstairs, and Eleanor stormed off to sort her out.

Beth got up, planning to leave the house and not come back. A Barbie shoe cut into her foot and she flung it at the wall. She heard the door slam and Eleanor and Ciara bickering their way into the car.

When Eleanor got back that evening there was a note from Beth saying that she'd gone to Ballinasloe for a few days, family stuff, that she'd call when she got back . . . but Eleanor had an inkling that she wouldn't. That night she dreamed Ciara was running towards a lake and she was shrieking at her to stop, but Ciara wasn't paying any attention. When she woke she was sweating all over. Ciara had crawled in beside her and was sleeping peacefully. Barbie and Action Man were locked in an embrace on the edge of Eleanor's pillow.

Beth did call in that week, but it was with news. She was going to Amsterdam to do a photography course in September.

'Well, I can't hang around in the bookshop flirting with all the beautiful women in Galway for ever.' Beth was being flippant, but looked as if she'd been crying shortly before.

'How will you live?'

'Oh, I'll take a job waitressing or something. I'll be fine. Apartments are much cheaper over there. Come visit. It's a cool city.'

'Will you come back here?' Even as she asked the question she knew that it was foolish. Though she was born thirty miles away, Beth was a blow-in. She had no particular ties to Galway; she could live anywhere. Beth shrugged.

'What about us . . . ?'

'There isn't an "us", Eleanor – there's you and Ciara. Maybe when she's a bit older you might have room in your life for someone . . . but it's not working now. It's not enough for me – you're like a day-tripper. It's not like that for me. It's more important. And I can't compete.'

Beth left a package for them in the hall, with her house key resting on top. Ciara spotted it, and pocketed it. When they unwrapped the parcel it was the photo of the rock fissure and an encyclopaedia of *The Simpsons* for Ciara.

'Cool!' Ciara said, holding up the photograph, adjusting the angle so her reflection landed at its centre. 'Can I hang it on my wall?'

# Space

Cuan ran the Setanta for the three weeks while James recovered. He took over Martina's old desk and took an active interest in the programming. When James returned in August, they ran a multicultural festival with African drummers, Indian dancers and a Chinese dragon. Though a handful of critics considered it politically unfocused and soft-centred, about 500 children participated in the festivities and loved it.

Martina received an invitation to the dragon and the fireworks, but she declined. She came up to Dublin once the festival was over, when she knew Cuan had a few days off. She met James for lunch and fished for subtle clues as to how Cuan was getting along, but they couldn't stick to subtlety.

'Well, he's not screwing anyone, if that's what you're asking.'

'No, it bloody wasn't!' Martina protested, poking him with her bread roll. 'I was just wondered if things worked out for him, that's all.'

They were in a tiny vegetarian restaurant that they used to go to a lot when Martina worked at the Setanta. They both seemed cramped by the tight seating. It suited their palates, but not their personalities. Usually they ended up sharing a table and having animated conversations with loud gestures and hoots of laughter beside serene, whippet-thin men and woman who all looked like yoga teachers in comparison. Martina and James could be entirely oblivious to other people's hang-ups – this was something Cuan loved about both them and something he envied them for at times.

'He's working hard and being an excellent support to me,

and he's doing a great job. I'm taking a few months off after Christmas and I'm going to recommend to the board that they leave him in charge.'

'You think he'll manage without a babysitter?'

'I think you're being unfair,' James said.

Martina shrugged.

'Just be careful it's not the pheromones clouding your judgement.'

James meowed loudly and the bald man beside him spluttered his spinach soup.

'Or yours, dear!' he said, as he patted his neighbour on the back.

Cuan was enjoying the Setanta again. He loved working alongside James, sharing an office and sitting at Martina's old desk. Sometimes when James went out, he opened up the bottom drawer and fiddled with some things she had left behind – a deodorant that smelled like tea-tree oil, a bracelet that used to rattle against the keyboard when she typed and drive her crazy, a purple clicking pen which she fidgeted with on the phone. Sometimes he pretended she was still there, and he would tell her things.

He spent time with Ciara and Eleanor. Eleanor chose neutral places for them to meet, and tried to keep quiet and let them get on with it. They met up three times, and Cuan and Ciara clicked instantly. They could play games together, imaginary games, with no difficulty. While Eleanor put great effort into explaining to Ciara how the world worked, wrenching her away from her fantasies, Cuan just drifted into Ciara's world until Eleanor said it was time to go, or time to eat, or time to do something tangible.

In November Cuan's mother was diagnosed with cancer of the colon, and died within two weeks. No one had noticed she wasn't well. She hadn't been to her GP in five years.

Michael blamed himself for not recognizing the signs. Brian blamed himself for being away all the time. Cuan knew the real blame lay with him. He had caused her the most heartache and confusion over the years, and he should have told her about Ciara. There was this beautiful child she would have held on to life for, but she never knew.

Martina came late to the funeral, and sat beside Eleanor and Ciara. Martina found Sarah's funeral almost unbearably painful. She hadn't been inside a church since her own mother's funeral and the smell of the incense was making her retch. Cuan, Michael and Brian sat at the front, looking alone and disconnected. The church was packed. There was a lunch in a nearby hotel afterwards. For once Cuan looked all of his twenty-seven years as he tried to make small talk with cousins and elderly relatives.

Ciara hugged him and he tried not to cry.

'Will you come and meet my dad on Sunday, come to Blackrock? He's too sad to talk today.'

'Sure,' Ciara said, glancing at the tall man in the dark suit, 'if it's OK by Ellie. He looks nice.'

'He is,' Cuan said, though he felt he hardly knew him.

Martina wanted to leave as soon as she could after the funeral. Her legs were shaking when she went to commiserate with Cuan in the hotel, and to say goodbye.

'How come you're going?' he asked.

'I have to, sorry,' she said. She hugged him, too briskly. He pushed her away. He knew she was making strange and he didn't accept it.

'Why didn't you phone?' His eyes were full of anger. She couldn't look in them.

'I've been really busy – the refuge and other stuff.'

'Are you seeing someone?'

'Yeah, an academic, archaeologist –'

'Is that two people or one?'

'One, just one.'

'Good.'

There was an awkward silence and Cuan glanced towards the door. James came in, carrying suitcases and obviously had just come from the airport. He rushed straight to Cuan and hugged him. Martina felt jealous – mean and jealous. When her mother died there was no one to hold her like that, and she couldn't touch and comfort this person that she loved. She couldn't do that simple thing that James just did. All she could do with Cuan was be confused and complicated – she was a bad, selfish friend.

She looked around the room. There were extended family, colleagues of Brian's, and friends of Michael – all doing or saying the right thing. She hadn't commiserated with either Brian or Michael, and she was going to sneak away before she had to. She didn't belong in a room where people seemed to understand death. Cuan was lost and frightened, and she could do nothing, or say nothing. She would write to him or post him some poetry when she got back to Limerick. She'd try to explain it to him some day. She vanished out the door while Cuan was safe in James's arms.

# Lifesaving

When Cuan was twelve, he did a lifesaving course at the swimming pool in Monkstown. It was the summer. His parents were trying to keep him and Michael busy. Michael was going to Irish college, but Cuan had flatly refused. The lifesaving course was the compromise. He was a good swimmer; it was a useful skill.

He was partnered with a girl called Anne-Marie, from Killiney. She was fourteen and about a foot taller than him. She had red hair and freckled arms, and ginger hair in her armpits. He had no difficulty dragging her the length of the pool, and she swam like a fish. He loved the feeling of her dragging him. He felt utterly weightless and safe when she held his head firmly, one hand over each ear, and he loved the ripples of water her legs made under him. They joked around; he made her laugh. When the instructor told them that sometimes you had to hit a drowning person in the face to shock them out of struggling and drowning you, too, she looked him straight in the eyes and boxed him gently on the chin. He dived under the water in a mock faint and tickled her on the way back up. The instructor blew his whistle.

'Concentrate, you two. These are life-and-death situations we're talking about!'

On the last day they did mouth-to-mouth resuscitation. For hygiene reasons there was to be no mouth-to-mouth contact, just mimicking it to the right rhythm. Anne-Marie kept giggling when Cuan tried it, so he found it almost impossible to concentrate. His hands were shaking when he held her nose and tilted her head to the side in case of vomiting.

She was very confident when it was her turn. She leaned close enough into his chest so he could feel her breasts, her nipples hard from the water, rubbing against him. He could feel himself getting an erection and he was mortified. She was unperturbed; if she had noticed it didn't faze her. The final act she had to perform was 'the break'. In extreme situations it was necessary to employ a deft blow upwards with the heel of the hand to the stomach. They were to mimic it gently. When she ran the heel of her hand from the line of his togs to his chest bone, he did in fact faint.

Three days after his mother's death Cuan fainted again. He was staying in Blackrock for a few days. Brian had asked both sons to stay, to sort things out, but really there was nothing to sort. It was as if Sarah had been preparing for this for years, and left things as easy as possible. They cooked her food from the freezer – lasagne, fish pie – until they could no longer bear it and started eating takeaways. On Sunday Brian dislocated his shoulder trying to fix a rattle under the car – he had been obsessed with it for two days, though Cuan and Michael couldn't hear it. Cuan made him a makeshift sling from a scarf of Sarah's and Michael gave him some anti-inflammatories. He sat most of the morning nursing his shoulder, the one that had carried his wife's weight in the coffin.

Michael cooked brunch, but no one had an appetite. Cuan went back to bed; the lingering smell of greasy bacon was sickening him. He had a dream in which his mother was still alive. He was helping her in the garden. They were making a pond and, as soon as they had built it, magic fish appeared from beneath the water lilies. Sarah laughed with delight and winked at Cuan, and he wondered which of them had made the sparkling fish . . . He woke and stood up, utterly confused – it took about fifteen seconds for him to remember that Sarah was dead. When he did he collapsed on the ground.

He had been out cold for about ten minutes when Michael found him.

Michael checked him out for head injuries, but there was none. 'You're fine,' Michael said, with his efficient doctor's tone. 'You feel OK now?'

'No, I feel crap. Fuck, what time is it?'

'Two o'clock. Dad's gone for a nap, too. What time is Ciara coming?'

'Three ... Christ, I hope it goes OK ...'

'Whatever way it goes, they're family. They should meet.'

Ciara was coming to meet Brian for the first time. Cuan had told him about her the night before – though Brian had recognised Eleanor at the funeral, he hadn't realized the blonde girl who held her hand and kept whispering questions was in fact his granddaughter.

Eleanor parked outside the house at ten to three. Eleanor was usually early. Ciara wanted to get out straight away, but Eleanor said no, the arrangement was for three. Ciara kicked the seat and sulked for the ten minutes, annoyed with Eleanor for being so particular. She'd do the same if they arrived to school early – even though other children would be chasing around the yard, Eleanor would quote some note she got when Ciara was in senior infants, which said the children weren't insured to be on the premises until eight-thirty.

'Why did you fuss and make us leave so early so?' Ciara would say, her legs itching to stretch and run.

Eleanor was anxious. This was the first time she was leaving Ciara alone with Cuan. She was due to pick her up again at eight. She knew that Cuan wanted her to spend time with Brian and Michael. They would talk about Sarah, and Ciara would learn about the grandmother she'd never met. Eleanor had liked Sarah; she'd always made her welcome in the house. When she stayed over at weekends, Cuan's parents were so

83

busy they'd always be out early in the morning, so she'd hardly ever see them. Yet when she'd come down for breakfast with Cuan, there would be a place set for her at the table.

Eleanor was learning to trust Cuan, slowly. She knew he would never harm Ciara, and it was clear that Ciara loved and trusted him, understood him even. But still she felt uneasy dropping her off – letting Ciara relate to this family, to her other family, independently. Even though she'd dropped her off to parties where she hadn't even known the parents' names, and walked down driveways hearing twenty-five small children shrieking with exuberance. She did what she used to do then – she folded up her mobile number into the front pocket of Ciara's dungarees.

'Call me. I'll be nearby if you need me to come and get you.'

'Muuuum!' Ciara protested. 'I know your number in my head!'

Cuan opened the front door and Ciara rushed inside with enthusiasm.

Cuan was nervous. He had no idea how to manage this situation, but in fact he didn't have to – Brian and Michael's impeccable manners made it easy. Ciara looked at Brian's injured arm and warmed to him instantly. She sat beside him on the sofa for an hour, while he showed her photographs of his wedding, and some from his days as an amateur actor. Watching them chat, Cuan realized that Ciara would never see a bombastic patriarch, just some benign wounded grandfather. Brian dug out another album, this time with photographs of Sarah as a child and a young woman. Cuan waited for Ciara to say what people invariably said, which was how like his mother he was . . . but Ciara didn't say that. She wasn't given to saying things just for the sake of it, particularly obvious things.

Michael opened up their old games cupboard – as a child

he had loved these games, but he could rarely cajole Cuan into playing. Cuan's childhood fantasies didn't include being a property magnate, an army general or a private detective. Ciara was happy to play. She enjoyed games and they played Monopoly while Cuan cooked some food. There was laughter in the house for the first time since Sarah's death.

After dinner Ciara asked to see Cuan's bedroom, like she'd do when she went back to a friend's house after school — somewhere quiet to chatter, away from the grown-ups. She smiled at the posters, asking him to explain each one. It was getting dark. Ciara thought the moon looked like a jellyfish.

'Not a flat one, like you get when the tide goes out,' she said, showing him with her hand. 'One with trailing bits, a stinger.'

Cuan turned on a lamp and they sat on the floor, making hand shadows of sea creatures.

'Cuan, what's the easiest hand shadow to make?'

'I dunno,' he said, twisting his graceful fingers around. 'A bird? A snake?'

'No,' she grinned, 'a hand!'

He made one, too, and their shadows touched.

# 2
# January 1999

# The Poetry Section

Beth was getting on well in Amsterdam, and eventually she had got the knack of riding her bright yellow bicycle without a handbrake. She knew the back-pedal brake was logical, but it was not an instinctive reflex. The course was excellent and she'd already had two of her photos published by local presses. She had planned to come back to Ireland for Christmas, but changed her mind and stayed put. Her sister Rachael was doing Christmas this year; Beth couldn't abide her husband Jack and the two toddlers who screamed incessantly. Anyhow, they'd hardly notice she wasn't there.

Everything was going well, but she was miserable. She had to drag herself out of bed in the morning. It took her two coffees and three cigarettes to face getting dressed. And at night she couldn't sleep. Leaving Eleanor was one of the hardest things she'd ever done. Though she made it seem as effortless as possible, it hurt so bad that for the first few months she felt like screaming. She'd been in Amsterdam fourteen months, and still Eleanor haunted her from time to time, every day.

Galway had been good; she'd been there five years. She had sex with loads of women, lesbian and straight – lots of Americans, for some reason. Always women passing through for a few days, for the Arts Festival, the Film Fleadh, or Cuirt, the literary festival. She picked them up in the shop or at the trad music session in the pub down the road. She knew after five minutes of meeting a woman if there was a chance. Usually she'd bring them back to the shop after the pubs closed. She'd leave the lights off, so as not to alarm the elderly couple who lived upstairs. She'd lay her leather jacket on the floor in front of the poetry section. Whisper a few sonnets, if they were that type. Then fuck for about an hour, very quietly, as if they were in a library.

Sometimes they'd spend the night on the shop floor, then go for a huge breakfast, hang out for a few days, if it didn't seem too messy. If it was a woman's first time with another woman, and some women really surprised her in that regard, she'd always say goodbye on the steps. Tell them she was going away, or that she had a psychotic girlfriend. Keep it simple. Eleanor was totally different. She loved her from the moment she saw her. And she waited and waited . . . it must have been a whole year.

When her friends from work spotted her in the super-market with Eleanor, they teased her unmercifully.

'Our little Beth's got married . . . have you heard?'

'Fuck off, Sean. The last time you had a shag your hand got bored.'

'Oh, we are tetchy today . . . and a pretty younger woman by the looks of things?'

They'd tease her when Eleanor came into the shop, humming the wedding march. Beth paid as little heed as possible.

'OK, guys! No more muffins or doughnuts for anyone who teases *and* I'll make you deal with all the psychos and smelly people.'

This was Beth's speciality – she was skinny and five foot four, but she was the best bouncer the shop had ever had. The most brazen book thief would zip up his shoulder bag at the sight of her. Her knowledge of world literature was profound, but it paled in comparison to her ability to make troublemakers turn on their heels and walk meekly out the door.

She loved Eleanor, way too much. She was intimidated by

Ciara at the start, but she liked her and they got along, negotiating the jealousies between them. But then it became too much. She stayed over too many times and Ciara put the boot in every chance she got. Keeping herself awake for hours. Feigning stomach aches. Calling the shots. Eleanor is a great mother, Beth thought, but way, way too indulgent. She'll create a monster.

Then there was Cuan turning up out of the blue, being welcomed with open arms like he was a soldier returning from the front, having battled on their behalf for years. When it was so clearly El who did the battling – she looks a decade older than him. What fun did she have through her twenties? A few parties with Ciara and jelly and ice cream. What freedom? None. And now that it's in sight she was looking to her parents, who were certainly getting on a bit, and how she's going to look after them for the next ten years. Beth had written four letters to Eleanor since she got to Amsterdam. Eleanor had let her walk out of her life like she was the plumber or the car mechanic. Thanks. Good job. No further services required. She hadn't written once. No one in Eleanor's life knew she was lesbian; the celibacy charade had been pulled off beautifully.

# Exhibition

The kiln made a clicking noise as it cooled down – rhythmic at first, then random and infrequent. Martina liked the noise. Often she'd click her tongue against the roof of her mouth to accompany it, or sometimes to pre-empt it. She looked at the batch of pots they had just fired. Two had cracked, but most had survived. One of the women from the class had stayed to help her fire them. Dolores had been in the refuge four weeks. Unlike most of the other women, she had no children staying with her. Hers were teenagers and they were with a cousin, she told Martina, then she told her about her abuse. Martina got angry, and found words to describe the man who had beaten her. Dolores held her hand and tried to touch the anger. Even though she had been working for over a year in the refuge, Martina still got angry. The full-time refuge workers seemed inured to stories of violence. Martina planned to leave the job before that set in.

Martina looked at the lopsided pot she had made as a sample, and she smiled – she was definitely a better teacher than practitioner. Maybe if she didn't try to talk so much while she turned the wheel . . . or perhaps she shouldn't even attempt something symmetrical. Dolores had made a mask, and it had survived the kiln. The other women thought it was a witch's face – but Martina knew it was Dolores's husband's face, contorted with hate.

Martina turned out the lights in the workshop. It had become an Aladdin's cave of jewellery, pottery and painted glass. Last month she had suggested to the refuge manager that they mount an exhibition in January, if the women

92

agreed. When she discussed it with the class they were all in favour, but they didn't want it in Limerick or Ennis – too close, too many extended family of the men that beat them living nearby. The men themselves, some still raging over barring orders or custody issues, were also too close. The Setanta with its eclectic mix came to mind. She phoned James and he told her Cuan was still running it.

'He's doing a good job, in fact,' James said.

'Good. Great,' Martina said, and she got off the phone before James prodded her with questions. She knew he didn't approve of her having broken the friendship with Cuan, and she usually had trouble finding words to justify it.

She hadn't spoken to Cuan in over a year. She had posted him some books of poetry – Patrick Kavanagh, Raymond Carver, Paul Durcan – with yellow sticky notes on the covers, suggesting pages that dealt with grief. Would she be able to work alongside him? She reckoned that enough time had passed, that their lives had separated enough to make it safe. She wrote to Cuan at the Setanta, the first letter ever, and it was a business one about the exhibition. It broke the ice. He wrote back and booked her in for January. As soon as she knew she'd see him, the rest of her life started to dissolve.

Seamus wanted them to move in together. He'd suggested it two months earlier. She wasn't ready, but she was running out of excuses. He wanted to have the boys for Christmas. Christmas was never a good time for Martina. Before her mother died it had been rough; afterwards it was intolerable. She thought about cooking for Seamus and the boys. She pictured herself with an apron on, basting a giant turkey, the noise of young men and a television in the background. She'd met them a few times at this stage. One was like an athlete, all tracksuit and runners and boyish thrashing about of limbs. He talked about tennis and soccer incessantly. The other was into computers, thin with eyes that blinked uncomfortably when looking at the real world, not a screen. He talked about the Internet and computer games. She wondered if such opposites happen in families by accident, or if they grow up like that, deliberately polarizing themselves, to prise their personalities apart. Seamus couldn't relate to either of them. He was a self-proclaimed Luddite when it came to computers, and he looked like he'd never kicked a ball in his life. She couldn't do it. She couldn't sit through another meal where no one connected.

She rang Seamus and said she was going away for Christmas.

'Where?' he asked, stunned.

Berlin was the first city that came to her mind. She booked her ticket the next day. The flight was from Shannon on the nineteenth of December. She rang Cuan's mobile from the airport.

'I can't . . .' he said.

'Why not?' she asked, knowing she'd given him at least thirty seconds to come up with an excuse.

'I can't leave Dad and Michael,' he said. 'They need me right now.'

'I fucking need you, too!' she said.

'Martina, you can't just ring me out of the blue and expect –'

And she hung up. It wasn't out of the blue, and she thought he'd understand that. Although she hadn't spoken to him in over a year, he was still present in her head all the time. Whenever she went to Dublin she looked for his face in the street, often passing people she knew and not recognizing them. She shouldn't have phoned him from the airport because for the ten days in Berlin she looked for his face amongst strangers.

# Field Trip

Beth went on a field trip to the wetlands, to photograph waders, despite her protests that she was not aiming for a career with *National Geographic*. She had very little interest in waterfowl and trying to differentiate between them, so she just photographed spoonbills, the lanky extroverts amongst the speckled brown masses. She was doing better. Eleanor had written twice and even hinted at a visit in August.

Beth had built a few friendships and thrown herself into a few projects. On the last night of the trip she went for a beer with Andrea, the youngest on the course. She was twenty-two and about six foot tall with bleached orange hair. Probably a dyke, Beth reckoned, although her radar had been inactive for so long she wasn't sure. They were on their third beer and their earnest discussion about art and photography had lingered upon what made an image erotic for rather a long time.

Andrea was wearing a white, very open-necked shirt, and a turquoise pendant that hovered distractingly, drawing Beth's attention to the fact that she hadn't touched another woman's breasts in what seemed like a very, very long time. Andrea's skin looked silver in the light. It caught Beth off guard.

'God, you've beautiful skin!' As soon as she said it, she regretted it. Now they were on a slipway, but she wasn't planning to go anywhere.

'Thanks. I used to be a model. That's what got me into this whole photography thing. I wanted to see what it was like to be on the other side.'

'So, do you like it on the other side?' Beth said, flirting by rote.

'Yeah. It's good. Don't know if I'll do it for ever, but it's good for now ... I loved the modelling, though. I miss it. There's great freedom in taking your clothes off, don't you think?'

Beth just smiled and knocked back the last of her beer. She needed to get going, otherwise she'd be leaning over and kissing this flirtatious woman within moments. She started looking for her jacket.

'Have you got your flash with you?' Andrea asked, preparing to leave with her.

'Ahh, I think so ... why?' Stop now, please, Beth thought.

'Well, if you like ...'

Andrea was going to spell it out.

'If you like, I could model for you tonight? An hour or so. No charge!'

Beth shrugged.

'Look, my room's very draughty ... I don't think it would work.'

'I never feel the cold.'

Beth was shaking her head and zipping her jacket.

'Just scared ... ?' Andrea persisted, unused, obviously, to rebuttals.

'No, thanks, great offer – but no.'

Beth blew her a kiss and walked out the door. Well, there's a first time for everything, she thought. They probably would have had a fun night. Beth was tempted, but her mind was on Eleanor. Maybe Eleanor was finally ready to let her be part of her life, an important part, an acknowledged part. When they argued in the past about keeping the relationship secret, Ellie would say it was because of Ciara, or her mother, or various other excuses that rang around Beth's head like a house alarm.

Beth had been hurt before, badly hurt by someone who wanted their relationship kept secret. She learned the hard way that when a relationship is separate, it's dispensable. When she was twenty-two, she was with Laura – Laura was an actress, very beautiful and had left her boyfriend to live with her. Beth was in London at the time and it was her first serious relationship. They moved in together and Beth worked in a sandwich shop by day and a pub by night to pay the rent when Laura wasn't working.

Laura didn't tell anyone about the relationship – she had plenty of excuses along the lines of it was hard enough to find work as an actress without being pigeonholed – and she insisted that Beth keep it secret also. Beth agreed – she was so in love she didn't care. Then Laura started to get more work and was out a lot . . . Beth got suspicious, and so jealous it nearly drove her crazy. She couldn't sleep if Laura wasn't home, but she couldn't keep turning up to collect her, either, because her friends would talk. She used to go to sleep with a Walkman on. Otherwise she'd end up listening for every car – maybe that's her taxi – or every slight sound – maybe that's her key in the lock.

Then one night they were making love and Beth noticed a different scent to Laura's skin. She said nothing. Maybe she'd made a mistake. Maybe there was no man in the background, or just some one-night stand. Then Laura disappeared. Beth rang the theatre where she worked and they told her that Laura was turning up for her performances. Three weeks later Alan, the stage manager, showed up to pick up her stuff. She'd just had some clothes. Beth realized they'd lived in the flat for over a year, and all Laura had was one bag of clothes. She was like a tourist, ready to move on when the weather changed.

# History

The exhibition was called 'Breaking the Silence'. It ran for three weeks at the Setanta and was a resounding success. Cuan invited local groups to contribute and the issue of domestic violence was picked up by the media. Cuan was wary about the media interest, but Martina said it was fine, as long as the helpline numbers were included – that every time a woman told her story on the radio or television the helpline got loads of calls.

'That may be so, but I think some of those television producers are voyeuristic wankers,' Cuan said, sounding like Martina and hoping she'd notice – but she was trying not to listen. She and Cuan had worked coolly and efficiently together over the three weeks, almost impersonally. She didn't mention the phone call from the airport and Cuan didn't either.

When the exhibition came to a close, they went out together for a meal. Two refuge workers from Limerick were due to come up and join them, but they cancelled because the weather was horrendous. Martina and Cuan walked to South Street from the Setanta. It was freezing on the streets, and started to hail. Martina was fine. She'd bought some hi-tech hillwalking jacket in Berlin, which stretched up around her face, leaving only her eyes uncovered.

'I'm glad it's just us,' Cuan said.

'What?' The rustling around her ears meant she couldn't hear him. He stopped her gently and leaned in to her hood.

'I'm glad the others can't come . . . so we can catch up.'

He was shivering so Martina lent him her scarf, and they

giggled as he tried to dislodge it without opening her zip. As they got to South Street they saw Frank stumbling out.

'Jesus, early for him,' Martina said.

'Liver must be packing in,' Cuan said.

They paused while Frank lit a cigarette; they weren't in the mood to talk to him. A pretty redhead came out and linked her arm in his.

'Well,' Martina said, 'seems his other organ's working fine.'

Cuan talked about Ciara over the pizza. Martina talked about Seamus.

'He even sounds like an old man,' Cuan said.

They got a honey-pot ice cream to share. It was their habit, too cute to break.

'No, he was fine, nice. I just got tired of pretending.'

'Like we pretend?'

'No, Cuan, not like that.'

'What were the other men like, the ones you never talk about – the two before the guy from Cork . . . Richard, wasn't that his name?'

'Haven't you a good memory?' she said, trying to patronize him and put him off.

'Just updating the files,' he grinned.

Martina sat back on her chair. She had drunk three glasses of wine; so had he. He rarely asked her anything as direct as that.

'Well . . . there was Barry, he was a journalist. We were together about a year, then we fell apart. He was busy, manic, and I suspect had slept with his editor a few times. We had fun together. We were in our twenties, lots of receptions, parties, free drink. We didn't feel much for each other. Odd, really, in retrospect. One day he said "Will we take a break?" I said, "Yeah, sure," and he just picked up his *Chambers Dictionary* and a couple of videos and I haven't seen him

99

since. Whenever he's having his drink problem it's not on the same beat as Frank!'

She smiled. But Cuan still looked serious.

'And before that . . . ?'

'Oh, Joe. Well, that's a whole other kettle of red herrings! I've to go to the loo.'

She came back and saw the waitress hovering, chatting . . . Jesus, what was it about him? You can't leave him alone for five minutes. She was a little drunk. She should go home . . . she had forgotten to ring Karen to ask her to leave a key out, but Karen was the kind of friend who probably had that covered.

'How about cappuccinos?' Cuan asked.

'Yeah, whatever.'

'And Joe . . . ?' he prompted.

'Christ, Cuan, what's got into you tonight? Are you doing some fucking psychotherapy course?'

He smiled. 'Actually I have been doing some counselling since Sarah's death.'

'Oh, shit, sorry.' Now she felt mean. Bitter and twisted, she was turning into Frank. She should book her table in the corner over there now.

'Let's just chat like kids, like we used to.'

'I'm nearly thirty,' Cuan said. 'I'm not a kid any more.'

'You're nearly twenty-nine, Cuan. There's a big difference.'

The cappuccinos arrived. The waitress winked at Cuan.

'And you can stop flirting with everyone. It's getting on my nerves.'

'She's an actress.'

'Oh, of course, like every waitress.'

'No, Martina, she did a show last month at the Setanta. *Medea*. She was great.'

'Well, go ask her about the first man who broke her heart.'

She couldn't shake him off. Where was the old petulance?

He was oozing this new-found patience. It must be the parenting. It was unnerving her.

'OK, OK, Joe lived down the road from me. We grew up side by side, but never played with each other. He was mousy blond, sallow skin, grey eyes. He wanted to study engineering, but he fucked up his exams and ended up doing arts in UCD, which he hated. He was two years older than me, but I was only a year behind him in school. So when I went into first arts he was there, too, repeating the year. We did everything together, lived in each other's pockets. Wrote essays together, sat beside each other in lectures, rigged things so we got into the same tutorials. We travelled home together and more often than not had sex in the clump of trees at the corner of the avenue. I hardly met anyone else in UCD for about six months. Joe was a bit misanthropic, or shy, or just a loner – I don't know. Anyhow he had no interest in joining any of the societies, and discouraged me every chance he got. My mother was drinking a lot around then and I had no wish to go home, so sometimes we'd stay in the trees until four or five in the morning. Then go home to our separate houses, have a nap, shower, some food and hook up on the bus back into Belfield. I got pregnant in March.'

Martina paused and reached for the last of the wine, knocking over Cuan's glass in the process . . .

'Fuck!' she muttered, mopping it up.

'So, you've had two abortions . . . ?' Cuan asked, gesturing that the wine didn't matter and that he didn't want any of hers.

'Nope – you want the fucking Greek tragedy, you can have it. I knew I was pregnant, about two months gone. I got sick on the bus one morning. Joe said nothing. That evening, instead of going home he said why don't we go to the pub – it was odd. We never did that. We never had any money anyhow, not like the kids nowadays. He had a pint and a whiskey. He bought me a gin and tonic. I threw up in the toilet. He had this odd leer on his face. We walked home and stopped at the trees. He was being much rougher than usual, not that he was ever very gentle. He lay on top of me and I cut my arm on some glass. He raised my arm up, but instead of checking the damage he started painting with the blood on my arm, writing stuff. I screamed and he put his hand over my mouth and kicked me. I struggled and got away. I got home, shaking too much to use the key. Mum was up, and sober for once. She let me in and gave me some stuff for my arm. I miscarried the next morning. There was blood all over the bathroom. I was vomiting. I never told Mum, never told anyone. It was ages ago. I was nineteen. I dropped out of UCD, moved out of home that summer. Did some FÁS course and night classes and finished up my degree as a mature student when I was twenty-five.'

Cuan spoke slowly.

'What about him?'

'Oh, he finished up the arts degree, went on to do law. He's a hotshot barrister now. I see his name in the paper every now and again. I let him off. That's why I'm working in the refuge, Cuan. I can give something back now; I'm stronger.'

'How did you get so strong?'

'By not bleeding to death, or drinking myself to death or wallowing in self-pity for more than forty-eight hours.' She looked in his eyes. 'And by loving other people, I suppose. You're lucky. Ciara's a precious gift. I looked at you and her that day and I felt my heart breaking. I couldn't hold on to the first baby, or the second – I may never have a child.'

She looked around. There were chairs up on tables, a bucket and mop had appeared.

'Jesus, was I crying that much? Let's get out of here or we'll be barred.'

# Dates

'Ellie? You know when people write books, like J. K. Rowling, for instance. Do they know how those books are going to end before they get to it?'

'Dunno,' Eleanor said. 'Sometimes maybe they start with a particular end in mind, and sometimes not.'

Ciara was writing a story. Eleanor presumed it was for Cuan. As neither liked chatting on the phone, they wrote long, funny letters to each other – full of drawings and stray thoughts in bubbles around the edges. Eleanor carried around one of Ciara's in her handbag for two days, sealed with a Daffy Duck sticker, before she overcame her jealousy and posted it to Cuan.

'Is your story for Cuan?'

'No, it's for me,' she laughed. 'Do you want to hear it? It's only at the beginning . . .'

'Love to,' Eleanor said.

'OK . . .

Once upon a time there was a world. In this world everything was black or white or grey. It was a dark place and the people who lived there were always fighting or unhappy. Then a magical thing happened. A colour appeared in the world. It was the hair of a princess, and it was golden. People came from far and wide to meet her. And everyone who met her fell in love with her . . .

'That's as far as I've got. I've no idea how it will end. When is Michael's wedding?'

'In two weeks, the twentieth of June, at Glendalough.'

'Let's go buy pretty dresses tomorrow!'

'Mmmm . . . OK.' Eleanor used to buy all Ciara's clothes on her own – Ciara would wear anything, as long as it was comfortable and not black. Shopping together for clothes might lead to squabbles . . . but Eleanor would give it a shot.

'When are you going to visit Beth?'

'The second week in August, after your art course.'

'And I'm really going to stay with Cuan for a whole week?'

'Yep.'

'In Blackrock?'

'I think so . . .'

Eleanor frowned. She'd better check that. She didn't think the rough and tumble of Pearse Street would be suitable for Ciara. She looked up – Ciara was writing all the dates studiously into her diary. Well, that's not from his gene bank, she thought.


It was two months since the bank had been raided. Shortly before the bank opened one morning, two men with sawn-off shotguns had forced the manager to open the security door and made the other seven staff members lie face down on the floor. Eleanor could still feel the rough carpet against her face, the panic in her stomach. She didn't tell Ciara and she didn't tell her parents. She didn't want to frighten them and she didn't want to admit to being frightened. She was finding it hard to sleep at night, and became obsessed about locking doors and windows. The other staff seemed to get over it very quickly – within a few days they were cracking jokes about it, black jokes that Eleanor didn't find remotely funny. She wrote to Beth, but she didn't tell her what had happened. She just told her she missed her.

At lunchtime on the day of the raid, Eleanor had wandered the streets for twenty minutes, confused and frightened. People walked by her as if nothing had happened. She went into Beth's old bookshop. Even though she knew Beth was in Amsterdam, and she hadn't seen her for eighteen months, she expected her to be there – because Beth was the only person who would look at her and know something was different.

She remembered something that happened when she was eleven, not much older than Ciara was now. Her mother had popped next door to do a quick chore for a neighbour. Eleanor was making toast in their new toaster, and keeping an eye on Nancy. She put two slices in and pressed down the shiny chrome lever. She noticed that the flex of the toaster was lying over the top. She didn't move it because she couldn't believe that anything bad could happen – this was just a simple toaster, not a trap. The flex began to smoulder, and there was a putrid smell, a smell of danger. She just watched, in horror and disbelief that she could have made this danger. The fuse blew and protected her, the house and Nancy, who was playing with her dolls on the floor beside her. When her mother came back she blamed the toaster, but she barely looked at it, anxious only to hug her and Nancy and reassure them they were safe. Eleanor was nervous that when her father came home he would examine it carefully, ask her some questions and find out the truth – that she had made a foolish, dangerous mistake.

Lying on the ground for three minutes that morning she realized she'd made another mistake – she wanted Beth to hold her, to reassure her, to make her feel safe again. She thought there would be plenty of time to sort stuff out, that there would be plenty of people like Beth. But she was wrong. Perhaps there was only Beth, and perhaps she'd fucked it up.

# Director

June twentieth was a beautiful summer's day. Cuan was best man, directing events. He had invited six guests of his own – Ciara and Ellie; James and his partner, Eamon; Luke, a friend from the Setanta; and Martina. Cuan and Martina had chatted on the phone quite a bit since January, but they hadn't met up. He wondered would she turn up, and was delighted to hear the lawnmower roar of her Volkswagen as she approached.

She got out of her car in the usual way, winding down the window and opening the door from the outside. The inside handle had been broken for so long, she'd ceased to notice. She was wearing a black linen dress. He was taken aback – he'd never seen her in a dress before. She grinned, aware she had knocked him a little off balance. She went straight to him and hugged him. She could have greeted almost everyone else first – they would have been easier, even the strangers – but he was the reason she was there.

Eleanor and Ciara arrived in matching tie-dye dresses. Ciara's idea. They were ridiculously cute.

'I blame that hippie school,' Eleanor muttered to Martina, as they reluctantly posed for a photo. James and Eamon arrived, and Martina was pleased that Eamon was charming, and about forty. Most of James's lovers to date had been handsome young brats, impossible to have a conversation with.

Brian welcomed everyone in his gregarious fashion, kissing all the women that arrived European-style, a peck on each cheek. Michael kissed the women and hugged the men, with warmth and affable good humour. Martina was struck by how different their physical mannerisms were – Cuan just nodded and grinned, accepted hugs cumbersomely, but didn't proffer any.

Luke arrived. He had worked on a multimedia exhibition at the Setanta, and now was building a website for them. He was in his early thirties, about Cuan's height and build, but much heavier on his feet. Where Cuan moved like a dancer, Luke walked like a cowboy, as if his body had more gravity. He shook Cuan's hand vigorously. He chatted to Eleanor and was openly flirtatious. Martina was relieved to gather that he was heterosexual, though obviously not terribly perceptive. She couldn't have handled it if he had been Cuan's first boyfriend, not the whole twelve-hour wedding performance, and it would have been exactly Cuan's style not to forewarn her.

Sinead arrived in a red open-topped Morris Minor, with her father and her younger sister who was acting as bridesmaid. Sinead looked very beautiful, and exactly as Cuan had described her. Everyone poured into the small wooden church to allow her to make a dramatic entrance. Martina went to sit beside James and Eamon as directed by Cuan, but James insisted that she sit between them, so they could share her. Martina wondered was it OK to enjoy yourself so much in a church, surely it must be breaking some rule. There was music and poetry – Cuan and Ciara both read W. B. Yeats – and everyone cried.

There was a reception in a nearby hotel. Michael's friends all looked like doctors, and sat together. Ciara joked with Martina about it.

'One's not a doctor. See if you can guess which.'

'The one with the white carnation?'

'Nope.'

'The one with the blue sparkly dress?'

'Nope – she's a gynaecologist!'

Jesus, Martina thought, I didn't know that word until I was about twice her age.

'The one with the red hair, tapping his foot on the ground?'

'Yep!' she grinned. 'That's him, married to the sparkly dress. He's an anthropologist!'

Martina half thought that might be a kind of doctor, but knew better at this stage than to argue with Ciara.

Sinead's family and friends were impeccably behaved. The two sides were outdoing each other at mingling and befriending.

'What is it with weddings these days?' Martina asked Eleanor. 'Do they lock up the mad relatives somewhere for the day?'

'Give it time,' Eleanor said. 'I'm sure there'll be rows and drama before the clock strikes midnight.'

Cuan made a charming speech. Martina felt foolish tears running down her face and muttered to Eleanor that her tear ducts must have an allergy to champagne. Eleanor gave a wry smile. Ciara kept chirping, 'I don't get it. This is a happy day. I've never seen so many moping grown-ups.'

There was dancing. Michael and Sinead. Brian and Sinead. Michael and Ciara. Cuan and Ciara. Cuan and Sinead. Brian and Ciara. Luke and a reluctant Eleanor. James and Eamon had their first formal dance, which caused a few raised eyebrows from Sinead's family. Then Cuan asked Martina, and she accepted, though she felt uneasy at being physically close to him in such a public place.

'But the tricky question,' she quipped, 'who'll lead?'

'Oh, you do, of course,' he grinned.

They held each other and tried to dance together gracefully, like old friends should. He rubbed his cheek against hers, as if by accident.

'Feck you,' she muttered, pulling away. She knew she was too drunk to deal with this.

'I love you,' he said, 'but you can spend another few years ignoring the fact if you like.' He pretended to trip so she had to lean forward to catch him.

'Fuck you, Cuan. Just fuck you! Everyone's in love with you ... why don't you go play with somebody else? James's mouth waters when he talks to you. Sinead's kid sister has been trying to chat you up all day – you haven't even bloody noticed. Even Eleanor under that cool exterior would probably melt if you flirted with her. I'm nearly ten years older than you – and that's a decade too old to play these games.'

'Actually, you're just eight years older,' he said, 'and I'm not just playing.'

'Well, if you're finally ready to have sex, go find Jeanette – isn't she first in the queue?'

'It didn't occur to me to contact Jeanette – I haven't thought about her in about two years, but if you think that's the correct sequence, well –'

'Shut up.'

'You shut up.'

They both did and the dancing stopped. Martina sat down in the middle of an argument between Eleanor and Ciara. Ciara insisted that she had been up later than this when she had been younger, so why should she have to go to bed now. Martina could follow her logic more clearly than Eleanor's, but she kept out of it. She reckoned 'overtired' was an oxymoron only tired parents used ... She wondered would Ciara's other parent agree.

# Touch

At the end of the night, Cuan sorted out taxis for the wedding guests. Afterwards he looked exhausted. Within an hour only a handful of people were left, those that were staying in the hotel. Cuan and Martina were bickering over the sleeping arrangements. Martina was muttering about getting the last taxi back to Karen's house, saying she'd pick up her car in the morning. She was drunker than Cuan; she always seemed to get drunker than him.

'What's the problem, Martina? I've a twin room. I'd love you to stay.'

'Twins, cute. You just don't fucking get it, do you?'

'No, tell me.'

She shook her head.

'OK. OK,' said Cuan, linking her arm in his. 'Let's go have a cup of tea, then you can tell me. Seeing as we only see each other about every six months these days, I think this is as good a time as any.'

They made their way up the three flights of stairs, trying not to raise their voices.

'You love me, but it's not a sexual thing, and I can't deal with that.'

'What makes you so sure?'

'Jesus Christ, Cuan! I've slept with about a dozen men. I *know* when they want to sleep with me.'

'Fine, and how many of them did you want to sleep with?'

'All of them . . . well, most of them, at least.'

'How many did you want to sleep with more?'

'More than what?'

'More than they seemed to want to sleep with you?'

'Plenty.'

'OK, name one.'

She paused.

'Robert.'

'Oh, who was he?'

'An actor.'

They got to the top of the stairs. A night porter passed them and winked.

'You won't sleep with me because you love me – too big a risk.'

'Great observation, Cuan. Bring your psychotherapist a box of chocolates on Monday. He's a clever fucker.'

'Actually, I see Frances on Tuesdays, and Frances is a she.'

'Then bring her flowers.'

When they got to the room Cuan made the tea. He brought it over on a tray.

'Well, haven't you turned into quite the –'

'S-t-o-p,' he said gently, the word rising at the end, like a warning to a toddler about to endanger themselves.

'How'd you get so grown-up all of a sudden? I'm not sure I like this grown-up, competent Cuan. Makes me feel like the fucked-up one.'

'I'm more damaged than you are and you know it. I'm the one that doesn't have sex, remember? I want you to stay and maybe we should try stuff ... It's been a few years, so it's hardly a rash decision.'

Martina looked at him closely, for the first time all evening. He was shaking, and serious. She would have to call his bluff.

'OK. Well, touch me, then,' she said – because she knew he wouldn't.

'I can't. You start.'

She reached out her hand and touched him on the cheek.

'Nope, you're too like a brother. It would be all wrong.'

'OK, then. Touch me like you used to touch me in work – like it was by accident.'

Martina laughed.

'You are a strange, strange boy. No. I can't do that either. I'm crap at pretending . . . with you anyhow.'

She was nervous, and not feeling remotely drunk any more. Sex with the others had been easy – just a game where they kept to separate sides of the court. Where were the lines with Cuan and what were the rules? And what if he broke? If he was telling the truth, though it seemed preposterous, and hadn't had sex in a decade, wouldn't it shatter him after so long? Could Frances glue him back together? Too much of a risk.

'OK, which bed can I have? Can we squabble over that now?'

But Cuan wasn't giving up. He got out his laptop computer.

'Jesus Christ! Do you think Internet porn is going to help? Or maybe there's some step-by-step instruction website for confused friends – friendswhowanttotrytofuck.com.'

'Shhhhh. Now, what do you want to learn? Excel? Sql? How about something more fun . . . Microsoft Paint – perfect! Bring over your chair.'

'You're not joking? No, well, if you think I'm in any state to pick up one of Bill Gates's clever programmes at 2 a.m. after a wedding, you can think again!'

But she pulled over her chair. He shuffled his closer until their legs were touching. The computer was booting up. She rested her head on his shoulder. She relaxed a little.

'Now, this is how you make a canvas and this is how you select a colour, say, black.'

He picked up the tiny paint-can icon and touched the canvas, turning the screen black.

'There you go. Then you can drop in a text box like this.'

He made a rectangular space and typed in large letters –
*So why don't you touch me now?*

In a blink he made it disappear.

'Now you try,' he said.

She leaned over him and took the mouse. She made a canvas and turned it red. She paused, not certain what to do next.

'How do you do the text box thing?'

These few minutes had steadied her nerve, but he seemed terrified. He took the mouse and made her a box.

*Now? Are you sure?* she typed, and he nodded.

So she kissed him on the mouth, after years of circling, but he was frozen. She led him to one of the single beds and he crawled in with his clothes on. He moved close to the wall, allowing space for her to follow. She climbed in and held him. She rubbed his shivering body as if he were a child who had stayed too long in the sea. He shook with violent spasms as she held him close, but eventually he became still. The smell of his skin made her long to explore his body, but that would be wrong, and impossible now. She could count his vertebrae touching her stomach. She kissed the soft white T-shirt on his back once, like a promise. Eventually she drifted to sleep, with him curled into her like a cat, seemingly relaxed, but ready to leap out of her arms at the slightest threat.

Cuan kept his eyes closed and his body rigid until Martina was asleep. Then he lay awake for two hours listening to her breathing. He loved her, an absolutely overwhelming love, but he hadn't told her the truth. They should never have tried this. He should have told her about Luke – he should never have asked Luke to come to the wedding. And, worse, he had lied to her about Jeanette. When he told her he hadn't thought of Jeanette in two years that wasn't strictly true. She had been around last weekend, and two weeks before that. If he told her the truth about Jeanette, tonight might not have happened. And Martina might have bolted, yet again.

# A Pass

Luke had separated from his wife and two-year-old son three months earlier. He knew Cuan had asked him to the wedding because he felt sorry for him, thought he should get out a bit and meet people. What Cuan didn't know was that Luke was in love with him. Luke was thirty-four. He had never found another man attractive in his life. It screwed him up so much he stopped having sex with his wife. She thought he was having an affair and questioned him constantly. He would say nothing; there was, after all, no affair to admit to. She tried to catch him out – she looked at his mobile-phone bill for clues; she turned up at the Setanta to pick him up. After six months it became intolerable for both of them. She wanted answers or things back to normal. So he left.

Cuan had hardly talked to him all evening. Luke flirted with every beautiful woman there, but felt nothing. He was preoccupied at all times with where Cuan was and who he was talking to. At the end of the night Cuan drifted over to him and asked if he needed a taxi.

And that's when he said it. He felt an utter fool, but he had to say it.

Cuan was kind, but not interested.

Luke was quite drunk and got aggressive. He accused Cuan of being a flirt, then of wrecking his life. Cuan looked absolutely astounded, as if he'd never realized. As if he hadn't encouraged him.

Luke didn't leave in a taxi or take a hotel room. He wandered around the gardens, then left the hotel grounds and wandered in the forest. He saw a stag. At about 6 a.m.

it started to rain. Luke wanted Cuan so much the pain was unbearable. He rammed his fist against a rock until it bled – any pain was better than wanting someone who didn't want him. He felt humiliated. Wrecking your marriage for a lover was one thing; wrecking it for a fantasy held no dignity. He'd ditch the job for starters. Then he'd get revenge.

# Jeanette

Things had gone very badly for Jeanette in Berlin. She was working in a club, and harassed nightly by drunken men. Her flat was dingy and infested by mice. After a while she got a cat from a shelter – Casper, a longhaired black-and-white, with enormous eyes with white whiskers. He was like a cartoon cat, the way he pounced about the place and careered up the back of the sofa – so much so that Jeanette often wondered was he in fact just a figment of her imagination. She had no friends and spent most of the time she wasn't working talking to Casper or writing a journal. One night on her way home from the club a man she'd seen drinking an hour earlier cornered her in an alley. He trapped her against a wall.

'Come on, baby,' he grunted in broken English. 'You know you want it, dressed like that.'

She broke away and ran, leaving her shoes behind and splitting her skirt. Then she didn't leave her flat at all, and had to give up her job. She attempted suicide twice. The first time she took pills. A neighbour found her and she was rushed to hospital, then transferred five days later to a psychiatric hospital. They pumped her full of drugs. That was where she attempted suicide the second time. She stole a glass at dinnertime, broke it in her room that evening and slashed her wrists. She was put in a locked ward and not allowed to wash or go to the toilet unaccompanied for four weeks. She'd stand in the shower, with some boorish male nurse waiting behind the curtain, and want to die. She didn't see the sky or smell anything other than the hospital smell of antiseptic and boiled vegetables for more than a month.

Then Michael showed up.

'How did you find me?' she asked, groggy, not sure if it was just a dream.

'Instinct,' he said. 'Like I found you the last time, do you remember?'

'No ... I feel awful ... what shit am I on?'

Michael looked at the chart.

'Rough stuff. A right cocktail by the looks of things, but I'm no expert at psychiatry ... and before you ask, no, I'm not going to specialize in it just for you!'

'Oh! You must be nearly finished med school, what are you doing?'

'Gynaecology.'

'Well ... that might come in handy.'

'Jesus, let's not go there!'

'Will they let me out?'

'Not for a week or so – they want to get you off the Largactyl first.'

'Can you stay?'

'Yeah, I'll stay. What's your flat like?'

'Foul. Not up your standards!'

'Right. I'll stay in a hostel nearby ... Can I get you anything?'

Jeanette looked down at the bile-green, hospital-issue pyjamas.

'I don't suppose a nice nightie ... ?'

'Jesus – give me a break! I'm not going foraging for nighties in a strange city. Get some sleep. I'll see you tomorrow.'

Michael patted Jeanette on the arm gently, and left to talk to the doctors some more. The consultant was due in at four and he hoped her English was good because he hadn't a word of German. He should ring home, but not yet. Better to talk to Cuan about it first and see what's the best story to come up with. He was useless at lying; Cuan was, naturally enough, an expert.

Michael visited every day for a week and they talked and talked. Towards the end of the week things were a bit brighter.

'I hope you can get some thesis out of this at least! A lecture tour, maybe.'

'You can pay me back sometime, when you're stronger,' Michael said.

'You were always stronger. Tell me about the first time you rescued me.'

'The first time you disappeared you were seven. Bessie our dog got hit by a car; you were terrified. I made you give me your T-shirt to bind the wound. You ran off and disappeared for five hours. Mum and Dad called into every house on the street. The whole estate was on the alert. The gardaí were on their way to the house when suddenly I remembered there was a bush you used to hide in when we went to Blackrock Park. I went by myself because I didn't want to get Mum and Dad's hopes up . . . and there you were. Freezing and rocking yourself, like you were in a trance. I gave you my shirt and I made you climb on my back and I carried you home. You muttered gibberish the whole way home.'

'Jesus!' Cuan said, suddenly remembering. 'Casper! I have a cat. At least, I think I've a cat back at the flat . . .'

'Yeah, I dropped by – your neighbour has it covered. A neurotic animal by the looks of it. He is *not* coming back to Ireland!'

'The neighbour or the cat?'

'Neither! Hey, that's the first joke you've made – things are looking up!'

'Well, actually, the gynaecology thing was a joke, too. If I go through with the operation they don't actually add those bits in; they just remove bits . . . Don't look so squeamish. You're a doctor, for Christ sake!'

'Fuck it, Cuan . . . you don't even look like a girl! You're hairy and muscular. You're not remotely effeminate.'

'I know I don't look like a girl – but I feel like one. Gender dysphoria. Look it up in your medical tomes.'

'What will we tell Mum and Dad?'

'I dunno. What do you suggest, doctor?'

'That you got sick – something debilitating . . . say, hepatitis – and rang me from the hospital because you didn't want to worry them . . . They may be broadminded and liberal, but this is way over their heads.'

'Fine.'

'So you'll come back to Dublin, yeah?'

'Yeah.'

'And as, er . . . Cuan not Jeanette?'

'Yeah, Jeanette's going to lie low for a while.'

# Explaining

The only person that Cuan tried explaining it to was Eleanor. She was so strong and clever, and even though she was only seventeen like him, he felt she'd understand. She tried; she couldn't. She'd rooted round the libraries and bookshops and found absolutely nothing to help her understand it better.

'I don't get it, Cuan,' she'd say. 'You look like a boy, an attractive boy. To everyone else you work . . . as a boy.'

'I don't feel like a boy, inside, but I can't explain it any better,' he'd say.

'But you're not gay?'

'No, I don't think so.'

'So, when we're together, does that make us . . . lesbians?'

'Yeah, I suppose it must . . .'

They loved each other. They might have carried on for a couple of years loving each other, but then Eleanor got pregnant. In the beginning the irony was the worst part. She never told her family about Cuan's girl stuff — things were bad enough. So when her mother decided he was too young and too feckless to be part of Ciara's life, Eleanor gave in to her wishes. Ciara had two mother figures already, her and her mother — three, if you counted Nancy. She didn't need another in the mix.

Two days before Cuan reunited with Ciara, she met him in a coffee shop and questioned where he was at.

'Ciara's expecting to meet a father . . . Are you living entirely as a man?'

'Virtually all the time,' he said.

'And the times you're not . . . ?'

'Just a bit of shopping, dressing up at home – nothing to do with other people.'

'She's too young to deal with that stuff. You know that, right?'

'Yeah. I know. Of course I know.'

Eleanor looked across the table at him. He was fidgeting with the sugar, and jiggling his knee to some other rhythm that was making the teacups chink on their saucers.

'Stop bloody jittering!'

'Sorry.' He put his hands flat on the table, fingers splayed, like a creature who's just landed there, frozen.

'Are you planning any operations or anything like that?'

'No. You have to live entirely as the other gender for a while before they'll even consider it and I tried that in Germany, and it wasn't what you'd term a successful experiment.'

'Damn you, Cuan. I read every single book about transgenderism and transsexuals to try to find out what had happened between us. What does it mean about me that the first man I choose to have sex with isn't really –'

'I was the first?' he interrupted.

'Oh, yeah, you're not the only one with secrets. And I bet I'm the only bloody woman in the country who got pregnant by her lesbian lover! Anyhow, Ciara is great. When we were kids it seemed like the end of the world, but things have worked out. So, see how you two get on, but I'm happy to let you be part of her life as long as you don't dump that stuff on her – maybe when she's fifteen or so, but not while she's a child. And no disappearing. If things are getting on top of you, stick around long enough to explain to her that you won't be seeing her for a while. Deal?'

'Deal,' he replied, nodding his head. She looked directly at him, aware that he was making a supreme effort to keep still. Was this just a crazy idea that would bring pain into their lives? She had forty-eight hours to decide. She had said nothing to Ciara, so she could still back out. She wanted Cuan to say something, anything, that would reassure her, but he stayed silent.

'Fine. See you Saturday.' She got up abruptly and sent her teacup flying. Cuan caught it before it hit the ground.

# Broken Windscreens

When Martina woke, Cuan was in the shower – she wondered was he OK. She got dressed, ready to make a quick exit. Maybe she should have breakfast with him. They could talk a bit – it wasn't as if anything earth-shattering had happened. She just held him; it wasn't a bloody car crash. He emerged from the bathroom almost fully dressed, and he looked exhausted.

'Did you not sleep?' Martina asked.

'Not very well,' he said. 'The porter called me about an hour ago. There are windscreens smashed in three or four cars. They can't understand it – apparently it's never happened before around here.'

'God . . .' Martina said. 'Whose cars?'

'Er . . . yours, Dad's and Eleanor's.'

Fuck! Selfishly she felt a rising panic – that would mean hanging about for a bit talking to Brian and Eleanor for most of the morning. She had a threshold when it came to families, and she had reached it last night.

'That's fucking odd, isn't it? Was it just a coincidence?'

'No, I have a fair idea who did it. This may seem ridiculous, but Luke was very drunk last night and made a pass at me. I had no idea he was thinking about me – interested in me, whatever. He's straight, married. Anyhow, he got pissed off . . .'

'But he seemed so charming . . .'

'Yeah, I know. He wasn't so charming around midnight, though. I'm not sure. It could have been some random thing. Maybe the music annoyed someone in one of those fancy country estates nearby and they sent over their butler . . .'

Cuan was trying to joke, but he felt guilty and worn out. He sat on the bed. Martina had spent so much energy over the past few years trying not to touch him that she had skidded back into it by accident. She sat beside him and tried to hug him. His body felt tense. We're back to square one, she thought.

'Let's go face the music,' she said. 'I presume all the other victims of vandalism are munching their cornflakes at this stage.'

'Are you OK?' he asked.

'Yeah . . . it's a little weird, but I'm OK. Do you regret it?'

'No,' he said, but he looked so guilty she didn't believe him. She needed to toughen up.

'He broke all that glass because you wouldn't sleep with him . . . ? And all those times you rejected me and I never even broke a nail.'

'Do you regret . . . staying?' he asked.

'Not yet,' she said.

Please don't, he thought. Please.

# Fabrication

Luke turned up on his wife Sheelagh's doorstep five days after the wedding. He'd hardly slept or eaten in days. He was raving. Their three-year-old son Carl was having a nap. Sheelagh kept trying to quieten Luke, but he was paying little heed to her. He had just been to see his solicitor and fired her. He was trying to file a sexual harassment case against Cuan, but she refused to initiate it. There were no grounds, she said. So Luke tried to convince Sheelagh, but he was making no sense.

They'd had a very rough two years, mostly over financial matters. Luke had been burned very badly by the IT collapse. He'd had his own Internet company and at one point was worth an unreal amount of money on paper. It was a good business-to-business website and would have turned into a viable on-line business in time. He was profiled in newspapers and interviewed on radio. He got involved with investors. The media attention escalated the company's growth way too fast. He needed capital. He did a shares deal with a huge US company, but it crashed before flotation and brought Luke's company down with it. He was left with nothing.

The stress and the high-adrenalin work meant that he'd missed out entirely on Carl's first couple of years. He wasn't the type of dad who cycled to the park with his baby on the back, but he was a provider, a good one. When the business failed he started doing freelance work, but his confidence was shattered. What his clients took for wild enthusiasm was in fact desperation or a line or two of coke. The marriage was on the verge of collapse before he left. Sheelagh had put up with enough, and Carl seemed frightened of him.

He grabbed the Golden Pages and was looking up more solicitors. Sheelagh had met Cuan a few times at Setanta. She knew this was fabrication.

'No, Luke, stop,' Sheelagh said. 'Just tell me what happened.'

'He seduced me! That fucker seduced me! We went for a drink and he just . . .' Luke started crying. He sounded like he was choking.

'Did he touch you?'

'No, but he touched everything else. Jesus, Sheelagh! He ran his fingers along his pint, he touched his face all the time, he kept rolling cigarettes and licking them . . .'

Every time he closed his eyes Luke could see Cuan running his tongue along the cigarette paper. He slammed his fist on the kitchen table. He howled in pain – his fist was still wounded from the windscreens. He'd never broken glass before – so, for the first one, he used his naked hand. He didn't tell Sheelagh how he'd made abusive calls to Cuan, how he'd started stalking him. How last night he'd cornered Cuan as he locked up the Setanta and Cuan, petrified, called the gardaí on his mobile.

Eventually Luke fell asleep on the sofa and Sheelagh called their GP. Luke was admitted to hospital and spent two months getting his head back together. He wasn't gay, of course, the doctor assured him. When he was discharged from hospital, he did a six-week outpatient stress management programme, which he excelled at. In time the obsession with Cuan seemed like a bad film, like someone else had been through those feelings and he'd merely sat back and watched disinterestedly. The psychiatrist told Sheelagh that Cuan was just a catalyst – inadvertently, the experience made him crack. The stuff that spilled out was ugly – but often men like Luke don't crack, they just kill themselves.

# Fantasy

The business with Luke had terrified Cuan. On one level it was just a fantasy made flesh, a heterosexual man bewitched by him. Cuan was flattered, and enjoying the attention, because he was certain it wouldn't lead to anything. How could it? One night they went for pints and Luke told him about leaving his wife. Cuan said maybe it wasn't really over, maybe they'd still be able to work things out. Luke looked despondent and Cuan asked if he'd like to come to the wedding, take his mind off things. Luke seemed so eager, Cuan realized he'd made a bad move.

When Cuan suggested it was getting late, Luke got agitated and started quizzing him about his relationships. Had he had many boyfriends? Was he with someone at the moment? Cuan kicked for touch as he always did with this line of questioning. He avoided pronouns. Said he wasn't looking for a relationship – just sorting himself out at the moment. Usually that put a halt to things, with women anyway, but Luke wasn't backing off. Luke was staring at him intently from the far side of the table. Cuan rolled another cigarette, with difficulty as his hands were trembling. Time to go.

'Well, have you feelings for anyone, interest in anyone?' Luke persisted.

'I've been in love with someone for ages,' Cuan said. 'It just hasn't worked out.'

Then things seemed normal, right up to the night of the wedding.

After the wedding it turned into a nightmare. Luke didn't show up for work. No one apart from Cuan paid much attention – IT types were notorious for burning out. He rang Cuan's mobile five times one night, so Cuan started to switch it off. He never took a call from him. He'd listen to the messages in the morning. The messages were confused, as if Luke couldn't decide if he wanted to seduce him or murder him. Then there would be remorse – sincere-sounding apologies with excuses about work pressure, the break-up etc. Cuan let it go three nights, then he phoned James and asked his advice. James was clear-headed and said that obsessive behaviour was trouble, always trouble. He advised Cuan to send Luke an e-mail, fire him and tell him not to make any further contact. Cuan did all this, and that night Luke turned up outside the Setanta as he was locking up. It was ten-thirty and there was no one around. Cuan was terrified. Luke looked as if he'd been sleeping on the streets. He hadn't changed his clothes since the wedding. Cuan phoned the gardaí on his mobile. Luke fled before the call was answered, so Cuan just hung up.

Cuan went home and vomited all night. He went to stay with James for a few nights and told him everything. He told him about Berlin, the panic attacks, the drugs. James listened, made him hot chocolate, ran him baths with oils and candles. James was a qualified aromatherapist, but Cuan couldn't bear to be touched. James understood, everything.

They were having dinner a week later when Sheelagh phoned. She explained that Luke was in hospital, and passed on his sincere apologies for the inappropriate behaviour. There would be no more crazy calls, she assured him.

'Suppose that means I should go home?' Cuan said, reluctantly.

'Stay one more night for luck if you like. I'm getting into this parent thing . . . Lavender or sandalwood oil in the bath?'

'Oh, both, please . . .' and he followed James into the bathroom.

'Thanks, James, for everything.'
James ruffled his hair, and smiled.
'No problem. You're worth the effort.'

# Flying

Eleanor got on the plane for Amsterdam at Dublin Airport and felt her heart racing as it took off. She'd never had a panic attack, but reckoned whatever she was feeling now must be close. Cuan had turned up early wearing a Walkman. He brought one for Ciara, a pink one, and she was thrilled. Was she crazy to leave her? She'd never left her before . . . in ten years.

Anna wasn't well and she was livid that Ciara was spending the week with Cuan. You can see his influence on that child already, she said. But Eleanor ignored her for the most part. When Ciara was a toddler, Eleanor remembered, her mother had tried to convince her that her daughter was autistic because she could spend two hours playing with a bucket of water – dancing her fingers on the surface. Eleanor ignored Anna then, too – Ciara was happy, preoccupied, and they were just Cuan's fingers dancing.

Anna didn't know about her relationship with Beth. She thought they were just friends. She found Beth a bit bohemian, and a bit frank. Had she been male, Eleanor had no doubt that her mother would have made all sorts of negative remarks. The prospect of them being lovers wouldn't have entered her head. The word lesbian was probably not even in her vocabulary. Just as well. She'd put up enough barriers against the trip to Amsterdam as it was.

There was a baby shrieking in the centre aisle, with a harassed-looking young mother trying to soothe him. There was a disgruntled man in the seat next to them, typing something on a laptop. The baby shrieked louder and the woman put him to her breast. Five minutes of peace and the man's watch alarm struck, with some cheesy electronic tango. The baby let go the nipple in fright. The breast milk squirted in an arc and landed on the man's keyboard. He freaked. Eleanor giggled. The mother giggled, too. What else could she do? Even the baby started smiling.

'Oops . . . sorry, sorry. They make these bloody seats much too close together.'

The man was mopping it up with his tie.

'It's ruined,' he said.

'Maybe this kind of thing is covered by your insurance,' Eleanor said. And the whole aisle erupted in laughter. He insisted on moving.

Beth was meeting her at the airport. What if it didn't work? What if they rowed? Her mind was racing – it must be the altitude. She looked over at the baby again. He had fallen asleep on the breast. The mother was easing her nipple out of his mouth and he let it go, puckering his lips, then smiling gently in his sleep, his tiny fist still holding on to her T-shirt. Eleanor longed for a baby to hold. She hadn't breastfed Ciara. She had wanted to, and began to, but bowed to the pressure of her mother.

'Sure, you don't know how much the child is getting!' she said.

Eleanor knew now that Anna's attitude was just a spillover from the 1970s – she hadn't breastfed her or Nancy.

'Oh, it wasn't the done thing at all in my day,' she'd say. 'Sure, it's just fashionable again now. Well, you can keep your fashions. The bottles are much more convenient.'

Which was rubbish, of course, Eleanor knew, but she gave in because that was the way things were between her and her mother. Sometimes she'd fight it out and sometimes just capitulate. She wanted to mother again, entirely her own way, not by Anna's rules and regulations. She wanted a baby that she'd bring into the bed with her at night. A baby she'd carry round Galway in a sling, wandering into the galleries and coffee shops. Then she thought of Ciara – maybe she'd turn into Hitler and boss Eleanor about child rearing. Those liquid brown eyes could turn tough – Ciara's not Cuan's . . . She couldn't remember seeing Cuan look tough. She couldn't imagine Beth having much patience for babies; Ciara seemed to stretch her enough.

The plane was beginning its descent. Air travel is entirely unnatural, she thought. I'm not ready to be in a new place yet.

# A Message

The phone rang in Blackrock.

'Don't worry, Ciara,' Cuan shouted. 'It's probably for Dad. The machine will get it.'

He went downstairs and stood beside the machine while it played his father's resonant voice, calmly requesting a coherent message.

A woman with a Glasgow accent who sounded about twenty spoke.

'Hi, Brian. It's Lucy. I'm in town this week. Maybe we'll catch a film if you're about. Ring me on my mobile. Oh, and I need somewhere to stay on Saturday – presume it's OK if I come over to Blackrock. See ya.'

Beep, beep, beep.

'Beep, beep, beep,' said Ciara, coming in. 'Who was it?'

'I have absolutely no idea,' Cuan said.

'Haven't an ocean! That's what Ellie says . . . I used to say that when I was little and now she says it.'

'Yep. Haven't an ocean.'

He rang Michael.

'I'm about to deliver triplets, but, hey, what can I do for you?'

'Any idea who Dad's friend Lucy is?'

'Nope. Never heard him mention a Lucy. He mentioned a Catherine a while back. Some producer type, if that's any help . . .'

'No, sadly not. Some Lucy is coming to stay, or at least thinks she is . . .'

133

'Oh. Well, ring her and tell her Dad's in Donegal.'

'She didn't leave a number.'

'Dad's got caller ID – you know his love of gadgets.'

'Brilliant. Back to your labours.'

'Hers, actually. Mine's the easy job. This is the first triplet birth that I've ever delivered. The mother's been trying to have a baby for over a decade . . . See you for Sunday lunch. Give my love to Ciara.'

Cuan found the number and was about to call when Ciara came rushing in from the garden.

'There's this fantastic spider – it looks like a tiger. Over by the shed. You have to come . . .'

He went outside and they spent fifteen minutes watching the spider wrestling a wasp. Ciara found these dramas in nature more enthralling than any film or book. When the battle was over, and the wasp well and truly the loser, they went in and had some juice.

The phone rang again.

'It's like an office!' Ciara said, and she rushed to get it.

It was Brian. They chatted about the spider, while Cuan hovered to speak to him.

'Dad, there was a call for you. Lucy . . . She wants to come and stay – I'll ring her and say no, OK?'

Brian was silent.

'Dad? Did you hear that or did the wild weather in Donegal drown me out?'

'I'll ring her, Cuan,' he said. 'I may come back early, the weekend.'

'Cool. I'll put you in the pot for Sunday lunch. Michael's coming. It'll be like Christmas, only twenty degrees outside.'

'Could you pop Lucy in the pot as well?'

'OK.' There was silence, then Cuan said, 'She sounded like a vegetarian . . .'

'Yes, she is,' Brian laughed. 'Amazing what you can learn from a short message.'

Cuan rang Martina. If they were doing Christmas in August, he wanted her to be there.

# A Handbag

Eleanor was missing Ciara dreadfully. She missed her lightness, her inventiveness, her pure exuberance for things. Though being a single mother was undoubtedly difficult at times, Eleanor could coast on Ciara's energy and let it blind her to the trudge. She thought about what Beth had said, before she left for Amsterdam, and she was right – she had no room for her, not then and not now.

For the first three days in Amsterdam Eleanor just felt exhausted. She'd make excuses to Beth about a sprained ankle, something she did at the first gallery they visited. It wasn't really that sore or debilitating, just a reason to slow down. She also had a very painful heavy period – she could swear her periods were getting progressively worse month by month. Nancy had a whole cocktail of herbal remedies and vitamin supplements she took religiously – maybe she should try them when she got back.

Beth had assignments on two days while she was there, and these were the hours Eleanor relished. She'd laze in bed, then get up and wander into a coffee shop, or browse a gallery by herself, no one asking anything of her, no one expecting anything. She resented Beth just for being someone who wanted something from her, for loving her, for looking at her expectantly. What she had loved about Beth in the bookshop was how she seemed so funny, invulnerable, sparring with the male customers, flirting with the female ones, expecting nothing. That Beth seemed to have vanished.

Eleanor said to her, 'You're so different, when it's just us.'

'Of course I am! You spend forty hours a week in a public

place you need some defences. I was just in off of the main street, El. That's not a place to be all soft and sweet. You must find that, too, dealing with the public all the time, even if you sit behind three-inch glass. You can't possibly be nice all day every day, so you fake it.'

Sitting alone in a coffee shop in a strange city, Eleanor realized she hadn't a private life – ridiculous as that might sound. She was a bank teller, a mother and a daughter. She had to change jobs – it was foolish to spend thirty-five hours a week doing something that she hated. Some days she had a piercing headache by mid morning from the fluorescent strip lighting – so bad that the grating of the plastic grid hurt every time she pushed it to and fro. The bank was a steady job. It had allowed her move out of her parents' house and live with Ciara – to be in control. But the raid had eroded all that. It was a steady job, but that didn't mean it was safe.

Eleanor had filled out her college application form three days after she discovered she was pregnant. She was going to follow her father and put down engineering as her first preference, and he'd encouraged her in his abstracted way. Her maths was always excellent, and she'd taken technical drawing as an extra subject because she thought it would be useful. She changed her mind at the last minute – it must have been the nausea or the fear – and put down the business studies course. No one looked over her application. Other people in her class gave over control of such things to their parents; she was never like that. She was so capable, it never occurred to them she could make a mistake or not make the right choices. So capable, the tagline that haunted her. Nancy got to be the ditsy one, the silly one, the one that would lose her handbag, or her keys or lose track of time and be an hour late when she was suppose to meet someone. If Eleanor did that they'd think she'd been hit by a bus.

She looked at her handbag, a sensible bag that held her

passport, some money, her mobile, some useful items such as a nail clippers, a small calculator. Somewhere buried in there probably a toy of Ciara's, one she had grown out of like a plastic dinosaur. Could she just walk away from the bag, just pretend to leave it behind? Would the waitress notice and catch her at the door? Would the man with the ponytail in the corner be an opportunist and nab it? Would some Dutch policeman come knocking at Beth's apartment, with it tucked under an arm? Christ, no wonder she never spent any time on her own. She was going crazy. She was due to meet Beth at a museum in an hour. What if she just didn't turn up? Would Beth imagine she'd got lost, ring her mobile? What if the man with the ponytail had it at that stage? Would Beth think she'd been abducted? No, because she just wasn't the type to get abducted . . . Nancy, now, wouldn't be able to differentiate between a psycho and a nice man whom she met in a coffee shop in a foreign city who wanted to give her a lift to the museum. But Eleanor would know. Eleanor wouldn't look for a lift or directions from strangers, or any bloody thing from anyone because she was so fucking capable.

# Chess

Brian arrived back on Friday night. He looked tired from the journey. Donegal was mostly a holiday. He had scaled back his work a lot in the past year. No one mentioned the word retirement. Someone like Brian wouldn't ever take to golfing or fishing, but he was taking things easy.

He got up on Saturday morning and played a game of chess with Ciara. She won.

'Yeah, the boys always beat me, too,' Brian admitted.

'That's because we went for his queen,' Cuan said. 'He's entirely dependent on that. He can't do battle with the other pieces at all.'

'My strategy, too!' Ciara said triumphantly, and went off to ring her mum for a chat.

'So, how was Donegal?' Cuan found conversations with Brian went a lot better if he led them. Little by little over the past two years they were getting to know each other.

'Wild. It's like they've their own climate up there. Catherine came up for a while.'

'Who's Catherine?'

'A producer, a friend, a close friend. Don't fuss, Cuan. We're probably too old to get up to whatever you're imagining.'

'She's not coming to lunch tomorrow, too?'

'No, let's ease her in gently, shall we!'

'And who's Lucy?'

'She's from Glasgow. I worked with her mother years ago. She's at art college. She's good, I think.'

'She sounds about twenty.'

'Yeah, she's twenty-two.'

'And do you see her much?'

'Yes, quite a bit.'

'And is she a "close friend", too?'

'No.'

'Well . . . that's a little less complicated.'

'No, not exactly.' Brian was tidying up the chess pieces. 'I should have told you boys this years ago, but somehow there never seemed to be the right time . . . She's your half-sister.'

Brian looked calm – he'd rehearsed this, obviously. Cuan could feel his voice shaking. He couldn't get his head around the maths or the lies. Twenty-two . . . ?

'Did Mum know?'

'Yeah. She met her a few times. We dealt with it, Cuan. Your mother was extraordinarily strong.'

Cuan felt a rush of anger, but he carried on, mechanically, asking questions.

'Have you told Michael?'

'I'm meeting him today. I'll tell him then. You were the easy one to tell, for obvious reasons.'

'Why?'

'Well, you know how easily this kind of thing can happen . . .'

'Yeah, but I wasn't married, Dad!'

'Yeah, well, you haven't been married either, so don't judge me too harshly.'

'Does she know about us?'

'Of course she does! She's wanted to meet you and Michael for a quite a while now.'

'Does she know about Ciara?'

'Yeah, I sent her a photo a while back.'

Cuan's heart was pounding. He felt utterly betrayed.

'You had no right to tell her everything and us nothing,' he said.

'Look, I'm sorry. I could pretend she doesn't exist for another few years and let you all bad-mouth me at my funeral. Or we can all deal with this as adults –'

'Ciara's not an adult,' Cuan said.

'Well, then, don't tell her,' Brian said.

How can he say that? Cuan thought. How can he think it's OK to lie to children, make them fools? Brian was on his way up the stairs. He'd left the kitchen door open. Cuan could hear Ciara still chatting on the phone to Eleanor.

He was going to tell Ciara – he just didn't know how. Maybe he should ask Eleanor's advice, but not now – he'd ring her back later.

Martina had rung last evening and turned down coming to lunch. She said she'd love to spend time with him and Ciara, but not the whole circus. Once a year is quite enough for Christmas, thanks. He rang her and left a message. His hands were shaking so much he could hardly press the keys – please, please come to lunch. I need you.

Twenty-two, which meant she was born in 1977, so he would have been seven. That moment he got a flashback of Bessie being hit by the car, so graphic it was as if it was happening on the kitchen table in front of him, as if he was seeing it for the first time. He felt his chest tightening and saw the room swirling around. As he hit the cold tiles on the kitchen floor he heard Ciara's voice.

'Got to go, Mum. Cuan's just fainted, I think.'

# Lessons

Beth woke to the sound of Eleanor rummaging for her plane ticket. She was going to phone the airline to see if she could get an earlier flight. She had tried ringing back Ciara, but the phone was engaged. She told Beth what had just happened.

'Are they alone?' Beth asked.

'No. Brian, Cuan's father, is there.'

'Is he the capable type?'

'Absolutely, yeah.'

Eleanor explained how she had tried to get Ciara not to hang up, so she'd know what was happening. Typical, Beth thought, as if she could direct operations from a phone in the corner of the room.

'Oh, well, they'll be fine so. Does he do drugs?'

'No. He faints ... well, he used to faint a lot.'

'So did I,' Beth said, 'when I was in school at the convent. All those short skirts ...'

'Jesus, this isn't a time to joke, Beth.'

In fact Beth hadn't been joking. She'd passed out cold a number of times as a teenager, but it was obviously not the time to explain this to Eleanor.

'Ring back in a half an hour. Give them a chance to sort it,' Beth offered.

'I don't want Ciara to have to "sort it" – she's a child.'

'She's ten, Eleanor, and very clear-headed.'

'Yeah, ten. She shouldn't have to be a trained paramedic. This kind of incident could scar her for life.'

'Parents aren't these infallible creatures. Mine certainly aren't. Kids don't expect that ... they don't need that.'

'Well, they don't need this either. I'm going to go back early, Beth. Leave today.'

'Please don't, El. Give them fifteen minutes, then ring back, talk to Ciara, and things will probably be fine.'

For once Eleanor listened. When she rang back Brian answered. He told her everything was back to normal. It was all over in five minutes. By the time he got down the stairs Ciara had wet a tea towel and was rubbing Cuan's forehead and he was coming around. Michael was on his way over just to check him out.

'Did he cut himself. Was there blood?'

Eleanor wanted to see the incident herself, so she could second-guess the kind of fears it might evoke in Ciara.

'No, nothing like that.'

'Did he vomit?' Eleanor particularly didn't want Ciara to see him vomit.

'No, no, he's grand. Just passed out – sensitive type. He threw the vapours a lot as a child. My mother was like that, too . . . So, tell me about Amsterdam.'

Brian wanted to strike up a conversation about the marijuana laws over there – he was doing a documentary on the campaign to legalise cannabis soon.

Eleanor was curt.

'I know nothing about the drug scene, Brian. Put Ciara on.'

They spoke and Eleanor was reassured, though irked by Ciara's reluctance to prise herself away from Cuan's side. When Eleanor got off the phone she sat on the bed, and leaned her head in her hands.

'OK. OK. You were right. The drama is over.'

'Everyone survive it?' Beth asked, trying to pull her gently into the bed.

'Yeah, everyone's fine.' Eleanor lay back with a loud sigh. 'Is he just a drama queen or . . . ?'

'Oh, forget about it, Beth.' She shook her head, shaking the images of Cuan that were tumbling in.

'So ... tell me about how you swooned over the girls in the convent.'

'Will it make you jealous?'

'It might,' Eleanor said, 'I never did that. Does that mean I'm not a real lesbian?'

'It might,' Beth said, a little too seriously. 'Did you swoon over boys?'

'No, never. You obviously didn't pay enough attention to your lessons!'

'Yeah, suppose you're right. But most of the stuff they taught us in school didn't seem worth learning.'

Beth started to unbutton Eleanor's jeans, but Eleanor caught her hand and held it still.

'Did you know ... even then?'

'Oh, yeah,' Beth said, surprised by the coy way Eleanor asked.

'I didn't know the word lesbian, until I was about fourteen ... but I just knew, way before that.'

Beth didn't ask the same question back. Eleanor's frowns were a giveaway. Clearly she didn't know then, and still might not know.

# Instinct

Michael arrived shortly afterwards and checked Cuan out. He had sprained a wrist.

'Well, you won't be chopping any vegetables tomorrow,' Michael said.

'God, the lunch. Maybe we should cancel?' Cuan said.

'Not at all. Do frozen peas. Actually, if you've any in the freezer they'll help with the swelling. Sinead's looking forward to tomorrow. This will be the first time she'll have seen her new family since the wedding.'

Cuan told Michael about Lucy. He was shocked, angry, too. But unlike Cuan, Michael had an ability not to take things personally, even when they clearly were.

Brian and Ciara were waiting in the kitchen. Ciara was watching next door's cat do battle with a small rat. The rat was jumping and biting, but the cat caught it below the neck and the rat was immobilized.

'Look, Brian! Do you see how she's holding him? Where do you think she learned that?'

'From the last rat that bit her I expect,' Brian said.

'No, I think it's instinct. Do you believe in instinct?'

Brian was finding this a little uncomfortable. He suspected these were the kind of philosophical conversations he'd have had with Cuan at that age, except that Cuan hardly spoke to him from about the age of five.

'Well, yes, I suppose I do.'

'I do, too,' she said. 'For animals and for humans. I think there are loads of things we can do that we haven't been taught.'

Michael and Cuan were coming back into the kitchen.

'OK, the patient is fine,' Michael said. 'I'd say he'd be ready for a game of chess.'

Ciara rushed over and hugged him. Cuan explained that he wouldn't be up to the Natural History Museum, so could they leave it.

'Sure, next time,' Ciara said. 'Anyhow, there's plenty of wildlife action in Blackrock. It's like a nature programme out there!'

'Ciara, I'm really sorry,' he said.

'It's OK, Dad,' she said.

That was the very first time she called him Dad. He was always Cuan, and would continue to be mostly Cuan. Like Eleanor was Ellie, most of the time, but sometimes Ciara made the distinction and called her Mum.

Brian shook his head, bemused. Never one to be upstaged, he coined a new appellation for himself:

'So now that we're all back on track, how about a walk with your auld granddad?'

# Documentaries

Michael went to lunch with Brian. Cuan and Ciara played chess and watched a documentary about meerkats. Being forewarned meant that Michael asked many of the questions that Cuan hadn't. Martina arrived. She'd been in Dublin anyway – she was seeing Karen that night, but was free for a couple of hours, and would be there tomorrow. Cuan hugged her. Michael grinned.

'Thank God. A sane person!' Michael said.

'God! Standards must be slipping around here,' she said.

She looked at Cuan's makeshift sling.

'Christ, am I the cook . . . ?'

Michael and Cuan both looked sheepish.

'Oh, OK, I'll rustle something up – but, Michael, you pick up an especially nice bottle of wine for me to tipple on while I wrestle with the pots.'

Within twenty minutes Martina was in the midst of a game of Cluedo with Ciara, and Michael and Cuan took a walk to Blackrock Park.

'OK. Here's the story. Dad was shooting a documentary about supernatural phenomena in Ireland and Scotland – banshees, pookas, that kind of thing, and whatever the Scottish equivalents are. Not Dad's cup of tea leaves, but it was a BBC Scotland co-production, and the budgets were attractive. Fiona, Lucy's mother, was the production assistant working for the BBC. She was twenty-five on the first day of the shoot. Dad turned forty while he was over there, so they had some kind of joint celebration and, well, the numbers multiplied. They liked each other's accents, apparently, but that was it.'

'So, it wasn't a long affair or anything like that,' Cuan said.

'No, not remotely by the sounds of it. When Fiona discovered she was pregnant, she told Dad she was putting the baby up for adoption . . . Her family was strict Presbyterian, she'd have been ostracized, unsupported and generally she enjoyed her life as it was, and couldn't imagine how she'd cope with a baby. Dad said fine, your call, but put me down on the birth cert.

'Lucy was adopted by a Glasgow couple who had two adopted children already. She'd a happy childhood. When she turned eighteen she looked up her records – tracked Fiona, did not hit it off with her. In fact, it had gone so badly that she waited another year before she tracked down Dad. But they clicked instantly . . . Now, don't puke at this bit, but he said they were like soul mates, like you and Ciara.'

'Fuck him!' Cuan said. 'When did he tell Mum?'

'When Lucy turned up on the doorstep.'

'So that was only a couple of years ago . . .'

'Yeah. July 1996. She showed up the day before your birthday, apparently. And there's more, I'm afraid . . .'

'Jesus Christ,' Cuan said, 'how many lies can one family contain?'

'Mum seemed to have got on very well with Lucy, even though they only knew each other a short while. Dad says she'd always longed for a daughter. She told Lucy she had cancer, six months before the rest of us knew.'

'But she was diagnosed by Doctor Farrell, he told us, just a matter of weeks . . .'

'Yeah, she covered herself. Farrell knew only two weeks before she died. She'd another doctor, a woman doctor in Sandymount, whom she'd been seeing for a while. Though apparently this doctor urged her to tell us – the boys, as she referred to us, and that included Dad – she opted not to. She wanted to carry on as normal.'

'That was heavy stuff for a nineteen-year-old stranger to deal with.'

'Well, she wasn't your average teenager, apparently. Think of Ciara and add ten years. She thought about things a lot.'

'She did as Mum wished and didn't tell Dad, until after her death. She was at the funeral, but Dad didn't think that was the right time ... Anyhow, we had your mystery daughter among us for the first time. Maybe one at time was best.'

Cuan felt doubly betrayed. It was one thing for his father to have kept secrets from him, but quite another for his mother. And such important things.

'That's the place I found you by the way, when the dog ...' Michael said, pointing to a bush with a gnarled trunk that didn't look like it could shelter a child, much less hide one.

'Yeah, yeah, I know. That's what I saw before I passed out in the kitchen. The whole thing re-ran.'

'Have you ever taken acid?'

'No, Doctor! Jesus, my head is fucked up enough. Have you?'

'Just once. We med students try just about everything just once ... apart from unprotected sex! I promise you I've no mystery child about to pop out of the woodwork.'

'I can imagine why she didn't tell me, I suppose, but why not you?'

'Yeah, I asked that as well,' Michael said. 'He said that Mum figured you couldn't deal with it, and they didn't tell me because it would have driven a wedge between us. She saw how well we seemed to get on and reckoned we'd both be there for each other long after they're gone.'

They reached the park gate and Cuan lingered for a few minutes. Michael waited patiently alongside him.

'That stuff you knew about me, did that drive a wedge between you and Mum and Dad?'

'No. The librarian in College looked at me oddly for a few years, though! She very sweetly called it "my area", and reserved anything new for me – well aware that the tomes I was borrowing fell way outside first-year med.'

They went home, or to Brian's home as it now was.

Cuan told Martina before she went out with Karen.

'God, scratch the surface of any suburban family and you find a whole soap opera festering underneath!' she said.

Later that evening he told Ciara. She loved the whole idea of Lucy, someone turning up in their lives like a lost princess.

# Rash

Martina was cooking a small turkey, roast potatoes, carrots and parsnip.

'Well, you said Christmas, Cuan, and whoever did the shopping took you very literally,'

'Michael, obviously,' Cuan smiled.

Martina was busy. She had her sleeves rolled up and a production under way, and she was playing mother, perhaps her easiest role around Cuan. She hadn't had much contact with him since the wedding. She was still trying to figure out what that strange night in the hotel meant. They hadn't discussed it and she knew they wouldn't, unless she brought it up. This was the stuff he couldn't articulate, and it had passed a point where she could either.

She tried talking to Karen about it the night before, but Karen seemed distracted or just disinterested. When Martina persisted, Karen just voiced her disapproval.

'Well . . . stage-managing someone's family drama isn't what I'd choose to do on my weekend off!'

They'd had a difficult evening. Martina had called Karen's fiancé by the wrong name twice, and apologized profusely. The third time she didn't even notice, and Karen didn't bother pointing it out. She got up early and sat drinking tea in Karen's near-perfect Dalkey apartment. The teapot matched the sofa and the curtains. She wrote her a note to say thanks and left at 8 a.m.

She walked to Blackrock, enjoying the morning sun and the quirky passers-by. She wondered where she fitted in amongst these strangers who got up that early on a Sunday morning – the health freaks and the elderly people with their pampered dogs. An anxious young father pushed a buggy on its two back wheels, the angle designed to keep the toddler with the grumpy red face asleep. Martina caught his eye and he looked aghast that she might utter some chirpy platitude about the weather and wake the sleeping monster.

When Martina got to Blackrock, Cuan and Ciara were eating breakfast. They were sitting at the kitchen table in their dressing gowns, and Martina was struck by how they seemed to have become more alike and more attuned to each other. Ciara went upstairs to get dressed.

'We might not see her for a couple of hours,' Cuan said. 'She wanders off in her head when she's on her own.'

'Well, she can't patent that characteristic!'

'I'd better get dressed, too . . .'

'Vanish for longer than ten minutes and I'm out of here. I'm not some dial-a-chef.'

'Thanks . . . I couldn't have gone through this perform-ance without you.'

Fifteen minutes later, Cuan was working by her side. He was finding her various implements and ingredients from the cupboards one-handedly, his other still in the sling. They were working closely, bantering and teasing each other gently. He was wearing a T-shirt Ciara had made for him, with a drawing of a grinning ginger cat. It was oversized and white, not his usual skimpy style.

Ciara reappeared, still in her dressing gown, and she brought in bunches of herbs from the garden. The remnants of Sarah's herb garden had survived, despite nobody tending it.

'Magic!' Martina said. Clearly delighted, Ciara went back out to find some flowers for the table.

Martina was chopping the herbs – sage, parsley, thyme – until the different greens dissolved into one.

'God, these are fantastic!' she said, and she cupped some in her hand and held them for Cuan to smell. He bent over and smelt them, then leaned lower and brushed his face gently against her hand like a cat.

'Oh, this bloody wrist is fine!' he said after a while, getting annoyed with the sling. 'But I think I'm coming out in a rash from the stress . . . Can you look?' he asked.

She was up to her elbows in vegetables, but he was looking for attention. She washed the muck from the potatoes from her hands.

'Where?' she asked, with exaggerated patience.

'My back,' he said turning around.

She lifted his T-shirt. What the hell was she supposed to do now – look, not touch? He had a rash, but it wasn't very angry-looking.

'Yep. Stress or those chemicals in the washing powder. It'll probably vanish in an hour or two.'

But he still wasn't happy – she was being too perfunctory, too practical.

'I think it may be on my chest, too. Could you check?'

He turned around and she raised his T-shirt with one hand, without looking in his face. She studied his skin briefly.

'Not a trace,' she said, 'and, whatever it is, I wouldn't say it's contagious.' She dropped the T-shirt, and ran her fingertips along his stomach as it fell.

'Thanks,' he said.

And she recognized it for the first time, clearly in his eyes, his desire to be touched by her.

Ciara came in with an enormous bunch of flowers for the table.

'Here you go!' she said proudly, and neither of them knew who should step forward and accept them.

# Research

Sunday was Beth and Eleanor's last day together. Beth had to get some prints developed and was heading out for a couple of hours to a tutorial. They were due to meet at a museum later. They had spent very little time talking about what might happen next. Beth felt the time had come to broach the subject. Things had gone OK, but a lot of the time Eleanor had been edgy, unable to relax. Beth had let a lot of things pass. She knew Eleanor was missing Ciara, like an actor floundering a little without her director.

Eleanor had got a call from her mother and Nancy last evening and she was still reeling from all their news. She had been away for a few days, and she felt they surely could have told her some of this before she left. Her parents were going to move to Dublin permanently. David was doing well, and had been offered part-time work supervising a PhD student. Nancy had just got engaged to a man called George. He was handsome, thirty-one. He worked in insurance and played golf, already.

'He sounds just the ticket,' Beth said.

'There's no need to be sarcastic. It's what Nancy wants. She's young, but she's ready to settle down.'

'What about you, are you ready?'

'What do you mean?'

'I'm finished up here in October. What do you want, El?'

'I need more time to think.'

'I've been here for two bloody years. If you still don't know at this stage, we're obviously not meant to be together.'

'You've had all this time . . . even the work you're doing,

your photography, is about you. I don't know what I want. I think I want to be with you. I think I want to stay living in Galway. I think I want to have a baby. I just don't bloody know!'

'A baby? You never mentioned that before!'

'Well, yeah, I know.'

'Well, go find yourself a fucking husband so.'

'I know I *don't* want that –'

'I'm not in the mood to joke around – I may be macho, but I don't produce sperm.'

'No, but there are ways. I read this article recently –'

'Jesus Christ! I'm sure you'd be the best lesbian partner if you only found the right book, but it doesn't work like that. This isn't research; this is life. My life, your life, and we're not facing the same direction.'

'What if we were to raise a child together?'

'I don't know if I want that kind of life and, even if I did ... you get pregnant by some anonymous sperm bank or cajole some nice man, it would always be your child, Ciara's brother or sister. So one day when we argued over whose turn to do the wash-up you could pick up the child and go.'

'You're so cynical. That's not how it would be necessarily – we'd be equal.'

'But we're not. We're not equal now. How would a child make us equal?'

'What do you mean?'

'We're not a couple – there's me and there's you and there's your entourage: Ciara, your parents, Nancy, Cuan, no doubt back in there, and me. Do you know you never talked to me about Cuan, never even mentioned his name, until Ciara got that letter?'

'You never asked. It's not like I was hiding it.'

'No, I'm sure you weren't deliberately "hiding it". Just like the way you don't deliberately hide the fact that we're together.

But you haven't told anyone – your family, your work people – that we're together. You're not out. That may not seem like a big thing to you, but, believe me, it is. The only people that know are Ciara, who's given another of her Barbies' hair the chop, and Cuan, probably, though I'm not sure he's that copped on. Can you see things from my perspective just for five minutes?'

'No, you're being unfair. Why should I make my life more difficult by explaining stuff to my mother?'

'Because you're pushing thirty. And if being with me "makes your life difficult", then that's that. I've had enough. We're not a couple – I don't think you even know how that structure works – and I want that, and if we can't have it I have to go find someone else . . . someone who wants to build a life with me, not dabble in some alternative lifestyle!'

'How could you say that?'

'Because I feel it – I love you and I know if you felt even ten per cent of that you'd want more from me.'

Beth was crying. Eleanor looked at the tears rolling down her face, tears like Ciara's, tears that could race each other. Tears that could trip over each other at the corners of her eyes. She had no tears like that, ever. She held her.

'I'm sorry, Beth, really, really sorry. It's not that I don't want you as part of my life, it's just that I like the way I'm different with you. That's why I want to keep it separate.'

Beth wiped away her tears and toughened up, she'd heard this too often.

'Separate, yeah. Cordoned off like the scene of an accident. Eleanor, has it occurred to you that you might not be lesbian – that you might be just hiding?'

Eleanor shook her head – it hadn't occurred to her that she was hiding, and she didn't think it was true.

'Why don't you tell me things? Take a few risks?'

'I don't know . . .'

156

'Well, I can't keep doing this – I can't keep waiting for you to trust me. It's like waiting to get hurt.'

'I'm not trying to hurt you, Beth. I'm just lost . . . Fuck it!' Eleanor looked at her watch. 'You have to go.'

'It's a tutorial; I can just not show up. This is more important.'

So they talked for another two hours. Eventually Eleanor rang Ciara and suggested taking another three days away, if it suited her and Cuan. It did. Beth and Eleanor spent an hour on the Internet finding where Eleanor would fly to next, on her own.

'Find a city full of dykes. Go to a club, see if it feels right . . .'

'Jesus, are trying to offload me on to some other unfortunate lesbian?' Eleanor laughed a little anxiously, but Beth was serious.

'No. But I want you to be with me by choice . . . How many lesbians do you know?'

'None, actually.'

'See, that's crazy, Eleanor. Galway is stuffed full of lesbians – you're just not looking.'

'But why the fuck should I be? I'm with you.'

'No, actually, you haven't been. We broke up, remember? I was too in love with you to put up with a small fraction of your attention. You've been single for a year and a half. I haven't a clue why you're with me – I'm actually not even sure why you're here now. I want you here, I'm not complaining about that – but I don't know why you came.'

Eleanor was silent. She wasn't sure either.

'El, when I was fifteen, the only dyke I knew was Martina Navratilova – I know that's a cliché, but there you go. I grew up on a farm in Ballinasloe – it wasn't exactly San Francisco. I couldn't even hit a fucking tennis ball on target, but I stuck her picture on my homework notebook, and I scrawled her name across my canvas schoolbag and bided my time.'

'But you might have been teased –'

'Fuck it, I'd have welcomed a bit of gentle teasing at that point. At least it was acknowledging the thing! The day I wrote her name on my bag I stopped fainting. That's why I kept passing out. I was thirteen, fourteen. I was denying the thing, just holding my breath. I'd a crush on someone in class and I'd see her throw her arms around someone, or take off her jumper – simple, tiny things like that – and I'd just get dizzy with wanting to touch her and end up flat on the floor. See, I'm even getting turned on now thinking about her. Susan O'Loughlin. She had a brace in her teeth and she used to suck her spit around her mouth in this sexy way. My mouth would just water when I sat beside her, so I'd do the spit-sucking thing, too, really quietly, and imagine kissing her. And, you know something, Eleanor – that's perfectly *normal*. Locking yourself away on a celibate kick for a decade isn't.'

'Did you ever kiss her?'

'Oh, yeah, eventually! I got incredibly brave and rang her just before a school disco, asking to borrow a pair of jeans – an excuse to be in her bedroom and take my clothes off. I just knew by the way she watched me that she was inter-ested . . . and brave, too. She asked to try on my T-shirt, the most boring ill-fitting black T-shirt you can imagine – but it did the trick. Before long we were both almost completely undressed and in her bed doing beautiful things. My instincts are usually right!'

'This time, too,' Eleanor said.

'I hope so, El, because I'm not always sure . . .'

Eleanor didn't want to hear any more doubt, or answer any more questions.

'Were you out then?'

'God, no. Have you ever been to Ballinasloe? I wasn't ready.

And even if I was, being out would have outed Susan, too, and she certainly wasn't going down that road in a hurry! It didn't last. We had about half a dozen beautiful nights together, before her mother copped on. Nothing was said. Sue lied to me and said she needed to study, that she was worried about exams. She said I couldn't stay 'cos we never got any sleep. She wanted us to be friends, but I refused. I just couldn't do it. It would have been such a lie. So we fought for while, then an endless hostile silence, awful stuff – blanking each other in the corridors. She moved school the following year. I'm sure her mother forced her – I hated her mother, hated both of them, for ages. Thought I'd never fall in love again. Hoped she never would. I spent about five years expecting her to come back to me. How crazy is that? Even after I'd slept with other women . . . for a while it was like I was practising for her.'

'Have we time to do some more practising?' Eleanor leaned over and kissed her, but Beth was still serious.

'I'm not practising with you, El. This is real.' Eleanor kissed her again.

'I know, and for me, too.' And every time she touched her, it was true.

# Table Talk

Brian was uptight all morning. He had gone to the shops and bought about five Sunday newspapers.

'When the hell is he going to read those?' Cuan muttered. They had been avoiding eye contact with each other, neither wishing to get into a row on the cusp of Lucy's visit.

Everyone, apart from Ciara, perhaps, was apprehensive about meeting her. She knew it was selfish, but even Martina felt resentful. Whatever the hell her relationship was with Cuan, most of the time they played brother and sister. The prospect of a real sister coming into his life filled her with jealousy.

Michael and Sinead arrived first and brought a chocolate cheesecake. They argued over who had made it, so Martina suspected they bought it on the way over. Ciara made melon wedges, with slices of apple and orange on cocktail sticks so each starter look like a sailing boat. After she made three perfectly she got bored, so Cuan helped her finish them.

'Brilliant!' Martina said. 'That should get us off on the right track.'

Then Lucy arrived. She was beautiful. She had short brown hair and long brown limbs. She had Cuan's eyes and grace. She had Michael's calmness and she looked physically strong in a way that Cuan never did. Cuan was strong – he just didn't look it, so people would forget it. Even Martina forgot his strength, though she had seen him many times dismantling a theatre set and lugging large objects. Lucy looked it. She looked like she could lift the entire table. She was intense, a little like Ciara's intensity, but not as arresting, intense in a still way. Martina could imagine total strangers telling her their life story on a bus. She was a vegetarian. Martina had rustled up a cashew nut roast at the last minute. Ciara insisted on eating this, too.

'I should be a vegetarian,' she said with perfect logic, 'if I'm going to study animals I should stop eating them.'

Lucy spoke of her travels. She had Brian's confident way of speaking – no apologies or nervous tics, no clearing of the throat as Michael did, or trailing off mid sentence like Cuan.

She'd just come back from backpacking in Asia. Ciara was fascinated.

'Oh, have we got an atlas so I can see exactly?' she asked. Cuan shook his head.

'Nope, I've a map of the stars and planets upstairs some-where, but no atlas.'

'Me neither,' Michael said. 'Though all my old medical text books are in the attic . . . How about a map of all your blood vessels?'

'Cool,' Ciara said, 'but not now.'

Brian must have an atlas somewhere, but he didn't offer one. He was enjoying Lucy's company too much, perhaps, to prise himself away and rummage around the bookshelves. He was obviously enjoying presenting her to the rest of his family, too – this was the intelligent, artistic child he under-stood. Lucy produced a photo of her sitting on a camel. Brian put it on the mantelpiece beside photos of Michael wearing robes and holding scrolls and a photo of Cuan, taken the year he left school. It was an odd photo. Cuan never looked right in photos to Martina, even recent ones – as if he were too fluid for the camera to catch him.

Brian looked over at Lucy with pride as she recounted her adventures and Martina felt angry with him. She'd seen him look at Michael like that, too – but not Cuan. She realized that it wasn't a matter of him getting to know Cuan as an adult, patching things up. She knew that he'd never love his youngest son unconditionally, always warily. As if Cuan was less real than the other two. For Martina, Cuan was the most real person in her life. He was confusing, exasperatingly so at times, but she was most aware of him being in the world.

The talk around the lunch table was a little stilted, for the most part. Aside from being attentive to Ciara, Cuan was at his most diffident, even towards Martina. They had got to the dessert stage, and Michael and Ciara were fixing it up in the kitchen. Martina hated the diffidence and tried to reel him in a bit.

'You should give Michael a look at that rash,' she said.

'It's fine!' he said, not even looking up at her.

Martina was finding his bad temper tiresome. He was making no effort to be pleasant. She turned to Lucy and asked about Glasgow, and Lucy in turn asked her about her work and about Limerick. Then Lucy made an innocent mistake, obviously misled by something Brian had told her, or not told her.

'And that's OK with your boyfriend,' she said, nodding good-humouredly at Cuan, 'that you live over a hundred miles away?'

'I'm not her boyfriend,' he interjected, in a tone that didn't hide his contempt for her presumption. Brian frowned at his excessive reaction, but said nothing. Michael rolled out the cheesecake in a valiant attempt to break the tension, but it was too late. Martina let Cuan know he was a cranky bollocks and left shortly after.

# Mixed Messages

Martina sat back on the train and closed her eyes. Surely now she had her answer; there was no ambiguity left. The message in his eyes earlier may have meant one thing, but, even if he was attracted to her, clearly he didn't want to be. Fuck him, let him mess up somebody else's life, not hers.

When she got back to her flat there were three messages on her answering machine. The first was about a job that had come up in a Dublin refuge – she had an interview slot on Tuesday. The second was from Cuan – a long apology, so tactful and comprehensive that Martina reckoned Michael must have scripted it for him. He asked her please to come back up to Dublin soon. He needed to talk. There were important things he needed to tell her. He could have rung her on her mobile, of course, but he obviously wanted the uninterrupted platform of a recorded message. She played it three times, before listening to the final message.

The third was from the refuge to say that a woman who had been through her workshops had committed suicide the previous month. Martina knew her well – it was Dolores Fagan. Martina remembered the night they talked, while the pots fired in the kiln. Dolores had two teenage children, almost adults at this stage. She had been violently beaten many times by her husband, and endured years of psychological torment from him. He was alcoholic, a binge drinker. He could be off drink for three months and things would be tolerable, the children would banter with him like normal teenagers, then every so often he wouldn't turn up for dinner on a Friday night, always Friday. Instead he would show up at 2 a.m. or 4 a.m.

and wake the whole house – when they were little, the children would pretend to be asleep; as they got bigger, they'd try to come to her defence. He never raised his hand to them – she had that marked as her threshold. If he ever did that she'd leave, she'd say . . . Then one Friday he was particularly drunk and he belted her across the face in the bedroom. Their collie Moll was in the corner of the room and pissed herself with fear. He picked her up and threw her out the window. She was seven and survived the fall, but her legs were so badly broken the vet suggested putting her down. Dolores ignored the advice and nursed her back to health. She felt it was crucial that Moll lived. The dog had been witness and, in fact, the dog had been the threshold. Dolores killed herself last month, three days after Moll had died.

There was always a question mark over Martina's father's death. That's how they would say it, relations gossiping in front of her as a child, and presume that this would be an oblique enough reference to suicide for her not to understand. But she picked it up and knew they were wrong. Her father wouldn't have left her – not like that. He had asked her to mind the towel. A blue towel with an orange sun at the centre. He had asked her to stay put, not to wander over the rocks. She did what she was told. She had no memory of him drowning, only vanishing. Often when he'd swim he'd do tricks for her – lie on his back and make enormous splashes with his feet. Tumble in the water or dive deep like a whale and show up again twenty feet away. When her mother came to her on the shore she wouldn't leave her spot, certain he had learned some new trick where he could stay under longer and would reappear any moment. They found his body five days later. Martina was never brought to the funeral, so she never saw him dead. For years she hoped that they'd made a mistake, found the wrong body, that he could still reappear as if by magic.

# Plaster Cast

Cuan wasn't well. He was breaking. The business with Luke had fractured him. The week in Blackrock had been almost impossible for him. He had planned to be there on his own with Ciara, but in time they were surrounded. Cuan's life depended on hiding things. To be surrounded meant he was existing three-dimensionally as a man, not as a woman. Jeanette was real; Cuan was just the front. If he became fully surrounded as a man, he would die. Because she would die. He believed that Martina would love Jeanette – she just needed to meet her properly. When she touched him in the kitchen, when her fingers traced across his stomach from one hip to the other, he wanted to tell her there and then. He was ready, but there was no time. He rang her and left a ten-minute message on her machine.

He moved out to Pearse Street with Ciara for the extra days. It was very unusual for Eleanor to alter her arrangements, but Ciara seemed happy at the prospect of more time with him. He was getting on very well with her, but he felt utterly drained of energy as soon as she went to bed. Though he loved her and loved her company, sometimes the fact that he was her father struck him as entirely impossible. He brought her into work on Monday and introduced her as his daughter for the first time to people. She looked so grown-up with her new denim jacket, her hair tied back and her composure, that they both enjoyed watching the jaws drop with incredulity.

He was feeling particularly low on Sunday night when Michael dropped him and Ciara to his flat. They talked for two hours after Ciara went to bed. Michael offered him drugs, but Cuan refused – the last time the drugs had been so hard to get off. Michael suggested the alternative might be a short stay in a psychiatric hospital.

'But they'll drug you there, too. It's how they work,' he warned.

Cuan thought back to the last time – it was a siege. Jeanette had taken the handsome young Cuan hostage, and the doctors and nurses all waited by the bedside with their scalpels and their needles to force her to release him. He had learned so many of the bad things about being a woman in Berlin – being humiliated, objectified, threatened. But to walk on the streets and be recognized as a woman thrilled him – not the clothes, not like a transvestite where it's about the stuff on the outside, but the inside, to be recognized for what you are on the inside. Cuan had become like a plaster cast cracking and peeling. Take him away, Jeanette screamed for weeks, just take him away. Wash him off me. He feels nothing; it won't hurt.

'I really don't want to go to hospital, Michael. Do I need to?'

'We'll see in a few days. Are you OK to mind Ciara?'

'It's just two more nights, and Martina's coming up tomorrow. She'll be here at lunchtime.'

'Does Martina know this stuff?'

'No, not yet.'

'She loves you, Cuan, you know that? I mean, it's obvious . . .'

'I love her, too.'

'But not in the same way, right?' Michael was off familiar territory here. He was great on the medical stuff, and he'd obviously read up on the gender stuff, but complicated love relationships were not something he could profess to be an expert on.

'I dunno. I mean I'd like to be loved, but as a woman, not the way I am . . . Does that make sense?'

Michael didn't understand. Cuan didn't really understand it either. He just knew it. He'd always known it. It wasn't a sexual thing – he thought very little of sex. He wanted to be loved and desired, but almost any touch was false because people believed they were touching a man.

'And what about Martina?'

'I'll find a way to explain it to her,' he said.

# Separate

Eleanor picked Glasgow because at least then she could eavesdrop on conversations, and because she'd heard it was a little like Dublin so it wouldn't feel too foreign to her.

'Be yourself for a while,' Beth had said. 'See what it feels like.'

It felt numb, dead. Eleanor found it incredibly difficult. Three days seemed like a daunting stretch of time. She got up before everyone else in the small hotel and went shopping. She went for coffee and got a paper – she'd go to as early a film as possible, she didn't care what, as long as it was at least two hours in length. The Glasgow Film Theatre was running Mike Leigh films back-to-back. Perfect: that was four hours taken care of, from 6 p.m. until bedtime.

She went into second-hand record shops, mostly old vinyl stuff, and thought how much Cuan would love it. She flicked through the singles from the 1980s, remembering particular summers and people. She went into an antiquarian bookshop and bought a Kate O'Brien first edition for Beth. She looked at the shelves and couldn't remember which books she'd read. She went into an art shop and thought of Ciara and bought her pens that had smells attached – peppermint and strawberry.

The Mackintosh Tea-Rooms were next, and she thought of her mother and bought her a mug, but she wasn't even going to tell her mother she'd been to Glasgow. This must be what it feels like to be cracking up. She looked around her to see was anybody staring, the way she had stared from the arrogance of total sanity at the less fortunate. She found all the space around her suffocating.

She sat in a park and the sun came out. She felt calmer. Ciara phoned her on her mobile.

'I'm not in Blackrock, Ellie. I'm at Cuan's flat in Pearse Street, OK?'

'Sure. I'm not in Amsterdam. I'm in Glasgow!'

'Glasgow, cool! You must visit Lucy.'

'Who?'

'Lucy, my new aunt. Well, I suppose she's not my new aunt exactly, but new 'cos we just met her yesterday, but she went back on a plane last night. She lives in Glasgow and she's at art college and she works part-time in a gallery called something funny – Cuan will know. You could just call in!'

'Well, I'm not sure that –'

'Oh, please, please, she's really nice!'

'What's her second name?'

'Ooops, I don't know that. Cuan, what's Lucy's second name?'

'Haven't an ocean,' he said.

'OK, ask him the name of the gallery.'

'OK. Hang on!'

Eleanor heard Cuan and Ciara laughing in the background about 'Sauchiehall Street' . . . What the hell was she doing in Scotland? Ciara didn't seem to miss her at all.

'Socky Hall Street, Mum. It's in the middle of everything, apparently.'

# Boxes

Martina rang Cuan back and agreed to call to him on Tuesday. She left a message on his answering machine to say that she'd mind Ciara for a while and they'd make time to talk. When she put down the phone, she wondered had he chosen not to take her call. Sometimes Cuan liked things to move very slowly, just step by step, her move, then his move. She had learned how to play the game, though often it irritated her intensely. She discovered that the easiest way to reach him was to ring his mobile and leave no message – then he'd ring back.

On Sunday evening she went for a couple of drinks with friends from work, and on Sunday night she got drunk in her flat alone. She passed her bathroom mirror and saw her mother. Not resemblance or a look around the mouth, but her mother exactly. It wasn't unusual for Martina to drink alone – she'd often have a few glasses of wine – but it was unusual for her to get drunk. She fell into bed with most of her clothes on.

She woke on Monday morning with a thundering headache. She went to the bathroom to throw up and realized she had vomited the night before, but she had no memory of doing so. She threw out all the drink in the house, even the sickly liqueurs that she'd been given as presents over the years. She tied them into three different plastic bags and chucked them in the outside bin. The house was a mess. It had been deteriorating since she moved in, but it looked particularly depressing that morning. The fridge was full of festering things. She always kept bits of things and didn't throw them out in time. Sometimes she'd end up throwing the whole container out, rather than try to clean the mould from it.

It was the same when she lived in Dublin. Cuan was one of the handful of people who'd been into her flat. He'd always do the washing up. Sometimes he'd call from the kitchen, 'Do you want me to do anything about the science experiments in the fridge?'

And she'd let him.

She had stuff in cardboard boxes that had moved flats five or six times and never been taken out.

'Do you need all this stuff?' Cuan would ask.

'It's my mother's stuff,' she'd say, and some of it was. But some was all her own.

'You know psychotherapists use the word baggage as a metaphor,' Cuan joked. 'For you, it's literal!'

If she had a family home with an attic she could store them there, but she didn't. When she was ten, her mother had drunk the house in Rathfarnham away. She had brought her to a meeting with the bank manager and burst into tears about the debts and the worries. Martina just sat there, not really recognizing this side of her mother, not sure what she was suppose to do or say. Her mother hadn't given her a script for this drama. So she just sat silently, fidgeting with the buttons on her coat.

They sold the house and lived in rented accommodation after that. Martina remembered travellers calling to the door and buying some of the furniture. They loaded the old brown sofa onto an open-topped van. She had a photograph of herself aged about two, sitting on her father's knee on that sofa. After he'd gone, she'd sit and brush her face against its velvet – smooth one way, rough the other, then smooth again. She wanted to scream and run down the road after the van. Climb on the back and curl into the sofa and be taken anywhere.

She got the train to Dublin on Tuesday. She still felt too fragile to drive and the headache hadn't lifted. She hadn't been in Cuan's flat in Pearse Street for ages and was surprised by how colourful and personal it had become. He had hung up photographs and paintings of Ciara's, and posters from his favourite shows at the Setanta. They had some lunch, and her headache eased. Cuan left for his meeting.

She was minding Ciara for a couple of hours, before her interview. They were reading and listening to music. Ciara could be full of questions and animated, or relaxed and self-absorbed like now. Martina was glad it was the latter mood, so she could settle herself for the interview. She wasn't sure if she wanted a job in Dublin. She had considered cancelling the interview that morning, but she tossed a coin instead of reasoning it out.

A mouse appeared and ran under Cuan's bedroom door. Martina shrieked, but Ciara said she'd look after it, she loved mice. Ciara tracked it to the wardrobe, which was open just a crack. She held her breath and listened. It had burrowed into a large cardboard box. She pulled out the contents of the box and found it cowering in the corner.

'I've got him now, Martina!' she called. 'Oh, he's really scared.'

'Careful!' Martina shouted from the safety of the living room. 'They can bite, you know.'

'It's OK. I know how to hold them,' Ciara said.

Ciara caught it by the tail. It was squeaking and squirming around.

'Don't look, Martina! I'll pop him out the back.'

The mouse scurried up the back wall and burrowed into the ivy on the top. It settled under a leaf, and was almost camouflaged among the grey ivy stems. Ciara watched it for a few moments, just a few feet away. Its beady eyes were facing forward. It could so easily turn its head and see her, but it chose not to. Ciara could have rustled the leaves around it, and forced it to move again, but she didn't. They both stayed still, as if they'd made a pact.

'Wash your hands!' Martina said, when Ciara came back inside. She didn't want to hear a blow-by-blow account of the capture.

'They don't have half as many diseases as rats, you know. Michael was telling me there's this thing called Weil's disease –'

'Agghhh, not now, Ciara, please! Tell Cuan all about it when we get to Bewleys.'

'Oh, OK. Were they your clothes in the box? They looked nice.'

Martina went quiet. She had to say something, some lie, quickly.

'Props . . . from a play. Cuan saves stuff in case it can be used again.'

'Oh. Good idea,' Ciara said.

Then Martina had to distract the most alert ten-year-old in the country, a child that could catch a mouse in her bare hands, so she could take a look.

'Have you seen the Irish Wildlife Trust website? It's great.'

'No, we don't have a computer at home.'

'Oh, you'll love it – I'll get it up for you.'

While Ciara was absorbed by the social life of the elusive pine martin, Martina went into Cuan's bedroom. On the far side of his bed there was a cardboard box and the contents lay strewn on the floor. Skirts, dresses, tights, make-up and, in the middle of a torn black velvet skirt, a journal, with Jeanette scrawled in red on the front. She flicked though it – drawings and poems, loads of line sketches of a cat and mutilated bodies. She was obviously a very disturbed woman. The last entry was a suicide note written when she was twenty-two . . .

*I'm doing this so Cuan can live.*

Jesus, Martina thought, why did he never tell me about this?

# Matching

When they got to Bewleys, Cuan was waiting for them at the door. Ciara ran to hug him. A woman buying coffee was staring at them. Yeah, what kind of newfangled family is this? Three people born in consecutive decades, all wearing faded denim jackets, like a cult. Martina rarely noticed other people when she was with Cuan. Normally he eclipsed the whole room for her.

Ciara and Cuan were having an animated conversation about the mouse. Martina felt like an outsider – Cuan was the person most familiar to her, and yet he was a stranger. They bumped into James, entirely by accident. Because it was their last night together Ciara was urging Cuan to bring her to a film. Martina jumped at the opportunity to spend the evening with James instead, after her interview.

The interview went well – too well because they offered the post to Martina on the spot. Her instinct was to turn it down, but it seemed ridiculous to have applied, only to reject it. She asked for a couple of days to make up her mind and they agreed.

James cooked her dinner. Eamon was away on business; Martina was delighted to have James to herself for the evening. They talked for three hours about drink, men and Cuan. By the end she had agreed to go to an open AA meeting and not drink for a month, just to see what happened. And she told him that she planned to walk away from Cuan, again.

'I can't see him, James. Five minutes and my thinking goes haywire. I tell him everything and he tells me lies, I know he does, all the time. After we slept together, and I mean just *slept* together – not sex now as you or I would define it – he switched off his phone for about five days. I was so angry with him.'

'That wasn't because of you, Martina. I know that for a fact. It was because of Luke. Talk to him – he'll tell you.'

'It's not so different, James! It's all unwanted sexual attention. I know Luke behaved psychotically and I don't, at least not most of the time. But we both want to drag Cuan kicking and screaming into the grown-up world and he's just not ready!'

'That's because he has other stuff to deal with first –'

'Jesus Christ, James. He's nearly thirty! I'd slept with a dozen people by that age and I'm sure you could multiply that figure. That's the age to have sex, not to play the coy virgin. Whatever about him, I'm much too old to play those games. I've tried to pretend I don't have these feelings for him, to convince myself that it must be an illusion – and a lot of the time that works – but then it creeps up on me again, slowly or like a bolt, and I'm not going though it again. Every time I leave him it hurts – see, I'm sounding like a bad pop song. You know you're fucked when you start sounding like the stuff you'd usually switch channels on the radio to avoid.'

'Maybe you just want a fantasy?'

'Oh, well, you can bloody talk!'

'Touché! Sure, I've had a host of fantasy lovers. I had a great time. But tanned hunks turn pale very quickly if you're looking to share your life with someone. Eamon's real – he leaves smells behind him in the bathroom, but I still love him.'

'OK, OK, OK, and what about Cuan? You're attracted to him and he flirts like hell with you. How come it doesn't stop you two having a friendship?'

'I love when he flirts with me, but that's all it is. That's why it's so safe. Martina, you can have sex with anyone, really anyone, but who can you meet for brunch in Bewleys on a Sunday and laugh for three hours with? Who can you ring from the video shop for advice about really kitsch B-movies? Who will I ring when my mother, eventually, eventually dies? Or when Eamon walks out 'cos I've folded his clothes once too often?'

'Well, I have that with him, too – so why do I want more?'

'Well now, Dr James doesn't have all the answers. I suspect I get more of a kick out of playing the parent with him than you do. When he does the cute stuff I just ruffle his hair.'

Martina thought about how physically relaxed Cuan and James were with each other. How readily they'd hug goodbye . . . maybe they'd just got it out of their systems.

'Have you ever had sex with him? Look, I'm sorry to be so paranoid, I just have to ask.'

'No, really, even if Mr Secretive had said nothing I'd have told you that! He has taken his clothes off many times in that very bathroom, but I haven't even peeked. He's a private person, very private.'

'Mmm, very bloody private. Now, tell me what you know about Jeanette. She's a figment of his imagination, right?'

'No. Ask him. Let's not blur lines here. I love you both. I want you both as friends. I wish the hell you weren't in love with each other because it will all end in tears.'

'In love? For fuck's sake, I'm thirty-six – spare me the teenage romance shit! It's some perverse lust on my part and some crazy mummy fixation on his.'

'Be a tough old wagon, Martina, if that's what you want. Blame him for being too young. But I've seen you both act like teenagers. You both even look like teenagers – the hormone buzz makes your skin shine. Unfortunately, I think it's chemistry without possibility. Cuan will probably never want to have sex, so where does that leave you?'

'Fecked . . . celibate . . . pathetic . . . bitter.'

'OK, stop.'

'Lonely. Bored.'

'Stop!' James said, and they both started to laugh.

'Fuck it, James, am I just making it up?'

'Some of it, certainly! How about a foreign holiday? Eamon has a small villa in the south of France. It's empty for the next two months. Why not take a break?'

'I can't bear being by myself. I'd succumb to all that cheap wine.'

'Actually, I meant the two of you, if you promise not to fight over sex. See if you can manage a sane friendship.'

'Maybe. Let me think about it for a few days. I'll go back to Pearse Street tonight, see if he'll talk.'

'I'll drop you back. I've got to get back by midnight, though.'

'A Cinderella thing?'

'Sort of. Eamon always rings at twelve when he's away.'

'Cute.'

'Well . . . I hope so. Though I think he may be checking up on me.'

'God, is any relationship free from paranoia?'

'No. But a good one can absorb a fair bit.'

# Detour

Eleanor called in to the gallery on Sauchiehall Street, mostly out of curiosity, an hour after Ciara had suggested it. She reckoned that if she was meant to meet Lucy, they'd meet. For Eleanor, who usually planned everything down to the last detail, this was a huge shift.

There was a photography exhibition on. The white walls were covered with harrowing black-and-white self-portraits by a woman who had committed suicide at twenty-five. Eleanor moved about quietly, eavesdropping on a talk in the next room on the life of the photographer. The young woman with the Glasgow accent was critical of the selection. Apparently the estate hadn't released some of the best work for exhibition. The father of the artist now had full control over her work. The same man that committed her to a psychiatric hospital at the age of eighteen, the place where she hung herself seven years later. Eleanor rounded the corner. The young woman giving the talk looked like such a surreal hybrid of Cuan and Ciara that Eleanor gasped.

'Can I help you?' Lucy asked, looking closely at her when the small crowd dispersed.

'Lucy? Hi, I'm Eleanor, Ciara's mother. She suggested I drop by.'

Lucy was delighted. She said she was about to go for a break, so they went for coffee. They talked for an hour. Lucy explained how extraordinary it was to have so many blood relatives sitting around a table yesterday – Ciara, particularly, because she could see a physical resemblance. Everyone commented on it. For Lucy having grown up without ever having that, it was overwhelming.

Eleanor talked, too, more openly than she would usually talk. She told Lucy that she was visiting her girlfriend in Amsterdam – this was the first time ever she had called Beth her girlfriend, and yet the word came out quite easily.

On Eleanor's last night in Glasgow they met at an Indian restaurant. Lucy explained about her art project for her MA. It was like a photo album, based upon something she had done as a child. She had painted imaginary parents and a brother and a sister when she was nine. Now she was painting the imaginary relations and the real ones side by side, adjacent like in a mirror. She was working from photographs of Michael and Cuan, but she had wanted to meet them.

'It's very confusing because I'd studied their faces so closely, yet they look very different moving and talking and three-dimensional.'

'Did you tell them about your project?'

'No. But I will sometime. Anyhow, the project is less important than getting to know them – at least I hope it is! They're very different, Michael and Cuan, aren't they?'

'Totally different. Opposites, in fact, but very close.'

'Cuan seemed distant. It was all a bit of a shock, I think.'

'Give him time. You two would probably get on.'

'Maybe . . .' Lucy paused, clearly wrestling with a question she wasn't sure how to ask.

'Is he . . . different?'

Eleanor smiled, wondering was this direct young woman about to unravel everything.

'Absolutely,' she said.

Lucy still looked perplexed.

'Sorry. Maybe I should ask Brian this – it's just a bit awkward. Is he autistic or some other condition like that?'

179

'No. Nothing like that.'

Eleanor pictured the Sunday lunch. This earnest young woman surrounded by a family gelled with lies, who are polite to the point of hypocrisy. No wonder Cuan seemed out of step – he played the game only when he felt like it. Maybe this was her moment, to tell the stuff she'd been carrying for years. Start the dominoes rolling, betray Cuan. She felt giddy with the sudden rush of power, then exhausted by it.

'Brian said you lost contact with him for a few years . . .'

'Eight years. Not lost as much as blocked. I had to, for various reasons. But when I see him and Ciara together I feel terrible guilt sometimes, that I stopped them having this when Ciara was little.'

'They seem so relaxed with each other. The time apart didn't harm that.'

Eleanor suddenly missed Ciara so much she got a pain in her throat and tears started rolling down her face.

'Sorry – Jesus, I never, ever do this.'

Lucy was still fixated on her enigmatic half-brother, and presumed the tears were for Cuan.

'Did you love him?'

Eleanor looked across the table at Lucy, who'd gone a little out of focus since Eleanor had started crying. Was she real? She was such a confusing jumble of her daughter and the seventeen-year-old she'd loved, it was as if she'd invented her. Though she had denied it to herself and everyone else, she did love Cuan – and for a few minutes she let herself remember what it felt like.

'So much that I felt physical pain for about two years. At first I thought it was the pregnancy, but it continued long after Ciara was born.'

Cuan had knocked her off balance. Eleanor, who was always so stable and sure-footed, tripped up. He was responsible as far as she was concerned for all vague, inexplicable things, coincidences and magic. He made her irrational, but she could hide it brilliantly. She'd pick up a book from her shelves and say, 'Page thirty-nine, fourth line, third word,' and look for something to connect to him. It was like they had a dialogue running between each other all the time – after a while Eleanor couldn't remember what they had said to each other and what they hadn't, and it ceased to matter. He talked about sex in terms of colours, gender in terms of ways of letting the world touch you. He belonged in a sensory world where music and films were the most real things, and John Lennon and Jim Morrison were still alive. She entered his world for a short while, and when she had to leave it was as if everywhere else was lit by hard white fluorescent light.

'But why didn't you stay with him?'

'Because I knew he didn't feel the same way. I had engineered the relationship – he was on his way somewhere else. I just took him off on a detour.'

'Seems like you got lost going off the road more than he did.'

'Yep, sure does.'

Eleanor smiled at the irony. Instead of betraying Cuan, she'd betrayed herself. She'd spent over a decade proving that she was solid and reliable, the antithesis of Cuan, and this young woman was looking straight through that. So what? Lucy might vanish for six months to South America next month, as she was planning to do, or maybe she'd just vanish at the end of this evening.

'I put my foot in it about Martina,' Lucy said. 'I just presumed they were together.'

Eleanor shook her head. This was stuff she wouldn't tell her, not yet at least. 'So do most people, but I think they just pretend.'

# Really

James and Martina arrived at Pearse Street. Ciara was asleep. Cuan was on the couch, looking a bit dazed watching MTV. James kissed them both and left. Martina was determined to confront him. She had had enough of him circling everything back into himself. Oh, another emotional crisis – I must go buy a CD or read a book to get me through it.

'Ciara show you where she found the mouse?'

'Mmm . . .'

'Was it a one-off, do you reckon?'

'Dunno.'

'OK, Cuan, wake up – or I'm getting a taxi to fucking anywhere but here.'

'Sorry. Sorry. I've had a rough day. She found some stuff in my cupboard . . . You saw it, too, right?'

'Yes.'

'I was making her a toasted sandwich earlier and she came out dressed up in a black skirt and blouse – it freaked me out completely. I shouted at her for the first time. She burst into tears. It was awful . . . She just thought it was dress-up stuff she said and flung it on the couch.'

'So, what is it?'

'They're my clothes, my make-up and stuff – Martina, I'm really a girl . . . I know that maybe doesn't make sense, but I've always felt this way . . . I've always been like this.'

Martina was mostly silent, watching him fidget, trying to concentrate on what he was saying. He looked nothing like a girl. He was wearing T-shirt and jeans. She looked at the thick fair hair on his arms, the shape of his muscles beneath, the stubble on his chin. If she moved a little closer she'd smell his male smell. Is he just crazy?

'So, what are you going to do?'

'I'm going to start taking hormones in a few months or so.'

'What will they do?'

'Make changes – gradual but immediate, apparently. Then after a year or two I can have surgery, if I decide to.'

The word surgery made Martina's heart lurch in her chest. He's not talking about dressing up in women's clothes, blurring gender lines here; he's talking about suicide – Cuan is going to destroy himself for some fantasy.

'Do you talk to Frances about this stuff?'

'Yeah . . . though for the first six months she walked a tightrope with it, so I didn't have to fix on a gender. She didn't want to pin me down . . . so I could choose.'

'She thinks you should choose rather than accept?'

'She wants me to be happy and lead a fulfilling life . . . I don't as a man – you know that.'

Martina felt numb. She couldn't speak any more, but her mind was racing. How can he think by destroying his body he'll be happy? Surely it's just like a compulsion, a denial, an illness, like anorexia? How the hell would Ciara come to terms with it? How would any of his family, and how would she . . . ?

'Tea?'

It was 2 a.m. She nodded, then shook her head. Cuan decided that was a yes, and made them two mugs. She didn't look up when he placed the mug in front of her, so he crouched down on the floor close to her.

'I'll make a good girlfriend, right? You've always said you don't think of me as a man . . .'

'I didn't mean like that! I mean you don't behave like a boorish thug . . . but I do think of you as male, just – nice . . . male . . . Oh, Jesus Christ, Cuan!'

183

'Well then, I'll make a nice girl, yeah?'

But then there won't be any men like you, she thought ... but what could she say?

'Why didn't you tell me before this?'

'Because I knew you loved me, like no one else had. The way you looked at me, looked in my eyes, I knew you loved me completely and it felt great, but it still wasn't enough.'

'But you're beautiful ... Loads of people love you – women, gay men, even straight men – you can take your pick. If you go through with this you'll just paint yourself into a corner.'

'Please, don't say that.'

'What the fuck can I say, Cuan?'

She felt exhausted. They sat for ten minutes in silence. Martina scratched her head.

'Oh, bollocks. I meant to tell you, Ciara has head lice. I found two on her earlier and she found four tiny ones on me. Do you want me to check you? Better, in case they lay eggs overnight ... Martina?'

She nodded.

He put a cushion on the floor at his feet. She sat between his knees. She snapped back to herself.

'Great, all this and parasites, too. I picked them up from kids at the refuge last year and it took me three months to get clear.'

Gently and meticulously he brushed her long hair; it crackled with static because of her acrylic jumper. Then he inspected it with a fine comb, slowly and thoroughly. He was being so gentle it made her eyes fill with tears.

'This is going to take a while,' he said.

'That's fine,' Martina said.

If it took for ever, she was happy to sit and be touched by him.

# Adhesions

Eleanor's flight landed in Dublin Airport at one o'clock. Nancy insisted on picking her up. She said she wanted to have a chat with her before they got Ciara. Eleanor was completely exhausted and all the talk with Lucy had made her feel fragile. She wasn't striding in her usual purposeful manner. Going through customs she started to feel anxious and guilty, as if she had some illicit items in her luggage. If Ciara had been with Nancy she'd have been rushing towards her – towards feeling something real.

She was trying to second-guess Nancy's need for a chat. Her father's health, perhaps, or the wedding plans, or Ciara or maybe one of those advice sessions where Nancy would get evangelical about her latest health fad ... Well, even in heavy traffic it was only maximum thirty minutes from the airport to Pearse Street.

Nancy ran towards her and kissed her. She looked older and thinner. It must be the stress of the wedding, Eleanor thought. They chatted about the wedding plans on the way to the car and Eleanor realized Nancy was enthusiastic about it, in her usual way, so that obviously wasn't the serious chat topic. When Nancy switched on the car it was still in gear and lurched forward before Eleanor had her seatbelt on.

'Oh, sorry, sorry. I'm a really good driver usually – you're just making me nervous. Must be a big sister thing!'

Eleanor grinned and tried to relax. Nancy was fidgeting in the dashboard for something as she careered around the first roundabout. It was a booklet on endometriosis.

'Sorry to dump this in your lap – it's just we never get time to talk what with Ciara and Mum, and I want this just to be between us for now.'

'Sure. What's it about?'

'Myself and George want to have children. We talked about it on the first date. I know that sounds corny, but he's that kind of man, and that's what I want, not some eejit who still wants to go clubbing at the weekend.'

'That makes perfect sense.' Eleanor smiled – Nancy always knew what she wanted with such certainty. Lucky George, never having to face ambivalence.

'Well, I'd been having awful periods. You know I've always had it bad, but these were really, really awful. I ended up flat in bed for three days with Ponstan or whatever painkillers I could find. So I decided to get checked out, just in case . . . You see, I read about this thing in a magazine.'

Eleanor glanced down at the booklet again – please let this be some magazine-based hypochondria, she thought, some kooky self-diagnosis. But Nancy was continuing at a rapid pace.

'My GP sent me for a laparoscopy at the Coombe . . . and things are not good. Basically, my fallopian tubes are full of adhesions and my ovaries are covered in what they call choco-late cysts – now I know that sounds revolting, but if you look at page five there there's a diagram. The problem is there is virtually nothing they can do and I haven't told George yet because I found out the results only on Monday, but what if we can never have children? What will that mean to him, to us? And I've looked up the whole IVF thing, but it doesn't look hopeful –'

'Hold on, Nance, slow down . . . You're telling me you have this condition, and you may not be able to have chil-dren?'

'Yes, I'm sorry for blabbing so fast. It's just I haven't talked to anyone about it and I don't know what the hell to do.' She braked coming up to an amber light, then changed her mind and accelerated.

'Well, talk to him. Take it one step at a time.'

'But what if he doesn't want to marry me if I'm infertile ... Ellie, you don't know George, but he loves kids, really loves them. He'd be a wonderful father. He's dying to meet Ciara. He's from a family of nine!'

'Nancy, if he loves you, and I'm sure from all you've told me about him that he does ... well, it's you he wants to spend his life with, not some children who don't exist yet.'

'Fuck, this is a one-way bridge – how do we get to Pearse Street from here?'

'Just take the next bridge up ... Look, let's park and go for coffee before we get Ciara.'

'But you must be dying to see her.'

'I am. Of course I am. But I've spent ten years solidly with her, apart from the past ten days – I think an extra hour won't make a difference.'

'Jesus, you've mellowed – are you taking Prozac?'

'No.' Eleanor laughed. 'Should I?'

'Well, maybe a few Valium before you get in the car with me again. Oh, and this condition is hereditary. Mum very likely had it – though I haven't discussed it with her, if you put two and two together, they're very devout Catholics and so I doubt she was on the pill all those years ... And you should get checked out.'

Nancy screeched into a parking spot.

# Atrophy

Martina went to France on her own in September. She panicked just before she left and tried to get Karen to come with her, but didn't manage to make contact. She turned down the job in Dublin, and quit her job in Limerick. For two weeks she swam and walked and read. But mostly she thought about Cuan. He had given her some website addresses and she browsed through them at a local library. There were some personal stories, but mostly there were cold facts: what the hormones did, the effects (growth of breasts, weight redistribution, atrophy of the male sex organs, infertility after six months) and the side effects (liver damage, mood swings, bone thinning).

'Atrophy'. The word kept preying on her mind. Atrophy. Some have 'gender-reassignment surgery' – where the skin of the testicles is used to form a vagina, and the penis is split somehow to form a clitoris, and the whole thing has to be kept open, like when you have your ears pierced, or it could seal up again. Some just take the hormones and opt for atrophy – after a while all spontaneous erections cease. The photographs on the various sites showed happy-looking, mannish-featured women, but none looked beautiful. Cuan was so beautiful. Martina had no photographs of him, but one night she sketched him from memory with a pencil. She sketched over and over until she got a likeness. She thought of the night of Michael's wedding when she held him and she drew him like that, curled up like a lithe cat, but naked.

She managed a month off drink as she had promised James. She'd been out a few times with friends of James who lived

188

nearby, and drank various mineral waters for the night. Fred and Edie were a batty but very happy English couple in their sixties, who had sold their house five years previously and travelled all over Europe in a camper van. They were having a party at the weekend, and Martina reckoned that might be as good a time as any to drink again.

The morning of the party she got a letter from Karen:

Dear Martina,

Sorry we didn't meet up before you left, but I had a hospital appointment I couldn't break. Thanks for your phone message – I would like to come over, but things are a bit complicated at the moment, and after I get through this letter you may not want to see me! I know this is probably not the way to tell you, but I can't do it over the phone either – I have breast cancer. I had a mastectomy last month, my left breast. I'm on medication and they think they've caught it in time. In about three weeks I'll know what's what.

There's something else I have to say because it's been on my mind for ages, and I've never been brave enough to say it before. We've drifted apart over the past few years. I know you're my oldest friend, but we've never really agreed over men or life choices. (Yes, I'm giving up the stressful job!) I've never liked Cuan – I think he's a manipulative brat who's never going to grow up. You've changed so much since you met him – it's like he's always there in the background, on your mind. In simple ways like you used never to leave your mobile on when we went out, but because of Cuan you have it on the table – I know when I leave you to go to the bathroom in a pub or restaurant that you're ringing him. I feel you're just passing time with me until you can see him. He doesn't like me either – I know you say he's shy and stuff, but what one person calls shy can come across as downright rude and sulky. He'll never make you happy. I know you think you found something when you met him, but actually you lost more. What has he given you, Martina? Some of the men I've been with over the past two decades have bored you to death, but they were always kind and loving and adults! Bill is great – he's been very supportive over this. We're going ahead with the wedding regardless in November. I'd love you to be there.

We're both in our late thirties – though you don't look it! Our friendship has survived almost two decades. I hope it can survive this stuff.

I need you now, if you can be there for me.

Sorry if this is all a bit harsh.

Love,

Karen

*I need you now . . .* Martina sat back on the bed, reeling with guilt. Karen was sick, maybe dying, and Martina hadn't even noticed. She had been sleepwalking through their friendship for the past few years. She put it down to the fact that Karen was leading such a conventional life – civil service job, buying an apartment, settling down while Martina was still in flux. Breast cancer. Martina thought that was what Karen's mother died from, too, but she couldn't remember. How could she not remember something as important that? How could she have been such a bad friend?

She wrote to Karen, saying she loved her and would be there for her. She ignored the stuff about Cuan; it belonged in a different world. Martina had stayed with Karen for two weeks after her abortion. They spoke about it every night. Karen was wonderful, completely non-judgemental and supportive. She even remembered to send her a card the week the baby would have been born. That baby would be six now, and her miscarried child would be seventeen.

Martina knew that Karen struggled to understand why she

needed to have that abortion, but Martina was clear that she did. She knew she had made the right choice for then, for the person she was then. But she was different now and maybe that was what Cuan had given her. He was undoubtedly selfish and childlike, but somehow he taught her how to love. She had let him closer to her than anyone, and they had both survived. She could need him, however awful that was for her. She had to let him go, over and over, without hating him. Now she had to let him go again, let him go and hold him safe at the same time – a mother's trick.

# Letting Go

Anna was getting ready for the move to Dublin. She was in Galway for a few days to sort things out. Eleanor and Ciara were going over to dinner and to help. She wanted Eleanor to give up her flat and move into the house while they were gone. They'd argued on the telephone. Logically it did make sense. Why should Eleanor be paying rent when the house was now empty – she'd have to keep an eye on it anyway? But she felt it was a backward step . . . and that was into the irrational stuff that she couldn't explain to Anna or Ciara. She was dreading this evening. Ciara was humming 'Big Yellow Taxi' to herself, slightly out of key.

'Ciara! CIARA! Maybe don't bring your Walkman over to Nana's house, OK?'

'Why?'

'Well, she has a bit of a thing about them.'

'Oh. Why?'

'I don't bloody know! Now get your runners on. We're going in five minutes.'

'OK, OK! Chill.'

'Don't say "Chill" – it's cheeky.'

'How is it cheeky . . . it's just a word?'

'OK, you can stay here if you're being such a smart alec.'

'Can I really?' Ciara asked, not sure if this was a threat or an offer.

'No.'

'Why not? I'm nearly eleven! I'll just watch TV and have a toasted sandwich. Come on. I'm nearly old enough to baby-sit and you don't trust me not to burn the house down!'

'It's not that. I do trust you.'

'Then prove it – bring your mobile. I'll ring you if anything comes up.'

*I'll ring you if anything comes up!* Jesus Christ, her authority was well and truly eroding. She was clutching at straws.

'Nana wants to see you.'

'She saw me yesterday when you were in work. We dug every weed up from the front garden together. Please, Mum, what could possibly be dangerous in leaving me for a couple of hours?'

She was right. Eleanor was scared of the irrational, terrified of it.

'OK.' She kissed her on the forehead.

Ciara hugged her tight and jumped into the sofa.

'Cool!'


Her legs felt shaky driving the car on the way over. This was ridiculous. Like the first time she left her in play school, that dizzy feeling of walking away against some kind of force field. She looked at her mobile – pressed the light button to make sure it was working. Would Anna give her hell for being irresponsible? Very likely.

'Is she with Sophie?'

'No. She's at home . . . by herself.'

'By herself! Well, I suppose she's nearly eleven . . . You were well able to fend for yourself at that age – and boss Nancy about. Gives us a chance to talk. The dinner wasn't vegetarian anyway – is she still at that fad?'

'Yep. Though she misses rasher sandwiches so much I'd give it another week or so before she caves in. She even dreamt about them last night!'

'So, will you move in?'

'Yes. Temporarily, it makes sense. Are you pleased with the apartment?'

'Delighted!' her mother said, and she described carpet colours and curtains, and all the old friends she had made contact with. Eleanor realized that things had changed. Her mother had become more independent back in Dublin. Perhaps the sudden move to Galway years ago had uprooted her the most, floored her, even. Building a life in a new city with two teenagers to look after, one pregnant, couldn't have been easy.

'Do you see much of Nancy?'

'Yes, lots. Nancy's a bit lonely. She likes us nearby. I'm not sure why they haven't opted for George moving in – everyone does it nowadays – but Nancy seems happy to go the more old-fashioned route . . . unlike some. I'm sure you don't approve of such –'

Don't fucking start, Mum, Eleanor thought, but Anna continued with a mischievous smile.

'Now what's the right word here?'

Anna was playing more than goading her, but Eleanor was too tired to rise to the bait.

'Let's not start this.'

'Right so. Tell me all about Amsterdam. All I know about it is people take lots of drugs there.'

'You watch way too much bad television! It's a beautiful city. People cycle everywhere, lots of museums and galleries . . .'

'And how's Beth?'

'Fine.'

'Is she coming back soon . . . her course must be nearly over?'

'Yes. Next month.'

'Is she coming to Galway?'

'I haven't an ocean, Mum.'

'Well, I'm just thinking –'

'Don't, Mum, really. Beth makes her own mind up about

what she does and where she goes – she's no responsibilities to anyone.'

'Shush, Ellie! All I'm trying to say is if you want her in the house with you that's fine by me. I've no prejudices about that sort of thing . . . I'd be a foolish woman if I had.'

Eleanor choked on the piece of pork chop she'd been swallowing. Anna clapped her on the back and went off to get some water.

'I remember you doing that as a baby – scared the life out of me. You swallowed a whole bread roll in your high chair one day and turned blue. I'd to turn you upside down by the feet, like I'd read in Dr Spock. My legs were shaking until your father came home. I told him I wasn't fit to be a mother; you'd nearly died. He looked at you and you giggled. "Oh, she's a survivor that one," he said.'

# Trust

Eleanor got back around ten and Ciara was asleep on the sofa with MTV on. She nudged her awake gently. She was too big to lift, so she just directed her sleepy trusting footsteps towards her bed.

'Night, Mum . . . thanks.' She smiled and snuggled down among her teddy bears.

'Oh, Beth phoned earlier,' she murmured.

Eleanor kissed her, and Ciara growled gently, protecting her sleep. Eleanor did trust her; she just wasn't sure how much to let her go. Ciara always thought she could do anything, everything. She remembered teaching her how to ride a bicycle. Ciara had insisted on learning without stabilizers. Eleanor used to hold the saddle, but that drove Ciara crazy because, once she built up momentum, it meant Eleanor was holding her back.

'No! Push me, Mum. Push me hard,' she'd say.

And that's just what Eleanor had to do – shove her hard away from her and hope that she'd steady herself. Most of the time she did. Ciara wouldn't take comfort if she fell; she'd throw a thumping fist in Eleanor's direction if she tried to hug her. She'd get up again even more determined, or storm off and not speak for a half an hour or so.

Eleanor made a cup of tea and sat down. She couldn't believe her mother had figured out about her and Beth. Maybe her father remembered it, out of the blue. Found it in his head one day, like a card someone had given him at the hospital. Maybe Ciara had said something, or Nancy. She told Nancy that day she picked her up from the airport, when they went for coffee. Nancy seemed OK about it. Did Nancy discuss everything with their mother? she wondered. How odd if she did, when Eleanor hid everything. Though why had she not discussed the endometriosis with her? She had made an appointment with Nancy's woman at the Coombe; she matched seven out of ten symptoms on the booklet checklist.

She should ring Beth back. She just didn't know what to say. She knew Beth loved her. Almost everything Beth had said to her was true – she was preoccupied with her family, she was way too busy in work, Beth wasn't part of her life, really . . . but surely that could change. Would Beth agree to stay at her parents' house? How would that work with Ciara? Would she just be torn in two by them? Once Beth started making demands on her everything changed. What did she expect, that Beth would just coast along?

Everything was fine in the beginning, when she was in control – when she chose Beth, and gently seduced her over months of book talk and coffees. But when Beth started loving her back, everything fell apart. Was it that simple – was she really that fucked up? Was it because of Cuan? He had never loved her back, never made demands, never desired her – he just wanted to be loved.

Cuan was barely aware of her body, but that didn't matter. She could look in his eyes and make him tremble from head to foot, make his whole body ache to be touched, and it made blood chase through her body like fire. She had that with Beth, too, at the start. Sitting in the cinema together that first time, whispering comments in her ear, feeling her brown curls, which smelt of coconut, brush against her lips. The thrill of finding that desire again, that she thought she'd thrown away after Cuan. But then it vanished, just as mysteriously as it had begun. Long before Beth went to Amsterdam, she had felt dead for months, like all those giddy blood cells had turned to lead.

Would it have vanished with Cuan, too, if they hadn't been prised apart? Probably not. Their structure would never have allowed Cuan love her back. Structures and labels mattered to Eleanor: Nancy was heterosexual, Cuan was transgender, Beth was lesbian – and she was a freak who couldn't let people love her.

Ciara stirred in her sleep and called out to her. She was having a nightmare about kicking rats around a football pitch. Her body was stiff with terror. Eleanor climbed in beside her and Ciara relaxed and went back to sleep. Ciara loved her – she battled her and disrespected her at times, but she loved her, unquestionably. Eleanor untangled them and climbed out of Ciara's bed. It was nearly midnight, perhaps too late to ring Beth; they were an hour ahead. Eleanor sat holding the phone for ten minutes before she made the call. They talked for an hour. She told her that her mother knew, and had suggested she could move in if she wanted.

'What do you want, Eleanor?'

'For you to come to Galway – for us to try to build a life together.'

Beth paused – she didn't believe her. Eleanor would have to be more convincing.

'OK, let me sleep on it and we'll talk in the morning.'

Beth rang back the next morning and agreed. She wanted to trust her, more than not. Lucy rang an hour later and said she was making a last trip to Ireland at the beginning of October, before she went to South America, could she come and stay a night with them and see Ciara. She'd cross over with Beth, but that was OK. Eleanor could deal with that.

# Cute

Fred and Edie's party was wild. Predictably they had friends of all ages and nationalities. Martina spent most of the night talking to an American architect called Josh, who was just one month older than her. They shared their late-thirties crises and they seemed to have the same soundtrack. Animated conversations about music made Martina relax. Josh was being like Cuan, and so she was being herself. He bombarded her with details about track sequences and original recordings – connecting things with facts. Influences couldn't be random – they had to be noted and explored until there was this complex labyrinth with Bob Dylan at the centre. Martina began to enjoy herself – she didn't need any of this information, but she needed to hear someone talk like that.

She had three or four glasses of wine and they shared a couple of joints. Josh sang a few ballads. He looked directly in her eyes and she felt it under her skin. Whether it was the drink or the dope or the sun on her skin for the past two weeks – whatever, she didn't care – it was proof she could perhaps desire someone, other than Cuan. Everyone cheered as he tackled another Dylan classic and Edie winked at her. She followed her to the van and got the story Josh hadn't told of the messy divorce and the broken heart.

'Oh, and she was Irish, too.'

'Edie, I'm here to get over someone, not fuck myself up again –'

'Love doesn't fuck you up. Guilt, jealousy, loneliness – now they do . . . Oh, but you young people know everything.'

'I'm nearly thirty-seven. So is he! And let's not call it love . . .'

'Fair enough!' Edie produced a tray of home-made jam tarts from the oven.

'God, they look surreal! I've never eaten a jam tart.'

'Tut, tut, and you're nearly forty – live a little!'

Josh walked her home and she could feel the heat of the day in the stone walls they passed. He put his arm lightly around her shoulder.

'We Irish would be very different if we had six months of sunshine.'

'What way different?'

'Less melancholic.' Martina still felt drunk and light-headed from the joints. His arm was starting to feel like an anchor.

They got to Eamon's house and suddenly she realized that she'd taken over the space with her drawings of Cuan and her notes on transgenderism were all over the place. She had written 'atrophy' in marker on the fridge. She couldn't ask him in for coffee, or sex. She simply wasn't ready.

She asked would he like to meet for coffee in a day or two.

'Are you playing here – is this an Irish thing, too?'

'No, this is just no, not tonight.'

'OK. You're very beautiful.'

'Thanks. You're cute, too.'

'Irish cute or American cute?'

'I suspect both!'

She left him without kissing goodnight. She lay in bed naked and felt the cotton sheets against her skin. It was as if she hadn't felt the bedclothes touching her for months. She thought about the night . . . was it the drink? She'd have to test it sober. If she found him attractive after two cappuccinos, she'd sleep with him. Why not? Casual sex and sunshine go hand in hand. Casual, Josh reeked of casual, right down to his crisp chinos and open-toed sandals.

She woke next morning with a headache and the sheets that had felt cool the night before were stuck to her and very uncomfortable. Fuck – all that time off drink just weakened my tolerance, she thought. By noon she was feeling a bit better. She planned to go for a swim and have some breakfast. She put the kettle on. Her mobile rang and startled her – though she'd kept it charged, it hadn't rung since she got there. It was Eamon. James's mother had died and the funeral was in London in two days' time. Would she be able to make it? James really wanted her there.

'Sure, sure, I'll be there.'

'We're leaving today, but Cuan will ring you with the arrangements this afternoon.'

'Fine, give James my love. Is he OK?'

'Bearing up. His brother asked him to organize all the readings so he's elbow deep in the poetry section at Books Upstairs at the moment.'

Martina pictured James involving everyone, the way he did, in his quest for appropriate poems. Cuan had lots of her poetry books – she should ask him to bring them to London when he rings. She had told Cuan not to ring her while she was away, unless it was an emergency. She knew he'd agree. She was always making rules for them, and he'd always kept them – it was a hangover from the days when she was his boss. Suddenly she missed him like hell. She felt absolutely lonely. Ridiculously she made two cups of tea – one black for her, and one for him, with two sugars and a tiny bit of milk. She put the milk back in the fridge and scrubbed off 'atrophy'. She looked at her mobile's blank screen – please ring, Cuan, please ring now.

# Packing

Cuan didn't ring. So at six o'clock Martina rang him. He said he'd tried umpteen times and couldn't get through. He was going over for the removal on Tuesday evening. The funeral was on Wednesday at 11 a.m. He had a place to stay for free – an empty apartment belonging to some friend of Michael's – could she come then, too?

'Sure, if I can get a flight. James's friends Fred and Edie have Internet access. I'll go book a ticket later and send you an e-mail with the details.'

'You OK? How's the detox going?'

Martina glanced at the drawings on the wall.

'Not the best! How are you doing?'

'Good. I think . . . I miss you,' he said.

She stroked his spine on the wall with her fingertip.

'Yeah, I miss you, too.'

Martina tidied the house and packed her stuff. Time to face the music; the holiday was over. She took down the drawings and put them inside her backpack. She went to Fred and Edie's, and booked her ticket for lunchtime the following day – there was a bus that would take her to the airport that left at eight.

They offered her dinner, but she turned them down. As she was leaving Josh arrived with a bottle of champagne in his hand. He looked surprised that she was going – the whole thing reeked of a set-up.

'I tried ringing you all day, but I couldn't get through – the network must be down.'

'Oh, must be. Another friend said the same thing.'

'You're going?'

'Yeah. I've to go to a funeral in London and I may as well head home straight after.'

'And now?'

'Now I'm going to pack . . .' – a white lie, but it seemed simpler.

'Oh. Need help?'

'No, not exactly.'

He had kind eyes; he probably would have helped.

'How about a walk on the beach when you're done?'

Josh, his name was like a sigh, Martina thought. He's handsome and charming, so why not . . .

'Yeah. Yeah that would be great. About ten?'

He smiled and handed her the bottle.

'This is for you. Do you have a refrigerator?'

Atrophy . . . *atrophy* . . . she was going to say the fucking word if she wasn't careful.

'Yep.'

He kissed her lightly on the cheek and handed her the bottle. She held it by the neck. A trophy.

Josh offered Martina a lift to the airport, but she refused. She needed as much time by herself as she could get to clear her head before she met Cuan, and she needed some sleep. So he left at 5 a.m.

He had turned up at five to ten in bare feet, and whether it was calculated or not that was the reason Martina chose to have sex with him. They had had a wonderful walk on the beach. They walked for an hour and paddled. He asked her about her work and he started the conversation she'd had many times with men – that surely as many men get beaten by women, that in his experience women could be just as violent as men. She stopped the conversation – she was going into autopilot and she'd argued it so often to so many deaf

203

ears she couldn't do it again. She couldn't do it and take him to her bed.

'Shhh,' she said, putting her hand gently over his mouth, 'listen to the gulls crying.'

He kissed her hand and she kissed his mouth. They went back and had tea. She said she didn't want the champagne – she wanted a clear head for the morning. They made love in her bed. He was a gentle lover and she relaxed and enjoyed it, but she was on autopilot again. He had a graceful stocky body, and his skin smelt slightly of cloves, but after the first five minutes Martina had just switched off. She wasn't sure if he had noticed. Even if he did he carried on and did his best regardless. Afterwards she told him she hadn't had sex in a while; she was a bit rusty.

'I bet you've made love more recently than me. Two years!' he said, with a certain resolute pride. 'Not since I left my wife.'

'Oh. I thought you were the seducing type . . . and I thought she left you.'

'No, well, she did in a way. She's manic depressive. She married me because she thought it would stabilize her, but it only made things worse. I walked away because I had to. She was seeing other men. She'd sleep with anyone when she was elated, then come back to me when she crashed. Sometimes it's better to break your own heart than have someone else do it over and over.'

'So why me?'

He blushed.

'You seemed in complete control of yourself, as if nothing would faze you or hurt you. You're different – I wanted to break her spell. That's why I rushed you. Sorry if that seems . . .' He trailed off. Martina was busy filling the blank. Cynical? Honest? Uncomplicated?

'So, why are you on your own?' he asked.

'A bad case of unrequited love. Maybe I'm not as tough as I seem.'

'Lucky guy. I hope he's worth it.'

They exchanged addresses, e-mails and no promises, and he left. Martina ran a bath and lay in it until the water grew cold.

# Uncomplicated

They met at six in a lesbian and gay bookshop on Charing Cross Road. Cuan emerged from the back of the shop plugged into his Walkman as usual. They hugged.

'You look great! Two weeks of lying in the sun or something else?' She smiled.

'Ah! Tell me all on the Tube!'

'Jesus Christ, do you have to read me like a book all the time.'

'Yep. Speaking of books . . . I heard they'd a good selection of trans stuff, but I can't find any.'

'Did you ask?'

'No, Mum! I'm not that relaxed about this stuff that I go blabbing it to every Tom, Dick and Harry . . . Anyhow, she doesn't look the most sympathetic . . .'

The six foot two blonde on the till winked at her. She looked the spit of one of the transsexuals Martina had seen on a website, but she said nothing.

'Want me to ask?'

'No, let's get going. James is a bit wobbly. We should get there early if we can.'

Cuan had the Tube route all sorted. They even managed to get adjacent seats.

'So, handsome Frenchman?'

'No.'

'Woman?'

'No. What the fuck is it? Have I some neon sign flashing?'

'No, just a gentle glow.'

Probably because of you, you fucking eejit, Martina thought, but this was an easier game to play.

'American man, divorced, sweet. Just a one-off thing.'

'Did he agree or are you breaking his heart as we speak?'

'Oh, his heart was well and truly broken before I went near him. I was just a salve of sorts, I think.'

'And for you?'

'The same, uncomplicated.'

'Mmm, very grown-up . . . OK, here we are.'


The service was beautifully done, but there were only about forty people there. Eamon had settled in beside Martina; he was obviously finding it all a bit of a strain. 'I suppose when you get close to eighty most of your friends have died . . . and Arthur seems the quiet type. He's the antithesis of James, don't you think?' he said.

Martina glanced over. James was standing at the front, wearing a bright orange shirt, his grey ponytail coming a little loose, his earring catching the light. His brother Arthur looked small, thin and sad. Like someone had deflated James and locked him in a darkened room for a couple of decades. Cuan was up shaking his hand, looking earnest.

'Absolutely. What does he do?'

'A banker. Never married.'

'Was he friendly to you?'

'In an absent, English sort of way.'

'Suppose I should go shake his hand, too. It never occurred to me that James was Catholic . . . well, Catholic background.'

'Yes, he even has some Irish blood on his father's side. And a trace of that guilt we're all steeped in.'


Afterwards they went for coffee in a hotel. Just an hour or so, then Cuan and Martina kissed James and Eamon and headed into the night.

'See you in the morning,' James said. 'Thanks for coming.'

'You guys heading out on the town?' Eamon asked with a wink.

'I'm shagged,' Martina said. 'I just need sleep. He can hit the clubs on his own.'

'Oh, shut up. You know I just want to drink tea and catch up.'

They linked arms and left. They decided to walk the mile or so to the apartment.

'Why do you do that stuff?'

'What stuff?'

'That patronizing me like a kid stuff.'

'Oh, stop being so touchy – I didn't mean to patronize you.'

'Why do you always try to push me off to play – when you know I just want to be with you and chat?'

'OK, now you're being crazy. I just thought you might like to go adventuring – dress up and go out. Big liberal city and all that.'

'You don't get it, do you?' He was shaking with anger.

'No. No. Explain it again. I must have missed something!'

'Martina, this isn't about furtive fumbling in some Soho club ... What difference would that make? This is about being accepted for what I am, for what I've always felt like, by people I love and care about, not some kinky sexual thrill ... not "dressing up", as you call it. I thought you'd understand.'

'I'm trying to understand. But I have to protect myself – I know you love me, but you're leaving me. When you get through all the hormones and operations and whatever the hell else, you're going to fly off in the night like a moth, and I may never see you again.'

'Don't be so fucking stupid!'

'No, you stop being stupid. You act like I'm always going

to be around – that I'll always be in the background. When did we agree that? I'm not your bloody mother! I can't bear you to go. Don't you see that's why I left the Setanta years back? I left because I knew it was easier than watching you go.'

'But I wasn't going anywhere – I'm still fucking there! You're not making sense.'

'But you could have just disappeared at any time.'

'But why would I have?'

Martina started crying. Cuan put his arm around her. He held her close.

'Because I love you, fuck you,' she muttered, hoping it would be inaudible.

'And whatever you muttered is something I should be punished for?'

She shook her head. They held hands and walked the last part in silence. When they got inside Cuan made the tea and produced a box of Jaffa cakes. The apartment was all ugly black leather and glass. Even the teapot was too angular.

'Why would someone make a mug handle a triangle rather than a semicircle? What is that? Does that look cool to you?'

There was an excellent library of old videos. Martina stuck on *Some Like It Hot* – they were talked out. They cuddled up like kids under a Mexican throw, the only thing of colour in the room.

Cuan curled into her lap and she rubbed his hair idly.

'No lice, I hope?'

'No, parasite-free,' he said.

After three minutes Martina felt herself getting aroused . . . Jesus Christ, give me a break, she thought. He was moving gently, maybe that was the problem.

'Stay still. You're wrecking my concentration.'

'Can you pass me a Jaffa cake?' he asked.

She held one to his mouth and felt his lips brush against her hand.

'Some like it a little less hot – let's get rid of the throw. I'm boiling.'

She pulled the rug off them, and he leaned to grab it before it hit the floor. And then she noticed.

'What's going on? You've an erection!'

'Well, I still have this flap of unwanted skin between my legs! Now, shhh ... don't shout at me any more.'

'What do you want? Is it Tony Curtis, or the pretty dress?'

'No, another Jaffa cake.'

This time he sucked the crumbs off her fingers.

'What, Cuan ... say it!'

'Shhh!' he said, snuggling down.

'No. You are a brat – and I'm not going to touch you unless you say it.'

'Can it be just once and uncomplicated?'

'Unlikely, but we can aim for that.'

'Then, yes.'

'Yes what?'

'Yes, please.'

And they had sex, for about ten minutes. Cuan turned off the light and took off his jeans. He had shaved his legs a few days previously and the stubble made Martina's sunburn sting like hell. Martina felt the strain in his body, and saw his face was full of pain.

'Do you want to stop ... ?'

He shook his head. His whole body was shaking. Martina realized that sex like this was never going to give him pleasure, or even comfort. It was like he was cycling up a steep hill with the brakes pulled. When he came inside her Martina felt herself orgasm unexpectedly, perhaps the relief that finally they could stop.

# Home

Cuan had to leave directly after the funeral the next day. There was a dance show opening at the Setanta, with a notoriously difficult choreographer – Jean-Luc Campion. The overnight get-in had been a disaster. Cuan got a call at eight-thirty from the lighting operator to say he was quitting if 'that bollocks' didn't show him some respect. Jean-Luc liked to work in the round. Considering the Setanta's theatre space was in the basement supported by large square pillars, this was virtually impossible. He always found fault with the technical stuff – the lighting board, the speakers – and he behaved appallingly towards all the staff. Cuan was convinced his bad karma caused things to break and fuses to blow. He would have to grit his teeth and face the music – the last time he swore he'd send Jean-Luc packing to one of the commercial theatres, but his work was brilliant and every dancer in the country wanted to work with him. Cuan looked pale and tired as he kissed Eamon and Martina goodbye. James ruffled his hair.

'Chin up, kid. I'm sure you can charm the pants off Jean-Luc.'

'Yeah, but he's probably even more trouble with his clothes off,' Martina said.

Cuan looked at her and grinned for the first time that morning. They had been awkward around each other, a little shell-shocked and raw. Martina decided not to try to talk it out. They analysed things way too much sometimes – better let it lie. They had to rush to get to the funeral on time. The Tube was down; someone had thrown themselves off the platform an hour earlier. They hardly spoke, but held hands in the church.

Martina was leaving at six and she spent the rest of the day with James and Eamon, apart from a quick trip back to that bookshop on Charing Cross Road. She found the transgender shelf and bought two books. She wasn't sure was she buying them for herself or Cuan. She browsed the books on the way back to James's mother's apartment. One was personal accounts – subtitled 'Travellers across the Boundaries of Sex' and from the introduction it was clear that these were the voyagers that survived – claiming that 50 per cent of people with gender identity disorder kill themselves before they reached thirty. Even if the statistic was slightly skewed, it still caused her to panic. She should have said something to him, but what? Acknowledged that he needed to change? She knew that now, and she knew she wouldn't stand in his way: the strange sex they had only brought her closer to his pain.

Back at the apartment James and Eamon were sorting through stuff. Boxing things, throwing things out. So this is how it's done, Martina thought. James obviously knows what's important and what's not – she just clutched everything to her like she was salvaging what she could from a shipwreck.

They found photo albums. Eamon was looking at photos of James as a child. James was looking at them for the first time in twenty-five years.

'You don't think of these things when you walk out the door in your early twenties,' he said, putting the photo album and some children's books carefully into a leather case.

Martina watched how comfortably James and Eamon got along. How they'd joke and flirt with each other, and the easy affection between them. Would she ever know this with someone? Was it always going to be defensive like most of the men in her life, or obsessive like Cuan? James and Eamon were attuned, but separate. She couldn't imagine them picking at words like she and Cuan did, dissecting them like they spoke cryptic poetry to each other. How often had he said to her, 'Remember the last time we were together and you said . . . ? or 'What did you mean by . . . ?'

And she'd do the same, as if they never had enough of the jigsaw. He told her Ciara walked by a mirror a week ago and stopped and stared and said, 'Cuan, have you ever noticed how your own face doesn't look as familiar as your friends or your family . . . like you don't know the expressions so well?'

Did he feel that way about her, or was he telling her because he knew she felt like that about him? Why did they say so much to each other, incessantly, when it was all just fishing line tangling them together? How could she separate from him? What was the route back out? She needed to, in order to be any use to him on his journey, and for her sanity.

'Gosh, you're very contemplative today. You've hardly said a word all afternoon.'

Martina jolted. She'd obviously been frowning to herself for the past fifteen minutes or so.

'Oh! Sorry, guys – late night, strange couple of weeks.' She yawned; she was absolutely exhausted.

'Yes, indeed. I won't even ask what you did to our cute boy, but he did *not* get his beauty sleep.'

Eamon's joke struck a nerve – Martina felt the tears coming. Fifty per cent commit suicide. Christ, that was just an even chance. What if she'd fucked him up even more? James noticed and put an arm around her.

'Don't mind that old goat. He's just jealous,' James said. 'Now, we've been hatching a plan we want to discuss with you. Eamon go make us some tea – but, for God's sake, don't use those tiny white cups with fuchsias – they make me feel as if I'm in an Oscar Wilde play.'

'But you are, my dear.'

While Eamon made the tea in the kitchen, Martina sobbed.

'I'm sorry, James. We buried your mother this morning – this day should be about you.'

'It's OK. It's all pain of one kind or another. I lost my mother long before today.'

'I can't bear the thought of losing Cuan – I know that's selfish, but what if it all doesn't work? What if he ends up a mess? What if he kills himself on the way?'

'He's a mess now, Martina. He'd be the first to admit that. I don't think he'll kill himself . . . You have to trust him. He's a lot stronger than that fucked-up twenty-five-year-old we all wanted to mother.'

'See, maybe that's it, James, I don't know that . . . and last night . . .'

Eamon came back in just as James was giving his most raised eyebrow expression to Martina –

'Well, I obviously missed the play's climax,' Eamon muttered. 'Typical!'

He poured the tea; James made a toast: 'To journeys, adventures and transgressions . . . that covers all of us, including mother, I think.'

They chinked mugs. James's eyebrows were still raised, but he covered it well by talking at speed of something he and Eamon had spent many hours gestating.

'OK, act two – here's the plan. Eamon's family home is in Westport. It's an old rectory – huge and, as they say in all the best property supplements, "in need of some repair". His parents live there at the moment, but are elderly and not coping terribly well. They're moving next month to a supported apartment in Glenageary – they'll have their independence, their own front door and that kind of thing, but there'll be panic buttons and nurses on call. Eamon's going to continue to live with me in Stonybatter, so he'll be reasonably nearby. In the next two years we want to convert the house into an artists' retreat. There are sheds, a couple of stables – loads of space. There are a couple of grants available, but mostly it will be a hard slog and a fair bit of money required. But at the end of it all it will be home.' James paused.

Martina wasn't sure what this all meant. 'Sounds good –' she began, but he was off again.

'Excellent! Now, we want you to help run it . . . There's a gate lodge with roses growing up the side like something out of a Laura Ashley photo shoot from the outside – looks like a chicken shed on the inside, however. That could be your place, once it's fixed up. There's a mountain of paperwork required because we want to set up some kind of a trust with charitable status. We may try to hook into an international gay and lesbian artists' and writers' collective, which would mean that at least fifty per cent of the spaces would be reserved for non-heteros . . . but all that's to play for at the moment.'

'Slow down, James . . . why?'

'Because we want to settle. I've had enough of Dublin, frankly. One stabbing doesn't make for a city of homophobes, but I don't feel the same going out and about at night. I never walk anywhere now – that's why I drove you that night to Cuan's, remember? Normally we'd walk, but I actually couldn't face walking home alone. And I'm getting older – I reckon I've about ten years of hard work left in me, health permitting, so why not do something I enjoy? I don't fancy running a venue again. I've been there, done that, and though it was wonderful in the 1980s when no one had any money and everyone had enthusiasm, now it's all frightfully conservative. Celtic tiger cubs want to go to late-night Disney films with nostalgic soundtracks, after their cocktails and tapas, not the kind of art or theatre that turns you or me on . . .'

'And why me?'

'Because you'd be brilliant at it . . . a bit of cooking, lots of chatting on the phone and sifting through applications – trying to keep the total loopers at bay, the ones that might come and never leave! Doubtless a bit of peacemaking every now again – all those complicated artistic temperaments bound to squabble like cats – but we'll love them mostly, I'm sure.'

'Eamon, what do you think?'

'Please do this with us, Martina . . . I think you may be the only person James ever listens to! I'll have to keep up the day job for another five years or so; I'll be more the sleeping partner. Westport's a great place – you'll love it. But don't let us push you until you see the place – we'll take a trip some weekend soon and you'll get a better idea.'

'Yes, OK. Count me in – chicken shed and all.'

Martina looked at James, who was smiling broadly.

'How come you never opted for that career in sales? You could obviously sell fridges to Eskimos.'

'Ah, you're obviously fairly persuasive yourself!' he said with a wink.

Christ, did she force Cuan? She felt a pang of guilt. She didn't, really, but no one would believe her. Like Alice in the dock: 'Off with her head.'

# Humouring

Eleanor was driving to Dublin for the day. There was one more carload of boxes that Anna and David needed. Eleanor's car was full of her father's books. He was hoping to begin a research project. His short-term memory had returned, and he wanted to exercise it. Anna thought it was a bit soon, that the PhD supervision was stretching him enough, but she was humouring him. Beth was minding Ciara after school. They were looking forward to a double bill of *The Simpsons*. Beth had been back three weeks, and things were tense already.

Eleanor felt elated driving to Dublin. For four hours she would have no demands. She left much earlier than she needed to. It was 8 a.m. and the roads were quiet. She'd got off ahead of the heavy traffic. She was dropping the stuff out to Greystones at around two, and she was picking Lucy up at the airport at five-thirty. She was going to call into Cuan first. She hadn't planned to, but as she got nearer Dublin she knew that was what she needed to do. The night with Lucy in Glasgow had unsettled her, and unsettled the past. Things were changing, the ground was shifting, and she wasn't sure where she stood. For the past few weeks she had felt an underlying nervousness, and she was finding it hard to eat or sleep.

Monday was Cuan's day off. She rang him to warn him that she was on her way over. He was always wretched in the mornings. Even though it was going to be close to eleven before she hit Dublin, she knew he could easily be still asleep.

She got to Pearse Street at eleven-twenty. He was yawning as he opened the door.

'Sorry, I only got your message about twenty minutes ago . . . Is everything OK?'

'Yeah. Beth's moved in, Ciara's having pre-adolescent mood swings every twenty minutes and Lucy's coming to stay . . . but at least it's not boring.'

Cuan looked at her warily. Eleanor wasn't herself; there was something fragile in her delivery.

'So, what's up?'

'I want to clear up some stuff. Can we talk about some stuff that happened years back?'

Definitely fragile, and it was making Cuan nervous.

'Well . . . yes, talking is good, but maybe you should find someone else . . . Now, don't take this the wrong way, but I've been seeing a psychotherapist for the past few years and she's fantastic.'

Eleanor was taking this entirely the wrong way.

'Don't patronize me, Cuan. I just want to ask you a few questions – about you, not me, and how's a psychotherapist going to know what's in your head?'

'OK, OK. Chill . . . I'll make some tea.'

Cuan didn't like her in his space – not when she was being hostile like this, particularly. Maybe he should ask her to leave or maybe they should go somewhere like a coffee shop – some neutral ground.

'Why did you not love me?'

*Oh, start with something subtle, why don't you* . . . Cuan was starting to feel dizzy.

'I did.'

'Not like you were supposed to.'

'Jesus, Eleanor, I was fucked up – I'm having a sex change, for Christ sake! I hated myself then, so how could I love you like the movies and magazines said?'

'Do you love Martina?'

'That's actually none of your business.'

'Tell me, Cuan, please.'

'Yes.'

'More than you loved me?'

'Look, I really don't believe we are having this conversation – it was twelve years ago. We were kids. We've all moved on . . . Lighten up, Ellie!'

'I can't.'

'Can't what – lighten up?'

'No, move on.'

'Then find a counsellor – I am the very worst person you should be discussing this stuff with. Talk to Beth, talk to bloody Lucy . . . get it out of your system.'

'That's what I'm trying to do now. I don't still love you – don't get me wrong, I'm not trying to rewind the clock here – but the problem is I don't love or trust anybody. I walked away from you because I believed you could never love a woman – I choked the love to death and now I see you and Martina and I realize I was wrong.'

Eleanor was starting to cry – Eleanor, who never cried. And what was so awful about being wrong . . .

'OK, OK, things are probably very different from the way you imagine them between Martina and me . . . but, yes, I do love her. But it's not the like the movies either. Please don't blame me for your stuff, El; I have a mountain of guilt without that. Look, I think you'd better go.'

She wasn't budging.

'Really, Ellie, I can't clear this stuff up for you . . . I'm sorry.'

He handed her some kitchen roll with Bugs Bunny on it. She looked at it and shook her head.

'I'm sorry if I fucked you up . . . even more.'

'OK,' Cuan said.

'Did I?'

'Probably!'

She looked miserable and utterly unlike herself as she walked towards the door.

'Don't say anything to . . .'

'No, sure.'

'And don't let's bring this stuff up again.'

'Sure.'

'Why are you grinning?'

'Because you're dishing out instructions again.'

'And you're just humouring me . . . ?'

'No, it was never that.'

'Well, what the fuck was it, Cuan?'

# Colours

Cuan shut the door behind her and slumped on the sofa for an hour. He turned off his mobile. He'd got her message at nine, but reckoned if he ignored it she wouldn't call in. Eleanor was usually way too pragmatic to go out of her way for a wild goose chase.

What possessed her to come and interrogate him like that, out of the blue? It was like she couldn't even see him. If he sent her a note – By the way, what was I wearing earlier? What colour are the walls of my flat? What music was playing on the CD player? – she wouldn't have a clue ... Black. Orange. And *Blue* by Joni Mitchell. Martina would know – she'd reply like a poem. That was the difference.

He had planned to go shopping. Clothes shopping. Early in the morning was best because the shops were quiet. He usually went to Oxfam and the other charity shops. If he left it too late, he ran the risk of bumping into people he knew – often he'd see costume designers and wardrobe crew. He passed himself off as that in many of the shops; the real ones would call his bluff. Noon – if he could stop shaking and get it together he still could go.

He got ready. He dug out the backpack he always brought. Those shops could never be trusted to provide an opaque plastic bag, if they had bags at all. He got out his bike gear, so he could get home quickly. Once when he was on foot he was convinced he was being followed. He shit himself going past Pearse Street garda station in his rush back home. No one could imagine how long that walk from George's Street to Lower Pearse Street had seemed. He didn't go shopping for another three months after that, and afterwards always took his bike.

The Cerebral Palsy Shop had very little that interested him – lots of flouncy blouses and baggy trousers from the 1980s with bold prints. The woman behind the counter looked about eighty. She smiled at him indulgently like a grandmother. He chatted to her a bit. He chatted to all the staff at these places, mostly out of nerves, mostly writing his alibi. This time he was looking for something for his aunt, he said. Something pink. She shrugged.

'Tricky colour, pink, not everyone can wear it.'

He moved on.

Action Aid was a bit better – a skirt that had some potential if he shortened it a little; a nice linen jacket, but with shoulder pads like something from *Dallas* that would have to be chopped out. He didn't buy, not yet, but told the thin woman with the pierced nose that he might be back.

'Will I hold them for your sister?'

'No, I'll be back in the next hour or so . . . Don't worry if they're snapped up.'

Snapped up. Jesus, how many other damaged creatures would be tearing their way through those shelves in the next sixty minutes. In the next shop he was known, as a freelance costume designer who usually worked on films . . . They'd got new stock just in, not processed yet, but would he like to trawl through it.

'Yes. Love to.'

This was the best. He got the cream – designer gear, slight seconds, straight from the manufacturers. A Paul Costello blouse, not too flouncy, in ice blue; a John Rocha linen skirt, black, straight and long enough to be ankle length, though perhaps designed as full length for a more petite lady; and an orange dress – the label was cut off, but it looked like a Quin and Donnelly – very plain and very stylish. He held the three treasures over his arm and went to Francesca, the Frenchwoman at the till.

'So, how much for this lot?'

'What's your budget like this time?'

'Not great – a bunch of film students from Dun Laoghaire . . .'

'Twenty pounds for the lot so . . . but come back to me when you hit the big time.'

'I will,' he said with a wink. 'I sure will.'

He tried the clothes on when he got home and they were perfect. A little loose, but that was OK because he'd fill out a bit with the hormones soon. He always bought size twelve, even though he'd often fit a ten, because he knew he'd gain a little weight over the next year or so. Martina had called and left a message on his machine. She was due to come up to Dublin that evening, but she cancelled, saying she had a stomach bug.

He was so elated with his purchases, he half thought of showing them to her. This was as good as it gets – lovely clothes, not the lurid red dress she probably pictured him in. The black skirt would suit her, too, but she wasn't really into clothes . . . She found *Vogue* on his sofa a while back and flicked through it scoffing.

'Look at that shite, look at those anorexic waifs! Look at her – I've seen heroin addicts in the shelter with two black eyes looking healthier than she does!'

'Don't blame me. I don't dictate what's fashionable!' Cuan protested.

'Whoever left that crap behind on the bus, Cuan, had taste. You shouldn't have touched it. You don't know where it's been.'

# Driving

Eleanor had spent almost all day driving, mostly in heavy traffic. Her right foot was stiff with cramp from hovering over the brake. By the time she reached Dublin airport, she had negotiated city centre rush-hour traffic, her parents bickering, and Nancy's tantrum because she wasn't staying for dinner. Ten minutes sitting still amid the frenetic white noise of the airport, drinking bitter, plastic-flavoured cappuccino, seemed restful.

She was dissecting her visit with Cuan that morning, line by line, and it seemed like a week ago. After her visit to his flat, she had gone to one of his favourite record shops. She clicked through hundreds of CDs, only recognizing a handful of names. She bought three, all ones she associated with him, and wondered how she'd hide them or disguise them from Ciara and Beth. If he wouldn't tell her, she'd have to find out somehow. This made perfect sense to her now. That box in her head that was full of his debris, his madness, his crazy notions had finally spilled over. She played the CDs loudly in the car all day, skipping through tracks, looking for something.

When Lucy walked calmly through the arrivals gate, with her well-travelled, tidy backpack, Eleanor felt a jolt of recognition right through her body. The giddy freedom she had felt earlier that morning returned. She was light-headed with hunger, and half-poisoned from bad coffee, but ready to hit the road again.

Eleanor's driving was more erratic than usual. Once she reached the N4, she tried to steady herself. It was straight all the way; she just had to keep calm. She'd been muttering to herself in the car most of the day, and now was trying to keep quiet. Apart from a few abrupt, inappropriate laughs she reckoned she was getting away with it. Lucy seemed physically present, and entirely imaginary all at the same time. All Eleanor knew was that she had to bring her home, then she could collapse. The others would know what to do.

Lucy chatted in her easy fashion. She was looking forward to seeing Ciara. She bought her an atlas as a present and brought some more of her photos to show her. She was delighted to hear that Ciara was off school for the next two days.

'Yes, lucky her, teachers' meetings – the kind of thing us single mothers usually have to jump through hoops to sort out. At least Beth is there now.'

She stopped at a petrol station.

'Do you want anything?'

'No, I'm fine,' Lucy said.

Eleanor paid for the petrol and bought a bottle of mineral water and a packet of sweets. This was way out of character – she usually bought sweets only for Ciara. Lucy held the water, passing it to Eleanor every now and again. It had a sports top on it, the kind you suck, so it wouldn't spill.

'Have some if you like,' Eleanor said, and she did.

And Eleanor got her to pass her sweets every so often, lifting her hand from the steering wheel to take them from her in the dark. She kept her eyes on the road as she was driving about sixty miles an hour. The cats' eyes on the road were streaking strange colours as she passed them.

She realized that in some odd way she was flirting with Lucy – she was obviously completely fucked up. She had a beautiful woman at home who loved her . . . Why would she flirt with a twenty-two-year-old, who looked like her own daughter, who'd come to see her daughter? She was sick. She was cracking up. She should never have called into Cuan – it had only made things worse. She should stop now before Lucy noticed and she embarrassed herself.

'So, has Beth moved in with you for good?'

'Yes, well, we'll see how things work out. Ciara has another year of primary school, then we might all move . . . or travel for a year . . .'

Eleanor was making it up as she went along, and was alarmed by what she might say next. She felt more psychotic than Cuan – so this is what it's like, she thought, when the stuff in your head is louder than the stuff outside it.

A motorbike was overtaking a van in the oncoming traffic. Eleanor just saw three sets of headlights coming towards her – she swerved towards the ditch, but it still knocked her driver's side mirror off. She was very shaken and pulled into the lay-by.

'Christ! Sorry.'

'It wasn't your fault.'

'I know, I just didn't see it coming.'

Eleanor, who'd spent her life being utterly responsible, had nearly got them killed. She felt like she did when her face was pressed into the carpet during the bank raid – unsafe and completely out of control.

'Will I drive for a bit? I'm covered by my insurance to drive any car I don't own – an odd clause, but it comes in handy when I'm travelling.'

'Yeah, actually, that would be great – my legs are still shaking.'

They got out of the car and swapped over.

Eleanor sat back in the passenger seat and finished the sweets, while Lucy drove with supreme confidence – as if she commuted these roads every night. They got back at eleven and had hot whiskeys with Beth. Ciara had tried keeping herself awake, but had dropped off to sleep with a book in her hand.

Within a half an hour everyone was in bed. Beth knew something was up, and quizzed her about Lucy.

'She's very beautiful . . . How come you never told me she was so beautiful?'

'I dunno. Didn't notice myself until earlier today. They're a fine-looking family, I suppose . . . Cuan's quite beautiful.'

Beth sighed. Maybe this was the time to push her, even though she was clearly exhausted.

'What is it with him?' she asked.

'How do you mean?'

'Don't keep fielding me here, Eleanor – what are you not telling me?'

Eleanor's head was still dancing to the rhythms of his busy music. She had to make it stop.

'OK. I may as well tell you. He's a girl.'

'Yeah, right.'

'No, really, that's it. That's the secret, Beth – the man I fathered Ciara with, the only man I've ever had sex with, is really a girl.'

'And you believe him?'

'Completely. He's changing – watch next time you meet him . . . slowly evolving into his ideal self – only I hope he gets there before he becomes a frumpy middle-aged woman. He wants to look something like Lucy, younger even, I suspect.'

'But that's grotesque – all those hormones and stuff . . . I've met guys over the years at clubs and they're just somewhere in between: they look like gay men, and not terribly attractive gay men.'

'Well, maybe you've flirted with others and not even realized –'

'I'd know,' Beth said.

'Don't be so arrogant. You wouldn't necessarily.'

'Does Ciara know?'

'No, and let's not tell her, for God's sake, until she grows up a bit. Maybe someone in the family will have a normal sex life.'

Beth was offended.

'So, being with me is abnormal?'

'No! Jesus Christ, no, Beth! If I could be with you ... love you like you deserve – but I'm a fucking mess. I don't even let you touch me half the time ... What the hell is that?'

Beth shook her head. She'd asked herself the same question many times. She decided that Eleanor couldn't think and feel at the same time, and that she thought way too much during sex. They made love when Eleanor initiated it and, though Beth couldn't remember signing off on that rule, it existed. She tried to break it and it simply didn't work. They'd had sex almost every night for the first week she got back, but not since. Eleanor was stressed to hell for some reason, and sex wasn't something that relaxed her, perhaps the opposite. She was completely overworked. Today was her day off and she drove up and down to Dublin – she couldn't seem to stop.

'Take the day off tomorrow. Come on, it's 1 a.m. already. You'll be shattered in the morning. Let Lucy and Ciara head off to Salthill and we'll take a bit of time ...'

Eleanor was starting to feel a rising panic.

'But I hardly know her – what if she ran off with Ciara?'

'OK, now I'm really starting to worry about you. She's her aunt, there's no question. She's the image of her. She looks utterly stable, but I'd have said that about you six months ago and now I'm not so sure ...'

'Do you think I'm cracking up?'

'Well, you're not yourself, not for the past few months. Why not go and see your GP in the morning?'

'My heart is racing, Beth – I don't think I'll sleep. I feel like I've drunk ten coffees.'

'Shhh, just curl up and I'll give you a back rub. This will all seem better in the morning.'

Beth touched her tenderly, careful to let her know she wasn't trying to arouse her, but Eleanor was oblivious to anything outside her head.

'There's something else: I have nearly all of the symptoms of that condition Nancy has, endometriosis. Maybe I won't be able to have any more children.'

'There's no point in speculating about that sort of stuff – just get checked out and see what they say. Those symptoms could all just be stress-related anyway.'

'But I always thought I could start again. I wasn't ready to be a mother when Ciara was born; I was completely over-whelmed by the whole thing . . . I wanted to do it again, do it right.'

'Ciara's great; you're a great mother to her. You did it right the first time.'

'I saw Cuan today – he's still a kid with his Tom and Jerry mugs and his Bugs Bunny tissues . . . his Wallace and Gromit toothbrush . . .'

'He's not a kid – he's nearly thirty like you, and probably been through a fair bit of crap himself.'

Beth couldn't believe she was defending Cuan. She was shocked that Eleanor had gone to see him. Was she still in love with him? Surely not.

'He's thirty, but he's starting again. I'm just ending, Beth.'

'No, El. You've your whole life ahead of you – you can do anything, go back to college, go travelling. I can't believe you're jealous of Cuan. He's not starting again, Ellie – he never started. He's just emerging from some ludicrously prolonged adolescence. Martina must have the patience of a saint!'

'Why do you think he loves her, Beth?'

What the fuck did this mean? Beth knew she would have to be really, really careful here.

'How would I know? Maybe he doesn't.'

'Well, what would you guess?'

'Jesus Christ, Ellie, I don't know! If I knew what made people connect with each other, I'd be writing pop psychology books and making a fortune.'

But Beth did know, even from the briefest of contact. Martina was real – she paid no heed to her appearance because she was naturally beautiful, and she knew it, with her long hair, clear skin and naked eyes . . . she was his total opposite. She looked at him with utter tenderness and he danced around her like a kite on a string.

'He never loved me, Beth.'

'Maybe people like Cuan don't love; they just take.'

Eleanor was sobbing into the pillow because Beth had got them mixed up. That was her – she just took. Cuan was going to be fine and she wasn't.

'I love you, El, you know that.'

Beth rubbed her on the back until she slept. For years she'd been wanting Eleanor to open up a little, to let go a little . . . now she had she seemed cut loose entirely. Beth looked around in the half light – this must be her parents' bed. She looked at the adjacent shelves. Ellie was on her father's side with a grey angle-poise lamp and the *Bones of Bridge*. She was on the mother's side with Catherine Cookson and a bowl of pot-pourri. Ciara was in Ellie's old bed, and Lucy was in Nancy's. It would be an interesting breakfast in the morning.

# Prognosis

The registry office was formal and cramped. Martina was surprised. She'd expected a church wedding. She'd never been to a registry office one before. Karen's prognosis was good. She'd had a fairly radical mastectomy and the doctors were confident that she should make a full recovery. There were sixteen people at the wedding – they were keeping it very small and stress-free, given the circumstances. Karen's father made a very moving speech and Bill was utterly charming.

They drank champagne and ate fresh salmon. Martina had come on her own. Though the invitation had said 'and guest', she had no intention of bringing anyone. Cuan was way too complicated, and Karen couldn't stand him. James was too colourful. He'd have dominated the whole occasion – he didn't know how not to. She RSVPed for one, and hoped that wouldn't be seen as been radical. She'd thought she'd nothing to wear, and considered ringing Cuan and asking to borrow the black velvet number, but sometimes he panicked trying to decipher what was truth and what was irony, and she'd lost the ability to tell him. So she dug up an old red dress she'd had in her cupboard for fifteen years. It was a little tight around the waist . . . Oh, great. Bye bye youth, hello middle-aged spread, she thought.

Towards the end of the day Karen sat beside her and they chatted. She looked drained. She'd looked great a few hours before, but obviously her energy bank wasn't up to long days.

'He's lovely,' Martina said, looking over at Bill, who was talking earnestly with Karen's father.

'Yeah, I'm lucky – but, God, I'm shattered!'

'Are you taking a honeymoon?'

'We're going to Florence for a fortnight. When I come back I'm going back to work on flexi-time, about nineteen hours a week – I should be able to manage it.'

'Do you need to?'

Martina wasn't sure what exactly Bill did, but she got the impression it was well paid.

'For my head. I'd drive myself crazy sitting at home dwelling on the health stuff. Bill's cutting back, too, so we'll have time together.'

'Sorry, Karen, for not being there for you . . . I've been a crap friend.'

'No, no. You're wonderful – I'm sure you do brilliant work with that women's organization . . . You just don't seem to mind yourself.'

'I do. I do now, at least.'

'Are you still seeing him?'

'I haven't seen him in a while. We were at a funeral together a month ago and I haven't seen him since.'

'Do you miss him?'

Martina decided to tell her the truth, though it would have been far easier to lie.

'Yep. I miss him like hell.'

'So, whose choice was it that you don't see each other?'

'Oh, I make all those choices for us.'

'For us? So you're still . . .'

'Yeah. I'm fecked, Karen. It's us, and it may always be us, unless he attaches himself to some nubile young woman or handsome young man.'

'How will you know if he has, if you don't see him?'

Because I'll feel my heart finally snapping in two, she thought, but she shrugged.

'Well, you've got a point there!'

'Why not just let him go?'

'I do, all the time.'

'But really, for good.'

They clinked glasses and knocked back the champagne. Martina felt sick. Mid-life spread and I can't hold my drink ... Oh, my forties are going to be such a barrel of laughs, she thought.

'For good, for bad. Look, forget about my crap – this is your day, Karen. I'm changing. Moving to Westport. Who knows what the hell my life will be like in six months' time. But it will be different.'

'Well, cheers to that!'

# 3
# January 2000

# Fertile

Cuan had his first appointment with an endocrinologist in late January, two days after Martina's rushed appointment with Michael in Holles Street.

'Do you mind seeing me this late in the day?'

'No, you're my last patient for the day – we can relax. So, how are you feeling?'

'Great – exhausted, but great.'

'Any nausea?'

'No, not really. I'm eating like a horse.'

'We'd best do a scan to get a precise date.'

'I know the date – I should be nearly four months gone. My sex life is intermittent enough for me to keep track of these things!'

Michael pressed her lower stomach gently.

'Well, let's do a scan anyhow.'

While Michael spread green jelly on Martina's lower stomach, she felt nervous – this would make it real, to see this baby on the screen.

'Cuan tells me you and Sinead are expecting in April.'

'Yes, fertile year obviously!'

He was frowning a little at the screen.

'Is everything OK?'

'Oh fine, absolutely fine. In fact, just as I expected . . .'

He was swirling the camera around at quite a speed. Martina was just seeing a black-and-white blur, but it was obviously making some sense to Michael.

'I don't need to know the sex . . . if that's . . . ?'

'No, that's not it at all. Congratulations! Take a deep

breath . . . Now exhale . . . That's just to relax you – Martina, it's twins.'

'Christ!' She was speechless.

'And everything looks perfect.' He pointed out two separate beating hearts.

'Is that OK . . . at my age?'

'Should be. No hi-jinx during the pregnancy, and they'll almost certainly be born before forty weeks – maybe even as early as thirty-two weeks. You'll need to rest a lot. But you're very fit. I specialize in multiple births here, and I'd be honoured to see you right through. Could I ask the awkward question . . . ?'

'Oh, money – you normally do private?'

'Jesus, no! The father . . . ?'

'Oh. Of course!' Martina laughed. She had been thinking about this stuff over and over in her mind for months. It seemed odd to be discussing it.

'Well, it's a little complicated. I had sex twice last year – but with different men and within forty-eight hours, so I suppose there's no way of telling . . . ?'

'No, not at this stage – it would be too invasive. Do you have a preference?'

'Yes. I had a fling with a nice American called Josh in France . . . but, er . . . I lost the piece of paper with his contact details.'

'These things happen,' Michael said, with a little irony. Not to you, Michael, Martina thought, not to you.

'And candidate number two . . . if you don't mind saying?'

'No – but in confidence, right?'

'Everything we've said today is in confidence.'

Take a deep breath, Michael, she thought . . .

'Cuan.'

'Cuan! My Cuan?'

Martina nodded. Your Cuan, my Cuan, and please don't look at me as if I've just committed child abuse.

'Does he know?'

That we had sex or that I'm pregnant. Martina was getting prickly. Michael was falling for the Cuan total eclipse trick . . . Now her life, her pregnancy, had drifted out of focus.

'No. I've hardly seen him, though we talk every couple of days on the phone. I've been working and, well, he's starting his hormone thing . . . If he gets the go-ahead from the doctor, and I didn't want to stand in his way.'

Michael was shaking his head.

'Look, don't judge me too harshly here, Michael. I love him. I didn't force him. Maybe it was a bad bloody decision to have sex, but we made it. We were sober, and adult at the time.'

'You support his plans?'

'I'm trying. I'm really, really trying. You?'

'The same. It goes way back. He fits the classic profile of people who need to do it or kill themselves. But psychiatry's not my area . . .'

'So, speaking of your area, do you still want to take me on?'

'Yes, absolutely. Look, sorry, Martina. It was just a shock. I think you're great. You've been great for Cuan.'

'Thanks – anyhow, it . . . Jesus, THEY . . . may not be his. And even if they are, he doesn't need to become involved if he's not able . . . I want this, and I can easily do it alone.'

'There's a very simple test when the babies are born to determine –'

'Oh, I'll know!' Martina said.

'Well, I wouldn't be so sure and there's a chance . . .'

Martina was laughing again.

'What now?' Michael asked.

'Josh was black.'

'Oh, OK, that might make it obvious all right. Anyhow, there is an outside chance, very unlikely, but I feel I should say it, that you could be carrying one by each.'

239

# Irony

Michael drove into St John of God's psychiatric hospital and smiled at the traffic sign. Still there – Cuan had commented on it ten years ago – *Caution one-way system in operation*.

'Have they no sense of irony?' Cuan said, and Michael remembered being cross with him –

'Work with these people, Cuan. At least they speak English. Or I'll get you a one-way back to Berlin!'

Michael wasn't sleeping very well. Sinead had only a few weeks to go and was restless. He was confident that she was doing fine, as was Martina. He was well used to keeping secrets, but this one was preying on his mind every night.

'Dr Bourke, thanks for seeing me.' Michael smiled and stretched out his hand.

'Michael, good to see you. Call me Andrew, for heaven's sake! I've your brother's file out. I remember him well. Smart kid, and far more handsome than that photo shows.'

Michael glanced over and was shocked by Cuan's long hair and his pale childlike face. He really had grown up a lot recently.

'What was it you wanted to discuss?'

'This isn't breaking any rules?'

'No. Not at all. Anyhow, he's pretty much history here. There were no readmissions and you say he's coping fine.'

'Yes. He's actually going down the gender-reassignment route. He's starting hormone therapy soon and seeing a psychotherapist on a regular basis. But there's something he doesn't know that may be of relevance. Really, I want to sound you out, if that's OK?'

'Go ahead.'

'I've been checking hospital records for multiple births in women over thirty-five, and I came across our mother's file. I discovered that Cuan was actually a twin – a girl baby died at birth. We were never told. I'm certain he was never told. My parents could be incredibly private about that sort of thing.'

'Have you spoken with your mother?'

'No, unfortunately she died a couple of years ago. I know little of psychiatry, but I think it could be of relevance to his gender dysphoria.'

'Certainly it could, but I suspect only if it had been addressed when he was a child. He's what – thirty now? Whatever impact it's had would be hard to untangle at this stage.'

'Should I tell him?' Michael asked.

'That's more a moral question than a psychiatric one – you could consult his psychotherapist?'

'She refused to see me, said it was inappropriate to meet with family members without the written permission of her client.'

'Oh, there's a very pure streak in many that enter that profession! So what's your instinct?'

'To tell him. I know there are hundreds of complex reasons why people are transgender – and he may be the only person ever that was a twin – but I feel he should know. By pure coincidence he may be the father of twins in a few months' time.'

'These things are rarely down to coincidence! Oh, well, that's a change – he wasn't sexually active when I saw him. Have you talked to your father – maybe he should be the one to tell him about his birth?'

'I doubt he was there! I'm seeing him this afternoon. He's been away for the past couple of months. Maybe you're right ... but my father has no tact.'

'Complicated people such as Cuan don't always need the pussyfooting, you know. I suspect he's tougher than you think.'

'You're right. Thanks, Andrew.'

'Anytime. There's a revolving door below – come back if you need to.'

# Prescriptions

Cuan's appointment with the endocrinologist had gone well. Despite all the prescription drugs years ago, his liver and kidneys were in good shape. His blood pressure was fine. He was in a position to start the hormone treatment right away. The doctor gave him a long spiel about the various different types – synthetic oestrogen, oestrogen derived from pregnant mares, testosterone inhibitors. Cuan nodded as if he was hearing this stuff for the first time, when in fact these were things he'd spent years researching.

'Well, you're the expert – what do you suggest we try first?' He said it a little too enthusiastically, and he paused, like waiting for a man in a sweetshop to pick out a chocolate bar for him, like he could guide his hand towards the right one with his eyes.

He left with his prescription tightly grasped in his hand, scared to put it in his bag because it was like a plane ticket and a passport all rolled into one, ridiculously valuable. The pharmacist raised her eyes above her glasses and commented, 'This could take a while, do you want to drop back?'

No, he'd wait. Best to wait. He browsed the shampoos and conditioners, memorizing the names to occupy his head. He invented television commercials for the moisturizers. He didn't dare go near the make-up, but he had a good look through the hair dyes.

He could hear them rattling in his bag as he walked home. When he got to his flat, he took out the bottles and put them in the centre of the table. Right away, the doctor had said – well, right away means just that. He took out two capsules from one bottle and one from another. He poured himself a glass of orange juice and swallowed them. He grinned to himself because he half expected a cartoon response – a flash of lightning and two breasts to pop out, his hair to grow suddenly long and curly, his penis to vanish in a wisp of smoke. But he sat back content, knowing this would all happen, in time.

He noticed there was post. An invitation to a play and he wondered how they got his home address, a mobile phone bill, and a letter from Martina:

Dear Cuan,
I was never the world's best letter writer, but somehow this seems like the best way to tell you this.

I'm pregnant with twins. They may be yours or they may be by Josh (that fling in France).

Or indeed one fathered by each of you.

So far the pregnancy's gone well. I'm seeing Michael at Holles Street, but I'm afraid he won't discuss it with you unless I expressly request him to, and I won't. I want to do this on my own, for now. I hope these babies will be born healthy and that I'll be a good mother.

I'm moving to Westport next week. My new address is at the top of the page. I got a skip and chucked out all the crap from my house in Limerick. You'd be very impressed if you saw my Zen environment!

I'm making space, Cuan. I don't want to talk on the phone or meet up for a while. I hope you can understand.

I hope things are going well for you, and that the hormone treatment is working out as you wanted.

I'll have blood tests done when the babies are born (May or thereabouts, Michael reckons) and let you know the results,

I love you, always.
Martina

Cuan lay on his bed for three hours. He thought he could hear the hormones chattering in his bloodstream. There was a ring at the door he didn't answer. It turned into an insistent knock. It was Michael, so he let him in.

Michael glanced over at the kitchen table ... He picked up the pill bottles and read the labels.

'So ... you've started?'

'Yeah.'

'I brought you some calcium and some B vitamins ... Oestrogen strips things from the system, too.'

'Thanks, I read that somewhere.'

'Want to go for a pint?'

'Nah, I'm tired.'

'A bit of an anticlimax?'

'No, I got a letter for Martina, an upsetting letter ...'

'Oh, well, that explains the mood, and I was worried it was the hormones.'

'She doesn't want to see me.'

'Well, give her time. She needs to come to terms with the whole thing herself, I'm sure.'

'Listen to you, speaking in clichés and circles around me! I trust you, Michael. We've always told the truth to each other – now you're playing circumlocution because you don't know whether she told me about the pregnancy or not!'

'Give me a break, Cuan! It's a professional thing – I can't tell you about it ... and in fairness she could have umpteen reasons not to want to see you at the moment.'

'Thanks, make it better, why don't you.'

'So, how do you feel about it?'

'Confused ... completely confused and angry.'

'With her?'

'With her, with myself for being so stupid ... and confused because who knows who their bloody father is. Some American prick is knocking back a Budweiser in his home town or wherever the fuck, oblivious to all of this . . . I could kick him in the head.'

'Well, the testosterone blocker has obviously not had much of an effect yet! Stop the blame shit, Cuan – she wants these babies; she's delighted to be pregnant. I know you're angry with me, but I'll make you a deal, you keep yourself together and do whatever Martina wants, and I'll pass her over to one of my colleagues if you want that.'

'You'd do that?'

'Yep.'

'Well, you don't have to. I want what's best for her, too, and that's you, right?'

'Well, multiple births are my speciality, so yes.'

'I love her, Michael. Why does she keep pushing me away?'

'Jesus, I don't know, Cuan! It's obviously very complicated . . . she loves you, too, though, I've no doubt about that. Oh, come out for a pint – there're plenty of B vitamins in Guinness . . .'

'OK, Doc! Can I wear a dress?'

Michael looked to make sure he was joking. Cuan grinned, and put on his leather jacket. As they went out the door Michael realized, as if for the very first time, that the brother he loved so much would disappear soon. This kid brother, who was handsome enough to attract attention wherever he went, would soon be turning heads for very different reasons. This kid brother . . . Before long Michael would have to cease introducing him as that.

# On the Road

'I'll have that, thanks!' Beth said, rather forcefully – holding her hand out for Jack Kerouac's *On the Road*. A blushing acne-covered sixteen-year-old shuffled back out the door, zipping up his now empty bag and turning his Walkman back on. She turned to explain to Alf, the junior staff member who was completing an economics degree, how to spot that situation again and deal with it.

He was nodding earnestly, but not taking in a word she was saying because some cute guy with torn jeans and a nose ring was flicking through a gay magazine nearby.

'Alf?'

'Mmm . . . ?'

'He's looking for the fisting article flagged on the cover – go help him out, will you.'

Beth had wandered into her old bookshop for a browse shortly before Christmas and was offered a job on the spot.

'Please!' the manager begged her, 'we're seriously under-staffed and most of the ditzy students who've applied don't even read books.'

Beth agreed to work for six months from January, and take it from there. She and Eleanor still hadn't a long-term plan in place, but they were working on it. Eleanor was much better. She'd been on antidepressants for a couple of months, and had started weaning herself off them gradually. Their relationship was changing. Beth was tearing up the rules one by one, and Eleanor was starting to enjoy herself. She had finally given up her job, and was starting an MA in UCG Women's Studies department, one she could do by thesis over two years. She had lots of research to do, but mostly in her own time.

She surprised Beth and Ciara one day by announcing that she'd got a part-time job in the college library. It meant that she was out four evenings a week. This suited them all, particularly Ciara who liked to listen to her Walkman and write her diary without the constant instructions that Eleanor was still inclined to dish out.

'Tidy your room, do you homework, don't read too late . . . blah, blah, blah,' she'd chant as she heard Ellie's car pull out of the driveway. 'Want to watch *The Simpsons* with me later, Beth?'

Beth was getting on well with Ciara, but that in itself caused rows. So Beth and Eleanor wisely spent time just by themselves, something Eleanor used to resist. They'd meet for lunch at the bookshop once or twice a week. Beth thought Eleanor would be loath to see her back at the bookshop, particularly as she had given her a rough sketch of her life as a single woman there shortly after they got together, but on the contrary it didn't seem to faze Eleanor at all. Beth enjoyed the constant stream of beautiful women, and she flirted from time to time, but nothing more. Anyhow, the poetry section was gone, replaced by popular fiction for commercial reasons – it simply wouldn't have been the same.

Eleanor had a scan of her ovaries and fallopian tubes and they were clear. The symptoms were a combination of stress and irritable bowel syndrome – lifestyle cramps, not endometriosis. Nancy was sniffing some hormone cocktail twice a day as a preliminary to her IVF. She was hopeful and determined, the right side of thirty, and the fertility clinic thought she was in with a good chance to conceive.

Though she was undoubtedly more mellow since she stopped the day job, Eleanor hadn't changed her personality entirely. She was gardening one day when Beth came back from the bookshop and saw a chain saw on the front lawn and Ellie inside at the computer ... She had borrowed it from next door to trim the hedge and, rather than ask how you switch the thing on, she was on the manufacturer's website printing out the details.

'You know, sometimes you really make your life difficult with that independent thing!'

'Nonsense,' Eleanor said, revving the saw triumphantly into action. Beth took her photo.

'Perfect for the next Pride exhibition – my lover and her chain saw . . .'

'Don't you dare!' Eleanor laughed.

Cuan came to visit for a couple of days. He explained his plans to Eleanor and Beth. Eleanor took it very well – she'd been expecting him to make this transition years ago, though she was still insistent that they shouldn't tell Ciara directly.

'It will come up, gradually. She'll notice things, ask questions – I think that's better,' she said.

Beth didn't agree. Cuan didn't agree either. So they decided to tell her in late September, after she had settled into her new secondary school, and after she'd turned twelve. Meanwhile she could spend a few weeks with Cuan in the summer and, if she expressly asked anything, well, fair enough, he could tell her.

'God, September is seven months away. Will you be very different then?' Beth asked.

'Well, I'll look different,' Cuan said.

# Other Half

Martina didn't actually move to Westport, but she needed to pretend that she was further away from Cuan than she actually was. She was cat-sitting in a house in Dun Laoghaire for a friend of James. It meant she was closer to Holles Street, and could attend all her antenatal classes and appointments effortlessly. Rene was a town planner who'd recently turned fifty and gone to spend two months on a Caribbean island. She had three cats: two young tabbies called Ginger and Nutmeg, and an aloof elderly Russian blue called Nikita. Martina's role was primarily can-opener and peacekeeper. None looked for affection from her – the tabbies were too preoccupied with chasing each other and imaginary mice, and Nikita was just downright disdainful. She'd stroll towards her china bowl, sniff the food and glance up at Martina as if to say, couldn't you make it a little more appetizing?

'Eat it, you wagon, or I'll give it to the kids.'

The tabbies would gobble their food first and have to be put in the garden, for fear their table manners would upset the Russian lady. She'd always leave food behind for them; she wouldn't give Martina the satisfaction of finishing even a quarter can. Then she'd paw the cat flap in a rather pathetic fashion. Obviously Rene was a total doormat . . . Repeat after me, Nikita:

'Open Sesame!'

'Miaaooo . . .'

'No. Open Sesame. Oh, use your head, you stupid cat.'

Martina loved the house. It had a view of the sea, but the company she could take or leave. James refused to visit – he hated cats – so she'd meet him for coffee in Dun Laoghaire Shopping Centre. It was very different from when she'd been there in the 1970s and 1980s.

*You know, it's strange . . .* she said one day, to Cuan in her head, *I suspect all these blue-rinse old ladies have killed off the punks . . .*

*No, they are the punks. You're just getting old,* he said in her head in reply.

How did that happen? She could conjure him so perfectly sometimes, it made her panic and want to ring him. After a while she stopped talking to him, and started talking to her babies. She wished desperately for them to be his, to love them, cuddle them, smell them and watch their eyes fill with love for her. She would know just how to comfort them and rock them when they cried, and how to delight them with funny games when they got older. She was getting soft, and more tearful than usual. She passed Ginger and Nutmeg curled around each other on an armchair, nose-to-tail, like a stripy yin yang symbol, and the tears just rolled down her face.

'What herbal tea would you like today, dear?'

James was heading towards the counter and a double espresso.

'Oh, I simply refuse to drink some shit called after an abstract noun – serenity or sensuality, Jesus! Just get me an apple juice!'

'So,' he said, settling back down, 'how are you, plural?'

'Good, a little sluggish – me, not them – but good.'

'When's your next appointment?'

'I've a class at lunchtime on Thursday.'

'Excellent! Eamon's cousin gave me a tape of dolphin noises for you – here you go. Now, I didn't ask was that to use during the labour or to put the little ones to sleep at night . . . but give it a listen and make up your own mind.'

'Thanks, she's too kind. Is she the psychic one?'

'Yep.'

'Did she say anything?'

'I thought you'd no time for that stuff! No, but if she did I wouldn't repeat it; she's spent way too long in San Francisco. When she met me first she turned to Eamon and said, "Absolutely, it's him!"'

'Meaning . . . ?'

'Meaning I was the other half.'

'Oh, cute.'

'No, not like that – she said people were really only interested in two things: the Big Buck and the Big Fuck . . . She'd already got his finances sorted, so I was the missing bit.'

'Well, it's still kind of cute.'

'I hope this sweet nature isn't going to last, or I'll have no one left to bitch with.'

'Will you come on Thursday?'

'Hold your hand in the waiting room?'

'No, come to the class, be my birth partner.'

James sat back in the chair, put his hands behind his head and twiddled with his ponytail.

'Well, I'm flattered, Martina, but I'm not the calmest person . . .'

'Well, that's fine – I'll do the calm bit.'

'And I'm dreadfully squeamish . . . I'd be useless down the business end.'

Martina laughed.

'Relax. That's what the midwives are for. If I wanted you poking around my fanny, I'd have asked you long before now.'

'You could say that a little louder – I don't think the woman with the headscarf at the corner table quite caught it.'

'I want support, and someone who'll understand my irony.'

'And I'm the closest thing to Cuan . . .'

'If I wanted Cuan, I'd ask him – I don't. It would be way

too complicated to have him there. I don't care if you faint. I'll almost certainly have a Caesarean, so there won't be screaming and roaring. There are only a half-dozen classes beforehand – I just don't want to face them on my own. They're for first-timers. I'd feel like the bad fairy amongst all those happy couples . . .'

'And I'm the counter-curse – the good fairy.'

'Exactly, that's what you'd be there for, to keep me entertained. Did I tell you his brother's my obstetrician?'

'Yes, the lovely Michael. I haven't seen him since the wedding – is he still as attractive?'

'Attractive, hmmm, I suppose . . . but not my type. He's put on a bit of weight – think rugby captain.'

'Oooh, you say all the right things.'

'He's wary of me . . . God knows what way he pictures me extracting Cuan's sperm.'

The woman at the corner table spilled her coffee, causing an embarrassing puddle of frothing cappuccino at her feet.

# Passing

The sun was streaming in Rene's back porch. Martina was having breakfast, and realized she'd never lived amongst so much light before. Nikita was sitting prissily by a rubber plant, keeping an eye on her, flicking her tail every now and again. Ginger and Nutmeg were cuddled up on their armchair, and just beginning to stir. They stretched and started washing each other. Martina had watched them do this a few times – it always ended the same way ... They'd keep going until Ginger would decide to wash the inside of Nutmeg's ears. Then she'd cuff him on the head, or bite him on the stomach, to make him stop.

'I'm with you on that one, Nutmeg. Ugghh, that scratchy tongue must feel horrible!'

She was meeting James in Holles Street at one-forty-five. It was only eleven – she had plenty of time. She had to get there a little earlier to have her blood pressure checked and hand in a urine sample beforehand. The sample was sitting on the table in front of her. She felt like peeing every half an hour or so – almost all the time, in fact, except when she sat in a cubicle in Holles Street. They gave her some sterile bottles so she could 'pass water' at home. Nikita jumped up on the table and startled her ... She sniffed at the bottle, and opened her mouth slightly as if it was too strong-smelling. Martina snatched it away.

'Don't look at me like that – I suppose you think I'm the one that pees on the red cushion as well. Well, I'm not – it's that fecker over there!'

Nikita rolled over to have her stomach rubbed ...

'You sure now. We've only known each other two weeks.'

Martina rubbed her and she purred. It was a louder, more resonant purr than the tabbies made, a sadder sound. She curled around on the table from the petting, overdid it a little and slipped off the edge. She fell on her feet and strolled off towards the cat flap, never looking back, as if nothing had happened.

Martina's old Volkswagen was acting up a bit. It was noisier than usual and overheating. She loved the car. She was proud of the fact it was more than twenty years old. If it broke again she'd have to get rid of it and buy a new car on one of those schemes, but she'd no wish to own an anonymous shiny hatchback. She was distracted by the rumbles and took a wrong turning. She usually went in the upper road, but was heading down Pearse Street. She'd pass Cuan's front door any moment. She felt shaky and started to break out in a sweat. The traffic was creeping along. It seemed to take forever to get past, and not look.

She glanced in her wing mirror and saw a woman coming out. Martina decided it was one of the Trinity students who lived upstairs. She was walking briskly, so she'd pass her out. Looking in the wing mirror was like watching a short film, where the perspective seemed slightly skewed. Then Martina realized it was Cuan, in a black skirt and some godawful brown wig. He was wearing a paisley long-sleeved top and he looked like he had breasts — how did he do that? Was he wearing a bra stuffed with something — his breasts couldn't have grown that quickly?

She had to turn left. She put her indicator on. He was waiting to cross. She might have to pass right in front of him. She tried to remember the sequence of the lights — Christ, how often had she walked these streets, surely she could remember? Her car was so conspicuous, he was bound to notice her. The green man flashed first. Cuan crossed, and paused at a shop window. Martina went to turn, but her engine cut out. The Land Rover behind her beeped and flashed. *You rude rich fucker,* Martina muttered, starting the car again. *Don't look behind, Cuan. Just don't look behind. I promise I won't look either.* She rounded the corner and managed to park at a meter in Merrion Square. She felt weak.

# Vice Versa

Two hours later she was lying in a bed in Holles Street. James had been let in to see her.

'I'm sure they're overreacting, James. They said my blood pressure was through the roof, so I told them it was just that the car kept cutting out . . .'

'How long are they going to keep you?'

'Dunno, Michael's on a day off . . . They say the babies are fine. They did a scan.'

'How do you feel now?'

'Awful.' Martina explained what had happened. James winced.

'But at least if he saw me, he would presume I hadn't seen him.'

'Probably less strange for him to see you than vice versa. At the end of the day, they're only clothes.'

'Oh, maybe I should have just beeped the horn – pop in, Cuan, come with me to the hospital to see how our babies are doing?'

'You're fairly certain they're his?'

'Nope, I've no grounds to believe that. Maybe you should try to find Josh's contact details for me from Edie . . . but, for God's sake, don't give them mine, and don't tell them anything.'

'Are you planning on telling him?'

'After they're born, if they're definitely his, I'd certainly consider it. He was nice.'

'Where in the States is he from?'

'Chicago, I think, or Seattle?'

'Bit of a difference.'

'Yeah, I haven't a fucking clue, actually. But I know his favourite Bob Dylan song and the first album he bought.'

'Well, that will come in handy when you're trying to track him down. I'm sure there's some database on-line that covers that stuff. But remember most people lie.'

'Yeah, I know – mine was *Arrival* by Abba, but I hardly ever tell people.'

'It's OK, that's gone round full circle and is cool again.'

'Look, I'm sure you've better things to do than sit here and listen to me moaning.'

'No, actually. Will they keep you in overnight?'

'I hope not – will you feed my adopted furry family if they do?'

'Oh, God, anything but that.'

'OK, they'll last a day without food. Go check up on Cuan instead for me.'

'Did I really say *anything*?' James groaned.

'Yep.'

'Martina, is this a good idea? I mean, aside from the ongoing psychological damage it might be doing to me – don't you think it would be better if you didn't have that kind of second-hand contact? Either see him or don't. Can't I go and buy you pretty pyjamas or something? I'd love an excuse to rummage around the lingerie in Marks and Spencers.'

'Oh, these yokes are grand!'

'They look like prison gear.'

'Now who's getting hung up on clothes.'

'OK, OK! I'll call around, on the condition that I can tell him you're in here. Once you stop lying, Martina, it's very hard to get back into the habit again. Don't ask me to do that.'

'OK. But he's not to call.'

'He won't. You know he respects lines like that. I've never

known someone so cautious about other people's boundaries.'

'What's that psychobabble mean?'

'That opposites attract! I'll ring the bell once. If he doesn't answer, that's it.'

# Semantics

The doorbell rang and Cuan went to answer it. He was expecting Michael. It was his day off and they were going out to Blackrock to have dinner with Brian. He wanted to discuss something with them. Michael had suggested it might be a good time for Cuan to bring up some stuff, too.

'What, that he may be about to have a couple more grand-children? Or that he's about to lose a son and gain a daughter?'

'Either. Both. He's got to find out sometime.'

Cuan looked at his watch. Michael was early – he'd only just got back in and changed into jeans.

He was surprised and delighted to find James on the doorstep with a bag of Danish pastries.

'Ohhh, combine those with oestrogen and they turn straight to cellulite . . .'

'If you're going to turn into one of these prissy waif-like girls who eat only sugar-free gum, you can forget about me inviting you to dinner ever again.'

'Only kidding – can I've the custard one?'

'I'll split it with you – I've had a rough day.'

They talked about Martina. James felt enormously relieved to be more open about things. Cuan was a little taken aback at him being the birth partner.

'I know I may not seem like an obvious choice, but she wants me to be there, and I adore her, so I will. She promises me if I pass out she'll get your cute brother to do CPR.'

'Did she say Michael was cute?'

'No, actually, she said he wasn't her type. God, you really are hilarious you two . . . I'm slap bang in the middle of a

play . . . People would pay good money to hear these semantics and I'll probably forget them all.'

'I won't, don't worry,' Cuan said. 'I presume she doesn't
want to see me.'

'Yep, she's keeping fairly much to herself these days. She's
doing well. Apart from the scare today, everything seems to
be going fine.'

'Should I say something to Michael? He's calling over soon.'

'Nah. I'm sure the hospital will bleep him if they feel that's
necessary. How are the hormones going down?'

'Reasonably. Do I look different to you?'

'A bit softer around the edges – even your face.'

'I think so, too. I'm passing better, when I go out.'

'How do you judge that?'

'Well, it's hard – especially around town because you get
all sorts, and people too cool to stare. Sometimes you can
tell best by children. They used to tug at their mothers and
point. I haven't noticed that happening as much.'

'How's Ciara?'

'Good. Eleanor went through a bit of a crack-up before
Christmas, but she's back on track.'

'Did Ciara tell you?'

'Sort of . . . she's getting on great with Beth, which helps.
I went down to them a while back and explained about the
hormones. They don't want me to tell Ciara, so I won't. We
went out for a walk and Ciara gave out about Ellie a bit, said
she was being too tough, too strict, too "instructional" . . .
cool word, huh?'

'She's like a frigging ice queen, but, yes, "instructional"
covers it.'

'Ah, she's not quite as hard as she seems . . . She called
around last November and effectively told me I'd fucked up
her life.'

'Well, you've spent enough time on the psychotherapist's

couch not to take that on . . . Does she blame Ciara, too, or have you solo credit?'

'No, just me. They're just going through the mother–daughter thing. Poor Ciara, she'll have to face it all over again with me.'

'Do you think that's what it will end up as . . . that you'll be more a mother than a father to her?'

'I don't know, James. This stuff doesn't make sense when I think of Ciara – so maybe Ellie's right, I'm not ready to tell her. I love her. I know she loves me. I don't think this will change things, but I don't know – look at what's happened with Martina.'

'That's not because you're changing Cuan; that's because she is.'

'You think? Oh, I've to take some pills before Michael gets here. Put on some music, will you?'

'Sure.' James flicked through the CDs.

'So, what was the first album you bought?'

'*Revolver*, by the Beatles.'

'Really?'

'Really, on my fourteenth birthday. Pop it on there . . . "And your bird can sing" . . .'

The doorbell rang.

'I'll get it!' James called, above the din of the music.

Cuan came out of the kitchen to find him explaining enthusiastically to Michael that he was Martina's birth partner. Michael, poker-faced, was nodding and smiling. Really, he should have given psychiatry a shot, Cuan thought. He was a natural.

# Moving

Brian looked suntanned and healthy. He was in a good mood, and he had news. He was moving to Donegal permanently, to live with Catherine.

'Huh! And we've never even met her,' Cuan said.

'Michael's met her – well, briefly anyway – a while back. Anyhow, I want to discuss what to do about here with you.'

'The house?' Michael said.

'Yes. As I see it, there are three options: sell it, rent it or one of you come and live in it.'

'What's your preference?' Michael asked, in his helpful tone.

'The last option. I wouldn't get under your feet, but it would mean I could come down the odd weekend if the wind and rain were driving me crazy. It's a bad time to sell, and renting would mean the place would have to have a radical overhaul, and I really don't fancy that.'

'Well, I'm fairly settled in Cabinteely at this stage. Sinead's done a lot with the house; she's all set for the baby. She's even made a ramp to get the buggy in and out the front door.'

'Cuan?'

'I'm a bit all over the place at the moment.'

Don't fucking roll your eyes, Dad, or I'll really give you something to chew on . . .

'Can I think about it and call you at the weekend?'

'Yes, OK. In fact, come out to lunch with me and Catherine on Saturday.'

'Er . . . just me?' Cuan looked hopefully at Michael.

He was shaking his head.

'Working, even if I had been invited.'

'We're getting married next month,' Brian said.

Cuan dropped his fork.

'Well, thanks for the warning,' he said.

'Oh, it's not going to be a big thing . . . just you guys, and Sinead, of course, if you'll all come, and Catherine's brothers, two bachelor farmers. Lucy won't be back from her travels . . . I think she'll be in Rio at that point. Are you on her group e-mail?'

Simultaneously Michael said yes and Cuan said no.

'Maybe Ciara would like to come,' Brian said, as if he'd just remembered her.

'Can you fucking believe the man?' Cuan was fuming in the car on the way back into town. 'What's she like anyway?'

'Nice, quiet, calm. I met her for five minutes. We talked about cloud cover in Donegal and global warming.'

'Jesus, the last thing I need right now is some lunch with them interrogating me.'

'Stop being so paranoid. She's the one who should feel as if she's on trial. Think about it.'

'Why are you dropping me into town – I can hop on a DART? You don't think I'm too panicky, do you?'

'No, not at all. I got a bleep to go into Holles Street. I can drop you on your doorstep.'

# For a Cat

James was on his way out to Dun Laoghaire. He'd picked up the keys from Martina earlier.

'I just want you to know I'm a living saint!' he said.

They'd kept her in overnight. Michael had been called in because her blood pressure was still high the evening before. James was back at her side when Michael called by. She started protesting again about the car cutting out and he said firmly, 'Martina, I've been in obstetrics for twelve years now, and I've never yet written car trouble on a chart.'

There was talk of her being let out today, if things improved. She was fussing about the cats so much James reckoned it would help matters if he fed the damn things. Cuan had rung him on the way out, to check how she was.

'Are you at the Setanta later?'

'No, another day off – the theatre's dark at the moment.'

'Good Lord, is anyone doing a full week's work these days? I'll call you later.'

He opened the door and went into the kitchen. The two tabbies hurtled themselves at the cat flap simultaneously to greet him and managed to squash through, although it confounded the laws of spatial relations. James sneezed dramatically and they raced out again.

'I'm allergic to you and I hate you. Now where's your bloody food and let me out of here.'

He found it, in its special cupboard, and dished it out. The tabbies bounded back in and fell on the bowls, growling at each other like wild creatures.

'Where's the posh grey one?'

James wandered around – beautiful house, he thought, and a lovely place for Martina to gestate. Then he saw Nikita, lying flat beside the rubber plant. Too flat for a cat.

Oh, damn it. He knew she was arthritic and at least fourteen, but still it would upset Rene no end. What the hell should he do – bury her in the garden? Have her cremated – can you do that in Ireland? This was just the kind of dilemma Martina would usually help him resolve, but best not to trouble her.

He rang the ISPCA, and after about five minutes they got helpful.

'Do you get a lot of crank calls, or was it my accent?' he asked.

They recommended burial in the garden. If the house was owner-occupied, most people opted for that. They even gave him the number of someone who'd make a small gravestone. If he wasn't going to do it for a few days – and some people like to gather the family together, to do it on a Sunday – he should put her in the freezer . . .

Lovely. He could just picture Rene coming back and looking for ice for her ginseng tea, and a cross whiskery face staring out at her. No, he'd do it today, but he wasn't going to do it on his own.

He rang Cuan.

'Get your pretty ass over to Dun Laoghaire. We have to bury a cat – at least you like the things.'

'Is it a full-scale funeral?'

'Yeah. I suppose so. You bring the poetry; I'll get out the shovel.'

Cuan arranged to meet him at four. James took a stroll on the pier and grabbed some lunch in a coffee shop. He'd left his mobile behind at the house. He rushed back in case Martina had been trying to contact him. When he got back to Rene's, there was a missed call from her, so he tried ringing. Her phone wasn't working – the battery must have run out. That was another of his tasks, to pick up her charger. He'd ring the hospital around five – she expected more results back by then. Cuan arrived and they had a cup of tea to psych themselves up before the ceremony. When they sat at the table, both the tabbies clambered onto Cuan's knee.

'Huh!' James said, 'Men, women and cats, too . . . Whatever it is, if you could bottle it, you'd make a fortune.'

At that moment Martina arrived.

'What the fuck are you both doing here? Is this some kind of set-up? James, you know damn well I'm not up to this at the moment!'

Cuan and the tabbies went into the garden while James tried to explain to Martina that it was just a series of unfortunate events. They argued for a full ten minutes with James telling her to calm down every second sentence and Martina saying she bloody well wouldn't.

'I'm going to lie down like I was told.'

Before she did she stuck her head out an upstairs window and shouted to Cuan, who had a tabby on each foot, 'I'm sorry. Really, really sorry, but I just can't talk right now.' She slammed the window shut.

James went out in the garden.

'Mum's gone for a lie down.'

'I know. She shouted something at me before she went.'

'Let's do the deed, shall we?'

'I've done it already,' he said, and only then James noticed the tidy plot and the tears streaming down Cuan's face.

'I had nothing Russian with me,' Cuan said, 'But I read a short poem by Nina Cassian; she's Romanian.'

'Ahh, that's close enough,' James said, 'for a cat.'

# Boy

Martina woke up three hours later and hoped it had all been a bad dream. She went downstairs and there was a long, apologetic letter from James on the table. No note from Cuan, but a book of poetry with a page marked which probably belonged to him, and no Nikita. The tabbies seemed subdued.

'Don't give me that crap. You never liked her anyway.'

Martina started crying. The tabbies inched towards her warily.

'And I saw the way you were fawning all over him . . . what is that – does he smell nicer? I've fed you for two weeks, you ungrateful feckers! Does that not count for something?'

They wandered out the cat flap. They'd do some tricks later to cheer her up.

She made tea, and broke the mug. That was the third she'd broken since moving in. She was normally much more careful. She reckoned the hormones were affecting her spatial judgement, and her concentration.

She picked up the book and smelt it – definitely Cuan's. The poem made her cry harder, and she rang James to say sorry. She said that she was fine, that Michael said she could go home for a couple of days, but she was to come back in on Monday.

'I'm sorry, James. I just panicked to see him there, in my space. I know it's not *my* space – it's Rene's house and I've never even met her – but, Christ, you've no idea how hard it is to get him out of my head. Now I'm fucked!'

'Well, it wasn't exactly fun for him either . . .' James sounded weary.

'And I'm upset about the cat dying . . .'

'She was an old, grumpy thing.'

'No, she was just . . . complicated. I should have noticed something, brought her to the vet.'

'She'd been off her food for ages. Rene said that before she left.'

'Cuan looked awful. Is he ok? Should I ring him?'

'Ring him if you want to, but don't mess him around . . . If you want a friendship make it that, where you can see each other from time to time. He needs a bit of stability and support, too, right now.'

'Whose bloody birth partner are you?'

'Don't fly off the handle – I'm both of yours.'

'But he may not be the father!'

'No, I'm yours for the babies and what he's doing is a kind of birth, too, and not an easy one. Come on, you know that.'

'And if you had to choose to support one of us?'

'Oh, get off the stage! You know, I'm beginning to wish you two had never met. I'm sick of the bickering. You've gone from teenagers to toddlers – the wrong fucking direction! I know circumstances are a little unorthodox, but what is the real problem here?'

She paused.

'I actually don't know.'

'Well, for fuck's sake, work it out for yourself and stop fighting. You actually don't need to blame him, Martina, because he blames himself for bloody everything.'

'James, I'm scared – the cat dying scared me. What if the babies die?'

When Martina got off the phone she cried for two hours solidly. She was crying for Cuan. She was finally letting him go. She would never see him again as a boy – the fantasy had shattered. He wasn't a boy; he was thirty. She had lost two babies by that age. Her father never even made it to that; he drowned at twenty-nine.

Cuan had glanced at her when she walked in – he looked her body up and down. He had never done that before. Some men do it all the time to women, some consciously and some entirely by habit. He seemed shocked. Of course she looked very different – he hadn't seen her since September. She was nearly seven months pregnant – her belly and breasts were huge. She was wearing a purple damask dress because it was the only item of clothing she possessed that didn't leave red weals on her skin. It was the first time she noticed him looking at her body, and she turned away from him and locked him out.

She would never see him again as a boy. His boyish body would no longer hold any erotic charge for her. He was a man she barely knew, who was turning into a woman. Funny, in all the times they had talked, he'd never used that word. He'd always said 'girl'.

# Magnetic

James had dropped Cuan back to Pearse Street. Cuan had been very quiet in the car. James knew to let him be when he was in that mood. He made small talk about the Westport plan, and was careful not to mention Martina's involvement. It wasn't certain, anyway, what her role would be. She told him she'd make a firm commitment to him in August, when the babies were a couple of months old.

'Eamon's parents have settled in well to Glenageary. His father's the frailer one, but he looks chipper these days.'

'When's Eamon due back?'

'Tonight, though he'll be worn out from all that conferencing, too much bad coffee and staring at flow charts.'

James glanced over at Cuan – was he angling to stay over, was he feeling really wretched?

'Ring me later if you feel like it.'

'Yeah, thanks. Though I think I'm just going to sleep. I'm shattered.'

Cuan shut all the curtains in his flat. He looked though his CDs in vain to find something that would be louder than the voices in his head. He wanted music he didn't know, music he didn't have. He wanted the total absorption of a new album by a favourite singer, where every note and lyric is familiar and autobiographical, but fresh.

Martina had never looked at him like that before. She just dismissed him. She had looked at him lots of ways – with anger, frustration, exasperation and all coloured with love. Then there was that look she gave him sometimes, more a stare than a look, like over the edge of a cliff with no fear of the water or the rocks. She didn't love him any more; he'd lost his edge. He looked away from her eyes as quickly as he could, so it would stop hurting.

He looked at her body. She looked totally different, like a parody of herself. He had two small cats in his lap that would wriggle around and jump off any moment. She had two babies in her womb – two babies trapped and safe that would look something like her. How could they be his? How could that strange night have changed everything? They were there because someone died, not to make more people in the world. Those brief times he had seen Ciara after she had been born, he never held her because Eleanor wasn't ready, and because she seemed impossible.

He took his drugs and had a shower. The drugs were giving him headaches and making him heavier. He had put on a half a stone, but they had made him much heavier than that sounds. He could feel his body hit off the ground more when he walked, as if the concrete ricocheted right up to his neck.

He dried himself with a rough towel. He should have shaved again. Though his body hair was growing much slower, it was still growing. It had got a little bristly around his chest. He looked at himself in the mirror and for a moment he barely recognized himself. He was nowhere. Breasts were forming, but they looked ugly, like the chests of fat old men on the beach.

He rummaged in the pocket of his leather jacket and took out his Swiss army knife. He ran the blade along his chest and cut one long hair that had escape being shaved last week. He held it against the light – it looked colourless. Was it silver? His body hair was usually dark. He traced the blade against his stomach, very gently. He liked that feeling always, that feeling of being nearly cut. He felt himself getting an erection – the first time in over a month. He ran the knife down lower, and his penis grew firmer. He looked in the mirror and smiled – it was as if it was magnetically attracted to the knife.

# Sequences

Ciara was in the garden, practising juggling, finding it frustrating. Cuan had sent her a set of three balls a couple of weeks ago – they were yellow and green, filled with sand. She had seen him juggling the last time she stayed. He had juggled three apples, then four, never dropping any. He juggled eggs, and she made him stop because it made her anxious.

'Sorry,' he said, not sure what had upset her, but he knew the feeling.

'It's OK. I just can't bear to watch you do it.'

She tried to remember what way he sequenced the apples. Next time she would watch him differently. She would watch so she knew how to copy. She wandered back inside. Ellie was at the computer, trying to find a subject for her MA. She wanted to find a pioneering woman scientist and research her life and document her work. Beth was out taking photographs. She had an exhibition coming up. A small exhibition in a coffee shop, and she had more than enough photographs already – but she felt something was missing. Ciara knew that feeling.

'Mum, I'm hungry.'

'Get yourself a bowl of cereal.'

'I had a bowl an hour ago! Let's have some proper lunch – it's two o'clock!'

Beth usually rustled up lunches. They alternated cooking dinners – Ellie's were usually the nicest. But Beth always rustled up snacks, brunches and lunches. She always had great ideas of things to try. She'd buy unusual breads and mix things up – experiment, so they'd have a Mexican wrap, with a Chinese style stir-fry or naan bread with tuna mayonnaise.

'Mmmm, OK. What do you feel like?'

Ellie wasn't going to have good ideas. Ciara decided to make it simple –

'How about cheese on toast?'

'Yeah, sure . . . I suppose I'm making it?'

'Cool! Like Beth does it with the onions and tomatoes? I'll get us some apple juice.'

'Put on the kettle will you – I need coffee.'

Eleanor was finding it frustrating – she was itching to get started and, until she found her subject, it didn't feel like real work.

'Sure . . . I wish coffee didn't smell so nice and taste so disgusting.'

They sat down ten minutes later and ate together. Ciara said the cheese on toast was delicious twice. Eleanor wondered was she patronizing her or just being her usual exuberant self.

'Mum . . . ?'

'Yeah?'

'Was I an accident?'

Eleanor sat back in the chair. Here we go – Ciara could always find new ways to do this to her.

'No, honey, that's an awful word.'

'It's just a word.'

'Well, it doesn't describe things right.'

'Well, what does then? Tell me the right word.'

'Cuan and I didn't plan to have a baby. We were very young . . .'

Eleanor paused and wondered should she say Lila's age. Lila was her baby-sitter, whom Ciara adored – would it make Ciara imagine Lila and a boyfriend together? Would it make her realize that Lila who was happy to watch kids' videos with her was probably quite grown up and having sex? Best not to go there . . .

'I know, you were only eighteen. No, that was when I was born, so younger . . . Were you both seventeen?'

'Yes.'

'Huh! Like Lila . . . is that the right age to have sex?'

'Sometimes yes, sometimes no – it depends.'

'And how did you know you were pregnant?'

'I just felt different . . .'

'Did it hurt?'

Christ, did what hurt? The sex? Being pregnant? The birth? Easier to blanket lie . . .

'No, it didn't.'

'What did you do, after you found out?'

'I told Nana, and I told Cuan and my friend Louise.'

'Who did you tell first?'

'Cuan, I think.' But in fact she hadn't. She'd told Michael, Nancy and that stupid priest her mother had sent her to, but somehow it seemed wrong to say that to Ciara.

'And what was the first thing he said when you told him?'

Eleanor couldn't remember him saying anything. She remembered his bedroom. It smelt of candle wax and he was playing *The White Album* by the Beatles . . . they were some-where between 'Dear Prudence' and 'Happiness Is a Warm Gun' –

'I really can't remember, Ciara. I don't think he said anything . . .'

'Maybe you just weren't listening –'

Beth came in – she'd been rained on. Eleanor hadn't even noticed the rain.

She looked at the two of them, sombre and still sitting at the kitchen table.

'So . . . did I miss anything?'

'Cheese on toast,' Ciara said.

# Casual Smart

Cuan was dressing to meet Brian and Catherine for lunch. He felt like cancelling. He had planned not to go to the wedding in a month's time, for reasons that had nothing to do with Catherine, so he thought it best to meet her now. Next month the changes in his body would be really noticeable. A family wedding, even a small one, was way too public a place to be in transition, and photographed. He'd be fixed for ever as the strange one, the fucked-up one.

He put on a loose cotton shirt – T-shirts were getting risky. He had bought some vests that were small for him. They were a cotton and Lycra mix, and they flattened and distorted the signs very well. He put on looser jeans than usual, and a linen jacket. He pinned a Daffy Duck badge Ciara had given him to the lapel – just in case Brian thought he was dressing like a grown-up now.

He got to the restaurant in Dun Laoghaire bang on time. He would prefer to be anywhere but Dun Laoghaire, but he hadn't known Martina's whereabouts when Brian made the plan. Brian was late. He'd rung Catherine and told her what to look out for.

'So he gave an accurate description?' Cuan grinned.

'Close enough!' She laughed.

They chatted and got past the platitudes – far easier than if Brian had been there on time. Cuan liked her. She was open and friendly, relaxed in herself. She had very short grey hair, and red-rimmed glasses. She wore jeans and a white cotton blouse, not unlike his own dress code, casual smart. She looked about fifty.

'So, how did you two meet?' Surely he should have asked Brian this, but she didn't seem to mind, even if she thought he was cross-comparing stories.

'On *The Rivers Run Foul* documentary . . . did you see it?'

'No, awful title, if you don't mind me saying.'

'No, I agree. Blame the other producer! What's the Setanta like? I've been meaning to go there often, but never made it.'

'It's a good place. There's a new play opening next week – a one-woman show about abuse. It's fairly rough going, quite harrowing judging by the script – but the pre-bookings are good.'

'I might try to catch it – I'm in Dublin all week.'

'Let me know if you can and I'll leave you a ticket.'

It suddenly dawned on Cuan that she might mean they'd go together. This was no ordinary woman; this was his father's fiancée. The last person he wanted under his feet in the Setanta, sipping wine and making comments, was Brian.

Brian breezed over, flushed and hassled-looking, but unapologetic for his lateness.

'So, you two had no trouble finding each other,' he said, as if it had been a fair, mutual competition, rather than just Cuan being the object described. They both nodded and Catherine poured him a glass of wine.

'Well, well!' Brian said. 'Nobody tells me anything! It's a good thing I've two good eyes left in my head and I'm not stone deaf.'

News, no matter what it was, was always about him. Cuan braced himself because he felt implicated by the angle of Brian's head, and the meaningful squint of his eyes in his direction.

'I just ran into Martina! She's pregnant – very pregnant – and she tells me it's twins!'

'It is,' Cuan said. Oh, fuck. Sorry, Catherine, say goodbye to the charming young man . . .

But a little insolence wouldn't dampen Brian over something so big.

'She looks extraordinary! No bother to her to be walking around – buying cat food, she told me. I suppose you've known for ages, though she said she hadn't seen you in a while and doubtless Michael knows . . . Now I know she's a frightfully independent woman, but is there a lucky man?'

'Yes, I think so,' Cuan said.

'See what I've to put up with Catherine? Just because he has a cute face he thinks he can be rude to the whole world.'

*Bollocks. Bollocks. Bollocks. Bollocks!* Cuan gritted his teeth, and contemplated walking out in as dignified a manner as possible.

'Are you ready to order, sir?' the waitress asked Brian. 'Oh, hi!' she said, beaming at Cuan.

'Hi, Rebecca,' he said. She was a dancer who had done a show at the Setanta the previous month. She was stunningly beautiful and ready to give him all her attention and ignore the man who was clearing his throat in response to her question.

Catherine, who hadn't said a word since Brian had sat down, said a resounding yes.

While they waited for the food, Brian probed further, saying how much he liked Martina and they should all meet up for Sunday lunch again. Maybe she'd even come to the wedding, if she hadn't popped at that point.

'She's due around then,' Cuan said.

'Oh, well, sometimes these dates don't match up,' Catherine said.

'Indeed,' Brian added, nodding at Cuan, 'he was four weeks early.'

Brian looked as if he hadn't meant to say it, as if Catherine's presence had duped him into some false openness.

'You never told me that . . . Was I premature, in an incubator, that kind of thing?'

'Yeah, all that,' Brian said, with his way of making that a clear full stop on the conversation. 'How come you haven't seen Martina in a while? Does she not cry on your shoulder about how awful us men are?' He winked at Catherine.

He'd love to blow Brian's theory out of the water: Martina stayed in the spare room in Blackrock – so Cuan's gay and Martina's the fag-hag. He'd even know the term.

Rebecca came back with the dessert menu, and asked him out for a drink.

He said no. Some other time.

What was that look on his father's face? Contempt? Jealousy? He thinks I'm gay and he's still fucking jealous because some pretty girl was flirting – Jesus Christ! Cuan gritted his teeth.

'Well, when you see Martina, *if* you see her, ask her would she like to come along – I think it would be appropriate.'

'Very appropriate, Dad – they may be your grandchildren she's bearing.'

Catherine gave a subtle smile, as if this made perfect sense. Cuan liked her. He really did.

# Priorities

Michael had four missed calls on his mobile. Sinead was in early labour and was coping well. They were hanging around at home for as long as possible – Michael's suggestion. He had seen far too many women come in too early. The hospital was overcrowded and not the place to be, unless it was entirely necessary. He checked his messages: Brian twice, Cuan and Sinead's mother. Well, they could all wait . . . there was no news.

His mobile rang again. This time it was Martina, and he took the call in case she was having trouble.

'Sorry to bother you, Michael. Are you busy?'

'Sort of – I think our baby's making a move!'

'God, that's much more important. Give Sinead my love and very best of luck.'

'I can chat for a while – she's actually hoovering at the moment.'

'Oh, well, I won't be doing that in labour, I can assure you! Listen, I ran into your dad today and he nearly fell over at the sight of me. I didn't say anything about Cuan – and from his look of surprise neither did either of you.'

'No. It's Cuan's place to tell him, really, and he's not the most forthcoming.'

'No, indeed. Does your dad know about the hormones yet?'

'Nope. He thinks Cuan's on antidepressants. He said that to me the other day, thinks he's slowed up and put on a bit of weight – classic signs he told me!'

'Oh, well, he's in for a bit of a land! Tell him whatever

you like, Michael, about the pregnancy, if he asks. I've no axes to grind with him; that's all Cuan's shite. He's always been nice to me.'

'Oh, hell!' Michael said, looking out the window. 'You can tell him yourself, if you like. He's just pulled up outside.'

'No, thanks! See you Monday . . . Oh, are you taking paternity leave?'

'A few days – but you're an exception. I'll be there for you Monday.'

'Thanks. Bye!'

Martina put down the phone. She was actually getting quite fond of Michael. Even if Cuan was top of his priorities, he still had plenty of time left for others. Cuan was self-absorbed like the dad, and selfish to a fault. They had the charm to offset it, so they'd always be loved despite the self-obsession. Michael was a straight-talker and a good man. Fuck charm, he'd be the best father of the lot.

Michael opened the door.

'Not a great time, Dad. Sinead's in early labour.'

'Oh, that's fantastic. I won't keep you long. I met Martina today –'

'Dad, surely this stuff can wait – I'm about to have my first baby!'

'No, please, hear me out, Michael – two minutes. I know she's pregnant with twins, and Cuan was a twin and we never told him . . . the girl baby – Aisling, we called her – died.'

'I know. I saw Mum's charts.'

'Well, isn't it relevant – hasn't it a bearing on Martina's pregnancy?'

'No. It's more complex than that. When your baby died, Aisling, she was a stillbirth, you know that – she may have died as early as thirty weeks. They couldn't track a heartbeat for her during labour. That death has no relevance to Martina's pregnancy, if that's what you're worried about.'

'Yes, it was. Sorry, Michael, I just couldn't bear them go through that. It ripped your mother and myself to pieces for months, years maybe. She never knew she was carrying twins, and we were never told why the baby had died ... It was a different time – there weren't scans, or questions –'

Sinead let out a cry of pain.

'OK, Dad – you have to go. We'll talk about this stuff again. I think you should tell Cuan.'

'Do you? Isn't he messed up enough?'

'Telling the truth doesn't necessarily mess people up. Now go, for Christ's sake – I've other priorities here.'

# Déjà Vu

When Cuan rang Ciara, she gave such a loud shriek that Eleanor and Beth both came running.

'A girl! Brilliant! Girls are the best! Can I come up and see her?'

'Yeah, if Ellie agrees.'

This would be the last time for a while, Cuan thought, maybe until the summer. He really wasn't great, and he didn't want Ciara to see him like that. He'd write to her, and send her stuff.

Ellie came on the phone, and Cuan told her the news.

'How's Sinead doing?'

'Fine. It was a fairly long labour and she had an epidural about halfway through . . . but fine. She expects to be home in about three days. I'm going in to see them tomorrow – let them get some rest tonight.'

'OK. Pass on my best wishes – our best wishes. Ciara can go up at the weekend, if that suits. Nancy's driving down on Sunday so she could bring her back. Hold on, she wants another word.'

'Sure.'

'Dad? I got a card from Brian this morning – you never told me he's getting married! He asked me to come.'

Fuck. Fuck him, Cuan thought. How could he not go to the wedding if Ciara was going? Brian had no right to do that.

'OK. Let's talk about it when you come up.'

'Will Martina be there? I haven't seen her in ages.'

'No, she's up to her eyes at the moment.'

'Awwww!'

He got off the phone and went to take his drugs. He was feeling more and more sluggish on them; maybe something was wrong. He put them back in the bottle – fuck it, skipping one dose won't make a difference. He should tell Martina about the baby. He rang her mobile, but there was no answer. He left a message, which was far less coherent than he'd have liked.

It was nine o'clock. He had slept half the day. Yesterday's revelations had taken a lot out of him. Brian had rung him twice, but he ignored the calls. He was due in work early the next morning. The one-woman show was previewing tomorrow night, and the set was arriving at 7 a.m. Maybe he'd get dressed and go for a short walk. He opened his wardrobe – he'd taken to hanging all his clothes together, not boxing any. He'd have to figure a way to keep Ciara out of his room if she was staying; things weren't as buried as they had been before.

So . . . trousers, jeans or skirt? He opted for a skirt and blouse. Was it dark enough to get away without the scratchy wig? He'd have to get a proper wig or do something to his hair – grow it maybe. It was still way too crispy and tight for girl's hair. He put on the wig, and suffered the discomfort.

He was out for thirty-five minutes. There was a new moon. He remembered that Ciara saw one the night of Michael's wedding – 'Look, Cuan – the moon's a grin,' she said.

A porter outside a nearby hotel nodded. 'Night, mam.'

That was the first time. OK, the man was probably about seventy and myopic, but still the first time he'd been acknowledged like that . . . it was a victory.

He dialled James on his mobile as he walked towards home. He was just getting through and only yards from his front door when they jumped him. Three of them – they must have been fifteen at the oldest. One knocked him to the ground and one kicked him in the ribs. One stole his mobile and punched him in the face. He could hear James's voice in the distance. His wig fell off, and one of them grabbed it . . . At that point a car slowed down and beeped the horn. The youths fled, but the car didn't stop. A BMW, a couple in their forties. They'd done their duty by saving his life, but they wouldn't dirty their hands by picking him off the street. He crawled into the nearest doorway and passed out. Twenty minutes later James and Eamon were by his side, with a garda. Cuan was terrified by the garda's questions.

'Just get the details, Officer, quickly. I want to bring him to the hospital,' James said.

Cuan wasn't coherent, but from shock and pain. He hadn't any blows to the head. James picked him up gently and took the garda's name; he'd call her later.

Eamon drove and James sat in the back with his arm around Cuan. He was in a lot of pain, and clutching his chest – he'd probably broken a couple of ribs. James had brought a pair of Levis with a thirty-six-inch waist.

'They'll be swimming on you, but less conspicuous if you'd like . . . No offence, but I didn't think you'd pass in the flourescent light of the waiting room.'

Cuan nodded, and lay back in the seat while James changed him. Clever friend, Cuan thought. He might have had some bloody psychiatrist assigned to him otherwise, when he just needed someone to stop the pain and the bleeding.

He was given priority in casualty because his nose was pouring blood alarmingly and upsetting the other thirty patients in the queue. He had two broken ribs and his nose was probably broken. They gave him strong painkillers. When he had to give an account of his medication, there were a few raised eyebrows, but no shrink called. By 2 a.m. he was cleaned up, in less pain and able to talk. Eamon had gone home, and James was still holding his hand.

'Thanks, James, for everything. I hate Dublin. That's it, I'm moving west with you.'

'They may have jumped you because they thought you were a woman – it may have started out an ordinary mugging.'

'Well, either way that means I'm easy meat to mug . . . Jesus Christ! You must have felt like this, same fucking hospital even.'

'Yep. At least you've no abrasions – I had to wait almost a week for the results from blood tests, in case I picked up something from his knife . . . That's the problem with bigots – there's no telling where he stuck the knife before me. Anyhow, life goes on. What practical things can I do for you?'

'I'm due in the Setanta at 7 a.m. to open up . . . Can I give you the keys? The stage manager's sound. If I give you her mobile, she'll be able to sort it . . . Just tell them I was mugged, I suppose.'

'No problem. I'll open for you at seven. Is the alarm code still the same?'

'Yep, very little changes, really.'

'The garda called while you were at X-ray – they got your mobile back. I'll pick it up for you and drop it in. You're going to be here for a night or two, I think.'

'Thanks – did we have to do the garda thing?'

'Yes.'

'It just means I'll have to make a statement . . . explain shit.'

'Cuan, you have as much a right to walk the streets as anyone. You didn't commit any crime – those thugs did.'

'Yeah. I know, I know.'

'Do you want me to ring anyone?'

'Oh, fuck! Michael's just had his baby. I'd better tell him, but we'll leave it until the morning. He can put a spin on it and ring Dad. What about Martina? I don't want to freak her out, James. It wouldn't be good.'

'No. I'm seeing her at Holles Street at ten. I'll tell her Cuan, but gently. I think she should know.'

'Yeah, I suppose . . .'

James leaned over and kissed him on the forehead.

'Get some sleep.'

'One last thing – would it be too much to ask you to bring some fresh underwear?'

'Nope. My pleasure. So girl or boy?'

'Huh?'

'Michael's baby?'

'Oh . . . girl! They're calling her Sarah, after our mother.'

# Curfew

Cuan lay flat in bed and touched his face very gently. His nose felt badly swollen. It felt as if he had a gash on his cheek, but it could just be congealed blood. He hadn't seen a mirror yet and was anxious to assess the damage. James dropped by with his mobile, new underwear, some clothes and a bunch of flowers. Martina's appointment had gone well; they let her go home.

'Thanks. You know, I think there's some CE scheme where you visit people in hospital all the time – maybe you should apply for it? How bad do I look?'

'Not great – do you want me to dig up a mirror?'

Cuan nodded and James vanished. He came back with a make-up compact.

'Jesus Christ, James! Pull the curtain will you.'

'Sorry, this belongs to a patient in the ward opposite. It's the best I can do; the nurses were way too busy.'

Cuan moved the small circular mirror around.

'I look awful – like some rough thug who had a drunken brawl.'

'It'll heal. I broke my nose a few years ago and it healed fine, perfectly straight.'

Cuan looked despondent, beaten.

'I ran into Michael at Holles Street this morning and I told him. I said you'd ring him later. The flowers are from Martina; she sends her love. Hey,' James said, 'don't go under with this! It's going to be tough, you knew that.'

'I didn't know I'd be beaten, hated ... I thought people

like my dad were going to have the biggest problem with this — not some fuckheads I've never even met.'

'Maybe you should stay in after dark for a bit . . . not go out on your own.'

'How can you say that to me? You, of all people, who's been on every bloody Pride march and soap box for gay rights? What are you saying, James — that it's cool to go through with this, but stay home and hide for the rest of your life?'

'No, just be careful. You're vulnerable at the moment. Do you think Martina should walk around Pearse Street at eleven o'clock in her condition?'

'No. I'd hate if she did. But I know you wouldn't be able to bloody stop her and anyhow her condition is short term. She'll be able to kick-box those young thugs in no time. I'm on my way to being a freak, permanently, so you'd better get me the fucking rule book . . . What exact time is curfew for freaks like me?'

At that moment Brian put his head around the curtain; Michael had phoned him earlier.

Even James was surprised. He left them to talk, taking the make up compact with him and dropping it back to the nice lady with the gallstones.

'Thanks for coming, Dad, but I'm really not up to talking.'

'I didn't expect you to be. How long are they going to keep you in?'

'I'm being let out tomorrow, I think . . . It looks worse than it is.'

'Come to Blackrock.'

'No, Dad.'

'Please, Cuan. Catherine's there for another day or two. You can't go back to the flat on your own like that –'

'It's just cracks and bruises — it's not life-threatening.'

'Please, I want us to spend some time together before I go to Donegal; there are things I need to tell you.'

'What sort of things?'

'Cuan, just give me a break here and say you'll stay – you can always leave if you need to. I'll come pick you up.'

'No, don't. I need stuff from the flat. OK, I'll stay for a couple of days. But I'll get James to bring me out.'

Brian left, satisfied. Cuan picked up his mobile and left Martina a message: Thanks for the flowers. I can't smell them, but they look pretty.

He had lost his edge, and now he was looking for her pity.

# Skin

Martina woke from her nap. The babies were kicking, though it felt as if they were wrestling. Thirty-five weeks – they would be born soon. They felt like strong, muscular babies when they kicked like that. They felt ready to be born. James had found her an apartment just down the road from Rene's house. Four bright rooms and a high ceiling; it sounded perfect. He knew the owners – James knew everyone. It was cheap, relatively, and they were looking for a six-month lease – just the kind of time block she could cope with. She liked Dun Laoghaire; it was peaceful without being suburban. She reckoned that she'd go out of her mind in the suburbs. They were going to look at it yesterday, but James had to go to Cuan.

The thought of him being attacked filled Martina with horror. She guessed James had underplayed the severity of his injuries and his trauma.

'He's OK, Martina, really. A bit of a bump to the nose and two fractured ribs. They should heal quickly. They've ruled out some godawful thing called flail chest, where the ribs break loose and damage lungs or spleen. He was fairly dazed through the whole X-ray business . . . but he was fine when I left him. Coherent and sharp, himself.'

'Was it an ordinary mugging or . . . ?'

'Who knows? And maybe it's best not to dwell on these things.'

'But it makes a difference.'

'Does it? Only if you feel he's more to blame – that he brought it on himself.'

'Just tell him to take care, James, please. Personal safety ahead of politics.'

'Personal safety is politics. Don't go all cloudy-headed on me. You work with victims of domestic violence, for Christ sake!'

James was being tough on her, unusually tough. He was worn out, she could see that, and worried about both of them. Did he blame her beneath it all? Cuan had rung at nine o'clock, just an hour before he was attacked, but her mobile was turned off. She wanted to ring him, badly, but she stopped herself – because she felt it would only bring more pain to both of them. She was settled into the sofa and she put her mobile on the ground and skated it across the carpet, as far from her as possible. The tabbies leapt out of their sleep to chase the strange silver mouse. Perhaps if she'd rung him back, he might not have gone out that night.

She wanted to go to see him, but Michael was adamant that she should do very little for the next while.

'It's only a couple of weeks, Martina – there's no point in taking any risks.'

He'd brought Sarah in. Sinead was in a ward on the next floor up. Martina found her overwhelming – she was real. Her skin was mottled purple and it looked so thin, skin that hadn't been touched by the outside world for twenty-four hours yet. She looked vulnerable but not fragile, not as breakable as Martina imagined. She was sleeping, unaware she was safe in her father's arms. Michael offered to let Martina hold her, but Martina declined.

'No, she's peaceful with you. Don't wake her.'

Actually, Martina was terrified. She had never held a tiny baby before. She had no cousins or nieces or nephews, not many conventional baby-making friends even. She had held robust toddlers at the refuge, but never an infant. She knew she'd learn to hold her two babies, and that they'd be safe in her arms. She lifted her T-shirt and touched either side of her belly, caressing them. These were babies she knew, that had lived in her body, that would rest on her body, it was just the other side of the skin.

Martina looked at her watch – five o'clock. She'd better get up for a bit or she wouldn't sleep later. The pregnancy had made her live like the cats – dozing half the day, then active at night. She went downstairs and looked for them . . . Nutmeg was chasing a butterfly in the garden; Ginger was looking for more food. No way! Go catch a fluttery snack like your sister.

She checked her mobile and got Cuan's message about the flowers. She would ring him soon. Surely she'd know what to say to him soon? She had asked James to buy bright, brash flowers, sunflowers or chrysanthemums – they probably didn't smell nice anyway.

# Double Bluff

A nurse came to check Cuan's blood pressure. It had been high last night, perhaps as a result of the hormones, but it was up to them to guess that. His arms felt cold, though the pins and needles had stopped. The bandaging across his chest must be cutting off the circulation. He had hardly been aware of them binding him last night. The doctors were anxious that the ribs healed straight, and they wanted to restrict movement in case one punctured a lung.

He looked at the white bandages – he was like a quarter Egyptian mummy. This is what some women who want to pass for men do – they bind their breasts down tight like this and put on shirts and ties and flirt with women. Now the binding was masking his small new breasts – it was like a double bluff.

The red-haired nurse was gentle, quietly efficient and confident, in his mid twenties or thereabouts. He said Cuan's blood pressure was fine, but he noticed that his arm was cold. He touched it in various places and asked him had he any loss of feeling. He did. He watched the pale freckled hand touch him. His arms were still covered in thick fair hair; it was a part he hadn't started shaving yet. He felt nothing. The nurse said he'd loosen the binding.

The sensation of the nurse slowly unravelling the bandages startled him. He could breath deeper, despite the pain. He'd hardly noticed how shallow his breathing had become since the binding. As each layer peeled down, he could feel his nipples grazing against muslin and he became aroused – in a totally different way. He had no erection, no feeling in his groin. It was like half his body was becoming aroused. His chest, hot from the binding and itchy from the shaving, was aching to be freed. The blood around his upper body was circling, following the calm hands of this nurse as he unravelled him.

As the final layer approached Cuan panicked: what if the nurse was repulsed by what he uncovered? What if he said something hurtful or asked questions? If Cuan had power, total power, he'd freeze things just there – just as the last thin layer of muslin lay veiling his secret. The beautiful lightness of that feeling. If he had total power he would pause it, hit rewind and feel that unravelling all over again – a few times, as many times, as it took for it to be known.

Shane, the nurse, winced – he was shocked.

'This bandage was far, far too tight . . . It's made an imprint on your back – you can see the pattern.'

He rubbed Cuan's back, gently but briskly, to encourage blood flow. Cuan felt thousands of blood cells dance under his fingers.

He couldn't think of anything funny or ironic to say.

# Careful

Ciara was having a snack before her homework, a mix of breakfast cereals. Beth was having yoghurt.

'You should try this, Beth. It's great!'

'Well, it looks colourful anyway.'

Cuan had rung that morning when Ciara was at school to say that he'd been mugged, and wasn't able to have Ciara to stay for the weekend. He sounded awful, despondent and miserable. He said he was staying in Blackrock. Ciara would be disappointed. She'd packed already, even though it was three days away. Ellie had gone to UCG library for the afternoon. Beth should wait until she was back and let her tell Ciara – Eleanor still liked to filter things herself. What would she say to her – the truth? Or maybe that he was sick? Or invent something entirely different, perhaps.

Ciara and Eleanor were arguing a lot these days. Ciara was growing up, and Eleanor often found that difficult. Ciara had called into the bookshop with her friend Sophie the other day. They chatted to Eric, the latest recruit, who had a blond Mohican hairstyle, and played in a rock band called Prick up Your Ears, though he probably had the wit not to tell them its name. Later she looked at Eric's dawny blue eyes pleading with her to come help, as he fumbled to put a book into a brown paper bag that was clearly too small. God knows what the two girls found so fascinating about him, she thought. Beth mentioned to Eleanor that they had dropped in.

Ciara was very different when she was with her friends, all giggly and whispery, cheeky to Eleanor, throwing her eyes up to heaven at her instructions. It drove Ellie crazy . . . to see her composed, philosophical daughter transform into a ditzy giggling blonde.

Eleanor was cross that she had dropped by the bookshop.

'You were supposed to be in Sophie's house – not wandering around town.'

'She lives in town; we virtually had to pass by the door! We just dropped in to say hello to Beth. No big deal.'

But Eleanor was clearly going to make it a big deal.

'You're not supposed to take detours.'

'Relax Mum, we won't drop by again . . . Sorry, Beth.'

This was a Ciara tactic, muddying the waters, the princess of ambiguity – sorry Beth that she wouldn't drop by again, or sorry Beth for the tedious argument, or sorry she had dropped by in the first place?

Beth found all the conflict tiresome – she hoped Eleanor would let it lie. Ciara could hold her own and argue this sort of stuff for hours. When she was Ciara's age she could disappear for half a day and no one would notice. There was a very useful diffusion of attention in big families; you could find growing-up space easier.

Everything Ciara did was monitored. Every minute of the day Eleanor knew exactly where she was. Maybe that was important now, maybe the world was a big bad dangerous place, but Beth felt that it didn't allow Ciara much space to breathe. Drama classes and art courses and a rigidly timetabled life at eleven didn't allow her much time to be creative either. *Maybe Ellie's as scared of that as anything else – the Cuan factor – that she'll get stuck inside her own head.*

Ciara and Eleanor started up again.

'Don't be ridiculous, Mum. Sophie's mother's not like that! Beth, did you hear that?'

'Don't hassle Beth about it – I'm just saying some parents would have a problem with the bookshop.'

Oh, Christ, Ellie let it go! Beth felt Eleanor was way too heavy-handed with this stuff.

'Because they sell books for gay and lesbian people?' Ciara sounded about forty.

'Yes.'

'Rubbish. And it's insulting to my friend.'

'I'm not saying Sophie's mother is like that . . . In fact, she very probably isn't. You just have to be careful.'

'Oh, right, careful to presume other people have prejudices!'

Oh, good line, Ciara. Beth was actually starting to enjoy the spat.

# Voices Carry

Cuan spent three days in Blackrock being bombarded by facts. Brian had a lot to get off his chest – the stillbirth, Sarah's postnatal depression, the shaky marriage, his own mother's 'problems' . . .

Cuan just listened as best he could, understanding little of what was said. Brian was too literal a man ever to be understood by a son who thought in metaphors and images.

'She would hear the child, Cuan. Hear your sister who never spoke, never cried, never breathed outside her womb.'

Cuan listened to hear Aisling and he thought he could hear a faint chatter above the clinking of the plates in the dishwasher.

'It nearly drove her crazy . . . It nearly drove us both crazy. She stopped telling me after a while because I just didn't want to know and sometimes she'd just gaze into the mid distance like a madwoman.'

'She wasn't crazy, Dad.'

'I know. I bloody know that. After three weeks or so I couldn't stick it any more. I made her go to the doctor. He put her on some drugs – which meant she had to stop breast-feeding you. She blamed me for that, of course. And all the while Michael was trundling around being a fire engine. At least it seemed to have no effect on him.'

Cuan tried to remember her breasts . . . He couldn't, not the shape or the colour. He thought of his own, and he moved slightly to feel them graze his shirt. He thought of Shane's hands, but couldn't feel them.

'Dad, do you mind if we stop now. I'm exhausted.'

Cuan felt like some bad disembodied therapist. He was finding these revelations very difficult. He wondered could he rig up some recording equipment for Brian, let him tell it to a microphone. As soon as Brian started speaking he went numb. The words would jumble into some incoherent mass, so the rain on the window sounded sharper, the dog barking in the neighbour's garden sounded closer.

'No, fine. I've to go and pick Catherine up.'

He was picking her up outside Blackrock Shopping Centre at three o'clock – it was ten past already. Catherine had not yet learned that the best place to meet Brian was bookshops or libraries, places where an extra half an hour is pleasure, not the side of the street in the rain.

'Will you be OK by yourself?'

'Perfectly fine. There's very little wrong with me.'

'You look awful, if you don't mind me saying. Your face is all puffed up.'

Cuan grimaced. He hadn't taken his hormones in four days now. His body was like a car struggling in reverse. He tried to take them last night – but he just couldn't do it. He'd have to tell Brian sometime, or cop out and get Michael to tell him. He had hoped that he'd just know. That it would be so bloody obvious he'd just know and accept, without the freaking out or the stupid questions.

'Michael and Sinead may call over with the baby later.'

Brian was saying this to cheer him up, but Cuan felt like a monster because he didn't want to see the baby. The last thing he wanted to see right now was a baby.

'Actually, I'm going out for a bit later . . .'

'Oh. Where?'

This was a normal question, he understood this question, but he had no answer. His dad knew James had gone to Westport for a while, so that lie wouldn't work.

'Martina – I want to see Martina.'

'Oh, excellent – give her my best. Do you need a lift?'

'No. Now go, Dad – you'll be late for Catherine.'

Brian stood up to leave. He looked happy – this stuff was actually making him feel better.

# Waking up

The tabbies came hurtling into the room, waking Martina from her nap. She had been dreaming of her mother's death, only not the way she had actually died, which was a relatively peaceful death in hospital, but a violent death, the death Martina had always feared for her – a drunken fall, an accident, where there was blood and screaming. Martina sat up in bed. Her heavy breasts were sweating so much there were two trails of sweat down her stomach – parallel streams, like tears on cheeks.

The tabbies knocked over a magazine rack. They were stalking each other to pass the time until Martina fed them.

'Oh, fuck off, you two! I'll be up in a minute!'

They were paying no heed to her – Ginger had Nutmeg cornered. He was slightly bigger and usually had the edge when it came to straight fighting. She was the queen of the ambush, however – she could find innumerable hideouts behind sofas or chairs to pounce him. She could make him jump four feet in the air, and land facing her, ready to fight. Their tails were twitching a warning beat in rhythm with each other on the stripped pine floor. They had a fixed stare. Martina knew if Nutmeg broke the eye contact Ginger would have her, and she'd lose. He tapped her with his paw, claws retracted. She hissed. He tapped her again and she leaped clean over him and they were gone – scurrying down the stairs.

The doorbell rang . . . an electronic 'Greensleeves'. Seems a bit out of character for Rene, Martina thought. Even if she's never met the woman, you can pick up quite an impression of someone by living in their house for a few weeks.

She picked up her mobile as she ambled downstairs, and checked her messages: Oh, fuck, it was Cuan.

She opened the door. Cuan had his head to the side, his cute-boy look – except his face was bruised, swollen and shocking to Martina.

'Hi . . . Come in. Sorry, I just got your message. I've turned into some semi-nocturnal creature who sleeps most of the day.'

Cuan said nothing.

'I have to have a shower – will you make us a pot of tea?'

'Sure.' The tabbies had already landed upon his shoelaces.

'Maybe feed those bloody cats as well! They might quieten down.'

She stood under the shower longer than usual. Feeling the water run down her body comforted her. The babies were asleep, or just being quiet. She angled her body so that her breasts broke the jet – that way the water wouldn't drum loudly on her belly and wake them.

Cuan was lost and broken. What could she say to him? He was doing his very best impression of a kid, but she couldn't see the child any more. He was at his oldest in London that time – fourteen maybe fifteen even, with a precocious command of the Tube timetable and a gift for directions. Excellent manners at the funeral, waiting until he got home to scoff the Jaffa cakes . . . He was too young to have sex, what he needed was a glass of milk. Are these his babies? Her instinct told her they were. However improbable or abhorrent that fact was to him. He was male and he was potent, just seven months ago.

When she came down the tabbies were in his lap, and a pot of tea on the table. He had opened the back door and there was a faint scent from the cherry blossom drifting in.

'You cold?'

'No, quite the opposite: the babies generate more heat then my Volks engine.'

'How are you feeling?'

'OK. Knackered, but OK. I'm really sorry you were attacked.'

He put his hand to his face.

'People on the DART were wincing at the sight of me – I've never had that before. Life's easier if you're inconspicuous.'

Cuan was never inconspicuous – but this wasn't the time for Martina to tell him. He was beautiful and graceful and therefore got to lead the kind of charmed life that beautiful people do. He got lots of attention, positive attention, whether he was standing at the checkout in a supermarket or negotiating funding with corporate sponsors. People liked him, on aesthetic grounds. However superficial that sounded, she remembered feeling it, too. Sometimes just looking at him made her happy – like a beautiful place that would never look as good in your memory or in a photograph, but just being there was magical. Now the bulldozers had moved in.

'Were you very frightened?'

'I don't really remember it. I passed out . . . Can I make more tea?'

'Sure – you hungry?'

'Not really . . . You should eat though, yeah?'

Martina nodded – she hadn't the energy to cook. She decided they'd ring for a pizza and Cuan agreed.

The babies woke up as soon as she started eating . . .

'Typical, my womb acts like it's in direct competition with my stomach for body space.'

'Er . . . I think it's winning.'

'Yeah . . . Do you want to feel them kicking?'

Cuan looked a little alarmed, but nodded, and didn't move. So Martina leaned forward and took his hand and placed it on her T-shirt, predicting where they might kick next. She was right.

'I'm not sure if that was an elbow or a foot.'

She moved his hand to the other side – running his hand unselfconsciously up and down like it was hers. She was focusing so closely on the movement inside, she hadn't noticed the tears in his eyes.

'This one's subtler, usually. Just rest your hand here for a bit – this is the favourite kicking spot.'

Martina left Cuan's trembling hand resting lightly just below her left breast and picked up another slice of pizza.

'Brian told me I was a twin. That a girl baby died at birth, or just before – she was a stillbirth.'

'Jesus!'

Martina looked in his eyes. This was the truth. This made sense.

The subtle baby kicked his hand from her belly.

# The Dark

They talked until it grew dark. Cuan looked exhausted. Martina didn't like the idea of him making his way back to Blackrock on his own, and she felt too tired to drive him. She asked him would he like to stay, and he said he would.

She put him in her bed, the spare bed. She decided to sleep in Rene's room. She went up to check if he was OK. The two tabbies had curled up under the covers. He had turned on the tape recorder.

'What the hell is this – some electronic crap?'

'Nope – dolphin sounds.'

'Christ, have you gone all New Age?'

'James, actually! I'm supposed to fit it somewhere into our birth plan.'

'Well, it frightened the hell out of the cats!'

She laughed, and realized she hadn't laughed in ages. She kissed him on the forehead:

'See you in the morning.'

She was glad not to be sleeping in that bed – the dream about her mother had been terrifying. Maybe Rene's bed would be a more restful place for her subconscious. Her mother had been on her mind since the dream, her death particularly. She had died when Martina was in France, picking fruit. It was where she met Richard. Her mother had been admitted to hospital, she knew that, but it was her fifth time in that year. It was early September, around the time of her father's anniversary. She died almost twenty-one years to the day after his death, alone in an overcrowded hospital. She was only forty-eight. That age seemed ridiculously young to Martina now; it didn't match the memory of the woman who had lived as a lonely, isolated widow for so long, for long enough.

She left Richard behind in France and came back to Dublin, catatonic and alone. Thinking back on that time, Martina had no idea how she organized the funeral. Because no one teaches you how to do that. No one tells you that one day you'll have to decide what is read and what said at that kind of ceremony. Or that you'll decide what type of sandwiches and where they'll be eaten and how many to expect. You'll need to know that, somehow, because you'll be asked by the hotel.

Martina tried to recognize people from every part of her mother's life, her life, one after another, as they shook her hand at the removal. Someone from college, someone from school, someone who worked with her father, someone she'd never met, but said they were a second cousin from Limerick, old neighbours – Joe's mother, that fucker who kicked the first baby from her stomach. She looked so clawingly sympathetic that Martina got a wild notion there and then to tell her what her-son-the-barrister did, the one that she was apologizing couldn't make it for whatever reason, the one that her mother opened the door to rescue her from, and saw she was hurt, saw her properly for the first time in years. And then the tears came, and Joe's mother leaned over to hug her and say, 'She was a good woman. A troubled woman, but a good one.'

Richard turned up on her doorstep two days after the funeral. She hadn't intended contacting him again, but there he was, so they made a go of it. He helped her box her mother's stuff as best he could – and they blitzed the rented house for the next tenants. They moved to West Cork and pooled their books and CDs. They had three copies of *One Hundred Years of Solitude* . . . how could that possibly have happened? Though they'd been through all that stuff together, she never felt connected to him. She felt numb from her mother's death, and continued to feel numb towards him – funny, he accepted numb quite well, and never looked for anything more.

Cuan was asleep. The one she didn't feel numb towards. She looked in and turned off his light. She was no longer in love with him, but she still loved him. She was glad he was nearby. Was it just a crazy fantasy or would he stay until she was ready to give birth? Just mooch about and watch videos with her, drink endless tea. She could let him back into her life easily now – because she no longer desired him, he was no longer dangerous. He looked so peaceful lying there in the dark. She wished she could crawl under the covers like the cats and rest with him. For all his torment there was something incredibly peaceful about his gentle body. So he was a twin, like her babies. He'd lived that close to someone in the womb. No wonder he was the loneliest person she'd ever met.

# House of Cards

James was delighted with the plan –

'All my eggs in one basket, so to speak. I won't ask how you both managed to mature in my absence, but I'm delighted!'

'Don't patronize us or we might squabble and revert.'

Cuan grinned. He was happy that things had worked out this way. He felt this was as it should be.

'*Us!* Wonderful. I love it.' James couldn't hide his glee.

'Shut up, James! Now, Ciara is coming for the weekend – she's staying in Blackrock with Cuan. Do you think he should tell her about the babies?'

'Well, that's a tricky one. To tell her maybe she's going to have siblings, or maybe not, is hard for a child to get their head around.'

'What if we told her they were mine, just mine?'

'I presume Ciara knows how these things happen. She's not been brought up with the cabbage leaves and stork theory.'

'I think you may be mixing your metaphors.'

'And your cultures.'

'Oh, stop ganging up on me! Actually, I think you're best holding off until they're born and the parentage established. Keep it simple.'

James was right of course, except that it would never be simple. Cuan was happy to stay on Rene's island in Dun Laoghaire until the babies were born. They were at home with each other again, bantering and squabbling of course, but allowing each other close. They could be happy for two weeks or so, like a holiday, with the promise of good weather. Martina believed the climate was too rough in the real world to let them be together. She had no idea what would happen when the babies were born.

The night before Cuan had suggested that she moved into Blackrock, and they argued around in circles. The house would be empty – Brian was moving permanently to Donegal. Cuan could keep his flat in Pearse Street, if that was what she wanted. Over and over they'd build a plan, until Martina panicked at her dependence and knocked it down.

'But what if they're not your babies?'

'I don't bloody care!' Cuan said. 'They sure as hell are yours, so let's make a home for them on that basis.'

And she'd follow his logic for a bit and they'd build again. They'd go as far as deciding which bedroom the babies would sleep in, what colour the walls should be . . . then make it crash down again. Martina leaving for somewhere else, somewhere no one knew her, or any bloody thing about her. Cuan was well used to Martina being like this. He knew these circles and he knew how to negotiate them – like a dancer, keep your eye fixed on one spot and you won't get dizzy or disorientated, you won't fall over.

'OK, let's start again. What I'm suggesting is that you move to Blackrock for six months – I'll get Brian to draft up a lease if you like – and just enjoy the babies and stop fretting about your independence. You are independent, you will be independent – you can see or not see whoever you like, including me – but we'll all be nearby.'

'I don't need you all to be nearby.'

'Yeah, I know you don't, but wouldn't it be nice . . . ?'

Martina stomped off and put the kettle on, muttering to herself.

Cuan had extraordinary patience. It was why he was good at fixing things. It was why he was prepared to go through with his sex change. He had started taking the hormones again, and was feeling stronger. The bruises had faded and the pain in his chest had lessened. He knew Martina wasn't bluffing when she threatened to walk away. She could and she had many times, but this time he knew she shouldn't.

'What is so awful about letting us be supportive? Me, James, Michael – everyone's on your side, you know. You don't need to fight everyone. What would you achieve by just walking away?'

'This crap is from someone who's having a sex change!'

'I'm doing this so I can stay, you know that.'

'Tea?'

'Yep.'

'So, when do you want me to change pronouns?' She was changing the subject. He was used to this, too.

'Whenever you want to! Now back to Blackrock for a minute –'

'No, seriously, do you want me to stop calling you "he"?'

'You don't. You call me "you" or "you fecker", depending on your sweet mood swings.'

'Strange to think, but the babies may only know you as female . . . Oww, fuck!'

Martina dropped another mug – she was having a pre-labour contraction. Michael said these were perfectly normal . . . and not to get excited. It didn't mean that labour was starting. Still, thirty-seven weeks – it was nearly time.

'Does it hurt?'

'No, these ones don't. The real ones do, I've heard.'

'Sit. I'll make the tea – I'm easier on the mugs.'

He came back with a pot of tea and a packet of biscuits. He was wearing a denim skirt today, and a top that was closer to a blouse than a shirt. He had taken to wearing skirts around the house, around Martina, and she accepted and became relaxed with it, as he knew she would.

'Do you conjure them out of thin air, or do you keep a hoard of them somewhere?' Martina asked, taking two chocolate fingers.

Cuan smiled.

'I went out to the shops earlier while you were having your nap. We needed more cat food. They didn't like the last stuff. They left it so long in their bowls and it started to get furry. I thought we needed some sugar.'

'Mmm, I used to love these as a kid.'

Martina wondered had he changed to go and changed back, or had he risked the skirt . . .

'I chickened out and put on jeans,' he said, reading her mind.

# Paradox

'Awww . . .' Ciara said. 'I like Pearse Street better – we're closer to things.'

'Not this time, I'm afraid. It's back to the sleepy suburbs.'

Cuan wished that he and everyone else could be honest with Ciara. That nobody lied or placated her – all the secrets made a distance between them which he was finding hard to bridge. They were walking down the quays from Heuston Station, along by the Liffey.

Ciara hadn't been too shocked by his appearance – she expected him to look different because of the accident. That was the spin Eleanor had put on it. She phoned him to make sure he'd comply.

'I told her you were knocked off your bike – I thought that was better than beaten up. I didn't want those pictures in her head.'

Control her subconscious, why don't you, he thought, but Cuan agreed.

'So, what was it knocked me off – a car or a truck?'

'Oh, fuck it, Cuan, I didn't elaborate! Look, I'm sorry for what happened to you – it must have been awful.'

Ciara had travelled on the train with Deirdre, a friend of Beth's from the bookshop, who was coming up to Dublin. Though Ciara reckoned she could easily go on her own.

'I'm nearly twelve – I've been on the train loads of times. What does Ellie think I'm going to do – jump out while the train is moving?'

'No, she probably just thought you'd like company. What's Deirdre like?'

'Nice, I suppose, though she kept talking to me like I was about five. Would you like some sweeties?' Ciara started mimicking a very patronizing, squeaky voice.

Cuan laughed.

'And I bet no one spoke to you like that when you were five either!'

'No.' And for a moment Ciara remembered what she was like at five, and that Cuan didn't know her then, so Cuan couldn't make that picture in his head. It confused her, so she changed the subject.

'When are we seeing Sarah?'

'Tomorrow morning – Michael's calling over. She's beautiful!'

'Cool! I can't wait to meet her.'

Brian and Catherine's wedding was in a week; Ciara had umpteen questions as they strolled through the crowds on their way to the DART.

'What's Catherine like?'

'Nice, clever.'

'Why are they getting married?'

'Because they love each other, I suppose!'

'Will it be like Michael's wedding?'

'No, much quieter. There's only about ten people going. Just family, not those noisy doctors.'

'Oh. Will Martina be there?'

'Probably not.'

'Will you and Martina ever get married?'

They'd got to the Ha'penny Bridge . . . Ciara was asking this sincerely, not jokingly. Cuan would have to answer it the same way.

'Probably not.'

'Why not – you love each other, right?'

'Yes.'

'Are you boyfriend and girlfriend . . . ?' Ciara paused, this was a premeditated question, and like all premeditated questions it was difficult to ask . . . 'cos Ellie says you're not.'

'What does Ellie say we are?'

'A paradox.'

Ellie could be glib, but not usually with Ciara – this seemed way out of character.

'Did she say that to you?'

'No, to Beth . . .'

'You know you shouldn't be –'

'Yeah, yeah, I don't usually. I was just on the stairs brushing my hair – I couldn't help overhearing.'

'Martina and I are not girlfriend and boyfriend, Ciara. We love each other a lot, a special love, but not like that.'

That was as close to the truth as he could manage. But then how the hell would he explain the babies? If Ciara was their sister, she had a right to know. She would presume that he had told her lies – that this 'special love' was a lie. He'd have to cross that bridge next.

'And what's a paradox?'

'I think it means something that's not meant to be true, but is – like a crazy contradiction.'

'Oh. Well, that can't be the right word. Cuan, can I ask you something else?'

Ciara was being her persistent self, but seeing as he hadn't really answered any of her questions properly, she was being unusually patient.

'Sure.'

'Was it a car or a truck that hit you?'

# Broken Net

James moved in with Martina for the weekend – she had got used to having company, and dependent on it, temporarily at least. She was being very careful, spending most of the time moving between the sofa, the shower and the bed. Her belly felt huge and tight. She'd got large purple stretch marks in the past few days, on the lower half of her belly – they looked like a broken net. She didn't mind that her body would be marked. That was one of the things she found difficult about the miscarriage and the abortion – there were no scars, no signs that her body had held two babies.

James was curious how she and Cuan had sorted stuff out, but she couldn't explain it.

'I don't know, James. Desire is an odd thing, like a trick of the light. We're back to where we should have started from, I suppose. He never wanted a sexual relationship; I know that now. I just wanted to believe something different at the time . . . for fecking years, really.'

'So what do you want now?'

'Well, I could do with letting these babies free soon! Then, I don't know. Maybe I'll fall in love with someone else in time, and maybe I'll be able to cope in a mature fashion if he does. If the babies are his, I hope he'll be a part of their lives – though I suppose he'll be more an aunt than a father.'

'Careful not to push him away again, Martina, when you have the babies for company.'

'James, I don't do it deliberately, I really don't. Sometimes I just can't handle him. Maybe now that the conventional relationship is completely off the cards things will be different.'

'Are you telling me that's what you wanted all along, a conventional relationship?'

'Well, obviously not, or I'd have chosen someone less complicated! Oh, make us more tea; you may be more mature, but he has the edge when it comes to making the tea.'

James went into the kitchen. The tabbies followed, though they weren't convinced that this large, noisy man was able to use a can opener. Martina yawned. It was eight o'clock – too late for a nap, too early to go to bed for the night. She wandered over to the shelves to see if there were any videos that she hadn't seen three times over with Cuan during the past few weeks. She put out her hand and picked one at random. She was too weary to make a decision – it should be fine. Rene's profile didn't seem right for anything too gory and entirely wrong for hard-core porn. She put it in the machine and, as she bent over, a gush of water splashed onto the wooden floor. Her heart skipped a beat, then she called to James:

'Take a rain check on the tea – we're heading in to Holles Street.'

# Focus

Cuan got the message that they had gone in to Holles Street while he was on the DART. It was nine o'clock, beginning to get dark. He was heading back to Blackrock having just dropped Ciara to Greystones. They'd had a great day. Michael and Sinead called over, and Ciara had been entranced by Sarah. The tiny baby looked at her cousin with big quizzical eyes, just beginning to focus.

Then the two of them went for a walk on Bray Head, all the way to Greystones. Ciara made a list of the birds they saw. Seventeen different types and three unidentifiable speckled brown warblers or fieldfares.

'Have you seen the different types of warblers in my bird book, Cuan? Even their relations must find it hard to tell them apart.'

Cuan was careful to wear the same kind of clothes Ciara would be used to – his denim shirt, though it felt rough and chafed his skin, and his leather jacket, which seemed to smell stronger, more acrid than it had before. Even so, she said that he looked different.

'What way different?'

'Dunno, maybe just older . . .' She looked at his hands – they were definitely the same. She looked closely at his face, and she couldn't quite figure it. Cuan looked at his watch – nine-fifteen. She'd probably be lying in bed now, he thought. Maybe she'd work it out in her dreams tonight.

Cuan decided to go back to Pearse Street. He'd be closer if anything went wrong. His heart was racing – he was trying to head off a panic attack. He rocked slowly back and forth, in rhythm with the DART. He hadn't been back by himself since he was mugged. He had popped in briefly with James to get some clothes and his drugs. He could hear his drugs rattling gently in his pocket as he rocked. He pictured himself inside his white plastic pill carton, watching them shift around.

He could feel things through his body more since he started taking the hormones – the movement of the DART, the noises of the brakes, even the breeze from the open window seemed more intense. He could feel the waistband of his new jeans like a perfect oval. He caved in last weekend and bought a pair of black Levi's with a two-inch bigger waist and a looser fitting cut. Even still they were a bit tight. They chafed his thighs, and a bout of thrush brought on by the hormones added to his discomfort. His old jeans were much too uncomfortable, but he couldn't bring himself to throw them out, not yet. He'd taken the same size in jeans since he was a teenager – maybe he should give up chocolate and biscuits. Go on a crash diet. Martina always scoffed at women on diets – have they little else to exercise their brain, she'd say, other than counting calories? ... Why are we still punishing ourselves after decades of feminism? ... blah, blah, blah. It was one of her hobby horses. She had a point, of course – Cuan could see that – but on the other hand she had a perfect body, at least before the pregnancy. She didn't have to watch what she ate, and with the tiniest of effort she could be a stone lighter, but she'd no wish to. She didn't know what it was like to hate your body – she couldn't even muster empathy for it.

She had some idea about his preoccupation with appearance, he knew that, but she didn't condemn him as shallow on account of it. In fact, she was quite tolerant of vanity in men. She was also one of the least observant people he knew when it came to appearance. She'd never notice if he got a haircut, or wore something new ... When James started wearing glasses it was about three months before she copped on. She always recognized people, though, better than he did, even from a distance – but she was working from some entirely different criteria, so maybe it wasn't a fair competition. She noticed mannerisms and body movement, any odd ticks a person might have, and something beyond the way they looked. He was having coffee with her once, when they knew each other first, and she handed him a biscuit. He had his hand up his sleeve and had to take it out.

'You always do that, or else you fiddle with the sugar,' she said. 'Mostly that, actually – both hands up your sleeves holding your elbows, straitjacket style.'

He liked the way she disarmed him, always. She knew him, best of anyone. But he was shallow. He was looking at the back of a *Hello* magazine across the way, trying to work out who the celebrities were and who made their dresses, while she was in some terrible pain and about to have her life changed for ever. No wonder she didn't want him there. He felt his heart banging against his ribcage, hurting the fractured ones. He had to keep reminding himself to breathe.

He tried to focus on what it must be like for her, right now. He had read about labour. She had a women's health book written by a feminist collective, which had graphic photographs of the blood and the pain. He dug his nails into his new stomach flesh. Imagine, her stomach was being cut open, to let these babies out. Martina, who didn't even approve of women shaving, would be cut. There would be blood, purple blood like Bessie's, everywhere. The babies might die. Martina might die.

Landsdowne Road – just one more stop to go. It was very dark. The walk from the station was about five minutes, three if he ran, which he would, then collapse for few hours – wake up and sort out the rotting things in the fridge, wait for news.

# Trust

'I am being calm – this is calm, Martina!' James had beads of perspiration on his forehead already.

'No, it's not, and try not to find anything else funny – they'll think we're stoned. They'll do a drug test on me in a minute.'

'Sorry, it must be nerves.'

Martina was in a lot of pain; the contractions had begun in earnest. She was waiting for the anaesthetist to come with the epidural. Michael was on his way; she'd very likely have a Caesarean when he arrived.

Martina had been assigned a male midwife, the only one in the hospital, who began by asking her if she had a problem with him being male. Martina found this funny, though it's hard to laugh when you're in so much pain, so she made a kind of choking sound, and James started to giggle . . .

Alan blushed.

'So, it's OK?'

'It's absolutely fine,' she said.

'And it's OK with your husband?' he said, turning to James.

'Not a problem!' James said with a grin. There would be plenty of time to explain all to Alan as the night progressed.

Then he and James started breathing together – in unison, like they had been taught in the classes, and encouraging her to join in.

'OK, OK, I'll try – but it is very bloody easy to do that when your body's *not* being ripped open . . . How about I do it between contractions and I bite into your arm during them?'

Alan was backing off.

'Oh, you're OK, Alan. I'm mostly vegetarian. Now, where is the guy with the needles? I'm actually looking forward to feeling a pain somewhere else – it'll be a novelty.'

Martina hoped they'd all have settled down a bit by the time Michael got there. It was ludicrous to be giddy and hysterical at a time like this.

The stultifying heat of the labour ward did the trick – after about twenty minutes they were much calmer and settling into a rhythm. The epidural was in place and it was working fine. Martina was still aware of the contractions, but there was no pain. They had hooked her up to various machines, which beeped and flashed rather disconcertingly. Every so often the ward sister with the pinched mouth would put her head around the corner and look at the screen, barely noticing the occupants of the cubicle.

'I can't bear all these machines, James.'

'Is everything OK, Alan?' James asked. 'Are these machines really necessary?'

'Yes, everything's fine,' he said, but in an anxious sort of way. 'They're just concerned about the babies' heart rate. They're just ensuring the babies are not in distress. Your obstetrician has arrived – he'll be in here in five minutes.'

'Great!'

'Dr McCarthy's nice – very calm.'


Michael strolled in and smiled, and cocked his head to the side like Cuan did . . . Martina felt tears of relief running down her face – this was someone she trusted.

'So, how's everyone?'

He looked at the chart and the monitor, then pulled out a small plastic hearing tube like something from the last century and listened to the babies.

'You're doing well; the two heartbeats are strong. You're

about three centimetres dilated, but the first twin is still breech – so we'd best do a C-section.'

'OK, whatever you think . . .' Martina was perfectly happy to let go at this point. She was ready, the babies were ready and she trusted Michael to deliver them from her, to her.

Forty-five minutes later the first baby was born – a girl, five pounds five ounces. She was small, but strong, with a shock of black hair. Her arms were flailing against the light, her voice was an indignant spluttering shout. Three minutes later there was a baby boy, five pounds three ounces. He had a little less black hair and his skin had a bluish tinge. His cry was like that sound a cat makes just before it pounces on a bird, intentionally gentle and a little misleading. They were perfect. They both looked like tiny versions of Cuan.

James sat down, completely overcome. Martina held the girl, who stopped shouting and looked up with a quizzical frown, flexing her long fingers. Martina crooked her other arm for the boy. Michael put him in gently.

'You want to call Cuan? I've my hands full . . . and Michael looks fairly busy from this angle.'

James rang Cuan and between sobs told him about the two beautiful babies.

Martina was being stitched back together, but she became oblivious to the procedure. She had lost very little blood – as C-sections go, it was a straightforward, uncomplicated one. Michael muttered something about the placentas – that some women liked to keep the placenta and do ceremonial things with it . . .

'Ceremonial?' Martina laughed. 'Jesus, Michael, you think I'm a white witch!'

The girl frowned at her for laughing, and made another shout.

'OK, OK! Honey, if you were hoping for a quiet mummy,

you popped out of the wrong belly. Should I try her on the breast?'

Michael nodded vigorously in approval. Martina looked at his steady hands stitching. He was truly unflappable, quite remarkable. This is the uncle of my babies, she thought, and his arms are covered in my blood. He has lifted them out of my body and given them to me – and he does this miraculous thing every day . . . and I've always said he was a bit boring.

The girl latched on like a limpet and suckled vigorously. The tiny boy was asleep. It was 3 a.m. Martina was exhausted.

Two nurses came to take the babies away for various tests, and to let Martina get some sleep. She rang Cuan before she dozed off.

'Come in when you can . . . I'm scared to go to sleep in case this is just an extraordinary dream.'

# Pressure

Martina was feeding the girl, who had latched on again with ferocity. The last person to suck her breasts was Josh, tenderly with soft lips, circling his tongue anticlockwise. At the time Martina's mind wandered, and she wondered did this mean he was left-handed. This girl was more like a Hoover in comparison, and she could do some trick with her tongue which made a strong vibration right through the breast.

After a while Martina broke the suction with her little finger and a nurse came to swap them over. Martina had very little movement. The gash across her stomach felt sore; she wasn't supposed to put any pressure on it. Her legs were still a bit numb from the epidural and she had a drip in her arm, and a catheter for her urine. It was like being marooned. She had never been physically vulnerable like this in her life. She was preoccupied by the babies, so she tolerated the pain and discomfort. The little boy was awake, but still reluctant to suckle – so she brushed her nipple against his cheek and he opened his mouth. She put her nipple into his mouth, but he wasn't latching on. She moved the breast slightly, pulled it a tiny bit away – and he got it.

Cuan hadn't sucked her breasts that night – in fact, mouths weren't involved at all in that strange sex they had. No talking, no tasting. There was no affectionate foreplay, no nuzzling or negotiation. Martina's clearest memory of it now was the violent pressure as they pressed their bodies together. They weren't gentle with each other; they weren't even careful.

Jill, the woman in the bed to the left of her, had just delivered her fourth child. Her first boy, ten pounds two ounces, almost as heavy as the twins put together, and he looked like a giant in comparison. Just before lunch there was a flurry of women admiring him. Her mother, aunt and two sisters, passing him from one to another, commenting on the nose, the hands, the shape of his head. Claiming his features quickly before the husband's side got a chance. There was no ill will between the two sides, just a need to assure that the eye shape was her Uncle Dan's, the nose her mother's father's. The bed was a sea of baby blue items, and cuddly toys from various cousins. Martina looked at her two babies who were fast asleep . . . she hadn't a single relative close enough to come and do this. She would be the sole source of her family's history for these babies. She hadn't even a proper photo album to show them. What was her mother's mother's maiden name? She didn't know; maybe she should know.

Jill would be out of hospital by tomorrow morning. She'd be back home and some of these visitors around her bed would be cooking and cleaning . . . 'I'll pick up Shelly and Rachael from school – that'll take the pressure off,' one said. 'I'll do a big lunch on Sunday,' another offered. Martina watched John, the husband, with his new son that morning. He held him outstretched along his arm, perfectly balanced – his heavy head resting in his large hand. Jill must be in her mid thirties; her husband the same – they were confident experts and they had a back-up team. She was alone and improvising, occasionally overwhelmed by the enormous responsibility. At times she was quietly confident, too. Somehow she knew that she'd manage, that they'd manage and be happy. She had decided to stay in Blackrock for six months. She had spoken to Brian on Cuan's insistence a few days ago. It was all sorted. Then she would move to Westport and build a life there, work there, support her babies. The Laura Ashley chicken shed would be their first real home, and her first since her father died.

*

327

When they had a quiet moment, Michael offered a blood test to establish paternity, but even he seemed to consider it entirely superfluous. Martina suggested they do one anyway.

'Have you heard that he's giving up the Setanta, that he's going to take up gardening?'

Martina didn't really approve. She worried that he was going to become a recluse, and she found it hard to understand how someone could suddenly develop an interest in something like that. He didn't even keep potted plants. She reckoned it was the hormones racing through his body sending odd nurturing signals to his brain, and she told Cuan that.

'Yeah, I said he could come and practise in Cabinteely. Myself and Sinead are hopeless gardeners . . . and Blackrock could do with an overhaul. Mum always kept the garden beautifully, but no one's touched it since she died.'

'But it doesn't make any sense. He's starting from scratch – he'll have so much to learn before he can make a living at it.'

'Yeah, I suppose, but he's changing – we have to let him change.'

It puzzled Martina why everyone else around Cuan seemed more accepting, more magnanimous, than she could manage. Surely they realized that he was obsessed with his appearance, his clothing, cleanliness? In the early days at the Setanta, if he got a stain on his clothes he'd nip out to Pearse Street on his lunch break to change them. That haphazard faded jeans thing, that just-tumbled-out-of-bed hair, that lazy two-day stubble were as choreographed an image as you'd find in *Vogue*. Now she seemed like the only one who couldn't envisage him in gardening overalls covered in muck. Was she the superficial one because she couldn't see beyond the urban teenager image? Was she the only one who really loved that side of him?

He was on his way in. He would see these babies for the

first time, his babies, who were just twelve hours old. Official visiting time wasn't for ages, but Martina had no doubt that he'd charm his way in. Cuan could get in anywhere with his gentle grin or articulate banter. Ten minutes later he popped his head around the curtain.

'Is this an OK time?'

'Yep. How'd you get by the nurses?'

'Well . . .' He came in from behind the curtain. He was wearing a skirt and blouse – but he wasn't even close to passing.

'I told them I was the babies' aunt.'

# Help

Three days before the wedding, Brian was hill walking in Donegal. It was a beautiful, misty morning. He could feel the low cloud against his face. He could almost taste it. He was looking forward to the wedding. Being with Catherine made everything perfect. He was a little concerned about Lucy. He hadn't had an e-mail from her in about ten days. It was possible she was still high up the Andes, and had broken her schedule, but it was a little out of character. He decided he'd send her an e-mail when he got back to the house – Catherine had her laptop with her.

He was near the top of the mountain when he slipped on a Lucozade bottle and hit his ankle hard on a rock. The pain was excruciating. He roared and, though the roar echoed around him, there was probably no one in earshot. He hadn't his mobile with him – Brian was the type who loved mobiles, but to contact people, not be contacted at inconvenient times. He hadn't brought it because he'd wanted to clear his head. The pain was so bad he thought he might faint. He'd never fainted – but the greens, browns and purples around him were swirling in a worrying fashion. He looked at his ankle – his foot seemed to be hanging at an impossible angle. He yelled again, as loud as he could. He yelled 'Help!' as his earlier cries were just cries of pain; they might be mistaken for animal noises when they muffled and bounced off the rock.

'Help. Help me!'

Fifteen minutes later he had passed out, and was found by a scout troop. Brian opened his eyes and saw Evan – a skinny, spotty young man wearing a ridiculous neckerchief and umpteen badges, with bad stitching. The scout leader was repositioning his leg, and ten boys were circled around making a chorus of ooohs and ahhhhs. Brian passed out again. Thirty minutes later a rescue party of burly men arrived with a stretcher. Evan was a hero, even if he hadn't spotted the twelve-year-old in his troop who littered his Lucozade bottle two hours previously.

Brian was admitted to Letterkenny hospital and informed that his ankle was badly broken. He needed surgery and pins inserted. He would be bed-bound for a while and in a wheelchair for several weeks. The wedding had to be postponed. Catherine, coolly efficient, tried to contact everyone from the hospital waiting room. She brought Brian's mobile for the telephone numbers. Cuan was out, but Catherine left a message on his machine in Pearse Street and Blackrock.

Michael said he would travel up as soon as he could. As she asked Michael directly about Martina, he told her. He said Cuan was probably visiting the twins this afternoon and that he'd probably phone later to tell Brian the news. He said probably a lot. Catherine realized that Michael knew his brother didn't always do the correct thing by his father, that he needed prompting and reminding. Was Michael presuming that she be part of this collusion, too – an intermediary between father and son? She'd liked Cuan straight off – more than Michael, even. Though he seemed wonderfully forthright and capable, there was nothing vulnerable about Michael.

She rang the number in Galway. Ciara answered, and Catherine told her the news. Ciara burst into tears. Catherine wasn't sure was she crying because she was worried about Brian, or because the wedding was delayed. She felt a sudden panic that she was marrying a man who had four grandchildren. Though she was aware he had three children, they were

331

very much in the background and up to this point she hadn't factored in being closely involved with their lives, and their children's lives. She was a little awkward around children. She had never felt the need to have any in her life. She was relieved when her friends got past the childbearing stage, both the ones with children and the ones that longed for them and talked about biological clocks incessantly.

She loved Brian. She loved the way his mind raced across topics. He was so interested in everything, ancient and new, from mummified bodies dug up in bogs to whatever synthesized drugs teenagers were taking nowadays. His mind was like a quality Sunday newspaper. He was arrogant and selfish like so many men his age, his generation, but he was charming and loving. Most of his working life was spent surrounded by obliging women — they spoiled him, they indulged him. She was tougher, and he respected that. She was confident they would have a good marriage. He was ten years older than her, but he was fit and healthy. He enjoyed rude good health, as he termed it, and he didn't look or act his age. It was easy to be duped into thinking they would have a long life together, when really they'd have only a handful of years.

He'd be an appalling patient — she knew that from the moment she got to the hospital. He'd moan and groan and blame everyone, grow a little bitter, grow older. But they'd manage, and the boys would help out. If Cuan rang her back she'd ask him to come to stay for a few days, sit by his hospital bed, keep him occupied. Martina would be in hospital for at least a week recovering from the C-section — maybe he'd be able to spare the time . . . it would be good practice.

# Names

Cuan stayed for two hours and Martina reckoned the babies knew. Cuan held them in turn, his arms trembling, saying nothing, just cooing a little, and they didn't wriggle or shout the way they did with the nurses. He and the little boy looked intently at each other. The little boy was wide-eyed and fully alert for the first time. Cuan passed him to Martina for a feed. The little girl was relaxed. Cuan put his index finger into her fist and she gripped it, closed her eyes and slept.

They talked about names. Martina hadn't mentioned it, but it occurred to her that they could call the little boy Cuan – little hound or little wolf. It would suit this gentle, tentative child. Children are often named after their father, but in this instance the legacy might be too much. She wasn't too sure when Cuan was abandoning the name in favour of a female one, but it must be soon. She wondered what her little boy would feel, growing up and carrying such a relic of his father's masculinity.

'I think the girl needs a strong name. I like all those romantic Irish names like Liadhain or Caoilinn, but none of them seems to suit her.'

'How about Maeve – warrior queen?' Cuan said, flicking through a name book with his free hand.

'Yeah, but how will I handle a fourteen-year-old warrior queen who wants to head off on the back of some boyfriend's motorbike?'

Cuan looked down at the frowning, sleeping baby who was cutting off the circulation in his finger.

'Nah . . . not going to happen. I think she'll own her own motorbike!'

'OK, I like Maeve . . . a definite possibility.'

Martina suggested Eoghan for the boy. It was close to his father's name, euphonious, without the baggage.

'Eoghan and Maeve – nicely separate. We should look up The Táin, though, and make sure she didn't slay an Eoghan in her travels.'

'OK, that's your job . . . I'm being dripped into and sucked out of at the moment.'

'How are you feeling?'

'Exhausted and exhilarated at the same time. Very strange – it must be the kind of buzz people run marathons for.'

'Can I bring you anything?'

'Yeah . . . but don't ask me to decide what! James is bringing me some nighties. I've covered three in blood already and I haven't even been here twenty-four hours. Something with buttons down the front, so I can get the breasts out quickly for these little guzzlers.'

Martina's breasts were starting to throb and heat up – the milk was coming in, and it felt heavy and uncomfortable. She looked at the buttons down the front of Cuan's blouse. They were pretty when they caught the light. They looked as if they were made from some kind of shell.

A young nurse popped by after Cuan had left. She was flushed and awkward.

'I hope it was OK letting your brother in?'

Martina looked at her blankly, and a little worriedly because this ditzy girl had been taking her babies off and bathing them.

'Sorry?'

The nurse fumbled with her stethoscope.

'Oh, yes! Sorry! Maybe I should say your sister. I'm not used to these things . . . I mean the babies' aunt.'

'Oh, that was fine, just fine. That was –'

My fucking sister, she thought, and what the hell do I call her?

# Angles

Catherine asked Cuan to come to see his father, and he said he'd check with Martina and get back to her. He knew Martina would be at least another four days in hospital. She didn't really need him around, and he could be back in time to help her get settled into Blackrock. Cuan's real reluctance was spending more intense time with his father. Doubtless Brian would be full of questions about the nature of his relationship with Martina, which Cuan couldn't discount as prurient interest. He was, after all, the babies' grandfather, and happy to have them live in his house.

Also, these days Cuan was dressing as a woman at least half of the time – Donegal would offer him no opportunity to do that. He could drift into Holles Street to visit Martina and the babies, knowing that Michael's shift was over, knowing Sinead was at home in Cabinteely and wouldn't choose that moment to visit Sarah's new cousins. For someone quite self-absorbed, Cuan could keep remarkable track of other people's movements.

'Is he OK?'

'Reasonably. They've given him morphine for the pain, but the title "patient" is a misnomer! How are the babies?'

'Incredible . . . absolutely incredible. Will you tell Dad the news? I'll bring up some photos . . . if I come.'

'Sure.' Catherine came off the phone, confident that he was in half a mind to come, the difficult half. She made up the spare bed in the cottage. She knew he'd like it there.

He needed to tell Ciara about the twins. He knew Eleanor would prefer if he told her first, but he didn't want to. He felt it was nothing to do with her, really, but no doubt she would see things differently. If he couldn't tell Ciara directly, he'd prefer to tell Beth, but Ellie wouldn't like that either. He could call the three of them together and tell them, but that seemed like a major drama. Fuck it, he'd no option. He'd go to Galway, then Letterkenny – 250 miles or so, an acute angle, almost a right angle.

When Cuan rang Galway to arrange it, Ciara answered and she was distressed.

'First you, then Brian, then Lucy. Cuan, everyone's having accidents!'

'What's happened to Lucy?'

'I had an awful dream about her, and we haven't got an e-mail from her in ages, so I asked Ellie to check hers and there was just a short note to say she had diss –, diss – Oh, that bad thing you get with diarrhoea.'

'Dysentery?'

'Yeah, and she collapsed on the side of a mountain some-where and she was attacked when she was unconscious and her money and passport were stolen. Isn't that awful, Cuan? Imagine someone attacking you when you're unconscious.'

'Awful.' Cuan had imagined it many times. 'And where is she now?'

'Stuck somewhere . . . a family rescued her, but she's still very weak and she can't travel until she sorts out the pass-port thing, but her father's going over – not Brian, her other father. Ellie's been trying to contact Brian at the hospital to tell him.'

'Let me give you Catherine's mobile – that's the easiest way to contact him.'

Ciara wrote the number down and repeated it back to him. She was still in tears.

'Cuan, why are so many bad things happening?'

'I don't know, Ciara. I'm fine, and Brian will be fine. I'm

337

going to see him tomorrow – but I'm going to pop over to you first, OK? I'm getting the first train, so I'll be there about eleven. Is that OK?'

'Yeah . . . suppose . . . Can I come with you to Letterkenny?'

Ciara wanted Cuan to mend things. He was the magic father who turned up out the blue. Michael could make people better slowly, if they could be made better. But Cuan was a juggler, a magician – he was even better.

'You still have school, right?' Cuan couldn't cope with being a father and a son all the same time, not at the moment. He couldn't bring Ciara to Letterkenny.

'Yeah, but maybe Ellie, she's not here at the moment, but maybe . . . ?' Her voice trailed off – even Ciara couldn't bluff that one.

'Ellie let you miss some of your last few weeks of primary school! Not likely, right?'

'No. See you tomorrow.' She sounded utterly despondent. He'd never heard her sound so sad or so adult.

When he got off the phone he developed his photographs. He made multiples of the best ones for Ciara and for Martina, Michael and Brian. None of the photos was perfect, but they'd do. His darkened bathroom looked bizarre with so many infants hanging on clothes pegs. So many tiny unfocused eyes catching him from every angle. Poor Lucy, that was horrendous news. Maybe he should make copies for her as well. For the first time he realized she was related to the babies, too. In fact, she was the real aunt; he was just the impostor.

# Visitors

Martina had lots of visitors. Cuan had been in early to tell her his plans and they'd had a fight. Martina was still reeling when Karen came with Bill. She looked stronger after her holiday, less pale. Bill looked blissfully happy, though a little awkward around a lactating woman. Bill was the decoy. They couldn't discuss Cuan or circumstances in front of him, and that suited both of them. Martina would invite Karen to Blackrock when things had settled, take the lecture on the chin. Sinead brought Sarah with her, who was now a four-week-old giant. Eamon came last and was happy to sit for hours holding the babies, cooing and gurgling.

'That's the man I can't get to sit still long enough to watch a television programme!' James said when Martina told him later. 'By the way, I'm bringing you a special visitor tomorrow.'

Martina looked at him warily.

'Some ghost from the early Setanta days?'

'Nope, Rene's back in town and she wants to pop in to say thanks for minding her babies.'

'And killing one! God, James. How was she about Nikita?'

'Sanguine. She knew it was on the cards. The other two greeted her with great affection – she was delighted with that. She said they wouldn't even be petted before she left.'

'Well, that's all Cuan's doing. Another time, another place, he might have had an excellent career as a snake charmer.'

'Oh, dear, do I detect a little testiness towards the cute boy again?'

'We really will have to stop calling him that soon! James, he comes, he goes. I've lost him again. He's gone off in his own head. He's mostly dressed in women's clothes around me these days, and that's OK by me. But he's not as sharp . . . have you noticed that? There's something spacey about him – like people on depression medication, or people up to their necks in religion. It freaks me out a bit because I'm starting to treat him differently.'

James knew exactly what she meant. He had noticed it, too. He put it down to the mugging, but maybe it was something else.

'What way are you treating him?'

'Like his family do – like some fucking casualty. I've never seen him as some kind of victim. He's one the cleverest people I've ever met, but I find myself sliding into it . . . Fucking gardening, James, it doesn't make sense!'

'Well, it doesn't do it for me, but all the glossy magazine's say gardening is the new sex.'

'Frankly, a bit of the old sex would be better for him!'

'Martina, you have to let him go . . . He doesn't want that life.'

'What life, James? I'm not looking for him to have sex with me, just someone! Actually, I think he should give men a shot. Jesus, he's only thirty! Am I the only one who thinks pottering around digging holes like some old granny is a bad idea, or am I the only one brave enough to say it?'

'Jesus Christ, you've more prejudice against gardening than the sex change!'

'Yeah, maybe I do! James, you know what his mind is like, all that sharpness and irony. What's he going to do with that – dazzle the earthworms and the slugs with his wit or just become some laid-back hippie in a kaftan, humming and giggling to herself?'

'He's not going to be digging holes twenty-four hours a day! The rest of the time he can dazzle us and all these babies with his wit.'

'No, he bloody can't because he's leaving. He's applied for a year to some yoga retreat place, somewhere in England. He'll garden in return for board and free yoga classes.'

'When?' James was shocked – Mr Secretive had really surpassed himself this time. He'd seen him a lot recently and he hadn't said a word . . . unless this was just a bluff to test Martina.

'September. He'll work with an experienced gardener and see the seasons full circle until the following September – then come back and live entirely as a woman. Bye bye, cute boy, for good.'

'What did you say when he told you?'

'Er . . . some fairly awful things – not what you might call "supportive comments". But, fuck it, James, he has a psychotherapist; we don't all have to do that role, too. I'm a friend. Friends aren't supposed to sit back and make helpful, nonjudgmental, platitudinous remarks – and if he wants that kind of friendship, well, he's better off hanging out with the hydrangeas.'

'Did he mention operations?'

'No, but chances are he's planning to do it in the UK while he's away . . . I'm worn out second-guessing him, but sometimes that's easier than asking him something he doesn't want to answer and hearing him lie.'

The babies woke simultaneously. They had slept three hours, a record so far. All that adoration from visitors must have tired them out. Martina took charge.

'You hold Maeve. I've taken to feeding her first because she shouts the loudest. That can't be fair. I'll get Eoghan started first this time, and you can walk her up and down the corridor a bit so she doesn't wake all the babies in the ward.'

James reluctantly lifted the squalling bundle.

'Oh, she may hate me for this.'

'Yep, but just for five minutes. Now he prefers one of the

breasts, I think it's the left one . . . it's a bit slower – the other one gushes for some reason and he splutters and chokes with it. I'll pop her on it in a moment; she handles it better.'

Maeve stopped crying in James's arms. Peace was restored. When they were all sorted, James kissed her on the forehead and left. She looked exhausted. The drama of the past few days had finally caught up with her. Her life was going to be very busy with these two.

Cuan said that he could move in for the summer, and help, before he went. Martina had said no straight off, but he asked her to think about it. It might be wonderful having another pair of hands around, but not if he was depressed and competing with the babies for her attention. She couldn't deal with that. She couldn't delight, like he could, in watching his maleness drip away. Every day he was getting closer to his fantasy, and destroying hers. It would be simpler to let him go, and to meet him again as a woman. Get to know this green-fingered, mellow person, rather than watch the frenetic boy-child she loved bleach into nothing.

# Looks

Cuan was on the bus to Letterkenny. Catherine was picking him up. She had insisted. The day was not going well. He'd been up since six and had two major rows already. He popped into Martina at seven. She had been awake and feeding the babies since five. She looked absolutely exhausted. She argued with him about the gardening again, as he thought she might. A whispered argument between clenched teeth because he wasn't meant to be there. She didn't understand. He reckoned she hated gardening almost as much as the Catholic Church, or chauvinistic men. He didn't understand. He was just trying to get out of her hair, but he didn't say that. He didn't really want to move away from his home, his friends, his family, but sometimes it's easier – because they can dig their heels in, resist change or try to nail your feet to the floor. He wanted Martina to love him like she used to, to look at him like she used to, but she wouldn't. She hadn't for months, so he knew he had to try to accept it. These days she even gave him the Brian look – the how-has-it-all-turned-out-so-wrong look – that acidic mixture of disappointment and guilt.

When Ciara, Eleanor and Beth sat in their tidy living room, he sat opposite and considered making up some wild story instead. The walls were covered with drawings and photographs by Ciara and Beth, equally proportioned, maybe measured by Ellie, or for Ellie by them. He wasn't sure what way the news of the twins was eventually broken. He had rehearsed it so many times on the train that the real performance merged with the practised one. His part at least. They

343

improvised in an entirely unpredictable way. Beth tried to referee, but it was an impossible task.

He had to say Martina didn't know the babies were his until they were born, otherwise he would have lied to Ciara for longer. Worse lies. This didn't make any sense to Ciara. She gave him that look she probably gave Deirdre on the train, only tempered by the fact that he wasn't holding any sweets.

'How could you not know?' she demanded.

She looked at him and he shrugged. He knew she didn't mean the biology, so he didn't try to explain it. He may have used the word accidental, but he hadn't intended to. Ciara looked at Eleanor, who looked like thunder. She looked at Beth, who was looking at the brown envelope Cuan was fidgeting with. So they all looked at the envelope. Cuan took out the photographs, the black-and-white indisputable evidence. Ciara glanced at them and burst into tears and ran up to her room. Eleanor was speechless with rage; she stormed off after Ciara.

'Congratulations, er . . . good photos. Jesus Christ! They look just like you,' Beth muttered.

'Thanks,' Cuan said, meaning thanks for not running out of the room like the others.

'Are you going to raise them together?' she asked.

'No. Martina will be the main parent. That's what she wants.'

'So you're not together?'

Cuan just shook his head. Beth was sound. He had dumped her in it; he knew that. She made him tea and sat with him for twenty minutes. No one came back downstairs.

Cuan had to leave to catch the bus to Donegal, so there was no time to explain, no time to make it less confusing. Ciara didn't want to come back down. She stood at the top of the stairs and said, over and over, 'You should have told me. You should have told me.'

344

'Ciara, I've only known four days.'

'Don't lie, Cuan. I'm not stupid.'

Cuan stood frozen on the doorstep. Nothing he could say or do would make this better.

'Just bloody go, Cuan,' Eleanor said, and he went.

He would write to her. Maybe Martina would write to her, too. He left the photos behind, but knew they wouldn't be allotted hanging space in the gallery.

As Cuan stepped gingerly off the bus, Catherine walked towards him looking concerned. The last time she'd seen him he was beaten up, spread-eagled on the sofa in Blackrock, nauseated by Brian's revelations. He gathered from her concern that he now looked worse.

'Do you get motion sickness?'

Emotion sickness, but what should he tell her? he wondered. Probably as little as she'll accept. She might be sympathetic or she might have a clear perspective, but either way she was in cahoots with his father. He couldn't build a friendship with her based on that first twenty minutes of relaxed conversation they had shared in Dun Laoghaire – it was an illusion; they were just waiting for Brian.

'No. It's just been a very long day!' he said, trying to put a brave face on. It was 8 p.m. If they rushed, he'd catch visiting hour at the hospital, but Catherine wouldn't rush him. Her instinct was to bring him back to the cottage and make him dinner. Let him get some rest. He could spend almost all day tomorrow at the hospital if he wanted. Tell Brian all about Martina and the twins. Tell him everything.

She U-turned the car and brought him home. He looked relieved. She could hear his pills rattling in his bag as they drove. She put on some jazz. Maybe he'd be strong enough to explain those to Brian tomorrow, too, she thought.

# Betrayal

Ciara cried in her room for about an hour. After a while Eleanor left her alone. She wasn't helping, she knew that. Then Ciara read for a while and wrote her diary. Eventually she emerged back downstairs. This wasn't one of her performance huffs. This was real and this was her drama, even if Ellie appeared to be trying to hijack it. She was the one who'd been lied to. She was the one who'd gained a brother and sister way too suddenly, and too shockingly. Surely the nine months are to help you get used to the thing. She reckoned she deserved at least some of that time. She sat on the stairs and listened to Ellie and Beth arguing. Their muffled voices sounded like out-of-tune opera, and she tapped a beat against the banisters to accompany it. Eventually she grew bored and went back to bed.

Eleanor and Beth talked for hours. Beth had swapped her afternoon shift in the bookshop, which meant she'd do a double tomorrow 9 a.m. to 9 p.m. Beth was trying to reason with Ellie, but Ellie wasn't listening to reason.

'Your anger's not going to help things, El. It's not like he's committed a crime here. He's not taking heroin or assaulting people – he's still the fucked-up kid he was last month. He looks wretched. That stuff can't be agreeing with him.'

'Stop being such a fucking liberal, Beth! It's an appalling betrayal. You must see that!'

Beth hoped Eleanor meant a betrayal of Ciara, not of herself, but she wasn't sure. When Eleanor spoke of her fantasy babies, Beth had never imagined that they would be Cuan's, but maybe Ellie couldn't imagine any other type. By the looks of him, that side of his life was over now. He was between genders now; he wasn't even masking it any more. Ellie had the first sex with him as a man; Martina had the last.

'I'm not sure what you're trying to tell me here, Eleanor – that you still love him?'

'No, it's not that. I just can't handle how things have turned out for him . . .'

'But you don't have to "handle" it – he's separate. He can live whatever life he wants, surely?'

But Eleanor shook her head. Cuan wasn't separate, at least not separate enough to father children. It was impossible.

'What the hell is it? How come you let him pull the rug from under you all the time?'

'He just does –'

'No, El. That's your choice.'

Eleanor shook her head. She was only half-listening to Beth.

'Sometimes I think you're just putting up with me – biding your time, harbouring some mad fantasy that you're going to sail off into the sunset with him.'

'No.'

'No? Well, if you want to adopt a fucked-up kid, there's half a dozen in the bookshop you can have. Black T-shirts and black rings around their eyes – my parents don't understand me . . . and Jeff Buckley and Kurt Cobain are dead. They spend their lunchtime reading Camus.'

Eleanor thought she heard the patter of Ciara's feet, an excuse to escape.

'Just fucking let him go,' Beth muttered, as Eleanor went upstairs.

Nobody slept well that night, but Eleanor's nightmare was the worst. She woke up terrified, with panic pains searing down her legs, as if she should have run away, but didn't. She was sweating, like she had a fever. She wanted water, but she just lay rigid in bed. Beth woke and tried to comfort her.

'Do you want me to get you anything?' she asked.

'Could you get me some water?'

Beth rolled out of the bed and moved towards the door.

'Hang on,' Eleanor said, 'I'll come with you.'

They sat in the kitchen sipping water. Eleanor was silent.

'Should I just give up?' Beth said, after about ten minutes.

'Give up what?'

'Give up on you, on us. You don't talk. You don't tell me things. So there are things I can't understand.'

Eleanor shook her head.

'Don't. Please, Beth.'

'Do you not see, Ellie? We have this same conversation over and over. It's not going anywhere. I'm not a bloody mind reader.'

Eleanor stood up and straightened the timetables on the fridge. She started making Ciara's school lunch.

'Eleanor, for Christ sake! It's 3 a.m.!'

'It'll save time in the morning.'

'You're fucking unbelievable,' Beth said, and went back to bed.

Eleanor made the sandwiches as she always made them. She had a simple routine. The bread and the jar of peanut butter felt solid in her hands. They felt real. Everything else at that moment felt vague and imagined.

# Semi-private

As Cuan entered the ward, he realized he was utterly sick of hospitals, their smell, their light, their clattering sounds. This was semi-private – just four beds. There must have been twelve in Martina's ward and all those cots; only the very skinny nurses could move between them. At first he didn't recognize his father. He looked smaller in the metal bed, and he hadn't shaved for several days. His face was covered with grey stubble, making him look ten years older. Cuan was dressed as boyishly as he could manage, but he could tell from Brian's expression that it didn't hide the truth. He pulled up a plastic chair, and felt two other sets of eyes watching him closely. There was an empty bed beside Brian; Cuan wondered could he just stretch out on it. Give up and sleep.

Brian kicked things off by telling him the news about Lucy. She was recovering. Her father was with her and they were travelling back together. The British embassy was helpful with the passport and visa issues. She'd be back in Glasgow by Sunday.

'Have you met her parents?' Cuan asked.

'No,' Brian said. 'I suggested it to Lucy at some stage, but she said they were a little reluctant. So tell me the news about Martina . . .'

Cuan took out another set of photographs, pointing out Maeve and pointing out Eoghan, realizing he hadn't got around to mentioning their names in Galway. Brian admired them with enthusiasm.

'They look like a fine pair,' he said. 'Will Martina be able to move into Blackrock soon?'

'Probably Monday. They have to be careful she doesn't get too run down after the Caesarean. It would leave her prone to infection. She's doing well. She'll be a great mother.'

'And you'll be a good father . . .' Brian refrained from adding 'this time', but still it sounded more like a question than a statement.

'Dad, things are changing. I'm changing.'

Brian stayed quiet. Cuan was impressed. Whatever pain medication he was on was opening his ears, so this should sound like a gunshot.

'I'm becoming female . . .'

Brian shifted to sit up, but moved his foot too quickly and sent a spasm of pain up his leg. He lay back down and gave a howl of pain.

'For God's sake, Cuan – changing gender?' He looked him up and down with utter horror.

'No, changing sex. My gender has always been female. I'm taking hormones and will have an operation – gender re-assignment, a sex change.'

'Don't be crazy! What can you possibly achieve by this nonsense, this mutilation?'

'A happier life.'

'Bullshit!' Brian spat. A nurse came by with a tea trolley. She offered Cuan a cup.

'You must be Brian's son. He told me you were coming today.'

Cuan nodded, and accepted the tea. Brian was apoplectic with rage, but the nurse paid no heed. She obviously understood that families could be complex. Cuan sipped his tea, while Brian delivered a monologue.

'From the moment you were born you looked for attention. If you'd been the slightest bit outgoing I'd have sent you to acting school . . . but all you ever wanted to do was listen to music and draw pictures. Fucking everything handed to you on a plate – you were handsome, naturally athletic, clever . . . but you engaged with nothing. No sport was good enough for you. All your teachers were fools. Any encouragement I gave you was shoved back in my face. First, you accused me of trying to make you like Michael, then of trying to make you achieve stuff for my own ego. You swallowed some Freudian mumbo jumbo and twisted it to suit your laziness. Have you any idea what it feel like to have a talented son waste his life? Just throw it away as if it didn't matter? And just as things drift towards some kind of normality – when things fell into your lap, the job, Martina, the babies – you have to find some way of fucking it all up. I've only a few more years left. The least you could do is hold off, or lie, for fuck's sake. But, no, you're too bloody selfish. You always were. Just go, Cuan! Just bloody go! I really don't want to know any more.'

Cuan stood up, numbed by the onslaught. It was as bad as he could have imagined, but he survived it.

'Will I come to see you tomorrow?'

'No. Frankly, I don't care when I see you again.'

Cuan picked up his bag, and it made a deafening rattle.

'Oh, and give me the bloody keys.'

'What keys?'

'The keys to Blackrock. Don't play stupid.'

'But that arrangement is between you and Martina. That's nothing to do with me.'

'More bullshit. I don't want to play any part in your sick relationship! Go find somewhere else to cohabit.'

'I wasn't even going to live there. Anyhow, I don't have them. That's the Setanta keys rattling.'

He was lying. He'd given back the Setanta keys last week.

'Well, if there's one place in Dublin that welcomes freaks, you found it. Congratulations.'

Cuan left and walked down the three flights of marble

stairs. He was dizzy and certain he'd throw up if he went in the lift. Catherine was coming in the revolving door.

'Oh, dear, that didn't go the best,' she said when she saw him. 'Want to go for coffee?'

'He may need you up there,' Cuan said. 'He looks worse.'

'He has umpteen nurses on call.'

Cuan smiled. This woman had fallen into their lives at just the right time.

Catherine had guessed, of course, the first time she saw him.

'How?' he asked, when none of his family or friends had guessed.

'Well, sometimes you're blind to these things only when you want to be. Also, I saw you with fresh eyes. Everyone else saw you as shades of what you were.'

'Brian's never going to accept it.'

'Maybe not, but he'll come around a bit in time.'

'He wants the keys back to Blackrock. He doesn't want Martina moving in.'

'That's just a knee-jerk thing. Let him sit with that for a bit.'

'But she needs to move in on Monday.'

'Well, let her move in. She can always move out again. He's not going to be in Dublin for at least three weeks, and even then only if I drive him down.'

'Sorry,' Cuan said, 'if this is going to cause conflict between you, upset the wedding plans.'

'Cuan, I love your father. He has a broad mind. If this had been my brother, he'd have accepted it without a problem. He adores you and Michael, and Lucy, of course. He'll probably grow to love the twins. He read you wrong, that's all. No offence meant here, but he had you boxed as a dope-smoking gay introvert, a bit of a dropout – and lots of his high-achiever friends have a kid like that. One that they rack themselves with guilt every so often over, then exonerate themselves in a bluster of pride at their other achievements.'

Cuan smiled at Catherine. She didn't mince her words – no wonder she was able for Brian's palaver.

'How long have you known?' she asked.

'Always,' he said.

# Responsible

Martina stood in the lobby at Holles Steet, feeling fresh air for the first time in over a week. Two nurses were with her holding a baby each, some insurance thing. Martina wasn't allowed to carry her babies down the stairs. It unsettled her slightly, cast doubt on her trustworthiness, but they assured her it was standard procedure. James was just pulling up the car at the front door. She could hear his jovial banter with a garda outside, promising he wouldn't block the traffic, that he'd be gone in a flash.

They bundled the babies into the car. Martina's heart raced as they pulled off. It felt more like an aeroplane than car. This was it. She was now entirely responsible for these two babies. No one on hand to bathe them, weigh them or answer questions. Surely they wouldn't have let her go if they thought she couldn't cope. She was so together she didn't even see the social worker. She thought that would have been common practice for single mothers, but maybe she fell outside of the vulnerable bracket. The nineteen-year-old in the corner bed had seen her three times, and had half a rainforest of leaflets for various associations and support systems. She was double her age, so she should be able to manage . . . But she had double the amount of babies.

They got to Blackrock in what seemed like ten minutes. The babies were brought in, still sleeping from the motion. They would wake up and see a bright clean kitchen, a tasteful wooden dresser with the best Irish pottery, and a beautiful wild garden slowly encroaching. The affluent side of the gene pool.

'Myself and Cuan have filled the house with food, all your favourite things. Olives and fresh fish; your local supermarket is very upmarket.'

'Cuan looks bloody awful. He needs feeding up as much as I do. Is he OK? He's being cagey with me.'

'Cagey? How uncharacteristic!'

'Much worse than usual – he's not even looking me in the eye. Things didn't go well on his round trip – I think he left a trail of emotional devastation in his wake.'

'Indeed and how uncharacteristic!'

'Oh, do I detect a little ill will towards the cute boy?'

'Martina, he's not telling me anything. But I love him to bits regardless. I think he wants some kind of powwow tonight, just the three of us . . . babies permitting.'

'Well, sure, but there'll be five of us. These little rascals don't switch off and get bundled upstairs at eight o'clock . . . I think that's just in the movies.'

'We'll work around them.'

'Work? I don't like the sound of that . . .'

'Yeah, it's something serious. But you know Cuan – that could mean anything.'

James hugged her and left, saying he'd be back in a couple of hours. This was the first time she was alone with her babies. She should have gone to the toilet before he went. She walked around and peered into the living room. Cuan had left a cot there. It looked handmade. Did he make it? When on earth would he have found time to make it? she wondered. The wood smelled freshly varnished. She thought she heard a baby stirring, but when she got back to the kitchen they were still sleeping. She made some tea, and beans on toast. The fancy food could wait for this evening.

# Answers

Brian rang Michael and asked him to come to Donegal, to discuss Cuan. He was angry. He knew Michael had known about Cuan for a while; he had no idea how long, however. Michael refused to come immediately, but said he'd be up next weekend with Sinead and Sarah.

'I can't lie here for a whole bloody week with no answers, Michael!'

Michael suggested a good book. Brian misunderstood, and thought he meant a crime novel and ranted some more.

'I mean a book about his condition. I'll post you up one.'

'His condition. Michael, I can't believe he's duped you with this! He's just looking for attention. If there's a book, he probably has it and is aping the symptoms.'

'Dad, give him a break. Nobody would do this to themselves unless they had to.'

Brian wasn't listening to that bit. He'd moved on to think about the next thing he wanted to say.

'I want to change the arrangement we made about the house –'

'Just wait. Nothing's in place and won't be for a few weeks.'

Brian, Michael, Catherine and Eugene O'Mahony, Brian's accountant, had met for lunch two months previously. Brian wanted to sign Blackrock over to Cuan and Michael, prior to the wedding. Catherine had lots of property. She had no interest in the house. She wasn't comfortable even sleeping there. The house had been Sarah's family home. Brian and Sarah moved in with her mother when they first married, while Brian was eking out a living doing freelance work. Her mother died the Christmas before Michael was born. The house transferred to Sarah, an only child, and there was never a mortgage. Whatever pressures there were on the marriage over the years, there were rarely financial ones. Brian trusted that Michael was steady, and would always be able to support himself. He reckoned that Cuan would need this safety net at some point, and yet would resist the plan because of his sheer contrariness.

Michael didn't agree. He felt Cuan should be told. Also, he was fed up with all the lies and conspiracies. Cuan had two time bombs ticking, Martina's pregnancy and the sex change. Michael knew one was certain to explode before the plan came to completion. Brian had agreed to say something to Cuan, but didn't. The lunch he and Michael and Cuan had was a set-up, an opportunity for either of them to spill the beans, but neither did. Brian shopped Michael by saying he'd met Catherine. Michael had to choke out some lie to Cuan about it. He said they had met briefly and discussed the weather, not property law and inheritance tax. Now Brian wanted to move the goalposts again, to sign the house over exclusively to him. To disinherit Cuan and disown him to boot. Even if Michael let him go ahead, and subsequently gave Cuan half, it would be wrong and damaging. So Michael bought a week, in the hope that Brian would come around, or that Catherine would talk some sense into him.

Michael also didn't want to face the barrage of questions Brian was certain to have about Cuan's gender identity disorder. How long have you known? would be one of his first questions – long enough for the condition to have changed names in psychiatry, long enough to accept it, long enough to love Cuan regardless. Almost always, in fact.

# Proof

*May 28th Sunday 9 p.m. The shock was the worse bit, like when you shove your hand under a tap and you're not sure if the water's scalding hot or freezing cold, but you pull your hand away anyhow, because for a split second it can feel the same. He should have told me. He should have told me lots of things . . . Why he wants to make a family with Martina and he couldn't with us. Why he looks different every time I see him . . . In the beginning he looked like Tony, Sophie's brother who has a motorbike and his hair in dreads . . . not exactly like him, but sort of messy like him . . . now he looks nothing like him. Sometimes I think I'm imagining it because nobody agrees – like mum says, Oh, (here she goes asking about Cuan-who-we-all-hate again) what way different, honey? Like I'm stupid . . . he's never given me any photos and Mum says she's none, which I don't believe (I'd keep a photo of my first boyfriend, even if I hate his guts now) and I just have one from Michael's wedding and it's all of us and he's kind of in the background . . . so's Martina . . . He lied to me, and I still don't know how much . . . and he's never told me the truth about some things, like how you can have so many stupid accidents.*

Eleanor heard a sound downstairs and snapped the diary shut. She put it back under Ciara's pillow, careful to put it at the same angle. She shouldn't have read it. Beth would freak at her and Ciara would hate her, maybe always, for such an intrusion if she found out. Eleanor heard the television switch on. She'd come home early from school . . . really early – she wasn't due back for another two hours. Eleanor picked up clothes from around Ciara's room, and bundled them into her arms.

358

'How come you're home so early?'

'We'd practice for sports day. I felt sick, so Ms Watkins let me go home.'

'Shouldn't they have phoned?'

'I said you weren't home, but that I'd a key. I thought you were in UCG this morning.'

'I didn't feel the best either,' Eleanor said.

Ciara looked at her with suspicion.

'You haven't done a wash in ages – me and Beth usually sort that stuff out now.'

Ciara used to enjoy Beth and Eleanor squabbling over it. Beth insisted there was a particular way to hang trousers and a particular way to hang shirts, and it drove Ellie crazy if she hung out a wash and found Beth reorganizing the pegs. Beth was right of course; Eleanor just rushed at it impatiently. But she found it impossible to learn from people, she could only learn things from books.

'Have you homework?'

'Yeah.'

'Well, maybe you should turn off the television?'

Ciara threw her eyes up to heaven, switched it off and stormed towards her room. She called from her platform at the top of the stairs.

'Ask Beth to come up when she's back, will you. She's giving me her old camera and she's going to show me how to use it.'

Eleanor just left the clothes on the floor. She didn't have the energy to shove them into the machine.

Beth wouldn't be back for ages. She'd gone to visit her brother; she might even stay the night. They'd had a dreadful row before she left. They'd booked a holiday to Greece for two weeks in July, the two weeks Ciara was due to be with Cuan. Now Eleanor wanted to cancel, and Beth was furious.

'This is like a bloody joke!' Beth said. 'This is our first real holiday, and you can just cancel it without a second thought.'

'Well, he's hardly fit to mind her *and* two squalling infants, and I'm not having Ciara spending her summer babysitting.'

'He was planning to go to Clare with her – remember? And Michael's family. I'm sure that's still the plan or he would have said. He's a fucking eejit, but he's not a bad person, Ellie. Just give this thing a chance.'

'Anyhow, Ciara may not want to go any more.'

'Well, ask her, but give her a few days, for God's sake. It's only Monday. Wait until she talks to him on the phone or gets her head around things a bit ... Nancy's wedding will distract her a bit next week.'

'Distract her! Beth this thing has run her over like a steam-roller and you think a bit of frivolity will take it away.'

'Yes, actually. She's nearly twelve.'

'And therefore her feelings are shallow!'

'No, Jesus, Ellie – will you just fucking listen. Not shallow, but resilient. He made a mistake by not telling Ciara about the pregnancy, but I get it! The ambiguity would have been too much for her; maybe it was too much for him. I think I'd make the same call if I'd been in his shoes. Now maybe things will sort out. Maybe this isn't just some huge calamity – maybe she'll get to know them, be close to them, less lonely because of them.'

'She's not lonely. Just because you grew up with people milling around, doesn't mean that being an only child is a bad thing.'

'Oh, let's just drop it. Anyhow, face it, Ellie, she's not one any more.'

And she left, exasperated and muttering. She'd be late for her brother's dinner. Eleanor knew that, by the time Beth got there, she'd have left this row behind her. Beth was sensible; she didn't let things fester. She forgave people incredibly easily. So much so that Eleanor took it for granted that she'd forgive her over this, maybe even come around to her point of view. She would see that Cuan had hurt Ciara, irreparably perhaps, the way he can hurt people, the way he had hurt her. So Eleanor read Ciara's diary for the worst possible reason, to prove that she was right.

Eleanor was dreading Nancy's wedding. Nancy had chatted to her on the phone and asked about her and Beth, what way would they be presenting themselves. Eleanor knew exactly what she was getting at, but played dumb.

'How do you mean?'

'Well, I just wondered if I should get George to forewarn his family . . . so they deal with it better?'

Nancy was actually trying to be helpful, but, like a lot of people who are well intentioned, she was saying all the wrong things. If Eleanor wasn't so upset about the twins she might have let it go.

'Oh, tell them, Nancy! Tell them we've got horns and devil's tails in our handbags, and make sure to keep the young cousins away from us because it's highly contagious.'

Nancy burst into tears and hung up. Eleanor took the phone off the hook because doubtless her mother would ring back and tell her to stop being mean to her. She was sick of it – the black sheep label, the single mother, now the lesbian mother . . . Fuck them! If any of those bigoted uncles and aunts and solicitor cousins said a fucking thing to her, Beth or Ciara, she would let them have it.

Nancy had told Cuan about the pregnancy. By accident, as she thought he knew already. She was fourteen and furious with him. She decided it was all his fault – that she was being forced to move to Galway, leave her friends, her school, every-thing, because of him. She bumped into him in a music shop, and she shouted abuse at him . . . every negative thing she'd heard their mother say, peppered with 'fucking' and 'shag-ging' until eventually they were both thrown out onto Dun

Laoghaire main street. Eleanor was livid – she thought she'd everything under control. She'd seen Cuan earlier that day, and just told him they were breaking up because it seemed simpler. She'd told him they were moving to Cork, not Galway, to muddy the trail. She'd spun stories to stop her mother contacting his parents. Then Nancy set off another bout of arguments and tears. It was twelve years ago – Eleanor shook her head at how naive she'd been. Sooner or later he'd have found out. Maybe it was time to forgive Nancy.

# Sorry

Beth stayed with her brother for three days, mostly bemoaning how difficult women are to share your life with. John's partner had gone back to Spain. She wanted to marry, have children. He just didn't seem to feel the rush. After all, he had only just turned forty. Beth loved John dearly, but he was just the kind of Irish male who needed a kick in the arse every so often. She kicked him, metaphorically, on Maria's behalf. Unfortunately John had no reciprocal advice to offer. On the bus back to Galway, she sent Eleanor a text message to check if she was home. Eleanor sent a message back to say she was working. Beth wanted to meet her for lunch, but her phone ran out of power before she could make the arrangement. She got off at Eyre Square and decided to walk to the college and just call in, on the off-chance.

Beth found the library with no difficulty. She hesitated for a moment before she approached the counter. Eleanor was the opposite of spontaneous, and might resent her for turning up. She'd been in the job a few months at this stage and never mentioned any of her colleagues by name. Doubtless nobody here knew she had a partner or daughter. That was Eleanor's way – everything was on a need-to-know basis.

Five minutes later Beth realized that the extent of Eleanor's deception was greater than that.

An hour later she was sitting at home with Eleanor, confronting the lies.

'Why, Eleanor? If you needed time we could have sorted something out.'

'I didn't mean to lie to you.'

'Don't give me that crap, Eleanor. It's obvious you made this thing up especially for me and for Ciara.'

'No. Christ, Beth, it just got out of hand. I was dropping Ciara to school before Christmas and I ran into Sophie's mother. Ciara had told her I'd given up the bank and she was giving me all these concerned looks and I couldn't stand it. She asked me to go for coffee. I said I couldn't, and she said some other morning so . . . and it just bloody slipped out. I said I'd a new job and she said where and it was the first place I could think of.'

'Hang on, Ellie, because you can't do the coffee thing, the chitchat shite, you decided to lie to everyone for four months . . . for ever, maybe, presuming you weren't found out.'

'It's not the chat thing — you should have seen the look she gave me. The same fucking look I got when I moved here, going round in the school uniform, eight months pregnant, all these old biddies shaking their heads at the slut and then this type, the tea-and-sympathy type, who were worse, actually.'

'Jesus, Eleanor! You're not the only teenager to get pregnant. You're being completely paranoid. And Janice is not like that — I met her with Ciara at the supermarket last week and she's nice, funny . . .'

Beth spotted the paranoia tumbling across Eleanor's face . . .

'No. Before you ask, I didn't introduce myself as your partner, nor did Ciara. Not because I get some buzz out of lying, but stupidly I thought you were on the brink of saying it yourself to people like Janice . . . but clearly I was wrong.'

'I was going to . . . soon.' Eleanor got up to plug in the kettle. Beth looked at her, standing beside her phoney work timetable on the fridge.

'No, you know something, I've believed that way too long.

I may be dim, Eleanor, but I'm not that stupid. Why don't I just go pack my stuff, and leave you to your parallel life. Be the fucking celibate, heterosexual librarian – I sure as hell can't compete with that.'

Beth went upstairs and sat on the bed. She was due in the bookshop in an hour. Not enough time to pack, to separate their lives back out. She'd have to do it later. Eleanor came in with two coffees.

'Don't go, Beth. Please, this is the life I want . . . with Ciara and with you.'

'How can I know that, Eleanor? How can I trust you? What's real – The MA? Or did you make that up, too?'

'That's real. That's important.'

'What did you do for the thirty hours a week? Are you seeing someone else?'

'No. God, no.'

'Don't know why you sound so shocked – a hell of a lot more people have affairs than pretend to be librarians.'

Beth thought about the times Eleanor left the house, rushing sometimes because she was late for her imaginary job. Was she just crazy?

'I did nothing . . . almost nothing. Sometimes I'd sit in the car by the river, with the engine running because it would get cold. Sometimes I went walking on the beach. I went to a few films. I went for coffee a lot and just sat there knowing you and Ciara were happy, watching *The Simpsons* or whatever. I can't do that, Beth – just relax, like everybody else seems to. When I was working in the bank I didn't ever have to – I was busy twenty-four hours a day.'

'You were exhausted.'

'Yeah. But that was better. Better than that awful blank feeling in my head. I was planning to tell you when the MA started, when I had a structure . . .'

Beth shook her head.

'I actually don't know what to believe, Eleanor . . . and whatever the hell lies you tell me, how can you do it to Ciara? She's sharp as knives. I'm amazed she didn't catch you out . . . or maybe she has and is biding her time – Jesus Christ, I'm in the middle of a minefield. For all the sanctimonious claptrap you go on about Cuan, at least he's trying to be truthful.'

'I'm trying, too, Beth . . . really.'


Beth went to work for the afternoon. She reorganized shelves with demonic energy for several hours. Customers scurried out of her way rather than ask for assistance. She caught one of the staff smoking a joint in the basement, and she sent him home. He rang her back nervously an hour later to ask was he fired.

'No, Jake, just clean up your act.'

'Thanks. You're cool . . . um, for a –'

'For a what, Jake?'

'For a boss.'

'Fine. If you're late at the weekends again, you're fired.'

'But my gig . . .'

'I don't give a fuck, Jake.'

'OK . . . sorry . . . really sorry.'

'Fine.'

'Sorry.'

'Enough sorries! See you Saturday.'

When she put down the phone, she realized Eleanor hadn't said it – not once. Maybe she wasn't sorry. She'd been caught out, but she wasn't sorry, just fucked up and full of excuses. Beth looked over at the till and Daphne was halfway through some sex-and-shopping novel, rather than doing the stock check. She walked briskly towards her.

'Go home.'

'Oh, sorry, I just got distracted . . . Oh, please, I need the job. I'm saving for my debs dress.'

'I'm not firing you! It's six o'clock – go home. I'm locking up!'

'Oh! Thanks!' Daphne flashed her a grin and rushed to the door, and crashed into Eleanor on the doorstep as she left.

'Let's go to dinner. I've dropped Ciara into Sophie's house. She's staying over.'

'Dinner?'

Eleanor nodded enthusiastically. She looked great, as if she'd just come back from holiday.

'And maybe a pint after – seeing as lunch didn't exactly work out,' she added.

'You honestly think we can get over the fact that you've lied to me for the past four months by going on a date? You're barking mad, Eleanor. Cuan's rock-solid sane in comparison.'

'I know this all makes no sense. I was stupid not to tell you, stupid to try to hide it . . . but it was like pretending to be dead. I thought it felt OK, better even, than being alive. But when you came crashing through it today I realized it wasn't. I wanted you to come.'

'And how do you think it felt for me?'

'I don't know. Awful, I'm sure.'

They went for dinner and Beth let Eleanor talk, and talk, her eyes shining like she'd found a religion. They went home and Eleanor slept for two days. They started again.

Beth considered not going to the wedding, but Eleanor was adamant that she would, that they would go as a couple: 'You promise not to be a wagon if everyone else seems to be enjoying themselves more than you?'

'Jesus Christ, am I really that bad?' Eleanor asked.

'Yep, sometimes.' Beth was tired. She leaned over Eleanor and turned off the lamp. As soon as she came in contact with Eleanor's bare skin, she ached for her, as intensely as when they had first touched. She knew that when Eleanor just relaxed a bit, she felt the same. That night she did and they made love for hours. Eleanor got up and went to college in the morning, smiling like she was stoned. Beth lay in bed, knowing if she told her friends a fraction of the crap that went on, they'd tell her to leave. But then there were the beautiful nights, when they were honest and utterly open, they held nothing back from each other. That open . . . When Beth was changing the bed she smiled to herself – there were perfect handprints on the navy sheet.

# Favourite Breasts

James arrived in Blackrock, hauling a top-of-the-range double buggy tied with a giant pink ribbon. Martina was surprised and delighted.

'The only problem is I think you need a degree in engineering to open and close the thing ...'

Martina undid the ribbon and it opened straight away.

'On the other hand, some people may just be naturals. This is from myself and Eamon, and it took us forty-five minutes to choose it, and suffer the giggling incompetence of two junior shop assistants who passed us over to one of the snootiest managers I have ever had to do business with.'

'What was the problem?'

'They didn't respect the purchasing power of the pink punt! I think they thought we were just wasting their time, that we were on some fantasy kick. Then they suspected there was something illicit motivating us, that they may be committing a crime by selling it to us. Really, I was on the verge of asking for a copy of the security tape and running it by our solicitor.'

Martina looked down at the colourful buggy, a little sadly –

'I hope it doesn't make it unlucky.'

'Not in the slightest – it is proof of our ability to triumph over ignorance! Now, any sign of Cuan?'

'I got a text message an hour ago saying he'd be here at eight ... You don't feel like cooking, do you?'

'Sure ... You feed the babies; I'll feed the grown-ups.'

Cuan arrived just as Maeve was giving out about wind, and Eoghan was giving out about Maeve interrupting his sleep.

'Take your pick!' Martina said, and Cuan lifted Maeve, who gave a loud, satisfactory burp as soon as he held her upright. Martina topped up Eoghan, and he drifted back to sleep. She lay him in the cot, and Cuan put Maeve in beside him.

'It won't fit the two of them for long, but it's great to lay them down together now,' she said. 'Where did it come from?'

'Oh . . . would you believe, Brian made it. He wanted it to be a surprise. He's never made anything out of wood in his life – I think he was trying to impress Catherine.'

'He made it before he knew they were yours?'

'Yeah, don't ask me why . . . Sinead was a bit miffed. She saw him whittling away at it one night. It's a bit wonky, but I suppose he knew that wouldn't bother you. It's the twins thing, I think.'

'How is he? I'll have to ring him to say thanks.'

'God, no, don't. He's fine – the ankle's fine at least. He may have to have another operation on it next week, though. But I told him about the sex change and he's gone ballistic.'

'How ballistic?'

'Completely . . . but let's not talk about that tonight.'

'Would it help if I rang him?'

'Absolutely not. Let Catherine listen to his bile – she's more of a stomach for it right now.'

'You still getting on OK with her?'

'Yeah. She's great, really great. She guessed . . . about me. Isn't that incredible?'

'Mmm . . .' Martina wondered would she have guessed, too, if she hadn't been so blind.

James lured them into the kitchen to eat his delicious meal, though he was modestly denying any flair with fish. They chatted about this and that over the meal, both glancing every so often at Cuan, who wasn't saying much. Martina knew James would never push him; he would just let him unfold stuff in his own time. She hoped she'd be like that with the twins, but it was too late to change her confrontational behaviour with their . . . aunt.

Cuan looked well – he must have been up to something this afternoon. He was dressed in a blue skirt and a white blouse. In certain light a full bra was evident underneath. Martina had found out his trick – he had bought silicone breasts on the Internet, complete with nipples, that attached with a special glue to his own. He showed her the website, and they laughed about the different types. His were 'teardrop', oval-shaped with the nipples quite low, but he could have opted for 'raindrop', rounded puberty style, with two perky nipples bang in the centre.

'Get a pair that can lactate and I'll be really impressed,' she said.

He explained quite earnestly that some transsexuals have tried to breastfeed – but it's contraindicated for pre-ops because the hormones aren't good for babies. She smiled – he could be circumspect or utterly candid. She leaned forwards and ruffled his hair because that's what people do.

'So, what's up?' She asked and looked him in the eye, realizing that he was getting quite knacky with eye make-up.

'I've been thinking about something you said, and maybe this is the right time,' he said. He was rustling in his backpack and pulled out her babies' names book.

'So that's where the shagging thing got to!' she said.

'I want to pick a name,' he said, 'and I want you two to be the first to use it . . . And we can change pronouns, too, if you're ready.'

'Yes, makes sense,' James said, 'if that's what you want.'

'Sure,' Martina said, not certain what happened to Jeanette, but gathering a while back that she belonged to history.

'OK . . .' Now he was looking a little tentative. 'I wanted a name that was clearly female, not a neutral one, and one that was Irish, ideally. So I've come up with two options – one's fairly obvious, and one's kind of ironic. I thought you two could throw in your opinions . . .'

The both nodded – neither was ever short of an opinion.

'Saoirse, meaning freedom, and Cliodhna, which this book says was the name of a beautiful goddess who fell in love with a mortal and left the land of promise to be with him, but when she arrived on the other shore she was swept to sea by a great wave.'

'Well, I like Saoirse,' James said straight off, 'but I'm the more in-your-face type . . . I'm not sure about the other name; the mythology seems to be working against hope.'

'That's the irony, James,' Martina said, and that's our bloody love affair to a tee, she thought.

'I like Cliodhna,' she said. 'I like the way it's different but similar to Cuan, letter wise you've just left out the U. Saoirse would be good if you were taking to soapboxes and daytime television championing gender politics, but you're not . . . unless you're having a personality change, too!'

Cuan smiled. He knew she'd get it.

'Actually, I kinda like Cliodhna best, too,' he said.

'OK, I may be missing something here,' James said, 'but I'm happy to toast to Cliodhna. It's pretty and musical. Hold on a moment until I top up our fizzy water.'

'Let's chink quietly, unless we want a squalling chorus,' Martina said.

And they did.

'To Cliodhna McCarthy, our friend,' James said.

'To Cliodhna,' Martina added. 'Aunty Cliodhna.'

'Oh, and I'm thirty today,' Cliodhna said.

'Fuck,' Martina said, 'we are *crap* friends. I never realized your birthday was so close.'

'No. You are undoubtedly the best friends, and this has been a great birthday.'

*

Shortly afterwards they got up to go and Martina felt a mild panic that she would be on her own for the night.

'You going to be OK?' James asked.

'Yep, I want to do this first night by myself, but maybe one of you come and stay tomorrow night, if you can.'

'Sure,' they both said.

'Well, sort it between you on the way home,' Martina laughed.

She hugged James, and heard a murmur from Maeve.

'That's just her first gear. She'll stop and start again in second in a minute.'

She hugged Cuan goodbye. She leaned closer in than she usually would, towards the more familiar musky smells around the neck, past the make-up smells and the moisturizers. Maybe everything would be OK. Just as her torn, bruised stomach would heal. Perhaps her body wouldn't be beautiful in an objective sense, but would have a different sort of beauty, and maybe Cliodhna's would, too. Scarred survivor beauty. Maeve began in second gear, and her favourite breast gushed over Cliodhna's crisp white blouse.

'Oh, feck, I'm leaking! Oh, God! First I can't hold my drink, and now I can't hold my milk.'

Martina grabbed a tea towel and tried to rub the slightly yellow milk away.

Cliodhna grinned, and watched the left 'teardrop' wobble under her touch. They just made irony together.

# Omissions

There was a thunderstorm the night before Nancy's wedding. Ciara was staying at Nancy's house. She woke up and looked out the window, enjoying the rain pelting down on the patio roof. She had made some kind of peace with Cuan. She had talked on the phone with him a few times. She wrote a card to Martina, and gave it to Ellie to post. She was planning to go to Blackrock and meet Eoghan and Maeve on Sunday afternoon. So far she had said nothing to Eleanor or Beth about it. She knew they weren't driving back to Galway until the following morning, so that wouldn't be a problem, but Eleanor might find other problems.

The day of the wedding was overcast, but at least it had stopped raining. Eleanor and Beth were staying in a bed and breakfast nearby. Anna had insisted – to offset any hysterical sibling rows on the morning of the wedding. Beth was getting dressed, ironing her red linen trousers and black linen top.

'I was going to wear a tux, but I thought that might make it too easy on your family – if they're playing spot the lesbian.'

Eleanor laughed. 'Lesbians, plural, surely?'

'Honey, you'll always pass for straight! Somewhere out there tonight there'll be lascivious men shaking their heads ... thinking you should have given them a shot!'

'See how truly subversive I am?' Eleanor kissed her, to stop Beth shaking her head in that exasperated way.

Eleanor didn't look the least bit subversive in her purple linen dress with spaghetti straps with a dramatic V down the back, which Ciara had picked out with her for her birthday. It was a little 'young' Ciara had suggested, but it suits you.

Damn it, Eleanor thought, I spent my twenties dressed like a forty-year-old, I may as well pull on the teenage fashions now that I'm thirty. Nancy was wearing a stunning white dress.

'Well, she would, wouldn't she!' Ciara said, good-humouredly, but with a hint of the family sarcasm. Ciara enjoyed Nancy, but she held her ground with her. Wild horses couldn't drag her into the hairdressers the previous weekend, and Nancy couldn't either.

A lot of George's siblings had emigrated to the States in the 1980s, all to the west coast, so they were having a second party over there during their honeymoon. His sister that was closest in age, Cassie, came back however. Cassie had short, bleached-white hair and was wearing an outfit very similar to Beth's, but the trousers were orange, with splits at the end. Beth spotted her at a distance, but said nothing.

At the meal they were put at the same table, along with Cassie's musician boyfriend from LA, so the game was up.

'Why do you look so familiar?' Cassie said, leaning flirtatiously towards Beth. She sounded American, the way some people do, even after a few months. She'd been there five years. Beth shook her head.

'So, where do you guys live?'

'Galway,' Ciara said helpfully, as everyone else was being shy or rude, particularly Beth.

'Galway!' Cassie said. 'That's it! I was there five years ago. We must have met.'

Please, God, don't let Ciara say the bookshop, thought Beth. At that moment the waiter arrived and they had to select their food. Luckily Cassie had enough issues with food to pause her reminiscence and try to get dishes with omissions – the pasta sauce without the cream, potato gratin without the cheese, and nothing that had touched seafood as she had an allergy ... The rest of the table were easier to

375

please. Once she'd made her choices Beth excused herself and went to the bathroom. Eleanor counted to ten and followed, like they were fourteen.

'What the fuck is it?'

'I slept with her, but she may have been drunk at the time. I was, but I have this godawful total recall when it comes to these things.'

'Well, you've slept with lots of women. I suppose if we went out more we'd run into them more often. We can't move tables – that would be terribly rude.'

'No. I'll weather it. She'll probably remember after the third glass of wine and be more awkward about it than me. Amm ... just out of interest, why aren't you jealous?'

'Because she's obviously bisexual and what is that sweet thing you say – you wouldn't touch them with a barge pole?'

'Well, I never said I was perfect,' Beth said.

'No, but you're close,' Eleanor said and kissed her, and Beth kissed her back, a kiss that lingered just long enough for Eleanor to spot her mother's handbag coming in the bathroom door. They yanked away from each other, and blushed.

'Why are you skulking in here?' Anna smiled knowingly.

'Adjusting our make-up?' Eleanor offered. Anna glanced at the two of them. Eleanor's make-up was perfect, as always. Beth's tanned face was decorated only with a handful of freckles.

'Well, there's no need to skulk, is there? This isn't that much of an ordeal, is it?'

'Nope,' Eleanor grinned. 'Actually, Mum, I'm quite enjoying myself!'

# Fine

Michael went to visit Brian at the weekend as planned. Like Cuan, he was struck by how the time in hospital was ageing his father. Apart from an appendix operation in his mid thirties, Brian was never in hospital. The ankle had to be reset, and he could be in for yet another week.

He was having difficulty getting the hang of the crutches: 'They should teach everybody to use these bloody things before they break something.'

'You're doing fine,' Michael said. Fine; not good or great. Fine was what he said to women who weren't dilating quick enough, and he needed to put on an oxytocin drip.

'No, I'm bloody not,' Brian replied.

Michael brought him *National Geographic* and a photograph of Sarah, Sinead and himself. It looked like a studio portrait, but in fact Cuan had taken it. Brian gave it pride of place on his locker.

Michael also brought an e-mail from Lucy. She was fully recovered and planning to take a trip over to see Brian. She had got a development grant for a documentary project about adoption. She was going to film him, if he was up to it.

'No. I'm not,' Brian growled. 'Why doesn't she try her attention-seeking half-brother . . . or can we call him that any more?'

'Did you read the book?' Michael had posted him a book of personal testimonies from transgender people, some who opted for hormones, some surgery, and some who just lived out their lives as part of what they called a 'third sex'.

'I dipped into it. Hardly the kind of book one reads cover to cover.'

'Do you see where he's coming from?'

'Michael, I know where he's coming from. I raised him. He's being contrary – he always was. Contrary and manipulative. How long have you known?'

'A while.'

'Have you ever seen him . . . dressed up?'

'Just once.'

Michael had taken Cuan to lunch for his birthday last week. They met in a hotel on the side of the Stillorgan dual carriageway. It was busy, as Michael had imagined. An extended family was leaving as Michael arrived and, while elderly grandparents were being gingerly assisted into cars, Michael caught a wayward toddler who was heading off at speed to play in the traffic. As he passed the angry redhead back to his parents, his little fists flying at the disruptive stranger, the parents recognized him – he'd delivered little Francis . . .

'Well, there you go,' Michael joked handing him over, 'I don't often do a reprise!'

The restaurant was full and the clientele could be divided into two groups – business people in suits having working lunches, and families with an elderly and perhaps difficult relative doing a duty. Cuan arrived dressed as a woman, as he had said. This was the first time that Michael had seen him dressed like this. Cuan was nervous; he'd spent hours trying to get it just perfect. He sat down – he even sat differently – and put a small satin purse on the table.

'That's just a prop. You're paying, right?'

Michael was speechless.

'Well . . . bloody say something!' Cuan said, and Michael, very uncertainly, began,

'You look –' but Cuan stopped him –

'I meant the happy birthday thing! It's two o'clock on my thirtieth birthday and no one's said it to me yet!'

'Happy Birthday!' Michael felt as if he was in a film, a Spanish film, perhaps. He looked around and half expected one of Sinead's sisters to appear and smack him on the face for having lunch with a strange woman – a very strange woman.

'So what do we do now? It's a carvery, so do we go up one at a time or together?'

'Let's do it one at time so we keep the table. You go first, OK?'

'Sure . . . keep an eye on my handbag.'

Michael sat back and sipped his mineral water. He was expecting some kind of drag queen. No matter what he read or researched the overriding image in his head was something like Tim Curry in *The Rocky Horror Picture Show*. Not someone dressed like a hotel receptionist, in a prim blue skirt and well-ironed cotton blouse. Cuan was never tidy. As a teenager he lived in oversized multicoloured jumpers, and for the last while that casual, dishevelled look where everything was a little frayed somewhere.

He was coming back with his tray, slabs of meat in gravy and a mountain of overcooked vegetables. From a distance he looked reasonably OK . . . As he got close something was just a little off – too square around the shoulders or jaw, maybe. He had manufactured breasts that moved as he walked, like real breasts. Michael fixed his eyes on Cuan's chest and realized the elderly man opposite whose family were off choosing food was following his gaze. He gave Michael an exaggerated, conspiratorial wink.

'What did he look like?' Brian asked.

'It will be a while, Dad, before he achieves the look he wants.'

'Jesus Christ, Michael! You sound like a fucking image consultant! What I want to know is did he look like an out-and-out freak?'

'No. He looked fine. Just give him a break, Dad. We nearly lost him. Fuck the embarrassment factor because you sure as hell wouldn't be embarrassed by a dead son.'

'How do you mean we nearly lost him? I gathered he was depressive, but not suicidal . . . ?'

'Well, I think he was, and could be again if we don't all support him with this.'

'But what about Martina, and those unfortunate kids.'

'Just get off your high horse. They're not going to have a conventional family, but Martina's doing great and Cuan will be part of their lives.'

'As bloody what?'

Brian's surgeon appeared and he introduced his son, the doctor, and they talked medical jargon. It was a welcome distraction from an argument that wasn't going anywhere.

# Black and White

*June 4th 10 p.m. I met Eoghan and Maeve, my half-brother and half-sister yesterday. They're fifteen days old. I helped Cuan feed them their first-ever bottles. Martina's going to mainly breastfeed them, but she wants them to be able to take a bottle every now and again so she can take a break. Maeve was the best, she drank lots. Eoghan hardly drank any, but Cuan said they'd try other types of teats and maybe find one he likes – Cuan says Eoghan's even fussy about which breast he feeds from! Then we changed their nappies and Eoghan peed all over Cuan. I brought my camera and took some photos. Cuan said not too many because the flash upsets them. I said I wanted to take his photo, but he said he hated his photo being taken and anyhow he'd have to change his clothes because he was covered in pee. I said, please, after you've changed, and he agreed. I took two photos of him in his favourite battered old leather jacket in the garden and then asked Martina to take one of me and him together. He started to fuss, but I said Cuan do you realize I haven't a single photograph with my father . . . people will think I've just made you up! Martina said while we're at it . . . and then he groaned really loudly, but she bossed him about the way she does sometimes and she took one of him and me and the babies . . . then I took one of just him and the babies . . . phew . . . the film was all used up and Cuan said he'd get it developed . . . oh no, I said, you might do some magician's trick and they might just disappear – I'll get them developed and send you copies!*

Eleanor looked in at Ciara and noticed she'd fallen asleep with her light on, and a pen in her hand. The pen was bleeding black ink into the white pillowcase and she removed it gently, careful not to wake her. She closed the diary without reading it, and placed it under her pillow. She was exhausted coming home in the car. It had been a hectic weekend, and an emotional one. She might keep her home from school tomorrow, if she'd stay. Before she went to bed, she asked Eleanor if they could do something quiet next weekend, just the two of them. Eleanor realized how unusual it had become for them to do something, yet they used to do stuff all the time and she wondered when they had stopped. Now Ciara was asking hesitantly. She used to say let's do this or let's do that, with wild enthusiasm, believing that Ellie would want to, too, even if that wasn't true. But now it was 'Could we . . .' or 'Maybe . . .'

Eleanor was tired, too. Things had gone well over the weekend, apart from the row about Ciara going to visit the twins. She'd predicted that Ciara would want to meet them; it just came sooner than she expected, sooner than she was ready. As far as Ciara was concerned, her timing was perfect; she was on her way out for a walk with Anna and David, leaving Beth and Eleanor to argue it out. Beth was adamant that it was wrong to prevent her. She offered to drop her off and pick her up, if that was easier. Of course it would be easier, but Eleanor wasn't convinced it was the right way.

'Shouldn't I be there for Ciara, in case she's apprehensive going in or distraught coming out?'

'Maybe Ciara would be just fine if you weren't there trying to second-guess her emotional response to the thing!'

Beth was fed up by how Eleanor constantly fucked things up by trying to do the right thing, mostly for the wrong reasons.

'Just bloody take her so!' Eleanor said.

'No, I'll take her, but you have to make some effort here. Don't let her think visiting them is some kind of betrayal. This is critical, Eleanor. You make it a black-and-white thing now and it will always be like that.'

Eleanor muttered about how come Beth got to be such an expert at this parenting malarkey, when she'd been doing it on her own for several years and clearly knew fuck-all.

Beth smiled; she'd grown used to this muttering. When Eleanor dropped the sharp direct tone it meant she was melting.

So Eleanor scribbled a card, wishing them well. She went to the shops and bought two yellow cot blankets, for Ciara to bring over on her behalf. A pink and a blue would have been perceived as pointed, by one of their parents at least.

# Hormones

Cliodhna spent most of June living in Blackrock and minding the babies. She wheeled them in the buggy to the shops, and from a distance they all passed. Up close it was obvious this wasn't your regular postpartum mum, but she ignored the begrudgers. She focused instead on how the babies gasped dramatically when a gentle breeze crossed them, or how the motion made their eyelids so heavy sleep was inevitable, whether they'd planned it or not.

In July she dug out her jeans and rough shirts, and prepared to wear them for what she presumed would be the last time. She had asked Eleanor could she tell Ciara, towards the end of the holiday, about the sex change. She was upset that Ciara was the last to know, and the last to be lied to.

'How clearly female are you now?' Eleanor asked.

'I think very, but maybe you better ask someone less biased.'

Eleanor wondered who in Cuan's life was not biased, besotted or hoodwinked.

'OK, Cuan, tell her. Tell her when she has Michael or someone available to talk to, if she can't talk to you about it. Tell her into the third week, when we'll be back in the country, in case she wants to come home.'

And would you like to write the bloody script, too? Cuan thought, but didn't say it because Eleanor very probably would.

So Cliodhna became strictly Cuan again for two weeks, while Ciara stayed in Blackrock. Cuan understood that this was Ciara's time, and wanted to do as much with her as possible. They went on day trips to Howth, Glendalough; they even got a bus to Newgrange one day because Ciara had wanted to see the tomb. They had an ideological discussion about visiting the zoo, and decided against it. Ciara suggested the Natural History Museum – at least they're dead and can't be oppressed any further, she said. Martina treated Cuan the same, perhaps a little more abrasively when Ciara was out of earshot. Cuan understood why she was abrasive. It was down to history – this was the one who hurt her, lied to her, impregnated her, betrayed her. She put up the photographs Ciara had sent, even though Cuan objected.

'I don't see why . . .' Martina protested.

'Because it's not me.'

'Of course, it's not, but it's a part of you.'

Cuan shook his head.

'I wish you'd bloody love the guy you were, Cuan, because we all did, and it would make things a hell of a lot simpler.'

Cuan was posturing in front of the mirror in his jeans, acting like a cowboy.

'You are such a fucking eejit!' Martina laughed, indulging him. 'Let's put them up for now. We'll take them down after, if that's what you want.'

And they both knew what after referred to, but didn't use its proper name.

For the third week of July Michael, Sinead and Sarah and Cuan and Ciara drove to West Clare for a week. They had rented a cottage, but Cuan and Ciara were planning to camp out in the garden.

'I might join you if this little lady starts shouting,' Michael joked. Sarah gave a dazzling toothless smile.

They had a good journey west, stopping at Kilbeggen for lunch and for a quick breastfeed for Sarah. Ciara watched closely, fascinated by how the milk was like a sedative. How

Sarah went from limbs flaying to being completely relaxed in a matter of minutes.

'OK, last stop for the toilet for another hundred kilometres,' Michael said. 'Everyone must go! I'd change princess's nappy, only the baby changing facilities are in the ladies. Dreadful sexism – I must write a letter to the *Irish Times*.'

'Or you could point it out to the management everywhere we go, only wait until after we've eaten!' Sinead said.

Sarah was passed from person to person while they ate their sandwiches. Ciara had a bit of a headache. She was a little grumpy and Cuan wondered if she was reluctant to go on the trip. Sarah was drowsy from the feed, but she had slept quite a bit in the car so was staying awake, just about. When Ciara held her she curled into her T-shirt and opened her mouth, wanting to suckle. Ciara blushed and hoped no one had noticed. She passed Sarah gently to Cuan and went to the bathroom.

'I'm going Michael, see. You can tick me off your list!'

After about five minutes she still hadn't come out, so Sinead went in. There was one locked cubicle.

'Ciara? You OK?'

'Erm . . . I just got my period.'

'Oh, have you anything with you?'

'No . . . this is my first. It's only a tiny amount of blood.'

'Oh . . .' Sinead wasn't sure what to say. 'Well, congratulations! I'll slip out to the chemist for you. Will I tell Cuan?'

'Yeah, sure.'

Sinead got sanitary towels – she reckoned it was easier to let Eleanor explain the tampon thing – and a tin of travel sweets in the chemist. Cuan waited outside the bathroom and hugged Ciara when she came out.

'I'm fine,' she said, 'but, er . . . could we stay in the cottage tonight? I think I'd like to have a real toilet nearby!'

For the rest of the journey everyone was mostly silent. Sarah fell asleep in her car seat in the front, and Sinead dozed off in the back, trying to catch up on all the broken nights. Ciara rested her head on Cuan's shoulder and thought about things, while they sucked their way through most of the tin of sweets. She didn't feel very different – she'd thought it would be more dramatic. Even so she'd write it in her diary that night. She had brought her camera. She might get Cuan to take her picture later on the beach – maybe it was the kind of difference that would show up in a photograph.

# Over and Over

Martina watched the rain streaming down the porch window. It felt like winter in the middle of July. Maeve and Eoghan were six weeks old. They had uncurled, and their limbs were rounder and stronger. Looking at them lying together, it seemed absolutely impossible that they had fitted inside her, even one of them. They were asleep in their cot, oblivious to the change in weather, and how quiet the house had become. Martina would miss Cuan . . . Cliodhna. She had changed names and managed not to slip up, but it was still very much a conscious effort. Cuan was still Cuan in her head, and still he rather than she. Though she knew it wouldn't be long before that changed. It would happen and catch her out unawares any day now.

The babies would miss him, too, this week. He had endless capacity for making idle fun with them. Two days ago the sun was streaming in the porch window while he was changing their nappies. He let them lie naked in the sunny window for a while and entertained them by swishing a sarong lightly across them. They gave broad delighted grins to feel the featherlight cotton against their skin, so he did it over and over.

She'd miss his company, too, particularly in the evenings. She loved that time together. Before Ciara came to stay, they'd slipped into a pattern where she'd take a long bath and he'd cook and juggle the babies. Then they'd eat and, while she gave the babies their last big top-up before bed, he'd go and take a shower. He'd wash off the make-up and shed the artifice, the bras and teardrops, that he'd have put on for the good people of Blackrock. Often he'd come back downstairs in a vest and tracksuit bottoms, and they'd watch an hour of rubbish on the television together. Or just sit and read, and listen to music, not very loud music so the babies' various sounds would be audible.

One night he fell asleep like that, stretched out on the couch. Martina glanced over and was struck by how beautiful he could look. Sometimes all the dressing up distracted her. It was like an overdubbed commercial on the television; it jarred. No matter how well it was done, you knew you were being duped, that some multinational was trying to pass off some product as indigenous.

That night lying on the couch, Martina could see all that was real in Cuan's new body . . . the slightly rounder arms, less muscular than she remembered them. In the half light he looked hairless, and she remembered their many arguments about shaving – I don't mind you becoming a woman, Cuan, but you don't have to look like bloody Barbie, she'd say.

His lithe body looked smooth, not shorn, and that was what he wanted. His small breasts looked almost cute under the loose vest. Up to now she hadn't looked at them properly, so as not to embarrass him, or herself. She couldn't quite accept the change, aesthetically or sexually, like when her own breasts grew at puberty and she spent a lot of time folding her arms and walking slower to stop them jiggling and people noticing. Who could she possibly have been concerned about noticing them? Like all early teens, she felt the whole world was staring into her goldfish bowl. Now Cuan spent half the day around her naked breasts and it didn't bother either of them a bit. It was different with the feeding, impossible to be embarrassed by something so bloody useful.

The night before, Maeve was shouting and Cuan came into her bedroom to help. He carried her over to the bare breast, her mouth open expectantly, and he just latched her on. Not quite like you'd plug in a kettle, but with all the subtlety something so basic encompasses. Maeve kneaded her favourite so it let down faster and her legs kicked at the other one, which made it start to leak. Cuan was watching and understood, and got a breast pad to stop it soaking her, and the bed. Martina ignored this helpfulness, for no better reason other than to see what he'd do next. And he surprised her by pulling back the covers and holding the pad in place.

'Jesus Christ, you'll be a counsellor with La Leche league soon!' Martina said, a little cross with herself for enjoying his touch. He just grinned, that bold grin he used to do when he flirted with her, and she realized that perhaps this was the first time he'd flirted with her as a woman.

He stirred on the couch and his vest lifted up a little, baring his stomach. Was he asleep or was he just pretending? Maybe it didn't matter, he was beautiful, still. She wished she could photograph him now, or draw him, and show him that beauty, that feminine beauty which needed nothing to enhance it, or colour it or doctor it. She put a cushion on the floor, sat down and lay her head against his stomach. He woke, if he was sleeping, without alarm, and ran his hands gently through her hair, letting it brush against his bare skin, over and over.

# Hatching

They got to the beach at about four. There was no one else on there. The torrential rain all morning had put them off, no doubt. There was good weather coming. There was an offshore breeze and the Aran Islands were glowing with the sun that was on its way.

'Look!' Ciara said, pointing to the break in the clouds. 'It's like someone unzipped the sky.'

Sinead went with Sarah to the cottage to check in and left the others on the beach.

'Oh, can we swim first?' Ciara said. This was her favourite beach, with its thundering Atlantic waves. She was dying to try out her new body board. Michael had given it to her. He had brought his surfboard along to play with, too. They got changed quickly, while Cuan made excuses.

'Mmm, you're a little better insulated than the rest of us,' Cuan said, as Michael got into his togs, noticing the way he slapped his stomach as if it should tone up a bit, all by itself.

'God, I'll have to join a gym . . . I look like I'm on my second trimester!'

'It's a bit chilly for me. I'll just watch, OK?'

Cuan simply couldn't take his clothes off until he explained things to Ciara. Otherwise he might shock her, or she might be repulsed by the changes. He would tell her tomorrow.

'Chicken!' Ciara said, and ran into the water first.

Cuan walked up and down the beach collecting shells while the other two surfed the waves, shrieking with delight. He saw another surfer in the distance wearing a wetsuit. Perhaps that was the answer as a stopgap, a second skin. But he'd have to be very discreet changing into it and changing back. Better if he could just twirl and change, Wonder Woman style, or wear it all the time.

The sea was rough, but Ciara seemed to be managing fine. Then Cuan noticed the wristband had come off her board. The board was rapidly moving out to the left and she was swimming out to catch it. He yelled out, but Michael didn't hear him over the din of the waves. Ciara was out of her depth and struggling now. Cuan rushed in his clothes towards her. As the waves rose he lost sight of her – but she could hear him and was calling to him.

'Just tread water. I'm coming,' he yelled.

He reached her and pulled her to shore. She'd got an awful fright, but was fine. He held her on his lap while she threw up whatever sea water she had swallowed. Michael joined them, ashen-faced. He wrapped a towel around them and went to ring Sinead to come and pick them up. He had to walk to the sand dunes to get a signal. From where he stood on the hill, Cuan and Ciara looked like a giant egg washed up on the shore.

'Owwww, Dad!' Ciara clutched her stomach. 'Owwww!'

'Are you going to throw up again?'

'No, it's a different pain,' she said.

'Owwww!' she yelled, biting down on the towel. 'I don't want to be a woman if it hurts like hell.'

And a trail of her warm menstrual blood seeped through his wet jeans and into the sand.


Pretend I've just hatched. Just pretend you see me cracking open my egg. You see my long neck stretching out. Say what you'd say if you saw me for the very first time.

# Acknowledgements

Thanks to Aengus Carroll, old friend and first reader (and attentive re-reader) of this: the manuscript landed in the right hands and heart.

And thanks to the following, who at crucial moments provided encouragement: Siân Quill, Ted Sheehy, Iseult Sheehy, Mary Montaut, Vivienne Parry, Jane Daly and Clare Dowling.

Special thanks to Sorcha Sheehy Williams, who read it before she was supposed to, and excused herself by saying she didn't read any of the boring bits!

Thanks to Caroline Davidson and Emma Barker for the rigorous engagement. All at the Irish Theatre Institute for being patient with my parallel life. Last, but by no means least, Patricia Deevy, Michael McLoughlin and all at Penguin Ireland, and copy-editor Siobhán O'Connor.